BACKSTAGE MURDER

"Missy could've gotten hurt on her way from the Arms hotel or she's lying unconscious backstage," Sloan said. "Take your pick."

"I don't like either choice," Nola said.

"Neither do I," Johnny agreed. "Whichever way you look at it, I'm out a leading lady."

"There's only one way to find out if Gram's right," Jinx said. "We need to split up and search the theatre."

Freddy and Sloan went to the kitchen, Nola and Johnny ran off to the stage left wing, and Jinx and Alberta climbed the stairs to the stage and quickly walked down the hallway off the stage right wing, turning right to continue behind the back wall. Without the working light behind the back scrim turned on, the area was pitch black, and they were about to retreat in order to get a flashlight when Alberta saw a light coming out of the star dressing room. When they stood in the doorway, it was evident that their search had come to an end.

They found their missing star lying on a settee, wrapped in a lace shawl, and holding a bottle of arsenic.

Missy Michaels wasn't lost, she was dead . . .

Books by J.D. Griffo

MURDER ON MEMORY LAKE

MURDER IN TRANQUILITY PARK

MURDER AT ICICLE LODGE

MURDER AT VERONICA'S DINER

MURDER AT ST. WINIFRED'S ACADEMY

Published by Kensington Publishing Corp.

J.D. GRIFFO

MURDER AT ST. WINIFRED'S ACADEMY

THE FERRARA FAMILY MYSTERY SERIES

KENSINGTON
PUBLISHING CORP.

www.kensingtonbooks.com

This book is a love letter to the theatre. It's dedicated to the actors, designers, stagehands, and everyone else involved in bringing magic to the stage. As you read, imagine you're in a dark theatre, the lights have just dimmed, and the show is about to begin. Hold your breath because in the theatre anything can happen. Especially when that theatre is in St. Winifred's Academy.

ACKNOWLEDGMENTS

As always, a big 'thank you' to my agent, Evan Marshall, my editor, John Scognamiglio, my publicist, Larissa Ackerman, and the entire Kensington Team. And special thanks to all the people in my life who instilled in me a life-long, unshakeable love of the theatre. My mom (who was also my first director!), Mr. Finley, Anna Brown, Miss Judd, Richard Sabellico, Pat DeFerrari, Joan Kashuba . . . the list goes on. They introduced me to the theatre, helped me find my footing in this world, and for that I'm forever grateful.

CHAPTER 1

Una vita molto diversa.

Alberta stared at the postcard. It was meant to bring happiness, but it only brought heartache. Sitting on her couch in her living room, she had never felt more alone in her entire life. And Alberta knew she only had herself to blame.

The postcard came as a surprise. Why was someone dressed in a Mickey Mouse costume waving at her underneath the entrance to Disneyland? When she turned the card over, she understood. Her son, Rocco, was spending the day at the world-famous theme park with his youngest child, Gregory, and he meant to share the event. He accomplished that and much more. His missive reminded Alberta of the distance—both geographically and emotionally—that had grown between them over the years. It also reminded Alberta of just how much she missed her family.

Living in Tranquility, surrounded by friends and relatives, Alberta Ferrara Scaglione was hardly alone. But her children were thousands of miles away and not part of her daily life. She was estranged from her daughter, Lisa Marie, and Rocco was focused on raising his own family and not maintaining ties with those he left behind.

After Rocco's first marriage to Annmarie ended in divorce, his former high school sweetheart moved to Los Angeles with their two daughters, Alessandra and Rocky. Unable and unwilling to be a long-distance father, Rocco soon followed his ex-wife so he could live close to his girls. Logically, Alberta understood the reason for his relocation—a good father based all his decisions on what was best for his family—but in her heart, she felt he had ulterior motives.

She could never quite understand why he didn't force Annmarie to remain in New Jersey with their children. It was where the estranged couple both had roots, it was where their families lived, it was where Rocco worked. Moving to the other side of the country didn't make sense for either of them. Alberta even consulted a lawyer and knew that Rocco could legally prohibit Annmarie from moving so far away because they had joint custody of their children, but Rocco claimed that his ex had wanted a fresh start and he didn't want to turn an already contentious divorce into an even more hostile environment.

Her power to control her son long gone, Alberta was forced to watch silently from the sidelines as Rocco made plans to change his life. He sold his home, got a transfer to work at his company's Los Angeles office, and said his good-byes, all to be closer to his daughters. Or, as Alberta felt, to get farther away from her.

She never voiced her beliefs because she knew how petty they would sound. She knew she would be labeled a controlling, unsympathetic, and selfish mother. And she *was* being selfish. But the main reason she didn't give her fears a voice was because she didn't want confirmation that they were true. What if she was right and her son had relocated to the other side of the country to get away from her? Was that something she really wanted to know? Alberta had already lost one child when Lisa Marie packed up and moved her family to Florida in a desperate attempt to end the constant fighting that had become an ugly war between mother and daughter; she didn't want to know that she had lost another child for similar reasons. She and Rocco did not have a volatile relationship like the one she had with Lisa Marie, but ever since he was a little boy there had always been a distance between them.

Rocco wasn't the typical Italian son; he wasn't a mama's boy; he took after his father in every way. Looks, mannerisms, thoughts, and, especially, how he treated Alberta. He was never abusive—not overtly—but he could be dismissive and disinterested and, as a result, their relationship was disappointing.

Sitting on her couch, the postcard clutched tightly in one hand, Alberta traced her gold crucifix necklace with the other. She looked up and saw Rocco's class photograph from third grade, and despite the sadness that filled her heart, she smiled because it was her favorite. His hair was disheveled, his tie crooked, his smile mischievous. Sammy hated the photo because he couldn't believe Alberta had let Rocco out of the house looking like a *teppista,* a roughneck, but Alberta loved it because in her mind, her son was so full of life it couldn't be contained.

She knew this *forza di energia*, this little boy with the devilish smile, would do great things with the life God had given him. She still felt that way, even though Rocco had proven, ever since that photograph was taken, that he was ordinary. It was one thing he had in common with his mother.

He was remarried to a woman named Cecilia, who Alberta hardly knew, and had another child, his first boy, Gregory, who Alberta had only seen twice. She knew Rocco was a car salesman but knew little more about his career. She couldn't remember his address without looking it up, and she didn't know if he still needed to take his blood pressure medication or if he still squeezed a lemon over his steak before he ate it like he used to. Her son's life was a mystery to her. Then again, Alberta's life was a mystery to her son.

A first-generation Italian American, Alberta Ferrara Scaglione was the middle child of her family and grew up in Hoboken, New Jersey. She obeyed her parents, got along with her sister, Helen, and her brother, Anthony, and was what was known as a *good girl*. She never caused any trouble, never gave anyone cause for worry. She wasn't invisible, only largely unnoticed, and, most definitely, ordinary.

Like most of the young women of her generation, she only left her family when she got married. She didn't want to become Sammy Scaglione's wife, but she couldn't think of a good reason not to, so despite misgivings, she went ahead with the ceremony. After a brief honeymoon down the Jersey Shore, she moved out of her family's home and into an apartment with Sammy to create one of her own. Because that's what all the good girls did.

Her marriage to Sammy was also ordinary. It wasn't entirely good, it wasn't entirely bad, it simply was. As a reluctant newlywed, Alberta didn't succumb to the belief that the fairy tales she read as a child had any bearing on the real world. She knew Prince Charmings didn't exist, she knew endings weren't always happy, and, most of all, she knew the worst enemy a person could have wasn't a witch with a tempting yet poisonous apple, it was their reflection in the mirror. Most women looked at themselves and saw a fantasy version of who they wanted to be smiling back at them. When Alberta looked at herself in the mirror, she saw the truth.

With only a high school education and little job experience, Alberta had few choices for her future other than marriage. It was her only option, she believed, despite the fact that she knew other young women had defied the odds and created lives for themselves that ignored traditions and stereotypes. They became surgeons, lawyers, actresses, authors, athletes. They became something other than a wife and mother. But those women were extraordinary, and Alberta was not.

Part of her wanted to flee from her inevitable future, to escape the predictable next chapters of her life, but in order to do that she would have had to fight. Maybe that was what Rocco had done, she thought. Maybe he fled what he thought was an unlivable future of not being a part of his daughters' daily lives. If so, he was much stronger than Alberta. She had been unable to find the inner strength needed to battle her parents, her fiancé, society, and, toughest of all, her own fears and doubts. She didn't run from a future she didn't want; she accepted it.

The irony was that, deep down, the strength Alberta needed was there for her, impatiently waiting to be roused, but she didn't believe she possessed what it would take to forge into unknown territory. Like so many others, she chose the familiar.

Rocco's smile looked down upon Alberta from his photograph, and she averted her eyes to escape his stare and found herself looking at Lisa Marie on her wedding day. Alberta had always thought she would become one of the women she used to see growing up, the grandmothers dressed in head-to-toe black mourning for their dead husbands, walking a few steps behind their children, and yelling at their grandchildren. She never thought she'd be living by herself in a house on a lake in a beautiful town like Tranquility, New Jersey. Wasn't she supposed to be living in the basement of her daughter's house? Wasn't she supposed to be adapting her schedule to the needs and whims of her children and grandchildren? Wasn't she supposed to be living in their shadow instead of casting shadows of her own?

She slumped back into the couch and let the cushions soothe some of the pain she was feeling. Maybe she was being too harsh. Maybe she was just feeling sorry for herself. She always knew memories were dangerous things; they distorted the past and manipulated the future. It was all the postcard's fault. How could she read her son's handwriting and not remember what had come before and imagine what could come next if only their lives had taken a different shape? She had forgotten what her mother used to say about walking down memory lane, that it was like *entrare in guerra*, walking into war. You put yourself right into the line of fire, except there were no bullets to wound you, only guilt and shame. And Alberta had plenty of both.

She could live with not being the perfect daughter, she long ago forgave herself for not being the perfect wife, but the one thing that still filled her with regret was that she'd failed as a mother.

Again, this wasn't a unique quality that Alberta possessed, as she was hardly the only mother in the world to display shortcomings, nor the first mother to disappoint her children. It was a rather ordinary feeling for a woman to believe she wasn't the perfect mother. Still, it was a source of constant pain for Alberta; there was always the doubt that she had truly done the best she could and the suspicion that she could have tried harder.

"Ah, *Madon*!" she cried.

Alberta rose from the couch with such passion, it made her cat, Lola, wake up from her third nap that morning with a loud meow. And because Lola hated to be woken up from her naps so abruptly, the meow did not sound pretty.

"I know exactly how you feel, Lola," Alberta said.

Unconvinced, Lola stretched out on the couch on her back, her legs pointing to the left, her head turned to the right. Her right eye was closed, but her left eye was wide open, her black pupil surrounded by a larger circle of white. Her expression made the white streak of fur over her left eye look like an exclamation point. It was as if Lola was saying to Alberta, *Oh really?*

Smiling, Alberta scooped Lola up in her arms. She cradled her like a baby as she always did, rocking her side to side as her eyes moved from photo to photo on the wall, and she watched the generations of the Ferrara family come to life before her eyes. Her parents, her grandparents, cousins, pets, her Gumpa Tony, her mother's godmother who wasn't a blood relative but was beloved by everyone, her children, her sister Helen, her sister-in-law Joyce, her granddaughter Jinx, and all the friends she had made since moving here.

Slowly, memory faded and the past, in all its fictional glory and factual heartache, gave way to the present. Rocco was still thousands of miles away living with his new wife and raising a son Alberta barely knew. Lisa Marie was living almost as far away, still refusing to bridge the gap that kept them apart. There was nothing Alberta could do to change what had come before, but she could stop wasting time dwelling on it, wondering where she had gone wrong, if she should have acted differently, or why she made certain choices. Why focus on the past when the present was filled with hope and promise?

Alberta laughed out loud because for most of her life she was not the kind of woman who grasped on to hope or believed tomorrow held the promise of a better day. But ever since her Aunt Carmela left her millions of dollars and the house on Memory Lake, she had changed. She no longer strived to be perfect, she only wanted to be the best version of herself that she could possibly be. She took charge instead of waiting to be told what to do, she discovered she had skills she never thought she possessed, and she took chances.

When someone asked her opinion, she offered truth instead of a mindless platitude. If something needed to be done, she did it herself instead of waiting for help. Her children might not recognize her, but that was okay. Just as they were living their lives the way they wanted to, Alberta had to do the same. It had taken her over sixty years, but she was finally answering to just one person: herself.

"*Una vita molto diversa,*" she said.

Lola meowed lazily, and Alberta translated, "A very different life, Lola, that's what I'm living."

When the phone stopped ringing, Alberta smiled because it was nice to hear her son's voice even if it was only a recording.

"Rocco, it's your mother," Alberta said. "Thank you for your postcard, it sounds like you and Gregory had a wonderful day. Give my grandson a big hug and kiss for me and tell him that I love him."

She had to take a deep breath before she could continue. "I miss you and I love you too," she said. "*Addio, figlio.*"

She stood in the kitchen for a few minutes, looking out the window and marveling at how beautiful and large Memory Lake looked. After all this time, the sight of it still surprised and delighted her. She wondered if her voice message would cause the same response from her son. Taking a cue from the sunshine that filtered in through the window and enveloped her, she chose to believe that it would.

The ring of the cell phone startled Alberta and made her jump. "*Dio mio!*" she exclaimed.

Hopeful that it was her son calling her back, she was smiling when she reached for the phone. Despite seeing that it was someone else calling her, her smile remained; in fact, it grew a little larger.

"Hello, lovey," Alberta said, answering her grand-daughter's call.

"Gram!" Jinx shouted. "I need to see you."

"Why?" Alberta asked. "What's wrong?"

"Nothing's wrong," Jinx replied.

Without thinking, Alberta tucked her hair back over her ear as she often did when she was nervous. It was a habit acquired from the time she was a young girl, and while it was soothing to run her finger through her still thick hair, let it travel around her ear, and trace her jaw-line, it didn't alleviate anxiety. Despite Jinx's protestations, Alberta was still concerned.

"If everything's all right, why do you need to see me?" Alberta asked.

"Because I have some superincredible, *stupefacente* news to share!" Jinx shouted.

"Wow, you're breaking out the Italian words, this must be terrific news," Alberta said. "Share it with me now."

"No! I want to see your expression when I tell you," Jinx said. "Come over to my place."

"Ah *Madon*!" Alberta cried. "Fine! I'll be right over."

"Great! You are gonna flip when you hear what I have to tell you!" Jinx yelled. "Love you, Gram."

Jinx ended the call before Alberta could reply. But it didn't matter, Jinx knew her grandmother loved her just as much. She also knew that Alberta would be at her place as quickly as she could simply because Jinx had asked her to come. Alberta was incapable of refusing her granddaughter anything. The reverse was also true, and even though Jinx could be unpredictable at times she was always a dutiful granddaughter. Neither one had expected their relationship to become so vitally important, but neither one could imagine living without the other in their lives.

Alberta's life might be very different from what she had envisioned it would be, but in some ways it was better.

And it most definitely wasn't ordinary.

CHAPTER 2

Guai in vista.

"I think Jinx is going to tell us that she and Freddy are engaged!"

Even though Alberta had promised she would immediately race over to Jinx's apartment to hear her good news, she had to first inform her sister and sister-in-law that good news was about to be shared. After Jinx hung up on her, Alberta called Helen and Joyce, explained the situation, and within fifteen minutes they were in Alberta's kitchen, where they were now. Standing side by side, the two women stared at Alberta with the same stunned expression plastered on their faces. They looked the same, and yet they couldn't have looked more different.

A former nun who had spent forty years living in a convent, Helen was thin, her short hair completely gray, and she stood about five foot seven thanks to the thick-heeled, sensible shoes she always wore. Her complexion, untouched except for a healthy application of pink lipstick, was fairer than the typical Sicilian's, and her blue eyes were more pale than vibrant, which, combined with her skin tone, made her appear like a soft, watercolor painting. The look belied Helen's much stronger and some might say cantankerous personality.

On the other hand, Joyce was African American, had black, close-cropped hair, black eyes, a curvy figure, and stood at five foot nine in her stocking feet. Her outfits were tailored, usually colorful, and always coordinated with eye-catching accessories, like the emerald stud earrings, avocado faux alligator belt, and cluster of Bakelite bracelets in varying shades of green that perfectly accented the khaki jumpsuit she was currently wearing. The only accessories Helen ever wore were the staples to her wardrobe: a gold crucifix necklace and a sturdy, black pocketbook.

Physically, they made an odd couple. Emotionally, they were in sync. And at the moment, they were in shock.

"Did you hear what I said?" Alberta asked.

This time when Alberta spoke, Helen and Joyce stared at each other. And then they screamed. Joyce's shriek was much higher pitched than Helen's gruff roar, but they were speaking the same language.

"Jinxie's getting married?" Helen asked.

"She only told me that she had wonderful news to share," Alberta said. "But I'd swear on Daddy's grave that she's going to tell us her boyfriend finally popped the question."

"I can't wait to take Jinx shopping for her gown," Joyce said. "I have a former client whose son owns a bridal shop in Brooklyn. I convinced the father to invest in *The Phantom of the Opera* and he's made a mint. The man owes me."

"We owe Jinxie a celebration," Helen said. "Do you think we have enough food?"

The ladies surveyed Alberta's kitchen table, which was overflowing with food Alberta had assembled while waiting for Helen and Joyce to arrive. There were Tupperware containers filled with leftover lasagna and eggplant parmigiana, platters of antipasto covered in Saran Wrap, two boxes of Entenmann's cakes—a Louisiana Crunch loaf and their classic golden cake with fudge icing. There was enough food to feed a hungry family of twelve and still the ladies weren't sure there was enough for an impromptu gathering of four.

"As long as no one wants seconds you'll be fine," Helen said.

"Something's missing," Joyce claimed.

"*Dio mio!*" Alberta cried. "I don't have time to make anything."

"Do you have a pitcher of Red Herring in the fridge?" Joyce asked.

Nervously, Alberta opened the refrigerator door, and when she saw a full pitcher behind the carton of nondairy almond milk that she always kept on hand so Jinx could have it for her coffee, she sighed. She pulled out the pitcher and raised it overhead like a trophy. "Found it!"

Whenever the ladies gathered to play canasta, discuss clues on their latest detective case, or just gossip about family or the denizens of Tranquility, they had to have two things: an Entenmann's dessert and something alcoholic to drink. For years they complemented their boxed dessert with flavored vodka, but when they ran out of new flavors to try, Jinx created their own signature drink. A Red Herring consisted of vodka, prosecco, cranberry juice, some orange juice, a splash of tomato juice, and a mint garnish to give it some extra visual oomph. No gathering of the Ferrara ladies would be complete without a pitcher of their very own liquid concoction, so they were relieved that Alberta had an extra one on hand to bring to Jinx's.

Alberta was about to close the refrigerator door when she spied something else that made her scream.

"What's wrong?" Helen asked.

"Nothing's wrong," Alberta replied as she pulled out a bottle of champagne. "Now we have everything we need to celebrate Jinx and Freddy's engagement in style!"

When they arrived at Jinx's apartment, the only one not ready to celebrate Jinx and Freddy's engagement was Jinx.

"I never said I was getting married," Jinx said.

"You did too!" Alberta shrieked. "You told me that you had the best news ever and you wanted to share it with me. And naturally I shared it with Helen and Joyce."

"I'm glad you got hold of them," Jinx replied. "I left messages, but neither one got back to me."

Helen and Joyce looked at their phones and saw that Jinx had, in fact, left them text messages telling them to come to her apartment so she could share some happy news with them.

"It's right here in black and white," Joyce said.

"Show us the ring," Helen demanded.

"What ring?" Jinx asked.

"The engagement ring Freddy gave you," Joyce clarified. "Let's see it."

"I'm sorry to burst the crazy little bubble you all live in," Jinx said, "but Freddy didn't give me a ring."

The three women gasped at the same time and instinctively reached out to grab one another's hands. In times of shock, a woman needed support.

"Don't tell me that somebody else gave you a ring?" Alberta said. "Poor Freddy will be devastated."

"Gram, you're talking *pazzo*!" Jinx cried.

"*I'm* crazy?" Alberta asked. "You're the one who tells us to race over here because you have important news to share, we come to celebrate, and you claim you're not getting married. You tell me, who's the crazy one?"

"You three are obsessed with marriage," Jinx declared. "Do you realize that?"

"Of course," Alberta replied.

"A smidge," Helen said.

"Also too, I can get you a primo discount on a wedding gown," Joyce added.

Jinx smiled because even though she knew she was staring at three women who shared an almost unhealthy preoccupation with her personal life, she knew they also loved her unconditionally. It filled her with both pride and gratitude.

"I pledge to you right now that if Freddy ever gets down on one knee and proposes marriage to me, you three will be the first to know," Jinx promised.

"We better be!" they replied in unison.

Surveying all the food that was spread out on her kitchen table, Jinx shook her head. "I can't imagine what you're going to whip up when I actually do get engaged. We're going to have to rent a catering hall."

"I have a friend whose daughter owns a place in Morristown," Joyce said. "I'll make a reservation tonight."

"In the meantime, now that you have a captive though slightly disappointed audience," Helen said, "tell us about this exciting news."

"It's actually not even my news to share," Jinx shared. "It's Nola's."

On cue, Jinx's roommate, Nola Kirkpatrick, came out of her bedroom and stood looking at the Ferraras as if she was on trial. Which was ironic because the last time she was in their presence she was the prime suspect in a murder mystery they were trying to solve. Nola wasn't a dangerous woman, but she did always seem to find herself in predicaments. And she usually dragged all those around her into her crisis as well.

Essentially an orphan after her adoptive parents died when she was a freshman in college, Nola didn't have any other family to speak of, so her friends had become her family. Because her best friend and roommate was Jinx, she had claimed the Ferrara clan as her own. Even though they bore no physical resemblance—Jinx was taller, darker, curvier, and had long, wavy black hair, while Nola had a tomboy's physique and long blond hair that remained straight no matter how long she used her curling iron—the two shared a sisterly bond. The rest of the Ferraras didn't share Jinx's opinion of Nola and considered the girl to be more like a distant relative. Better to be heard of than seen.

"*Guai in vista*," Helen muttered.

Those in the room who understood Italian knew Helen

was speaking the truth. Trouble had most definitely arrived.

"Hi, everybody," Nola gushed. "I'm so glad you could all come over."

"Jinx said it was important," Alberta replied.

"I figured you'd be more inclined to accept my invitation if it came from Jinx instead of me," Nola confessed.

"You've come to know us so well," Helen said. "You're a terrible director, but you're perceptive."

A beloved English and creative writing teacher at St. Winifred's Academy, where she'd been named teacher of the year four times in a row, Nola also ran the theatre department at the school, directed the high school shows, and was the artistic director of the Tranquility Players, the town's community theatre. Nola's productions delighted the entire town, except Helen.

"Aunt Helen!" Jinx chided. "Nola's a wonderful director and you know it."

"You really are, honey," Joyce said. "Your decision to set *Guys and Dolls* in a gambling addiction rehab center was inspired."

"Thanks, Aunt Joyce," Nola started. "I'm sorry, is it all right if I call you Aunt Joyce? After everything we've been through, I really do consider you all family."

"Of course," Joyce replied. "I'd be honored."

"You can call me Helen," Helen said.

The comment made everyone in the room cringe and hold their breath, except for Nola, who burst out laughing. "Duly noted . . . Helen," Nola replied.

"Now that we've gotten that out of the way," Alberta said, "tell us what this emergency gathering is all about."

"You should sit down for this," Jinx instructed. "You're all gonna freak out!"

Alberta and Joyce sat down on the couch on opposite sides of Helen and all three ladies braced themselves for whatever words were going to come out of Nola's mouth.

"The Tranquility Players are putting on another show," Nola announced.

Those were not the words they were expecting to hear.

"That's the opposite of good news," Helen barked.

"Nola isn't directing," Jinx offered.

"That's slightly better news," Helen said.

"I'll only be producing and probably acting as the stage manager, because no one ever wants to do that job," Nola clarified. "But yes, after a slight hiatus, the Tranquility Players are back in business."

"That's wonderful news, Nola, it really is, and we fully support the arts and your, um, artistic endeavors," Alberta stammered. "But Jinx, you could've told us this news on the phone."

"This isn't any run-of-the-mill show," Nola interjected.

"You're the producer of the show," Helen said. "Of course you'd say that."

"No, Aunt Helen, she's right," Jinx said. "This show is going to put the Tranquility Players on the map, and I guarantee that all three of you are going to beg to sit in the front row at every performance."

Shrugging her shoulders, Alberta said, "Your captive audience is intrigued. What's so special about this community theatre production?"

Nola and Jinx looked at each other and squealed. They were acting like they were just told the secrets of the Vatican by a loose-lipped priest. It was time they shared their classified knowledge with the rest of the group.

"This show is going to be headlined by a real-life

star!" Nola exclaimed. "I got a bona fide movie actress to be in the show."

The ladies looked at each other and couldn't conceal their growing excitement and skepticism. What famous actress could Nola have lured to act in her play? The Tranquility Players put on a good show, but it was hardly Broadway caliber entertainment. Or off-Broadway. It wasn't even off-off Broadway. Then again, actresses were desperate to perform and would go anywhere to perfect their craft if the part was good enough. Maybe Nola tantalized them with a role they couldn't refuse. But who would've taken the bait?

"Is Ann-Margret coming out of retirement?" Alberta asked.

"Maybe Sophia Loren is tired of relaxing in her palatial villa," Helen said.

"How do you know her villa's palatial?" Joyce asked.

"It's Sophia Loren," Helen answered. "What other kind of villa is she going to live in?"

"Maybe it's Claudia Cardinale," Alberta said. "I loved her in *The Pink Panther*."

"Nope," Nola replied. "None of them."

"Who, then?" Alberta asked. "Elke Sommer?"

Nola shook her head.

"Dyan Cannon?" Joyce asked.

Nola shook her head again.

"Anne Bancroft?" Helen asked.

"Anne Bancroft's dead," Nola replied.

"So's my interest," Helen said. "Enough of this guessing game, Nola. Who'd you get to star in your little show?"

"Missy Michaels."

Alberta, Helen, and Joyce looked as if Nola had indeed revealed the secrets of the Vatican. They all stared at the young woman, their mouths agape, their eyes widening slowly. They remained like that until the excitement building inside them could no longer be contained, and then they let out three shrieks that, combined, created one deafening blare.

"Missy Michaels is going to perform right here in Tranquility?" Alberta asked.

"Yes!" Nola shouted.

"Didn't I tell you this was the best news ever?" Jinx asked. "A heckuva lot better than my impending nuptials, which are not impending, by the way."

"Let's not get carried away, lovey," Alberta said. "Nothing would be better than hearing that you're going to get married, but this is a very close second."

"How in the world did you pull this off, Nola?" Joyce asked.

"It must've been blackmail," Helen said.

"No," Nola said. "I asked her."

"You just asked her to come to New Jersey and perform in a show you're producing, and she said yes?" Alberta asked.

"Yes!" Nola shrieked. "Can you believe it?"

Again, Alberta, Helen, and Joyce all replied in unison, "No."

"Well, it's true!" Jinx shouted. "And it's all happening because Nola is very persuasive."

"If this really is true," Alberta said, "this is the most exciting celebrity news since Dinah Shore took up golf."

"Since Elizabeth Taylor and Debbie Reynolds patched things up," Helen said.

"Also too, since Twiggy cut off all her hair," Joyce added.

"I have no idea who any of those people are that

you're talking about. The truth is I didn't even know who Missy Michaels was until Nola told me," Jinx confessed, "but I knew that if she was as famous as Nola said, you would be thrilled that she was coming to Tranquility."

Jinx had no idea how right she was.

To anyone who grew up in the late '50s, there was no one more famous than Missy Michaels. Starting in 1957, when Missy was only seven years old, she began starring in movies as Daisy Greenfield, an orphaned heiress who lived with her grandmother in a swanky apartment on Central Park West in New York City. Daisy might not have had parents, but she did have enormous wealth, an extra bedroom where her army of dolls slept, an infectious giggle, and a doting grandmother who catered to Daisy's every whim. Missy could cry on cue, had a deadpan delivery that left the audience in stitches, and when she smiled, her dimples lit up the screen. She was the little girl all America loved. Now, the one-time child star who dominated the box office before she hit puberty was coming to Tranquility, New Jersey, to headline a community theatre production. It was thrilling news. It also made no sense whatsoever.

"Why don't you tell us how all this came to be?" Alberta suggested.

Nola explained that because the Tranquility Players hadn't produced a play for over a year, she needed to find a surefire hit that the audience would instantly recognize and make them waltz out of the theatre with smiles on their faces. After a long decision-making process, she decided that the hilarious comedy *Arsenic and Old Lace* would fit the bill perfectly as the Tranquility Players' comeback production.

"But I knew the show would have to be extra special,"

Nola said. "And I thought the best way to create some excitement would be to get a celebrity to play the role of one of the spinster aunts."

"That's smart, Nola," Joyce said. "You really do think like a producer."

"It's not as if she thinks like a director," Helen quipped.

"Aunt Helen, I'm not going to remind you again!" Jinx yelled. "Be nice."

"That's all right, Jinx," Nola said. "An artist always has her detractors."

"But it isn't always the case that an artist sees her vision executed," Joyce said. "You should be proud of yourself, Nola."

"Thank you, I am," Nola replied. "I didn't doubt myself or worry that Missy would hang up the phone once she heard my request, I just called up and asked her."

Alberta smiled listening to Nola's enthusiasm. It reminded her of why she did like the woman in spite of Nola's tendency to lead Alberta into the danger zone. "I'm glad to hear you sound so confident."

"I knew it was a long shot," Nola admitted, "but when I offered Missy the role, she immediately accepted. It was like taking candy from a baby."

"Except Missy hasn't been a baby, a toddler, or even a young woman for decades," Helen said. "Just how old is she?"

"She'll celebrate her seventy-first birthday a few days before opening night," Nola shared.

No one had to speak for Nola to understand what they were thinking, their concern was written all over their faces. They were worried that Missy's advanced age would somehow compromise the production, but Nola informed them that they were wrong.

"Missy sounded great when I spoke with her," Nola said. "She was funny, she told me stories about her past, and she has a real understanding of the play and her character. Plus, she looks amazing. She e-mailed me a photo of herself and she doesn't look a day over seventy."

"Neither does Berta," Helen said.

"Ah, *Madon*! I'm only sixty-seven!" Alberta yelled.

"I know," Helen replied.

Ignoring her sister's jab at her age, Alberta still didn't really understand why someone like Missy would want to work with someone like Nola. They came from completely different worlds. Nola brought the joy of the arts to her small community, but Missy had been a worldwide sensation. Alberta understood that having a well-known celebrity perform in her production would be a triumph, but for Missy, it could only be described as an epic fall from grace.

"No offense, Nola, but it still seems odd to me that Missy would accept," Alberta said. "Tranquility is a long way from Broadway and even farther from Hollywood."

"Which is precisely why Missy accepted my offer," Nola stated. "She's wanted to perform again for quite some time, but she's been too intimidated to return to the public eye in a big vehicle and be under such large-scale scrutiny. Our small venue is perfect for her."

Alberta finally saw the brilliance of this unconventional pairing. Nola and Missy really did benefit each other.

"Missy gets to make her comeback," Alberta said, "and the Tranquility Players reap the benefits."

"More commonly known as a win-win situation," Jinx added.

"Exactly!" Nola said. "Now, let's open up that bottle of champagne you brought and raise a toast."

Joyce did the honors and uncorked the champagne bottle. When all their glasses were filled with the bubbly, they raised them high in the air.

"To Nola!" Alberta cried. "May she and Missy Michaels find nothing but success together. *Salud!*"

"*Salud!*" everyone repeated.

And then Nola proved once again why she was the type of woman who gave everyone around her agita. She just couldn't keep her mouth shut.

"Missy and I are the perfect combination," Nola said. "What could possibly go wrong?"

As Nola blithely drank her champagne, Alberta looked at Jinx, who looked at Helen, who looked at Joyce, and together they shook their heads. They knew the answer to Nola's flippant statement could be summed up in one word: *everything*.

CHAPTER 3

Sono pronto per il mio primo piano.

One of the many good things about growing old was that wisdom really was age's traveling companion.

Standing in Jinx and Nola's living room holding a half-drunk glass of champagne, Alberta could sense that the women around her had become nervous thanks to Nola's offhanded comment. Nola truly thought that bringing Missy Michaels to Tranquility to star in *Arsenic and Old Lace* would be an uneventful event, that it would run smoothly from start to finish. Nola believed that because her intentions were good and that both she and Missy would benefit by the collaboration, no problems would arise and there would be no obstacles as they moved closer to opening night. Alberta knew better.

She also knew there was no way to prevent the inevitable roadblocks that would pop up along the way. But having dealt with past hardships during the first six decades of her life, Alberta understood that there was strength in numbers. Whether dealing with a problem child, a sticky situation, or a hopelessly naïve woman, it was always wise to call in reinforcements.

"Because we have all this food, let's invite the boys over and make this a real celebration," Alberta suggested.

"That's a terrific idea, Mrs. Scaglione," Nola said. "If I've learned one thing from my life, which you all know has had its share of ups and downs."

Jinx reached out and grabbed her friend's hand. "That's all in the past, Nola."

"I know," Nola replied, giving Jinx's hand a squeeze. "But it's important to share the good stuff with as many friends as possible. And this coup I pulled off definitely falls in the good stuff pile."

"*Amen a quello,*" Alberta said.

Jinx took out her phone from the back pocket of her jeans and said, "So I assume by 'the boys' you mean the regulars?"

"Yes," Alberta replied. "Vinny, Freddy, Father Sal . . ."

"And don't forget Sloan," Joyce added.

"How could Gram forget her boyfriend?" Jinx asked.

"Don't start with that," Alberta chided. "Just start making phone calls."

"Not yet."

Helen hadn't raised her voice, but she had used a tone that indicated her words were not to be dismissed. In response, the rest of the group stopped what they were doing and turned their attention to Helen, who sat on the couch and held her champagne glass with the same authority she typically held her pocketbook, looking as if she had something very important to say.

"What's wrong, Helen?" Alberta asked. "Why do you want us to wait?"

Helen drank the last mouthful of champagne and turned her head to face Nola. "Have you cast the rest of the play?"

"Not yet," Nola replied. "Auditions will take place next week."

"I'm going to play the other spinster aunt," Helen declared.

"Well, a . . . confident attitude is good when preparing for an audition," Nola stammered.

"I'm not auditioning, it would be a waste of time for both of us," Helen said. "I was born to play a crotchety, old spinster aunt. It's who I am. You're not going to find anyone else better to play the role in this hick town, so let's cut to the chase and give the part to me now."

Nola looked at the other women in the room, one by one, for support, but found none. She was foolish to think that Alberta, Jinx, or Joyce would disagree with Helen— she was their family after all, and family stood together. But they most certainly understood the protocols of theatre, didn't they?

"First, let me say that I hear your passion and I applaud it," Nola said, actually placing her champagne glass between her knees and clapping. "But I can't just give you the part, Helen, I have to hold auditions to choose the cast. That's how we do things in the theatre."

"That's not how you did it with Missy," Helen said.

"Yes, that is true," Nola replied. "I did offer her the role of Abby Brewster."

"Then offer me the role of Abby's sister, Martha," Helen said. "You know I'm perfect casting, and if you give me the part, I'll never say another bad word about your directing again."

Everyone was stunned by Helen's words. They all, including Nola, knew how much she despised Nola's direction, so for her to agree to keep her negative comments to herself for the rest of her life meant she truly wanted this role. Alberta was shocked by Helen's desire to be a thespian at this stage of her life, but not by her determination. It was what she had come to expect of her sister.

"Not another bad word?" Nola repeated. "Spoken or in writing?"

"Nothing but praise and adulation," Helen affirmed. "And the sincere kind, not the phony worship the rest of the town usually offers."

"Then you, Miss Ferrara, shall star opposite Missy Michaels in my new production," Nola announced.

Once again, they all cheered and raised their champagne glasses. No one looked happier than Helen. Although the reason for her cheerful glow was laced with a small, but potent dose of spite.

"I can't wait to see Father Sal's face when I tell him I'm Missy's costar," Helen cackled.

"Father Sal is a fan too?" Jinx asked.

"Lovey, anyone over the age of fifty is a Missy Michaels fan," Alberta said.

"Start making your phone calls, Jinx," Helen ordered, "and let's get this party started!"

Within thirty minutes, the population in Jinx and Nola's living room had almost doubled. Vinny, Freddy, Father Sal, and Sloan all raced over when they received Jinx's text that she had an emergency and needed their help. It was a fib, but it got the job done. With the men scattered throughout the room, the only thing left was the reveal.

"Thank you so much for coming, gentlemen," Nola said. "Why don't you each grab a glass of champagne or Red Herring before I explain why you've all been summoned here this evening?"

Obediently, the men poured themselves glasses of their beverage of choice, hoping it might penetrate the cloud of confusion encircling their heads.

"Sounds like we were summoned here under false pretenses, Alfie," Vinny whispered to Alberta.

"Trust me, Vin, it'll be worth it," Alberta replied.

Adding a splash of champagne to his glass of Red Herring, Vinny said, "Well, if I've learned anything after all these years, it's to trust you."

Radiating confidence as a result of her longtime friend's compliment, Alberta's cheeks started to turn the same color as Vinny's drink. When Sloan stood in between them and gave her a kiss on the cheek, they burned even brighter.

"I know we're in mixed company, but I couldn't control myself," Sloan said.

"Restraint is a highly overrated trait in the Sicilian heritage," Alberta replied.

The clinking sound of Nola's fork hitting her glass interrupted their banter. It was showtime.

"As some of you already know, I am going to produce *Arsenic and Old Lace* as the Tranquility Players' next production," Nola announced.

"A fine choice, Nola," Father Sal declared. "Brava."

"Thank you," Nola said. "What you don't know is that I've lined up a superstar to play the lead role."

"No kidding," Sloan said. "Who?"

"You'll never guess, not in a million years," Nola declared. "Go on and try."

"Missy Michaels."

The gasps heard in response to Freddy's outburst sounded as if a bomb went off in the middle of the living room. A bomb that stole all Nola's thunder.

"Freddy!" Jinx screamed. "It was supposed to be a surprise."

"Dude!" Freddy screamed back. "You told me the old lady was coming to star in the show, you never said it was a secret."

"I'm sorry, Nola," Jinx said. "Boys are dumb."

"That's okay," Nola replied. "At least now everybody knows. Isn't this fantastic news?"

"You're not serious, are you?" Sloan asked. "*The* Missy Michaels?"

"The one and only," Nola answered.

"*Mucca sacra!*" Vinny cried.

"Holy cow is right," Sloan said. "I haven't heard that name in decades."

"No one has," Nola said. "That's what will make this production so special. After being out of the public eye for generations, the incomparable Missy Michaels is going to make her acting comeback on my stage. What do you think of that?"

"Yes, Sal, what do you think of that?" Helen asked. "You're being awfully silent."

Everyone turned to face Father Sal, who had remained

motionless since Freddy prematurely exposed Nola's news. He was holding his glass of champagne in midair, his jaw had dropped so his mouth hung open, and his un-blinking eyes stared straight ahead. He looked paralyzed, but was it with fear or shock?

"*Santo Dio del cielo! Non avrei mai pensato di vivere abbastanza a lungo per ascoltare notizie così meravigliose!*" Sal shouted.

"I think he's speaking in tongues," Joyce declared.

"He's speaking in his native tongue," Helen clarified. "I agree, Sal, you have lived long enough. And this is the most amazing news you've ever heard." Helen raised her glass to Nola. "I told ya he was a fan."

"Helen Ferrara, do not insult me!" Sal exclaimed. "I am more than a Missy Michaels *fan*, I worship at the altar that is her stardom."

"And now he sounds blasphemous," Joyce added.

"That *old lady*, as you, Freddy, jeeringly call her," Sal started, "is perhaps the biggest star to ever grace the silver screen. The movies have not been the same since her early, and much lamented, retirement."

"With all due respect, Nola, how's this possible?" Sloan asked.

"It's a long story," Alberta interjected. "Let's all sit and eat while Nola fills everyone in on her great accomplishment."

They all gathered around the table, and because Jinx and Nola's table was smaller than Alberta's, they had to share seats and cram close to one another so they could all fit. Chattering excitedly, they started to fill their plates with cold cuts, olives, chunks of cheese, and recently re-heated lasagna and eggplant parmigiana, and they refilled their glasses to the rim. Armed with sustenance, they fell silent and turned their attention to Nola, who sat at the head of the table. It was as if they were packed into a crowded theatre and the houselights began to dim.

For the next fifteen minutes Nola regaled them with the full account of how she persuaded a movie star to grace her stage. They were all impressed, even those who already knew the story, and when she finished telling her tale, their excitement led to reminiscences. For most everyone sitting around the table, Missy Michaels was a member of their past and they couldn't wait to be reunited with her again.

Jinx and Freddy were fascinated to learn that the young actress had been even more popular than Shirley Temple, who came before her. And as Father Sal pointed out, Missy had all the wit and charm of Shirley, but without the annoying curls and tap dance routines. Even though Missy played an outrageously rich orphan living in a sprawling Central Park West penthouse with her grandmother, every kid in America thought they could be her. She was accessible, she was welcomed, she was the cinematic embodiment of the girl next door.

Vinny seemed to have the best memory, much to Sal's chagrin, and remembered almost every detail about her movies starting with *Daisy Greenfield: Orphaned Heiress*. He quoted her opening line—"You sure don't look like a grandma"—and they all recalled how beautiful and nongrandmotherly Teddy had looked.

In the films, Theodora Greenfield, Teddy for short, was Daisy's paternal grandmother, and after Daisy's parents were killed in a private plane crash while flying home from a ski vacation in the Swiss Alps, Teddy took

Daisy in and raised her as her own. She was sophisticated, smart, well-dressed, well-bred, and a bon vivant.
An Auntie Mame without a boozy best friend and poor
accounting skills. Most important, Teddy loved Daisy
with all her heart and soul. It was the combination of this
lonely young girl who needed to be loved and this grandmother who was overflowing with enough love to warm
the hearts of generations of children that made the series
such a roaring success.

They argued over which movie was the best. Was it
Daisy Learns a Lesson or *Daisy's the Toast of Hollywood*? Alberta and Joyce voted for *Daisy Joins the Circus*, but Sloan and Helen claimed that no film was better
than *Daisy Visits the White House*. However, they all
agreed that the most poignant film in the series was *Daisy
Finds True Love*. The film showcased Daisy's marriage
to Willie Mueller, the butcher's son from Hell's Kitchen,
a triumph of love over class distinction. The couple wasn't
sure their families would approve of their union because
they came from different worlds and, at first, their suspicions were validated. But when Teddy and Willie's widowed father, Milo, got locked inside the butcher store's
meat freezer, the two realized they had more commonali-
ties than differences, starting with their shared dream that
Daisy and Willie would find true happiness.

The movie ended with Daisy and Willie's lavish wedding and the two leaving for a six-month honeymoon
traveling through Europe. It also signaled the end of the
film's franchise. While Vinny, along with many other
young men at the time, hoped Daisy's marriage would
end in divorce so she'd be free to appear in their fantasies

as a girl they could make their own, the only thing that ended was Missy's career.

"She never made another movie?" Jinx asked.

"Not another Daisy Greenfield movie," Vinny replied.

"She made some B movies and did the talk show circuit in the '70s," Sloan added.

"Other than that, Missy has been out of the public's eye since then," Alberta said. "And I don't recall her ever doing a play."

"She never has," Nola confirmed. "This will be her first."

"Missy must be one brave woman," Joyce said. "I hate to be ageist at my age, but will she be able to remember her lines?"

"If my sister can do it, so can she," Alberta said.

It was the moment Helen was hoping for so she didn't have to make the announcement herself, and she was thrilled that there was a dramatic pause after Alberta's innocent remark. She fought the urge to speak and allowed the words to settle in until she was sure that everyone understood their meaning. She had been practicing her next line and wanted to make sure it had the proper impact.

"*Sono pronto per il mio primo piano,*" Helen announced.

"What close-up?" Sal asked. "And why are you ready for it?"

"Because Missy Michaels is gonna be my costar!" Helen declared.

As expected, Father Sal showed signs of apoplexy. He coughed, he sputtered, he gesticulated wildly, and when he finally spoke, he sounded roughly the same age as Missy did when she made her screen debut.

"I wanna be in the play too!" Sal shrieked.

Nola made a futile attempt to advise Sal that the auditions were the following week, but he declared, as Helen had earlier, that he would not audition and that Nola had to give him the part of Jonathan Brewster, brother to the spinster sisters, the role originated on the stage by Boris Karloff.

"I'm sure you'd be wonderful as Jonathan, but I can't give parts away willy-nilly before the auditions start," Nola said.

"Give me the part, Nola, or I will tell everyone everything you've ever shared with me in the confessional," Sal declared.

Everyone was shocked that a priest would use his priestly duties in such an unpriestly manner. Everyone except Helen.

"I told ya he'd be jealous," Helen said, grinning from ear to ear.

"Oh, how you vex me, Helen!" Sal seethed.

"Please, Father Sal, you can't tattle on me," Nola pleaded. "That goes against every oath you've taken."

"There are very few things I would cross a line for," Sal said. "A bottle of 1811 Chateau d'Yquem, a pair of Testoni loafers in buttery calfskin, and the chance to star opposite Missy Michaels."

Throwing up her hands in defeat, Nola yelled, "Fine! But that is it. If anyone else wants to be in the show, they'll have to audition, and the director has final say!"

"That reminds me, Nola. If you're not going to direct like you usually do, who will?" Alberta asked.

"My boyfriend," Nola replied.

Immediately, Alberta felt a knot grow in the pit of her

stomach, a feeling she had learned not to ignore. Whenever she experienced this sensation it was a harbinger of doom, a physical foreshadowing of bad things to come. Alberta didn't know who Nola's boyfriend was, but she sensed very strongly that he was going to do more than direct this show. He was going to bring trouble to Tranquility. And when he did, no one in town would be safe.

CHAPTER 4

Tutto il mondo è un palcoscenico.

A star was reborn.

The entire town of Tranquility was buzzing with the news of Missy Michaels's imminent arrival. At first no one could believe that the former child star was coming out of retirement and making a beeline to perform on the stage at St. Winifred's Academy. But when they heard how Nola dangled a carrot in front of Missy, assuring her that she could make her comeback in relative obscurity, everyone understood why the aging actress had chosen their town as the place where she would once again perform for an adoring public. The realization, however, had made Tranquility a bit less tranquil.

All over town the denizens were making plans to celebrate the arrival of Tranquility's most famous, if only temporary, new resident and conjuring up ways to give

Missy a queen's welcome. Ignoring that the primary reason Missy had agreed to perform in *Arsenic and Old Lace* with the Tranquility Players was the assured anonymity of her presence, almost every small business owner was preparing to exploit the actress's name in the hopes of boosting sales.

The Tranquility Country Club put Missy's Manhattan on their cocktail menu, which was simply the standard drink garnished with a daisy along with a cherry. Alberta's hairdresser, Adrianna, added the Daisy Bob as a new style choice at A Cut Above so any customer could get the chin-length-bob-and-bangs look Missy sported in her early movies. Even the owner of the new Tranquility Diner, which was formerly Veronica's Diner but renamed once it was bought from the old owners, added the PBJ&F to their menu because Daisy's favorite food was a peanut butter, jelly, and French fries sandwich. There was no doubt about it, the town was experiencing Missymania.

At Nola's request, Vinny instructed his officers to remind the population that if they turned Missy's arrival into fan-hungry fodder for coverage on *Entertainment Tonight,* there was a very good chance that the actress would cancel her comeback before she ever set foot in town. It did the trick, and collectively, everyone agreed to corral their enthusiasm and wipe the stardust from their eyes. They kept their Missy-centric items on their menus and available for purchase but didn't advertise them so boldly. In other words, they put the tranquil back into their town's name.

When Alberta told Joyce about Nola's latest stunt, her sister-in-law didn't react with the same amount of tranquility.

"What do you mean, she *used* me?" Joyce asked.

"She really had no other choice," Alberta replied. "I know it isn't fair, but we need you to take one for the team."

"Berta!" Joyce cried. "Are you suggesting I agree to an indecent proposal?"

"Indecent?" Alberta questioned. She repeated her comment in her head, and this time she heard the indecency that was slathered over her words. "*Dio mio!* I didn't mean it the way it sounded. *Gi urso su Dio.*"

Laughing, Joyce reassured Alberta that she didn't think she was really suggesting Joyce compromise her virtue. However, she still didn't know how she was being used.

"Nola has arranged for Missy to stay at the Tranquility Arms for the rehearsal period and during the run of the show for free," Alberta explained.

"How'd she ever manage to do that?" Joyce asked. "Sanjay is a notorious tightwad."

While the Tranquility Arms had a reputation for being a cozy and inviting bed-and-breakfast, its owner, Sanjay Achinapura, was well-known for being a miser.

"That is true," Alberta agreed. "He does have the first rupee he ever made framed and hanging behind the front desk."

"Then why did he agree to let Missy stay at the Arms for free?" Joyce asked. "And even though I'd rather not know, how exactly am I involved?"

"Because Nola promised him an opening-night ticket sitting right next to you," Alberta replied.

The second thing Sanjay was well-known for was his not-so-subtle crush on Joyce. He had asked her for a date on numerous occasions, but each time she gently reminded him that she was a married lady. He would always respond that his wife was a married lady too, so they had something in common. As expected, Sanjay was unsuccessful in convincing Joyce that because his wife, Urja, was living back home in Mumbai with his parents and their three children, she wouldn't interfere with their romance.

Another woman might be furious by such a misogynistic comment, but Joyce didn't survive working on Wall Street in the '80s by having thin skin. She was used to men like Sanjay. She didn't particularly like them, but she knew from past experience that Sanjay fell into the category of annoying yet harmless. If sharing an armrest with Sanjay during the opening night of the play would help out Nola, she was up for the challenge. She was also secure in the knowledge that if he crossed a line and she had to change seats in Act II, causing Sanjay to renege on his bartered deal to provide free housing to the show's star, she was rich enough to pay the remainder of Missy's hotel bill. Who says money can't buy happiness?

"That's fine with me," Joyce said. "If it will give Nola one less thing to worry about, I'll be Sanjay's date for the opening."

"Are you sure, Joyce?" Alberta asked. "I am not a fan of the man. You know I don't trust anyone who isn't generous."

"Once you get past the miserly thing and his penchant for infidelity, he isn't so bad," Joyce confessed. "Also too, he makes a delicious shrimp curry."

"When have you tasted the man's shrimp curry?" Alberta asked.

"He made a bet with me once," Joyce explained. "He told me that if I loved his shrimp curry, I had to go on a date with him."

"But you just said he makes a delicious shrimp curry," Alberta said.

"You know that and I know that, but I never told *him* that," Joyce said. "I keep telling Sanjay there's something not right with it and he should try again. I think he's on his fifth recipe and each one is better than the last."

"*Volpe furba,*" Alberta said. "I can't believe he keeps falling for it."

"I may be a sly fox," Joyce declared. "But like Jinx said, boys are dumb."

Jinx, on the other hand, was turning into one smart reporter. Whether a story fell into her lap or she had to go searching for it, she was learning to use every opportunity to her advantage. If she overheard an intriguing conversation, she followed up on it to determine if it deemed further investigation. If she read an article about an event taking place in another part of the world, she researched the topic to see if it had local ramifications or would be of interest to her readers. She had trained herself to be prepared to sniff out a story before it even was a story.

When Nola told her that a major celebrity was going to star in her production, her first reaction was that she was thrilled for her friend. But as Nola started to tell her more about who Missy was and what she had accomplished in her career, Jinx knew a large portion of *The Herald* demographic would love to read more about the long-forgotten star. Within minutes, Jinx had secured an exclusive interview with Missy, and when she told Wyck about her scoop, her boss spun around in his chair several times before banging his fist on his desk and shouting, "I can always count on you to give our readers what they want!"

"Thanks, Wyck," Jinx said. "I really do feel like I know how to reach them. Even if I had no idea who this Missy person was a week ago."

Troy Wycknowski, Wyck to everyone who knew him, was the editor-in-chief of *The Upper Sussex Herald* and a man who had a flair for drama whether in print or real life. He threw himself back in his chair and clutched his heart as if he had just been shot. This time when he spun around he did it slowly, with his head hanging to the right and his tongue hanging out of his mouth. It was like a scene out of an old melodrama and, considering their topic of conversation, not entirely inappropriate.

"That wounds me to hear you say that, Jinx," Wyck said. "It really does."

"Should I call a medic?" Jinx asked.

"I'm serious," Wyck said. "Missy Michaels is a living legend. She should be widely known, not on the verge of being rediscovered."

"Save your spiel, I've already heard how wonderful she is from my grandmother, my aunts, Sloan, and the chief of police," Jinx replied. "I think Father Sal has a shrine to her hidden in the tabernacle."

"And don't forget Teddy!" Wyck shouted.

"The grandmother?" Jinx inquired.

"Yes!" Wyck shouted even louder. "She was the best part of the series."

"I thought Daisy was the character everybody loved," Jinx said.

"She was, but Teddy was single, rich, and owned a

New York penthouse," Wyck said. "That grandmother was the woman of my dreams."

The next day, when the director of *Arsenic and Old Lace* met Helen on the first day of auditions, he felt like he had just met the woman of *his* dreams.

"I never thought I'd find a method actress hiding out in the suburbs," Johnny gushed. "Thank you for dressing in character. It shows true commitment to your craft, and that is rare to find these days."

Helen gave herself the once-over from head to toe and realized that she was giving her director the wrong first impression. "This is what I always wear," Helen said. "Including my pocky."

"Your pocky?" Johnny asked.

"My pocketbook," Helen replied. "Does no one understand slang?"

"Nola!" Johnny cried out. "Look who I found to play Martha Brewster."

Clutching her clipboard to her chest, which held the names of all the local hopefuls waiting to audition, Nola bounded over to the back of the theatre where Johnny and Helen were standing. She had not yet found the courage to inform Johnny that Helen as well as Father Sal had already been cast in their roles, so she was thrilled to hear this news.

"Helen Ferrara as Martha Brewster is brilliant casting!" Nola squealed.

"I couldn't have picked a better actress to play opposite Missy Michaels," Johnny said. "They'll complement each other perfectly."

"You're a genius, Johnny," Nola declared.

Helen understood the dynamic playing out in front of

her, and while she wasn't an advocate of fabricating falsehoods, she didn't want to contradict her director and her producer before the first day of rehearsal. When she witnessed Nola's next move, Helen realized just how savvy and manipulative the schoolteacher could be. She wasn't sure if she was impressed or made uneasy by the skill in which Nola sidestepped the truth.

"And I found the ideal Jonathan Brewster!" Nola exclaimed. "You must meet Father Sal, I know you'll agree he should be cast in the role."

Johnny's face lit up like one of the million lights on Broadway. "We really are the perfect team, aren't we?"

"On- *and* offstage," Nola replied.

"Consider yourself cast as one of my leads, Helen," Johnny announced.

"What a wonderful surprise!" Helen exclaimed, continuing to lie. "I couldn't have cast it better myself."

Helen couldn't help but cast a conspiratorial smile in Nola's direction that Johnny, still in director mode, didn't catch.

"Now if you'll excuse us," Johnny said. "I need to meet the man who's going to play your brother."

Although Helen had never been in a relationship with a man, she didn't think lying to your boyfriend was the foundation for a healthy partnership. In this instance, however, it had yielded favorable results. Helen had the role she wanted and Johnny had no idea that his power as director had been usurped, so they both came out of the negotiations feeling victorious. As Helen watched Nola take Johnny by the hand and lead him to the other side of the theatre to introduce him to Father Sal, she could sense even more victory. If body language was any indication, the couple was indeed standing on very solid ground. Helen didn't realize that they had been ever since their first encounter.

Johnny Fenn met Nola Kirkpatrick when they were both waiting in line to snag last-minute tickets to see an off-off Broadway production of *Long Day's Journey into Night* starring former sitcom stars Tony Danza and Joyce DeWitt. They wound up sitting next to each other, and by the middle of the four-and-a-half-hour performance they felt their journey into downtown theatre had lasted long enough, so they split during intermission and spent the rest of the night at The Scratcher, a dive bar near the theatre, talking about how they would've directed the production and the necessary cuts they would've made to Eugene O'Neill's ingenious, but wordy, script. After their third drink they agreed that either one of their interpretations would've been smash hits that would have made the leap to Broadway.

By the time they shared a cab back to Grand Central Station so they could catch their respective trains to New Jersey—she to Mount Olive, the nearest station to Tranquility, and he to Parsippany—they had shared their first kiss and made plans to meet the next night for dinner at a more respectable establishment. They had been practically inseparable ever since.

They both were obsessed with theatre, they both were directors, and they both felt they had something important to contribute to the world through their artistry. They might not be the next Lunt and Fontanne, but they felt like they could be. A cynic might say they took themselves a tad too seriously, but they were young and hungry to make their mark in the world. They were also guarded about their pasts and kept large chunks of their personal histories secret. Recognizing a kindred spirit, they didn't press each other for details and facts about their lives, they accepted that certain truths were better left unspoken. Like the subtext in a complex drama, not everything needed to be heard to be understood.

Some people, however, needed to be introduced.

Nola climbed the small set of stairs on the left side of the theatre that led up to the stage and walked to the center. She stood motionless, still holding her clipboard, and stared out into the audience. Slowly, everyone in the theatre noticed that someone was onstage waiting to be noticed and the chatter and activity subsided until the entire theatre was silent. Following the rest of the auditionees, Helen took a seat in the back of the theatre, and this time she was fully impressed by Nola's skill. Without uttering one word, without moving a limb, she commanded everyone's attention. Maybe she wasn't such a bad director after all.

"Ladies and gentlemen, thank you for coming to the auditions for *Arsenic and Old Lace,*" Nola began. "As you know, I'm the producer of the Tranquility Players, and it gives me great pleasure to introduce the man who will bring this production to life. Our director, Johnny Fenn."

Instead of taking the stairs to take his place next to Nola, Johnny placed his hands on the stage, swung his legs to the right, and hoisted up his body onto the platform. Part flashy, part boisterous, it was a move that endeared him to the gathered crowd, who applauded loudly. Almost every member of the audience anyway.

"Talk about cocky showmanship," Jinx muttered under her breath as she slid into the seat next to Helen.

"Jinxie," Helen whispered. "I didn't see you come in."

"I just got here," she replied. "I want to talk to everyone involved in the show so I can get additional material for the article I'm going to write about Missy."

"You can start with the director," Helen said.

"He looks like a walking cliché," Jinx remarked.

Helen looked at Johnny and realized Jinx was right. He was wearing faded jeans, worn-out sneakers, and a loose-fitting, white T-shirt, and his long, straight black hair was tied back in a ponytail. His navy-blue baseball cap, which was the de rigueur accessory for any serious director, was adorned with a capital M embroidered on it in gold, which Helen thought was a fitting tribute to the star of the show. This director had truly come to them direct from central casting.

"He might be, but I like him," Helen said. "He's a straight shooter."

Jinx wasn't convinced but was willing to give her aunt the benefit of the doubt until she got to know the man better. "If you say so."

"Thank you, Nola," Johnny said. "And thank you, Tranquility Players, for inviting me to be your director. I love this play, I love this town, and like all of you, I love Missy Michaels."

Johnny's speech was interrupted by a round of raucous applause. He understood that as the director he was technically in charge of the whole shebang, but the real star of the show was the star who had yet to arrive. Until then, he had to keep the excitement brewing to build suspense for her grand entrance.

"I guarantee you that if we all work together, our production of *Arsenic and Old Lace* will be a huge hit and will become a legend in this town," Johnny claimed. "I for one can't wait to get to work. So come on, Tranquility, show me what you've got and let the auditions begin! And to quote Jaques, the star of Shakespeare's *As You Like It,* in the melancholy Frenchman's own language, *Tout le monde est une scène.*"

"What's that mean?" Jinx asked.

"*Tutto il mondo è un palcoscenico,*" Helen replied.

"In English, Aunt Helen."

"It means all the world's a stage," Helen translated.

Jinx was by no means a Shakespeare aficionado, but she had taken a dramatic literature class in college that focused on several of the Bard's more popular works, and being Nola's roommate, she had read lines from many of his plays with her over the years. Recalling the full soliloquy that Johnny had referenced made her suddenly feel queasy. Johnny quoted Shakespeare to rally the troops, but Jinx took it as ominous foreboding.

Like most messages, the truth of the soliloquy had been forgotten and all that was remembered was the catchphrase because it was a more optimistic sound-bite and, therefore, easier to accept. Jinx knew the character of Jaques wasn't celebrating the world's desire to perform on stage; he was describing how every single one of us was marching toward our own inevitable death.

CHAPTER 5

Che cast intrigante di personaggi.

There is nothing that ignites the imagination more than an empty stage. Anything can happen in that blank space, and utilizing a bit of theatrical knowhow can transform a back wall and a wooden floor into the majestic hills of Austria, the bloody battlegrounds of the French Revolution, or a cheap but desirable apartment in New Orleans. Because where there is nothing there could be everything. And even on the modest stage of St. Winifred's Academy the possibilities were endless.

Built in 1954, the theatre was an addition to the school to commemorate the academy's tenth anniversary. Even though its architecture was simplistic and its design practical rather than ornate, it was greeted by the public at the time as a marvelous achievement and a symbol of what the future could hold. In a small but very significant way, it brought live entertainment to postwar Tranquility when all the world wanted to do was sing, dance, and act out fantastic stories.

Over the decades, the proscenium theatre was renovated, with some of the changes being cosmetic, while others technical upgrades. The main curtain, originally made of thick cotton, was replaced with one made of velvet. Its rich red color was maintained, but now a trim of gold brocade was added as well as a valence in the same color scheme. An apron was added to the stage with a radius of three feet, allowing for a larger playing area in front of the main curtain, and an elaborate arch was added to give the stage a more eye-catching frame. On each side of the stage, three gold columns rose and curved to outline the curtain. But what gave them their star quality was that on both sides just before the curve, the columns intertwined to create geometrical florets. An intricate addition to an otherwise standard design.

The sound system was upgraded to include twelve more channels, two new lighting trees were hung from the ceiling on either side of the stage, and a row of running lights was added to the crossover behind the back curtain so actors wouldn't have to cross from one side of the stage to the other in total darkness.

The auditorium saw improvements as well. Thanks to a hefty endowment in 1974 by Didi Joy McAllister—the then-mayor's second wife, who was much younger and more liberated than his first—every one of the 472 seats in the theatre was reupholstered in the same red velvet as the main curtain. Her generous donation also allowed for the male and female dressing rooms to be equipped with individual makeup stations and a shower, the addition of a private star dressing room, a ramp for wheelchair access into the theatre, and a portrait of Didi Joy with a plaque underneath identifying her as the founding president of the Tranquility Players and being a "humble benefactress of and proud participant in the theatrical arts" that still hung in the front lobby. Didi had written the quote herself.

Nola, as the Tranquility Players's current president, made it a habit to offer a smile to Didi Joy's portrait every time she entered the theatre as a way of paying homage to her group's founder. She was still smiling as she stood on the lip of the apron to welcome her cast.

"Welcome to your new home," Nola started. "For the next six weeks you'll be spending so much time here in this beautiful theatre rehearsing that you'll think you enrolled at St. Winifred's Academy."

Laughter erupted all around Alberta, who was standing in the back of the theatre by herself, although she didn't join in the merriment. She wasn't there to be part of the action, she was there to cheer on her sister.

"As for many of you, the theatre is my home," Nola said. "It's here where I find my passion, my peace, and, most importantly, my family. I want to thank each and every one of you for joining me in this journey, and while we may not be tied by blood, we're bound by something much more powerful: our love for the stage. Let's use this time before we start rehearsal to get to know one another, become comfortable in one another's company, and create bonds that will last forever."

Alberta was too perplexed by Nola's speech to join in the applause. What could be more powerful than family ties? Friends and community were treasures for sure, but nothing could take the place of family. As the clapping grew louder and more enthusiastic, Alberta realized she might be wrong. She felt, as many Italian women did, that life began and ended with family. Her opinion could never be swayed, but that didn't mean others couldn't have a different interpretation. Especially when that interpretation was born out of necessity.

Alberta remembered that not only was Nola adopted, but both her adoptive and biological parents were dead. Being an only child with no close relatives, Nola didn't have a traditional family, so she had created her own. Her close circle of friends, the people who shared her passion for theatre, became her brothers and sisters, her aunts and uncles, maybe even a new set of surrogate parents. Even Alberta and her family were part of that circle. Nola wasn't related to any of these people by blood but by choice. It filled Alberta's heart with joy that the young woman had found her own family.

Looking around the theatre, Alberta was delighted to see that she had found an old friend.

"Bruno!" Alberta cried.

Standing in the aisle, a tall, blond-haired man, turned when he heard his name. He recognized Alberta in an instant and flashed her his trademark smile: full, genuine, and a showcase for his pearly, white teeth. Alberta returned his smile and was glad to see that the public defender had finally decided to put his matinee idol looks to good use. Other than representing defendants who couldn't afford to pay for legal counsel, of course.

"Bruno bel Bruno, are you going to be in this play too?" Alberta asked.

"Yes ma'am," Bruno replied. "I've gone from being Nola's lawyer to being her Teddy."

"You're going to be her teddy bear?" Alberta questioned.

Bruno laughed so hard his blue eyes seemed to twinkle. "I've been cast to play Teddy Brewster, the nephew to the two spinsters, who thinks he's Teddy Roosevelt."

"Congratulations," Alberta said. "I had no idea you were interested in acting."

"There's a fine line that separates practicing law and strutting your stuff onstage," Bruno said. "I thought I would give the latter a try."

"If you command an audience the same way you command a jury, you'll wind up stealing the show," Alberta said.

"Don't tell that to Missy Michaels," Bruno said. "Rumor has it she's the real star."

"Trust me," Alberta whispered. "You're going to give the old lady a run for her money."

Bruno smiled again, but this time his lips didn't part to reveal his perfect orthodontia. His expression, however, revealed his absolute fondness for Alberta.

"At the risk of favoring my emotionally demonstrative Sicilian ancestry over my emotionally restrained Swedish heritage," Bruno stated, "could I have a hug?"

It was an offer no Italian could refuse.

Alberta embraced her friend and was instantly enveloped by two strong arms. At five foot four, Alberta was dwarfed by Bruno's six two, muscular frame, but the lawyer-turned-part-time-actor bent over, so it looked as if they were dancing cheek to cheek. Until Alberta's boyfriend broke up the action.

"Do I need to pour cold water on you two?"

Sloan McLelland wasn't as tall as Bruno and not nearly as wide, but his query elicited the desired response and Alberta and Bruno separated. And then they burst into a mutual fit of laughter.

"So much for the authority of the boyfriend," Sloan said, laughing along with them.

"It's great to see you again, Sloan," Bruno said, extending his hand.

"What?" Sloan asked. "I'm not worthy of a hug?"

When Sloan was hoisted two feet off the ground thanks to Bruno's bear hug, he was forced to rethink his request. "You can put me down now," Sloan said breathlessly.

When Sloan was safely back on the ground, Alberta tucked his dress shirt into his chinos and, in her best admonishing tone, said, "Be careful what you wish for, Mr. McLelland, you might just get it."

"I'll remember that the next time we're alone," he replied.

Alberta slapped Sloan playfully on the shoulder. "May I remind you that we have company," she said, tilting her head in Bruno's direction.

"I see the two of you have gotten closer," Bruno said.

"You would be right about that," Alberta replied, this time her eyes glowing in Sloan's direction.

"That makes me happy," Bruno said. "But what are you two doing here? Did you get cast in the show too? I didn't see you at the auditions."

"No, I'm helping Joyce with publicity," Sloan explained.

"And I'm here because I didn't want to be left out," Alberta said with a laugh. "Jinx is also here somewhere because she's going to write some articles on the production, and my sister, Helen, is playing your aunt. It's a regular family affair."

"Helen is a riot!" Bruno exclaimed. "I read some lines

with her for the audition and she doesn't need an ounce of rehearsal, she's ready to go on tonight."

"This is a role she was born to play," Alberta said. "I'm so happy she's getting her moment in the spotlight. It's long overdue."

"That's for sure," Bruno agreed. "And it's nice to see Nola in a different kind of spotlight, if you know what I mean."

Alberta knew all too well what Bruno meant and she too thought it was a nice change of pace for Nola to be standing in the footlights instead of waiting to give a sample of her fingerprints. A lot had changed since the last time Nola was a large part of their lives. When Alberta felt her stomach lurch, she realized a lot had also stayed the same.

Why was she getting that weird feeling in the pit of her stomach again, the feeling that she was about to step into another puddle of danger? Maybe it was the residual effects of being in a theatre, her imagination in overdrive. Forcing herself to focus on the real world and not the conjuring of precarious thoughts, Alberta steered the conversation to more mundane matters.

"It looks like you're not the only resident poised to make his community theatre debut," Alberta said. "I see Dr. Grazioso, one of the vets at the animal shelter, and Benny, the photographer who works with Jinx at *The Herald*."

"And isn't that Luke from the morgue?" Sloan asked.

Alberta had unfortunately visited Luke on several occasions at his workplace, so she recognized the lanky, long-haired orderly immediately. "It most certainly is."

"Having a morgue attendant cast in a murder mystery could come in handy," Bruno suggested.

Without looking at each other, Alberta and Sloan, responded as one: "Bite your tongue!"

Before Bruno could apologize for his bad joke, Johnny called out and asked for Bruno to join him on the stage.

"Sorry, my director needs me," Bruno declared. "I'll see you both later."

They watched Bruno follow his director's orders and hightail it up to the stage. Neither Alberta nor Sloan had ever participated in a theatrical event as part of the cast, backstage crew, or production staff, so they were amazed by the electricity in the air. The show hadn't even started rehearsal and the air was overflowing with energy. The feeling was infectious.

Sloan's blue eyes twinkled and looked even more youthful than Bruno's, even though he was more than twice the lawyer's age. He placed his hand on the small of Alberta's back and pulled her close to him. When she breathed, all she could smell was the cologne he always wore, which was a blend of pine and vanilla. As Sloan pressed his lips against Alberta's waiting mouth, the scent intensified, and she felt her body swoon into his. The physical contact was definitely unexpected, but not at all unwanted. Alberta wasn't used to open displays of affection in a crowded space, but she was old enough to know that learning new tricks was the trick to staying young.

And also capturing the attention of the police.

"Do I need to pour cold water on you two?"

"Tambra Mitchell!" Alberta cried. "Please tell me you're in the play too and you're not here to arrest us for disorderly conduct?"

"The correct charge would be lewd behavior," Tambra corrected.

"*Dio mio!*" Alberta cried. "I'd be like my cousin Rosa,

who brought shame on the entire family. God rest her soul."

"Vinny's right," Tambra said. "You really do have a colorful family."

"Vinny should watch his mouth," Alberta teased. "I know all about the skeletons in *his* family's closet, and some of them are in Technicolor."

"I'll keep that in mind," Tambra replied. "And to answer your question, I'm playing Elaine Harper; she's engaged to Mortimer, who's the nephew to the homicidal aunts."

"I can't believe this play is a comedy," Alberta said.

"One of the funniest ever written," Sloan replied. "I can't wait to spread the word, this show is precisely what this town needs."

Tambra went on to explain that that was precisely why she decided to audition. A self-described theatre nerd since childhood, she performed in shows all throughout high school and college, but stopped when she enrolled in the police academy to concentrate on her studies. Police work, even in a small town, was serious business, and she needed to bring some laughter back into her life.

"And because Vinny is too scared to get on stage," Tambra said, "he gets to live vicariously through me."

Alberta knew Tambra was being facetious, but she was still concerned by her comment.

"That man needs to get a social life," Alberta declared. "I'm starting to worry about him."

An impish smile grew on Tambra's face and Alberta knew there was a secret underneath, dying to be revealed.

"What do you know about Vinny that I don't know?" Alberta demanded more than asked.

As Tambra hedged to avoid responding, she was saved

by a pair of fellow members of her acting troupe: Nola and a young man neither Alberta nor Sloan recognized. Tambra, on the other hand, recognized the group's entrance as a means for her quick exit.

"Excuse me," Tambra said. "I need to talk to my director about my character's motivation."

"Hi, everyone," Nola announced, approaching the couple. "I wanted to introduce you to our leading man, Kip Flanigan. He's going to play Mortimer Brewster, the part Cary Grant played in the movie. Now please excuse me as I attend to a spill backstage. A producer's work is never done!"

Alberta and Sloan introduced themselves, and before Kip could reply, they launched into a discussion of the young man and acted as if he had joined Nola on cleanup duty.

"I don't think he looks like Cary Grant, do you, Sloan?" Alberta asked.

"No, he hasn't got the floppy ears," Sloan replied. "Freddy looks more like Cary Grant than he does."

"He does look like someone, though," Alberta said.

"Tony Perkins," Sloan replied.

"You think so?"

"Yes, squint your eyes."

Alberta squinted and then squealed, "Oh yes, I see it. He *does* look like Tony Perkins."

"From that *Psycho* movie," Sloan clarified.

"That was such a scary movie," Alberta declared. "And the fact that he resembles Tony Perkins will work perfectly in this play, won't it? Like Bruno said, it's a comedy, but it's all about murder."

"That's true," Sloan agreed.

"That's not *exactly* true."

They were so engrossed in their own conversation that when Kip spoke, they were startled.

"Mortimer is practically the only one in the play who isn't a murderer," Kip explained. "He's trying to stop everyone from killing people, not the other way around."

Now that they heard Kip speak, they immediately changed their opinion about which former movie star he took after.

"He *is* Cary Grant!" Alberta exclaimed. "He sounds just like him."

"The same high-pitched voice," Sloan said. "A bit clipped and almost frantic. Are you British?"

"No," Kip replied. "I'm from the Boston area."

"That's in New England, which is close enough," Alberta said.

Through their joint interrogation they uncovered some facts about Kip. He'd recently moved to the area and was a real estate lawyer who, like Bruno and Tambra, had a lifelong passion for the performing arts. He had been looking to become part of a community theatre and jumped at the chance to audition for the Tranquility Players when he saw the notice posted in the New Jersey theatre group he belonged to on Facebook.

Without knowing anything about his acting ability and comedic skills, it was easy to see why Johnny had cast Kip in the lead. He had a certain presence. It wasn't commanding, it was comfortable. At five eleven and roughly 175 pounds, Kip didn't cut an imposing figure, and his dark brown hair, green eyes, soft features, and fair complexion worked well together, but weren't striking. Kip was good-looking in a preppy, schoolboy way and not the dreamboat Bruno was. Women in the audience would think they could be his girlfriend and men in the audience would think they could get a beer with him. It was an important quality a director looked for if he wanted his audience to care about what happened to his leading man.

Alberta was curious to know what Kip thought of the play's leading lady.

"Are you excited to meet Missy Michaels?" Alberta asked.

Kip hesitated before he answered. "I know everyone's really pumped to have her in the show, and according to Google, she was pretty famous a long time ago, but I hate to admit this and please don't tell anyone, I've never heard of her before."

"You sound like my granddaughter, Jinx," Alberta said, laughing. "She has no idea who Missy is either."

"Jinx is the reporter who's going to do a piece on the show, right?" Kip asked.

"Yes, she's the star reporter of *The Upper Sussex Herald,*" Alberta declared.

Kip thought for a moment and then replied, "She realizes the shortcut for that is *TUSH,* right?"

"Yes, but don't ever say that in front of Jinx's editor," Sloan warned.

"As long as you guys don't tell anyone I never heard of Missy before," Kip said.

"Your secret's safe with us," Alberta said.

From the stage, with Johnny by her side, Nola spoke into a microphone so her voice would be heard over the din of conversation and asked the entire cast to join her onstage. Kip, Bruno, Tambra, Helen, Father Sal, and the rest of the members of the company did as they were told and assembled behind their producer and director. As with most community theatre ensembles, it was a motley, if not joyful, crew.

"*Che cast intrigante di personaggi*," Alberta whispered in Sloan's ear.

He attempted to translate, but knew he'd get it wrong. "You think they have character?"

"Yes, of course, but what I said was, 'What an intriguing cast of characters,'" Alberta corrected.

"They do look like a fun group," Sloan said.

With the most important member of that group missing.

"In a few short days Missy Michaels will arrive," Nola announced. "And then the most exciting period in the history of the Tranquility Players will begin!"

She had no idea that it would also be the most notorious.

CHAPTER 6

Una sorpresa prima della sorpresa.

The days leading up to the movie legend's arrival were a bit of a blur. All throughout Tranquility, in the coffee shops, the liquor store, even the roadside fruit and vegetable markets, the conversation inevitably led to Missy Michaels. The star was making her presence known before setting one foot on Tranquility soil.

Those who remembered the child actress told stories about how they imagined themselves living out Daisy's pampered lifestyle. Being catered to by servants, having unlimited funds to buy whatever their hearts desired, and jet-setting from one glamorous location to the other. Of course, no one mentioned that her coveted life was the result of the deaths of her parents in a fiery plane crash, but such ugly truths would tarnish the memory. No, Daisy and Missy were seen as beacons of hope and not the results of tragedy that they were.

Not only was Missy Michaels the topic of every conversation, it also seemed that she was the reason behind everyone's latest jobs. Jinx had already published one article focusing on the comebacks of both Missy and the Tranquility Players, which would be the first in a series, with the highlight being the exclusive interview she would have with the star herself. Helen, Father Sal, and several other members of the community were in the cast, Sanjay and his staff at the Tranquility Arms were preparing to make Missy's stay with them as memorable as her movies, and Joyce and Sloan were spearheading the marketing and publicity efforts for the upcoming production. One of the few people who found themselves without a Missy-oriented task to complete was Alberta.

Despite being relegated to bystander and not participant, Alberta didn't feel left out or snubbed; she regaled in her new position. She might have been on the outside looking in, but that didn't mean she'd be letting everyone else have all the fun. Alberta had spent most of her life watching the world pass her by, but since she moved to Tranquility, she had become an active member of that world. She wasn't going to let that change any time soon.

Through the front glass doors, Alberta could see Joyce and Sloan sitting on folding chairs near the box office in the lobby of the theatre at St. Winifred's. They were looking through papers and files that were scattered along a rectangular, black-lacquer table with a classic Chinese design of interlocking boxes running the length of the underside of the surface. Joyce and Sloan were so engrossed in their work, they didn't hear Alberta enter until she knocked on the glass door. "I hope I'm not interrupting."

"Alberta, what a pleasant surprise," Sloan said.

"Have you gotten the theatre bug too?" Joyce asked. "Or are you still having flashbacks from the last time you were onstage?"

"Berta!" Sloan cried. "You never said you'd been onstage."

Sighing deeply and pointing a stern finger at Joyce, Alberta replied, "It was a very long time ago."

"It sounds like a juicy story," Sloan said. "And I want to hear every word of it."

Bristling at the memory, Alberta nonetheless complied. "In second grade at St. Ann's I played Mary in a Nativity play and dropped Baby Jesus right before the Three Wise Men showed up."

"Please tell me they didn't cast a real baby in the role," Sloan said.

"*Dio mio,* no, thank God!" Alberta exclaimed, making the sign of the cross. "But the doll's head popped off and rolled right off the stage and landed at the feet of Monsignor Valdaccini."

"It's become known as the headless Jesus story," Joyce explained.

"My performance got me in so much trouble with Sister Margaret that it soured me from ever wanting to perform in another show again," Alberta declared.

"You're welcome to sit in the dark of the theatre with the rest of us anytime," Sloan said.

Ignoring his flirtatious comment, Alberta wanted to know why they weren't sitting in the theatre and had made their office in the lobby.

"Nola and her stage crew are getting ready to build the set so there's going to be a lot of noise and activity inside," Sloan said. "We thought it best to sit out here to do our work."

"Looks like you're working in style," Alberta remarked. "That's a lovely table."

"Nola said it was from an old production of *Flower Drum Song*," Joyce explained. "I swiped it from their prop closet."

"Where's that?" Alberta asked.

"In the stage right wing space," Joyce answered.

"That's off the right side of the stage?" Alberta asked.

"Yes, you're getting the hang of theatre lingo," Sloan said. "Just remember that when you're standing onstage, stage right is to your right and stage left is to your left."

"But when you're sitting in the audience," Joyce continued, "stage right becomes audience left and stage left becomes audience right."

"Which is completely logical," Sloan said. "And downstage is in front of you when you're onstage."

"And upstage is behind you," Joyce added. "It's really very simple."

"I feel like I've just watched Baby Jesus's head roll off into the sunset all over again," Alberta joked, thoroughly confused by the lecture.

"Don't worry, by opening night all this jargon will be part of your vocabulary," Sloan said.

"Let's get through Friday night first," Joyce said.

"That's when Missy arrives, right?" Alberta asked.

"Yes, and Nola's decided to throw a party in her honor to welcome Missy to our little hamlet," Sloan explained.

"That's a wonderful idea," Alberta said. "I have a lasagna in the freezer I can defrost."

"Uh-oh," Joyce said.

"Uh-oh what?" Alberta asked. "What's wrong with my lasagna?"

"Nothing's wrong with your lasagna, you know I love it," Joyce confirmed. "But I don't love what Sloan said."

"What did I say?" Sloan asked.

"The name of the play you're not supposed to say," Joyce said.

Sloan took a moment to replay his words in his head and understood Joyce's confusion.

"*Hamlet*?"

"Yes," Joyce said. "Isn't there a superstition that if you say *Hamlet* in a theatre it brings bad luck?"

"No," Sloan said. "You can say *Hamlet*, but you can't say *Macbeth*."

"Sorry," Joyce said. "I got my Shakespeare mixed up."

"Sloan, watch your mouth!" Alberta cried. "You just said the word you're not supposed to say."

"*Macbeth*?" Sloan repeated.

"Now you've said it twice," Alberta replied.

"Don't be silly," Sloan said. "*Arsenic and Old Lace* is a fun little comedy about little old ladies who commit random murder. What could possibly go wrong?"

Alberta and Joyce looked at each other, eyes wide and eyebrows raised. They knew from experience that no matter the situation, anything and everything could go wrong, but they didn't want to smother Sloan's optimistic spirit. A perfectly timed text from Father Sal allowed them to change the subject.

"He wants us all to be at my place at eight tonight," Alberta said, reading the text.

"Why?" Joyce asked. "Did something already go wrong thanks to Sloan's slip of the tongue?"

"It's only a superstition," Sloan protested.

"Feel free to walk under a ladder on Friday the 13th after a black cat cuts you off," Joyce said.

"Aha! You've proven my point!" Sloan exclaimed. "Lola's a black cat and she's never brought anyone bad luck."

"Lola has a white stripe over her left eye," Alberta corrected him. "She's not all black."

"I give up," Sloan said, throwing up his hands and sitting back in his chair.

"We're only teasing you, Sloan," Joyce said. "But to be on the safe side, let's talk less about Shakespeare and more about Father Sal. Why does he want us all to meet tonight?"

"I don't know," Alberta said. "He only said that he has *una sorpresa prima della sorpresa.*"

"A surprise before the surprise?" Sloan questioned. "What kind of surprise?"

Shrugging her shoulders, Alberta replied, "I guess we'll find out tonight at eight."

By ten after eight that night they were still in the dark as to what kind of surprise Father Sal had in store for them because Father Sal still hadn't arrived. They were going to have to hold the proverbial curtain until the star made his entrance.

By 8:20 Father Sal was still a no-show and they were ready to give the star the hook.

"I say we give him five more minutes and then we eat," Vinny suggested.

"We've waited long enough," Helen said. "Berta, take the manicotti out of the oven, I'm starving."

Naturally, when Sal asked that they meet at Alberta's for a surprise, she'd whipped up a quick meal of fried meatballs, roasted vegetables, a bowl of macaroni, and manicotti. The usual array of breads, cheese, and olives was already spread out on the kitchen table and the invited guests had been nibbling, but not enough to satisfy their hunger. They had learned that when they went to Alberta's house, the only thing they were required to bring was a hearty appetite. Helen might have been the only one to express her desire to ignore etiquette and eat before the guest of honor showed up, but the rest of the group had no problem standing in a line behind her with plate in hand, ready to receive a homecooked meal.

Alberta doled out healthy portions to Helen, Jinx, Joyce, Freddy, Sloan, and Vinny. She even cut up a meatball and poured some gravy over it for Lola. The cat was meowing so loudly they didn't hear Father Sal come in through the front door until he was standing with them in the kitchen.

"I can't believe you started to eat without me," he declared.

"I can't believe you're half an hour late," Helen said. "Hold on a second, yes, I can. I forgot the Rosary Club nicknamed you Nine Fifteen Sal."

"Why'd they call him that, Aunt Helen?" Jinx asked.

"Because when he presided over nine o'clock mass, it always started at nine fifteen," Helen explained.

"Getting your vestments to fall just the right way can be tricky," Sal said.

"You want to know what else is tricky, Sal?" Vinny asked.

"What would that be, Vincenzo?" Sal replied.

"Leaving us in the dark all day long and then making

us wait on pins and needles to find out what this surprise of yours is," Vinny said. "Now tell us or I'll arrest you for obstruction of justice."

Sal waved one hand in the air to dismiss Vinny's empty threat, and with the other he dropped a small bag on the table. "Herein lies your surprise."

Reading the name on the bag, Joyce replied, "I think the surprise is on you, Sal. Tranquility Video and Electronic Repair closed up about fifteen years ago."

"I was the first one in line when they announced they were having their out-of-business sale," Sal said. "That's where I picked up this bit of movie history."

What he took out from the bag was the holy grail for any Missy Michaels fan. It was the DVD collection of all fourteen Daisy Greenfield movies.

"We are going to have ourselves a movie marathon!" Sal exclaimed.

Naturally, they started with *Daisy Greenfield: Orphaned Heiress*, the first movie in the series that marked the silver screen debut of the then seven-year-old Missy Michaels. They all knew the basic plot of the movie, even Jinx and Freddy, who had never seen any of the films in the series before, so no one was surprised when Teddy received a telegram announcing that her son and his wife were killed in a plane crash on their way back from their ski vacation in Switzerland. What they didn't expect was how devastated they would be by the news. And it was all thanks to Inga Schumacher's riveting performance.

The thirty-year-old actress was only cast in the role a week before the film went into production. The original concept was that the widowed Teddy was matronly but reserved, and it was Daisy who brought life to Teddy's antiseptic, orderly world. After endless screen tests with every notable actress over the age of fifty, the producers still hadn't made a choice and were starting to panic. They felt that they would never find the right woman for the role. Their failure was because they were looking for the wrong kind of woman.

After a particularly grueling day of screen tests in search of the perfect grandmotherly actress to play the pivotal role of the grandmother, Missy was sitting on the floor with the very nongrandmotherly looking continuity girl. At first Missy was pouting and tired, but within minutes the two were drinking chocolate milk, blowing into their straws to make chocolate milk bubbles, and giggling. It was then that one of the producers overheard Missy say, "I wish someone like you were playing my grandmother because then the little orphan girl's life would be all fun and games."

The producers immediately began a search for a less matronly, less grandmotherly actress to play Teddy. Thanks to Missy's insightful comment, they realized they had to reverse their initial thought of the granddaughter-grandmother dynamic because it wasn't Missy who breathed life into Teddy, it was Teddy who had to bring the orphan back to life. If Daisy was already perky, comfortable with her parents' sudden death, and wise beyond her years, there would be nowhere for the series to go, and the first film was always envisioned to be the start of a series. With Teddy in the role of mentor, the audience—through Teddy's eyes—would watch as Daisy gradually overcame the tragedy in her young life and found a way to incorporate joy to coexist peacefully with the sadness she would always feel at the loss of her parents at such a young age.

Inga was one of the last women to test with Missy and

the first impression she gave the huddled, worried group of men and women who greeted her was that she was too young to play a grandmother. Upon seeing her in hair and make-up, the second impression was with the right lighting she could pass as a young grandmother. After seeing her test, their third impression was that no one other than Inga could play Daisy's grandmother. The chemistry between Inga and Missy was undeniable both as their characters and themselves. By the time Inga had changed back into her own clothes, there was a multi-picture contract waiting for her to sign.

And that's how Inga Schumacher got to play a seven-year-old's grandmother when she was the ripe old age of thirty.

If Missy wasn't such a natural-born actress, she could have had a career as a casting director. But from the first moment Daisy came onscreen to the final shot, Missy's performance was completely unaffected and made the audience feel as if they were peeking into a neighbor's window. She had the magnetism of a young Judy Garland combined with the beauty of a young Elizabeth Taylor, and yet she appeared not to be a cliché or soaked in movie star magic. She looked both lost and grounded, real and imagined, youthful and old, but the audience didn't understand any of that. All they wanted to do was wrap their arms around the little orphaned girl to try to ease some of her pain.

The first time Daisy appeared onscreen she was wearing a black-and-white-houndstooth coat and black patent Mary Janes with white ankle socks. She was holding a suitcase and staring up at her grandmother with eyes that have seen far too much tragedy in her short lifetime. By the time she uttered her first line, *You sure don't look like a grandma*, the little girl with the jet-black hair cut in a bob with severe bangs had already won over the audience's heart. After Teddy knelt before Daisy, took her suitcase from her, and replied, *"Well, you better get used to it because I'm never going to stop being your grandma,"* the world had burst into tears. Which is exactly what Jinx did after seeing the pivotal scene for the first time.

"Oh my God!" Jinx exclaimed. "It's just like you and me, Gram."

"I never thought of that before, lovey," Alberta replied. "But I guess in some ways it is."

Through her tears, Jinx explained her rationale. "You don't act like a real grandmother—except for the food, of course—and we were both reunited when we desperately needed each other. It's like I'm watching myself, except for the bangs, which I could never pull off."

The group, a mixture of family and good friends, had known each other for so long that no one was embarrassed by Jinx's emotional honesty. Her relationship with Alberta wasn't completely parallel to the relationship between Daisy and Teddy, but there were definite similarities. Most important, the sentiment came straight from Jinx's heart. And in that respect, she was very much like Daisy.

By the time the closing credits for the third film in the series—*Daisy Joins the Circus*—scrolled on Alberta's TV it was almost two a.m. and they realized it was time to pause their marathon for another night. They needed to make sure they got their rest because tomorrow night was Nola's party at which they would finally meet Missy in person.

"I wonder what she's like now," Jinx mused.

"Nola hasn't said much about her, has she?" Joyce asked.

"No, they've only spoken on the phone and e-mailed," Jinx replied. "They've never even met."

"She's taking a big risk, casting her in the lead without even auditioning her," Helen said.

"She didn't audition you either," Alberta said.

"Because Helen didn't give her a choice," Father Sal said. "And before you say it, I'll do it for you: I didn't give Nola a choice either. But I did it all for Missy. Getting to be in her company, perform with her, and get to know her as a real person and not someone I've idolized for years will be a dream come true."

They all felt the same way. The little girl the world loved unconditionally and had watched grow up on screen, transforming from a scared, heartsick child into a strong, formidable young woman, was going to arrive tomorrow. No one knew if she'd be that same warmhearted little girl, or if she had turned into someone completely different, but it didn't matter. Whatever person Missy Michaels had become, they couldn't wait to meet her.

CHAPTER 7

Il tempo vola, ma rimane sempre lo stesso.

The day had finally arrived. A little bit of Hollywood was coming to Tranquility, and Alberta could feel the magic in the air. It was still hard to believe that a movie star would soon be in their midst. Then again, Missy Michaels was more than a movie star; she was a friend.

Because Missy played the same character for over a decade in movies that chronicled and highlighted a young girl's growth from child to young women, Alberta, and scores of other filmgoers, felt as if they grew up right alongside her. She wasn't some mysterious, untouchable film creation like Lana Turner, or Jean Harlow who came before her, nor did she play other film roles like Margaret O'Brien or Hayley Mills. Missy's only major role was playing Daisy, and because she played the role for so long the two became interchangeable. As a result, Daisy became less of a character and Missy became more of their contemporary.

Only two years younger than Missy, Alberta easily pictured herself in Missy's Mary Janes and imagined she was living in Teddy's Central Park West luxury apartment instead of the five-room apartment in Hoboken, but even as a young girl, Alberta felt sorry for Missy because the girl up on the silver screen didn't have a family.

It didn't matter that Missy had a closet overflowing with frilly party dresses or a bedroom overpopulated with stuffed animals, Alberta knew that the poor little rich girl would overturn her situation if it meant she could have her parents back. Missy had more *things* than Alberta ever dreamed she would possess, but Alberta possessed the one thing Missy would never have: parents.

Unbeknownst to her, grown-up Missy had tons of friends in Tranquility who were anxiously awaiting her arrival. Lost in a daydream where she was giving Missy a tour of the town's hot spots, Alberta came back to reality just in time to turn down the flame before the water started boiling over the top of the saucepan.

"Ah, *Madon,*" Alberta muttered to herself. "I'd better pay attention or else Missy will have nothing to eat."

From her vantage point lounging on the kitchen table, Lola watched Alberta quickly pour the box of spaghetti into the bubbling water with her head resting on an outstretched arm. Her body language was easily interpreted, and Alberta knew it was full of judgment.

"Don't you look at me that way," Alberta said, pointing a wooden spoon at her beloved cat. "This is a very important day and your mama's *ansiosa*. Now be a good girl and get off the table."

Lola had rarely been a good girl in her entire life, so

Alberta was not surprised when she rolled onto her back, lifted her four paws into the air, and played with an imaginary ball. Feline discipline would have to wait for another time; Alberta had more important things to focus on at the moment, like cooking the food that would be served at Nola's party that evening in honor of Missy's arrival. Alberta had cooked for hundreds of parties before, but this one was somehow more special and she wanted to make sure everything was perfect.

The third tray of lasagna, this one with sausage and hard-boiled eggs like her great-uncle Santino, one of the best chefs in their family's village in Sicily, used to make, was still in the oven, along with a tray of eggplant that had been cut into long strips that would serve as the main ingredient in a recipe Alberta created to satisfy Jinx's healthy diet. Vegetarian braciole consisted of layers of eggplant, green peppers, mozzarella, and portobello mushrooms all rolled together and cooked in Alberta's homemade gravy—the red kind, not the brown. The mushrooms had a similar texture and, remarkably, a similar taste to flank steak, which was the traditional meat used to make braciole, so when you took a bite it was almost as if you were eating the same thing.

In the refrigerator were trays of deviled eggs, a cold seafood salad, two large containers of pasta fagioli, bruschetta topped with spinach, goat cheese, and honey, escarole and beans, stuffed clams, stuffed peppers, and one of Alberta's favorite dishes, mushrooms wrapped in bacon.

There were also trays of sausage, peppers, and onions, and chicken parmigiana that would all be reheated in the kitchen at the theatre. Alberta didn't need help preparing the food, but because her refrigerator couldn't hold everything that was on her elaborate menu, she enlisted Joyce to get the antipasto and Jinx to mix up several batches of Red Herrings.

Nola thought Alberta was off her rocker when she volunteered to provide the food for the party because the entire cast and several invited guests would be attending, until Joyce explained that Alberta was used to feeding the entire Ferrara family, whose total number was closer to the number of seats at the theatre than the number of cast members in the play.

Alberta knew that she was an excellent cook, but she had almost exclusively cooked for her family, who loved her recipes. Cooking for strangers was always nerve-racking because they wouldn't tell you what they truly thought of the meal. If it was terrible, if there was too much garlic, or if the pasta was too al dente, a stranger would never offer a negative critique. Family, on the other hand, wouldn't hesitate to share a blunt opinion, which Alberta welcomed because it only helped make her a better cook. Plus, she'd rather throw away poorly cooked food than force someone to eat it just to spare her feelings. The only thing that induced more fear into Alberta, however, was making dessert.

It was a family truth that Alberta was a terrible baker. Over the years she had tried to follow her grandmother Marie's recipes for struffoli, bamboloni, tiramisu, pignoli, and failed every time. She even tried no-bake recipes for limoncello cheesecake, chocolate mousse, zabaglione, even a simple icebox cake, but there was always something off. The results were edible, just not Alberta-worthy. It had been years since Alberta attempted to make a dessert, but with Missy's impending arrival she thought it was the ideal time to see if she could break the curse.

Hiding in the back of the fridge in a Tupperware container Alberta bought at a St. Ann's fundraiser back in the '90s was a Neapolitan Baked Alaska. The traditional version of the dessert was Daisy Greenfield's favorite, and the first meal she had when she went to live with Teddy. Alberta thought it would be the perfect dessert to serve, with an Italian twist, of course.

She prayed to St. Lorenzo, the patron saint of cooks, to make her offering taste as delicious as the rest of the meal would most likely be. When she handed the Tupperware container to Sloan to bring out to his car for the drive over to St. Winifred's, she felt as if she was placing myrrh at Baby Jesus's feet. Hopefully he wouldn't lose his head after taking a bite.

"Do you think you made enough?" Sloan asked.

"*Per l'amor di Dio!*" Alberta scolded. "Who do you think you are? Shecky McLelland? This is no time to be a comedian, just pack up the car."

"You mean cars," Sloan said, grabbing a shopping bag filled with an assortment of plastic containers in various shapes and sizes. "Luckily, Freddy's right behind me with his truck."

Alberta scooped up Lola, who hadn't moved from her place in the center of the table, and opened the door for Sloan. Jinx entered before Alberta could close the door.

"Hi, Gram," Jinx said, kissing Alberta on her cheek. "Hello to you too, Miss Lola." She repeated the loving gesture and showered the cat in kisses, prompting Lola to meow rapturously. Her next comment provoked a decidedly different response from Alberta. "Gram, do you think you made enough?"

The string of Italian phrases and off-color words that flew out of Alberta's mouth were mostly indecipherable to Jinx, but she got the gist of the message and left the kitchen carrying a tray of lasagna while laughing hysterically. It took them fifteen minutes to pack both cars before Alberta, holding a container of the freshly made spaghetti drenched in red gravy, asked Lola to wish her luck, smiled in appreciation when the cat dutifully purred in response, and shut the kitchen door behind her. On her back, Lola raised her front paws overhead and stretched, yawned silently, and rolled onto her side to survey her domain. She was greatly relieved now that Alberta had left so peace and quiet could be restored to the house.

At the theatre, however, the calm, unfortunately, had been replaced by a storm.

"That sign is tilted!"

Nola's screech bellowed through the theatre's closed doors and filled the lobby. For a moment, Alberta wondered if she should turn and leave. She could spend a quiet night at home on the couch, drinking tea and eating the Baked Alaska she was holding with Lola. If the dessert tasted terrible, she knew her cat would only hold it against her until it was time for her next meal. Before she could give in to temptation, Sloan banged on the lobby door with the tip of his shoe and asked Alberta to let him in.

"I'm sorry," Alberta said. "Nola's yelling distracted me and I forgot to prop the door open."

It was Alberta's turn to put the tip of her shoe to use. She kicked down the lever so the front door to the lobby would remain open while they unpacked the car and brought in their bounty.

"Why's she yelling?" Sloan asked. "I thought that was part of the director's duties."

"Maybe she's lending Johnny a helping hand," Alberta said.

"I could use one of those," Jinx announced, entering the lobby. She was carrying two trays of food topped by a large shopping bag that hid her face from view. "Take the top bag before I trip and break my neck."

"Lovey, why'd you stack them so high?" Alberta asked. "You can't see a thing."

"Ask Freddy," she replied. "He did the stacking."

"Dude," Freddy said, entering the lobby behind her. "I'm trying to shorten the number of trips so we can get this party started."

"It sounds like the party has already started," Alberta said. "Though, honestly, it doesn't sound like much of a party."

Juggling the Tupperware container and the shopping bag, Alberta managed to open the lobby door. When she did she saw that she was right. The theatre was filled with people, there was a huge banner hung from the proscenium arch with the words "Welcome Home, Missy Michaels" written on it, and Nola was in the middle aisle screaming.

"I need someone to fix that sign ASAP! We can't welcome Missy back to the theatre with a droopy sign."

"Did Nola forget that neither the stage, nor Tranquility, is Missy Michaels's home?" Sloan whispered to Alberta.

"I think she's trying to be symbolic," Alberta replied.

"She needs to knock it off," Jinx said. "All week long she's been acting like this night is life or death and I have had it."

Jinx rushed past Alberta and Sloan to enter the theatre.

"The sign looks fine, Nola!" Jinx shouted. "Now stop your shouting!"

"I love when my girl takes charge," Freddy declared.

"I wonder where she gets it from," Sloan added. He winked devilishly at Alberta and then followed Freddy into the theatre.

Shaking her head but smiling, Alberta muttered, "It's gonna be a long night."

As she entered the theatre, something caught her eye that made all the noise fade away and stopped her in her tracks. It was a reminder of why they were all there in the first place.

At the entrance of the theatre just off to the right of the middle aisle was a large poster for the show propped up on a tripod easel. It said, "The Tranquility Players presents *Arsenic and Old Lace*, starring Missy Michaels, star of the Daisy Greenfield movies." In the center of the poster were two photos, one of Missy as the child star she once was and another, presumably, as how she looked today.

"*Il tempo vola, ma rimane sempre lo stesso*," Alberta whispered.

It was true, time flew, but at the same time, it remained the same.

The two images were complete opposites, but, oddly, completely the same. Together, they were bookends of an entire life, the before and after, the past and present of a person Alberta never met, but someone she felt she knew incredibly well. It was a silly thought, a holdover from her youth when she considered Missy a friend. But now, a much older woman, Alberta couldn't let go of the thought and felt a childlike spark ignite within her. She was actually going to be reunited with a long-lost relic from her past.

The photo of young Missy was the classic headshot Alberta remembered seeing advertised everywhere at the start of the girl's career. Her black hair in bangs and cut in a short bob adorned with her signature butterfly barrettes. The photo of old Missy had a different hairstyle, but one Alberta immediately recognized because it was her own. A bob about an inch longer than chin-length, parted on the left, with not a strand of gray among a sea of black. Alberta wondered if Missy used the same hair dye that she did, Clairol's Shade 2 Blue Black. Wouldn't that be a coincidence?

Based on the side-by-side photos, Missy still had the round, black eyes, pert nose, and the dimple in her right cheek that helped make her famous. Alberta suspected the current photo had been airbrushed a bit, but not much, because there were wrinkles on Missy's forehead, lines underneath her eyes, and crow's feet on their sides. Her neck drooped appropriately for a woman her age, and when Alberta looked further down, she gasped. Not because Missy was showing an inappropriate amount of décolletage for a woman her age, but because she was sporting the same gold crucifix around her neck that Alberta always wore.

"Dio mio," Alberta said. "Would you look at that?"

They wore the same hairstyle and the same jewelry, so Alberta wondered what else she and the elusive star had in common. Whether or not they shared any other traits or characteristics didn't matter to Alberta. All she wanted was for the star to arrive so she could see in living flesh the person she had only seen in celluloid.

She looked up at the banner hanging high above the stage and didn't care if the words weren't entirely true, she felt in her heart that the message they conveyed was accurate.

Come on home, Missy, Alberta thought, *everyone is waiting for you.*

CHAPTER 8

È meglio cadere dalla finestra che dal tetto.

An hour later everyone was still waiting.

Alberta sat in a seat in the left section of row K with Helen and Joyce on either side of her and surveyed the theatre. There were people everywhere, but Missy wasn't one of them.

Jinx, Freddy, and Bruno were standing at the far end of the buffet, which was made up of two long, rectangular tables, each topped with black, vinyl coverings trimmed with comedy and tragedy masks in gold. One end to the other was filled with all the food Alberta had prepared, as well as the pitchers of Red Herrings and six bottles of Dom Perignon, which were Joyce's surprise contribution so they could toast their special guest in style. If that guest ever arrived.

At the other end of the table stood Vinny, Tambra, and Father Sal, eating and drinking, but definitely showing signs of concern due to the absence of Missy's presence. On the other side of the aisle from Alberta, and closer to the stage, sat Sloan, who chatted with Luke, still dressed in his medical scrubs because he'd come to the party directly from St. Clare's, and Wyck, who claimed journalistic privilege as editor in chief of *The Herald,* and had invited himself to the party. Scattered throughout the theatre were the other members of the cast and some other notables from the town, but the lead of the show couldn't be found.

"Do you think Missy's gotten cold feet?" Joyce asked.

"Maybe she's just used to making a grand entrance," Alberta replied.

"She'd better not make me wait like this onstage," Helen said. "We don't stand for such unprofessional behavior in the theatre."

"We who?" Alberta asked.

"We, the theatrical community," Helen answered. "Of which I'm a member."

Alberta could easily have pointed out that her sister's membership in the theatrical community was still up for review because she had yet to set foot into the rehearsal room, but she wouldn't dare. This was her sister's moment to shine and Alberta wouldn't say or do anything to extinguish that light. She loved seeing Helen's eyes twinkle a little brighter and her posture be a bit straighter.

Missy might be the draw to ensure a sold-out audience for the play, but Alberta knew in her heart that by the end of opening night the entire town was going to be talking about Missy's costar. Then again, if Helen forgot every line and stumbled across the stage like a blind woman in an obstacle course, Alberta and the rest of the family would praise Helen's performance as if it could rival any role portrayed by Vivien Leigh or Suzanne Pleshette. The former being one of the greatest actresses of all time and the latter being Helen's favorite. She felt Suzanne did a perfect imitation of her gruff tone.

Looking around the theatre, Alberta noticed that Missy wasn't the only one who had chosen to make a fashionably late entrance.

"Maybe Missy doesn't want to arrive before her director," Alberta said.

Joyce and Helen turned around in their seats and looked at all four corners of the theatre. When they were finished inspecting the area, they realized Alberta was correct. Johnny Fenn, the man who was allegedly steering the ship, was nowhere to be found.

"Where's my director?" Helen asked.

"Maybe he's the one picking up Missy and bringing her here," Joyce suggested.

"If that's the case, why is Nola pacing up and down the aisle?" Alberta asked.

"And why does she look like she just sat through one of the shows she directed?" Helen observed.

"Also too, if she holds her cell phone any tighter she's going to crush it," Joyce added.

"Where are you, Johnny?!" Nola screamed. "And why aren't you here?!"

Standing in the middle of a theatre and shouting was one way to capture a crowd's attention. Unfortunately for Nola, it wasn't the way to elicit a helpful response to her question. All it did was create confusion.

"You don't know where our director is?" Father Sal asked.

"If I did, do you think I'd be calling him to find out?" Nola replied.

"I assumed he was going to pick up Missy and bring her over with him," Tambra said.

"Well, you assumed wrong!" Nola shouted.

"Calm down," Jinx ordered. "There's no reason to freak out."

"That's easy for you to say!" Nola screamed, her voice filled with the unmistakable sound that was made when a person freaked out. "You're not the one whose reputation is on the line, mine is! I have everything riding on this production and already it's a disaster!"

"Rehearsals haven't even begun," Wyck said. "A show needs to chug along for a little bit before it can be labeled a disaster."

"You're not helping, Wyck," Jinx said.

"Sorry, it's a side effect of my job," Wyck explained. "I can't help but speak the truth."

"If the truth is all you have to offer, why don't you keep your mouth shut?" Nola asked.

Jinx had moved from the food table where she had been standing and was now walking down the aisle toward Nola. "Listen to me," Jinx said, waving her finger. "You are getting yourself all worked up for absolutely no reason. What did you tell me when I said Johnny was rude for always being late when you two had a date?"

"That artists have a different concept of time than regular people," Nola replied.

Joyce leaned over to whisper into Alberta's ear. "I'm an artist and I'm always on time."

Helen leaned over to whisper into Alberta's other ear. "Tell Joyce that's because she isn't a very good artist."

"Will you two hush and pay attention to Jinx?" Alberta said.

By this point everyone was paying attention to Jinx.

They had moved from their positions throughout the theatre and congregated in the aisle that split the audience into two separate sections. Nola and Jinx might not be standing on the stage, but they were captivating their audience nonetheless.

"So why is this situation any different?" Jinx asked.

"Because this is more important than a date!" Nola exclaimed. "This is the *theatre*!"

"Get your head out of the footlights, Nola," Jinx said. "I know you love the theatre and you find it therapeutic and it's your way of connecting with your students, but nothing—and hear me loud and clear, Freddy Frangelico—nothing is more important than a date."

"That's because you have the best boyfriend in town," Nola said.

"Dude! Did you hear that loud and clear?" Freddy asked.

"Everybody heard her, Freddy!" Jinx exclaimed without turning around to face her boyfriend. "And you're right about Freddy, Nola. But if you don't think Johnny's a good boyfriend, why are you dating him?"

Nola's eyes lit up, and Jinx thought she might have finally gotten through to her friend and made her realize she needed to make better decisions when it came to relationships. But Nola wasn't responding to the words that had come out of Jinx's mouth, she was responding to the person who had come through the lobby door.

"Because right when I need him the most he shows up," Nola said. "Like my very own white knight."

All heads turned to see Johnny looking nervous and walking cautiously down the aisle.

"She does know that he's wearing a black T-shirt and jeans, right?" Helen asked.

"And that silly baseball cap," Joyce replied. "To an indoor function to boot."

"*L'occhio vede ciò che vede l'occhio*," Alberta said.

"Looks like her eyes see something different from what the rest of us are seeing," Sloan replied.

"What do you expect?" Alberta said. "The girl's in love."

Which meant she was not entirely in control of her emotions. One moment she was on the verge of swooning, the next she was about to attack. Her adoring expression had abruptly changed into a mask of fury and Johnny only had to look at her to know that if he didn't offer up an explanation for his late arrival, he was going to be on the receiving end of a very public tongue-lashing.

"I panicked," he said.

"What are you talking about?" Nola asked. "Why would you panic?"

"Because I've never done anything like this before," Johnny explained.

"You told me you've worked in theatre since you were a kid," Nola replied. "This cannot be the first cast party you've ever attended."

"Of course not," Johnny said. "But it is the first cast party I've ever attended where I'm the director and the leading actress is a legend."

"Why should it matter if Missy is a celebrity?" Nola asked. "You're a director, this is what you do."

"I know that, but on the drive over here all I could think about was that tomorrow I'm going to start directing what will be the most important production of my life because Missy Michaels is the lead," Johnny said. "And it hit me that this is the first time I'm going to meet her.

What if she doesn't approve of me? What if she thinks I'm a no-talent hack who just got the job because my girl-friend's the producer?"

Before Helen could reply that no one would blame Missy for thinking that because it was the truth, Alberta gave her sister such an ominous glare that she swallowed her retort and didn't utter a sound.

Although Helen remained silent, Nola wound up saying exactly what was on Helen's mind. "No one would blame Missy for thinking that because it's the truth," Nola said.

"What?!" Johnny cried.

"You are my boyfriend, I am the producer, and you don't have a ton of directing experience," Nola said. "It would be a fair assumption on anyone's part to think that you got the job because of our personal relationship."

"If you're trying to make me feel better, Nola, please stop," Johnny said, clutching his chest. "Oh my God, I feel another panic attack coming on!"

Nola moved closer to Johnny and grabbed his hands. "Trust me, you can't worry what other people think about you, you have to believe in yourself," she said. "I doubt Missy is going to think you're not up for the job, but if she does, prove her wrong. Show her what I already know."

"What's that?" Johnny asked.

"That you're the best darn director this side of Broad-way," Nola declared. "Missy and the rest of the cast are lucky to have you at the helm."

Nola threw her arms around Johnny's neck and kissed him like it was the end of a romantic comedy where the girl finally got her guy. Moved by their emotional embrace, the crowd applauded. The audible recognition reminded Johnny and Nola that they weren't alone, and the couple quickly parted, wearing identical impish grins.

"I'm sorry, everyone," Johnny said. "I swear that from here on in, I will be the director you deserve. Someone who is capable, confident, and not intimidated by a cast member. Even if that cast member happens to be Missy Michaels."

"You shouldn't be intimated. She's just like everybody else in this room."

The entire group thought Missy herself had finally arrived and was responding to Johnny's public promise, but when they turned around to see the woman standing in front of the lobby entrance, they knew they were wrong. The woman in view was a blonde, carrying a briefcase, and twenty years too young to be the woman they were hoping they would see.

"Donna," Nola started. "What are you doing here?"

"I heard the commotion on my way out and thought I'd investigate," she replied. "I forgot you were having a party tonight."

"Are you going to introduce us to your friend, Nola?" Alberta asked.

"This is Donna Russo," Nola said. "The new principal of St. Winifred's Academy."

Donna looked like a principal. Her thick, curly hair could've been unruly, but it had been cut to fall just above her shoulders, so it was manageable. Her five-foot-two frame could've appeared diminutive, but her well-tailored pink business suit and black pumps made her appear more powerful than she was. She looked like someone you didn't want catching you breaking a rule. She sounded like one too.

"Hello, everyone, I didn't mean to barge in and speak out of turn," Donna said. "But one of the hallmarks of a good education is a level playing field. No one student should receive a better education than another."

"Because they all deserve the best," Johnny said.

"Exactly," Donna replied. "Likewise, every cast member is a star in their own right and deserves to be treated that way."

"Thank you," Johnny said. "It's good to be reminded of simple truths every now and then."

"Then my work here is almost done," Donna replied.

"Almost?" Alberta asked.

"Vinny," Donna said, "I was going to call you in the morning, but now that I have you, I can ask you in person."

"You, um, want to ask me something?" Vinny asked.

"Would you mind speaking to the freshman class at an assembly next week?" Donna asked. "About the importance of the police-community dynamic."

"I'd be delighted," Vinny responded, looking relieved. "That kind of audience I can handle."

"Maybe you can wear your old uniform," Donna said. "A man in blue always cuts such a dashing and authoritative figure."

"Do you think you can still squeeze into your old uniform?" Father Sal joked.

"I'm sure his uniform will fit splendidly," Donna said.

Although her tone was far less suggestive than her words, she still managed to quiet the crowd. She might not have been an actress, but she had learned how to command an audience.

"I'll call your office on Monday to confirm a date,"

Donna said. "And with that, good ladies and gentlemen of the theatre, I bid you anon."

When no one returned the deep bow she offered them, she stood with one hand on her hip and used a thick, New Jersey accent to deliver her next line. "That was Shakespeare, ya numbskulls. I thought you *thee-a-tuh* people had class."

Laughter and applause followed Donna as she left the room but was quickly drowned out when Nola let out a scream. "Where's my leading man?!"

Once again, all heads turned and looked around the theatre, but Kip Flanigan couldn't be found.

"First my director is late, now my leading man isn't here," Nola cried.

"Hold on," Bruno shouted. "Kip sent me a few texts, but in all the commotion I didn't hear my phone."

"What did he say?" Nola asked. "Is he sick? Was he in an accident?"

"He's lost," Bruno replied.

"Does he need a police escort?" Tambra asked.

"I'm here!" Kip projected his voice so loudly and at such a high pitch, it sounded like a police siren. "I'm sorry! You should all know right now that I have the worst sense of direction in the entire world. I know my way around a stage like the back of my hand, but put me in a new town and I get lost going around the corner."

"Don't worry, Kip," Nola said, much calmer now that he had arrived. "The party hasn't officially begun yet."

"Good," Kip replied. "Where's Miss Michaels so I can say a proper hello?"

"She's the reason the party hasn't officially started yet," Bruno said. "We're still waiting for her."

After another fifteen minutes of waiting the mood shifted from mildly worried to greatly concerned.

"This is ridiculous," Vinny announced. "I'm going to the Tranquility Arms right now to bring Missy over here."

"Please don't, Mr. D'Angelo," Nola said. "Missy said that she preferred to make a grand entrance and come on her own."

"Once a star, always a star," Sal declared.

"The hotel is only a block away, so I didn't think it would be a problem," Nola said.

"Clearly it's become a problem," Vinny corrected. "Let me go over there and get her."

"She might feel slighted if you barge on over there," Alberta said. "A woman of her stature is used to getting her own way."

"We can't wait all night, what if something's wrong?" Jinx said.

"Nola, why don't you call the Arms and find out if Missy's ready?" Alberta suggested.

"Joyce might have better luck if she makes the call," Helen said.

"It's Sanjay's night off," Joyce said.

"You know the man's schedule?" Helen asked.

Ignoring her sister-in-law, Joyce said, "Talk to Brandon, Nola, he's the assistant manager, he'll be able to help."

Based on the escalating sounds of shock that clung to Nola's words, it appeared that Brandon was only making matters worse. When she ended the call, it took her a few seconds to collect herself before she could speak.

"Brandon said Missy left over an hour ago with her escort," Nola conveyed.

"Who was her escort?" Jinx asked.

"He said he'd never seen him before," Nola said.

"That's impossible," Vinny said. "The Arms is a five-minute walk away. We've all been here for hours, we would've seen her come in."

"What if she never made it to the theatre?"

Alberta's question prompted the group to take action. Luke called St. Clare's and confirmed that no woman who fit Missy's description was rushed to the hospital. Tambra and Vinny called their colleagues and reported that there hadn't been any car accidents or any 9-1-1 calls. To be on the safe side, Vinny and Tambra left the theatre to investigate the surrounding area to make sure Missy hadn't gotten into an accident nearby that had not yet been reported.

Reluctantly, Nola told the cast to go home and she would see them at ten tomorrow morning for the first day of rehearsal. Joyce drove Helen and Father Sal, and Wyck and Benny, who carpooled together, left the theatre with them. Bruno advised Kip to follow him in his SUV so he didn't get lost again, and Luke said he could take anyone who needed a ride in his car, but warned them there was a strange odor coming from his backseat ever since he had to take the cadaver bags to the laundry. Not surprisingly, he had no takers.

"Should we start packing up the food to bring back to the house?"

Jinx heard Freddy's question, but she was more interested in the questions that appeared to be racing through her grandmother's mind. "Gram, what's wrong? You look worried."

"She is," Sloan replied. "She thinks Missy is in real trouble."

"Why, Gram?" Jinx asked. "Do you know something we don't?"

"We don't know anything, which is what worries me," Alberta replied. "What if Missy did make it to the theatre but didn't come through the front door?"

"Where else would she go?" Freddy asked. "The only way into the theatre is through the lobby."

"She could've come through the stage door around the back," Johnny said.

"Or the side entrance that leads to the kitchen," Nola said.

"Or the storage entrance off the wings on stage left," Johnny added.

"I had no idea the place had so many exits and entrances," Freddy said.

"What if Missy got lost backstage and fell?" Nola asked. "She could be like one of those old ladies on TV who's fallen and can't get up."

"È meglio cadere dalla finestra che dal tetto," Sloan replied.

"Why is it better to fall from the window than the roof?" Freddy asked.

"That's the literal translation," Alberta said. "Figuratively, it means to choose between the lesser of two evils."

"Missy could've gotten hurt on her way from the Arms hotel, or she's lying unconscious backstage," Sloan said. "Take your pick."

"I don't like either choice," Nola said.

"Neither do I," Johnny agreed. "Whichever way you look at it, I'm out a leading lady."

"There's only one way to find out if Gram's right," Jinx said. "We need to split up and search the theatre."

Freddy and Sloan went to the kitchen, Nola and Johnny ran off to the stage left wing, and Jinx and Alberta climbed the stairs to the stage and quickly walked down the hallway off the stage right wing, turning right to continue behind the back wall. Without the working light behind the back scrim turned on, the area was pitch black, and they were about to retreat in order to get a flashlight when Alberta saw a light coming out of the star dressing room. When they stood in the doorway, it was evident their search had come to an end.

They found their missing star lying on a settee, wrapped in a lace shawl, and holding a bottle of arsenic. Missy Michaels wasn't lost, she was dead.

CHAPTER 9

Chi è più freddo? L'uomo o il cadavere?

The first thing that struck Alberta was that Missy looked exactly like the publicity photo she had seen in the back of the theatre. Same haircut, same black eyes, same slightly wrinkled face. There had been no airbrushing, no photo enhancement of any kind to make the image look younger or prettier; it captured Missy just as she had looked when she was alive, which, according to the information they currently had, was less than two hours ago. But maybe Alberta was overlooking a crucial detail? What if Missy was still alive?

"Stay here, lovey," Alberta instructed.

Before entering the dressing room, Alberta quickly surveyed the area. There weren't any footprints on the tiled black floor and the mirror attached to the vanity was spotless. The light bulbs that framed the mirror weren't turned on, but they were dust-free, and the flowers in the vase next to the mirror were freshly picked and fragrant. Besides the settee Missy was lying on, the only other pieces of furniture in the room were an occasional chair upholstered in a green-and-gold-paisley pattern, a black half-moon table to the right of the chair that hadn't a speck of dust on its surface, and a brass floor lamp on the left that was topped by an off-white lampshade trimmed on the top and bottom with black ribbon. It was the lamp that illuminated the small room.

Even though to the naked eye it looked as if they wouldn't find any fingerprints in the room, Alberta still took precautions to make sure she didn't contaminate any potential clues. The dressing room wasn't yet a crime scene, but there was a very good chance that was the next role the room would play.

She took off her pale pink espadrilles and tiptoed in her stocking feet until she reached Missy. Alberta placed two fingers on the wrist of Missy's outstretched right hand—the one that wasn't holding the bottle of arsenic— and felt for a pulse she was certain she wouldn't find. After thirty seconds she conceded that her instinct was correct. She looked at Missy's bloodshot eyes and silently commented to herself how sad it was that the former star died before she could make her comeback.

"She's dead," Alberta announced.

Jinx wasn't surprised by the news, and while this wasn't the first time that she had found a dead body in her midst, it was still a shock. Luckily, she hadn't yet become a jaded journalist. She turned away, made the sign of the cross, and started to say a Hail Mary. When she finished her prayer, she kept looking down the hallway to avoid looking into the dressing room.

"We'd better tell the others," Alberta said.

"I already texted Freddy and Nola to let them know we found Missy," Jinx said. "They should be here any second."

Alberta walked into the hallway and started to put her shoes back on. She placed her right hand onto Jinx's shoulder to maintain her balance while bending over and putting the index finger of her left hand into the back of each shoe so she could slip her feet back into her espadrilles. While she was bent over, she looked up, and Missy's eyes were staring right at her. Woman to woman, corpse to detective. Alberta heard Missy's voice loud and clear, as if the words had trickled out of the dead woman's lips.

Find my killer.

Alberta's body shook and Jinx, thinking her grandmother had lost her balance, grabbed her hands to steady her. Alberta was grateful that footsteps coming from the wings on stage left interrupted them because she wasn't sure she wanted to explain to Jinx that she thought she was hearing voices from beyond the grave.

As Nola rounded the corner with Johnny right behind her, the unlucky producer sighed with relief when she saw Jinx and Alberta standing at the dressing room door.

"Thank God!" Nola cried. "Missy, we've been worried sick."

Jinx put up her hands and stopped her friend from physically entering the room and pushed her back slightly so she couldn't look in. She wanted to prepare her for what would undoubtedly be one of the biggest shocks of her life.

"What are you doing, Jinx?" Nola asked. "I have to see Missy to make sure she's all right."

Jinx had a tendency to be blunt, which was an inherited Italian trait. It was a useful quality for an investigative reporter, but unsuitable when attempting to be a sensitive friend. Knowing Nola as well as Jinx did, however, she knew that despite the delicate circumstances a direct approach was needed.

"She isn't all right," Jinx replied. "She's dead."

"What?!"

Nola's scream was instantly followed by Freddy's.

"Dude! Where are the dressing rooms?!"

"Follow the hallway that leads behind the stage!" Jinx shouted. Then, lowering her voice considerably and adopting a much less shrill tone, she looked at Nola and said, "I'm so sorry."

"This can't be happening," Nola said. "Missy can't be dead."

There was no sense in arguing with Nola, so Jinx moved to the side so her friend could peer into the room and see for herself. Gasping, Nola covered her mouth with her hands to stifle another shriek and, seconds later, while instinct was still in control, she stepped forward in an attempt to walk into the room and get closer to Missy. Neither Alberta nor Jinx had to make a move to prevent her from entering the room and disturbing the area because Johnny did it for them.

"Don't," Johnny said. His hand was placed firmly on Nola's left shoulder, which prevented her from taking another step. "We don't want to disturb the room and destroy any evidence."

Alberta was about to ask Johnny why he suspected there would be any evidence that needed to be preserved when Freddy and Sloan entered from the hallway on stage right.

"It's so dark back here you can't see your hand in front

of your face," Freddy said. When he could finally see clearly and saw the group gathered outside the dressing room instead of inside, fawning over their star, he was confused. "Where's Missy?"

Sloan caught Alberta's eyes, and from her expression he knew exactly where Missy was and why the rest of them were waiting outside the room. "Looks like she's right in there."

"Then why is everybody hanging out in the hallway?" Freddy asked. When he stood in the doorway and saw Missy for himself, he understood. "Dude, she's dead."

It wasn't the most eloquent description of the situation they found themselves facing, but it was accurate. All that was needed now was the police's stamp of approval, which they received when Vinny and Tambra returned to the theatre a few minutes later.

The pronouncement, seemingly all the more final when given by an officer of the law, caused Nola to burst into another round of sobs. Johnny wrapped his arms around her, and she clung to him tightly. Sloan put his arms around Alberta and she gratefully held on to her boyfriend as she shed tears for the woman she would never truly get to know. Jinx buried her face into Freddy's broad chest and cried because death had once again made an appearance in her life. Despite their grieving, there was work to be done.

"I called it in, Chief," Tambra said.

"Thank you," Vinny replied. "And thank you, Alfie."

"Me?" Alberta said, pulling away from Sloan and wiping the tears from her eyes. "What did I do?"

"You acted like a real detective," Vinny said. "You had the good sense and the restraint to keep everyone out of this room."

"Don't shower me with praise just yet, Vin. I entered the room so I could find out if Missy was dead or alive," Alberta admitted.

"I know," Vinny said. "Which is what you needed to do in case she needed mouth-to-mouth to be resuscitated. But you didn't let anyone else in and you took off your shoes before entering."

"How do you know I took off my shoes?" Alberta asked.

"The back of your left espadrille is collapsed under the heel of your foot," Vinny said. "They weren't like that earlier, so at some point after we all split up, you must have taken off your shoes, then put them back on."

This time, Alberta held on to Sloan's shoulder for balance as she lifted her left leg to look at her shoe. "*Dio mio*! I was so overwhelmed with all *this* that I didn't even notice."

Tambra's walkie-talkie crackled and she gave instructions on how to find the dressing room backstage.

"I need you all to move out of the way so Forensics can do their job," Vinny said.

"What job?" Johnny asked. "We already know that she's dead."

"We need to find out how she died," Alberta interjected.

"That's right," Vinny agreed. "Tambra, could you take them all back to the theatre?"

"I'm not going anywhere," Nola announced. "This is my theatre and I have a right to know how one of my actors died."

"I understand how you feel, Nola," Vinny started. "But right now, I need you to follow my orders and wait in the theatre until my team is finished. I promise you all I'll share whatever we find with you."

"And we're supposed to just believe whatever you say?" Johnny asked.

"Yes," Vinny replied.

Johnny was about to protest, but Nola spoke first. "The chief is a man of his word. He can be trusted."

The tension in Johnny's body remained and he appeared as if he was physically reluctant to accept what his girlfriend said. Alberta and Jinx glanced at each other, and the intrigued look in their eyes told them both that they were surprised to see Johnny had an issue with the police. Maybe it was simply the strange circumstances they all found themselves in or maybe it was something more deep-rooted. Time would tell.

Forty-five minutes later, Vinny was ready to tell the group assembled in the theatre what the preliminary investigation had found. Unfortunately, it wasn't much more than what they had known before the experts arrived on the scene.

He conveyed that Missy had been dead for approximately an hour. It wasn't a stunning revelation, but nevertheless, it did leave the group stunned because it meant that Missy had died in the theatre while they were a couple hundred feet away. They didn't hear a thing—not her entrance through the stage door nor her exit from this world—and had they known she was going to make a pit stop in her dressing room before greeting everyone on stage, perhaps they could've gotten to her earlier and saved her.

"No one should blame themselves," Vinny said. "There was no way to know that Missy wasn't going to enter from the front of the house, and there's a very good indication that she didn't want to be heard until she was found."

"What do you mean, Vin?" Alberta asked.

"It appears that we may be dealing with a suicide," Vinny announced.

"That's ridiculous!" Nola exclaimed. "Why would Missy commit suicide? She was about to make her comeback."

"Maybe she was too frightened to go through with it," Sloan offered.

"So quit the show and go back home," Freddy said. "Don't go to the trouble of making the trip just to off yourself before the first day of rehearsal."

"If you'd let me finish," Vinny said. "I was about to remind everyone that just because it looks like a suicide, it doesn't mean it is. We won't know until we get the full report back from the medical examiner."

"Now I'm impressed, Vin, with how much *you've* grown as a detective," Alberta said. "We have to rule suicide out, but Missy was definitely murdered."

"Murdered!"

It wasn't lost on Alberta that the only people who didn't shout that word were either members of the police department or the director of the show.

"Alfie!" Vinny yelled. "How many times do I have to tell you not to get carried away and make a snap judgment?"

"I'm not getting carried away," Alberta said. "Did you see what was around her neck?"

"A lace shawl," Vinny replied. "Not particularly in style for a woman of any age, but she was probably getting into character. We won't know if Missy committed suicide, was murdered, or died of natural causes until we get the autopsy report, so until then, no one should speculate. And that means you too, Alfie."

Alberta opened her mouth to speak, but then saw the group looking at her, waiting to hear what she was going to say. As the widow of a man who hated to be contradicted, Alberta had learned that it was sometimes better to keep her thoughts to herself and allow others to think they had won an argument. She disagreed with Vinny but felt it wasn't the time to contradict him. She would do that once she had proof that she was right.

"I hope you put the autopsy on the fast track," Jinx said.

"Yes, I told the medical examiner to make it a priority," Vinny shared. "Now if you'll excuse us, we're needed elsewhere."

Vinny, followed closely by Tambra, retreated backstage while the six people who were the first witnesses to Missy's death gathered closer together. Most of the law enforcement workers were backstage with only two cops standing guard near the lobby doors, but they still felt they needed to speak quietly and maintain an air of privacy.

"I cannot believe Missy died right here in the theatre on the night before rehearsals were about to start," Nola said. "This show was supposed to put the Tranquility Players on the map."

"It'll probably still do that," Freddy said. "But, you know, for all the wrong reasons."

"This is an absolute disaster," Nola cried.

"Tell me about it," Johnny said. "This production was supposed to make my career and now it's going to ruin it. I mean, how selfish could Missy be to kill herself right before rehearsals? She couldn't wait until after opening night?"

Alberta wasn't able to tell if Nola shared her opinion that Johnny's comment was callous and inappropriate when she pulled her boyfriend away from the group in an attempt to calm him down. Regardless of what Nola thought of Johnny's point of view, it was clear that Jinx, Freddy, and Sloan agreed with Alberta.

"Dude," Freddy said. "That dude's rude."

"Also too, as Aunt Joyce would say," Jinx added, "he's a jerk."

"I don't disagree with either of you," Sloan said, "but we're not theatre people, and remember that old adage."

"*Chi è più freddo? L'uomo o il cadavere?*" Alberta asked.

"What's that mean, Gram?" Jinx asked.

"Who's colder: the man or the corpse?" Alberta translated.

"I'm going with the dude," Freddy said. "I mean, the man."

"You might be right, Berta," Sloan said. "But I was referring to the theatre motto: The show must go on. Despite Missy's unfortunate and ill-timed demise, the Tranquility Players still have a show to do. As the director, that's Johnny's top priority, which means he's under an extraordinary amount of stress."

"And stress does make people act funny," Alberta added.

"It certainly does," Sloan said. "And he and Nola both had a lot riding on this show."

The fate of their production of *Arsenic and Old Lace* would have to wait as a different type of show was currently taking place in the theatre.

Two men wheeled the gurney that held Missy's body across the stage. They moved from stage right to stage left and slowly rolled the gurney down the ramp that led to audience level. Like a funeral procession, the men moved down the aisle of the theatre, causing the group to part to either side to let the gurney pass by.

When Missy's body, covered in a thin, white sheet, passed them, they all made the sign of the cross. Everyone except Johnny. Alberta wasn't sure if he abstained from the gesture because he wasn't religious or if he wasn't sorry that Missy was dead. Maybe he was still angry with her because he considered her death to be more of an inconvenience than a tragedy. For the moment, Alberta pushed those thoughts out of her mind so she could concentrate on praying for Missy's soul.

When the results of the autopsy came in, she'd decide if she needed to pray for Johnny's soul as well.

CHAPTER 10

Scatta una foto, dura più a lungo.

A melancholy air floated above the ladies' heads, thick and heavy, until it descended and infiltrated their spirits, turning their moods from somber to heartsick. A woman didn't die alone, she took with her a collection of dreams.

Sitting around Alberta's kitchen table, the four women who made up the unofficial Ferrara Family Detective Agency stared at their glasses of untouched Red Herring and unopened Entenmann's boxes and wrestled with what had transpired only a few hours before. The event itself, as well as the collateral damage. Each of them had a reason to mourn.

Joyce had enjoyed Missy's movies as a child, but it was only when she was an adult, with her own children, that she felt a connection to the fictional character she hadn't previously recognized. Although Daisy was raised by her grandmother, she was an orphan and, consequently, on her own. As the only African American member of a large Italian family, Joyce often felt the same way. She was never alone, but oftentimes she felt isolated, not because of anything the Ferraras did, just the undeniable fact that she was an outsider. It was this kinship with Daisy that filled her with excitement to finally meet her. She was also delighted to be working with Sloan on the show's publicity and explore a professional skill she hadn't utilized in years.

Jinx didn't have a personal bond with Missy until she saw her movies, and then she saw herself as the little girl on the screen, forging a new and unexpectedly powerful relationship with her grandmother. She couldn't wait to interview the woman and delve into her connections with Teddy as well as her biological grandmother. But the opportunity would never come. Jinx had been in this situation before, where a professional gig was derailed due to circumstances out of her control, but the sense of loss was still maddening.

Helen admitted that her feelings about Missy's demise were largely selfish. At her core she grieved for the loss of life, but right outside that feeling was a more personal sorrow for the loss of her chance to appear onstage. She knew it was a petty and self-centered reflection that shamed her, and yet she couldn't shake the sense of utter disappointment that consumed her.

Alberta felt like a part of her had died along with Missy. Was she being narcissistic? Was she being histrionic? She didn't know. All she was certain of was that a woman her age who resembled her, a woman she'd fantasized was her childhood friend, had died before she got to say hello. It was devastating. It made Alberta contemplate her own mortality, and it put death with a capital *D* into a new perspective.

None of these losses were as significant as the loss of a human life, but nevertheless, having those dreams and hopes shattered so abruptly and completely left wounds that cut deep. Wounds that would take a long time to heal, especially if it turned out that Missy took her own life. A fact that the ladies vigorously debated.

"Do you think Vinny could be right and Missy committed suicide?" Joyce asked.

She said the last word softly, almost mouthing it, so Lola, who she was cradling in her arms, wouldn't overhear.

"I don't think so," Alberta said.

"We can't gloss over the obvious," Jinx instructed. "Missy was found clutching a bottle of arsenic."

"Don't you think that's a bit too on the nose?" Alberta said.

"She was going to star in *Arsenic and Old Lace,*" Helen started. "Maybe she felt it gave her death some kind of symbolism."

"Clearly, the woman loved symbolism," Jinx said. "I mean, she wrapped herself in a lace shawl."

"No, she didn't," Alberta said.

"Gram, we all saw it," Jinx said. "I'm not sure if it was hers or a prop, but Missy's body was wrapped in a lace shawl."

"I know that's what it looked like," Alberta said. "But that's wrong."

It could have been the late hour, or it could have been

that everyone was tired after a long and unfortunately noteworthy day, but tension started to grow between the ladies like a foul odor. It was unpleasant, but it couldn't be ignored.

"Berta, now you're getting carried away," Helen said. "I know you think you always know what's going on, but there's no way you could know that."

"Helen's right, Berta, you need to reel in your imagination," Joyce added. "Missy was an actress, maybe she was creating a scene. She drank some arsenic and then added a nice touch by wrapping herself in a lace shawl."

"Missy wasn't being subtle, nor did she kill herself," Alberta declared. "Somebody did that for her."

Jinx's face scrunched up, as if she'd just bit into a sour apple. "Trust me, Gram, I get it. If Missy was killed, that would make for a much better story."

"It isn't a story, lovey, it's the truth," Alberta protested. "Missy was murdered."

"Just because that's what you think happened, Berta, doesn't make it the truth," Helen stated.

"It isn't what I think happened, it's what I know!" Alberta shouted.

She didn't mean to shout, but she was growing tired of not being heard. Hadn't she proven that her instincts were usually right? Hadn't she solved enough murders to warrant devotion from her flock? Shouldn't all those around her offer up blind faith and simply agree to whatever she said knowing she couldn't possibly be wrong?

Instead of following up her shout with a rant, Alberta started to laugh. Acting foolish was better than saying something that would make her look like a fool. The women sitting around her kitchen table weren't part of her flock, they weren't her entourage, they were her family. And family didn't always temper honesty with sweet talk.

"I'm sorry," Alberta said. "I didn't mean to yell. It's been a stressful day."

"It's been a stressful week," Helen said. "But you're not off the hook, Berta. Why are you so insistent that Missy was murdered?"

"Because she was," Alberta replied. "And it was premeditated."

Now that Alberta was speaking in a quiet, almost resigned tone, her claim didn't trigger exasperation, it didn't make those around her indignant and combative, it made them curious.

"How do you know that, Gram?" Jinx asked.

"Because she wasn't wrapped in a lace shawl," Alberta replied.

"Yes, she was," Joyce said. "We all saw it."

"No, we all saw what the killer wanted us to see," Alberta explained.

"Berta, we're all tired," Helen said. "Just tell us what you're talking about. What did we see that we really didn't see?"

"Missy wasn't wrapped in a lace shawl," Alberta said, "it was a lace curtain."

"A curtain?" Helen said. "How do you know that?"

Alberta looked around the table sheepishly. She wasn't proud of what she had done, but it was time to confess, and prove that she had come to her conclusion about Missy's demise not solely based on instinct, but also on fact.

"I may or may not have taken a photo of the crime scene," Alberta announced.

"You did what?!" Jinx exclaimed.

"Berta, is that allowed?" Joyce asked. "I mean, is it a crime to take a photo of a crime scene?"

"Technically, when we first found Missy's body, the dressing room wasn't a crime scene," Jinx said. "However, I think it's fair to say it's generally frowned upon to use such a locale as a photo op."

"Wait a second," Helen said. "Jinx, weren't you with your grandmother when you found the body?"

"Yes," Jinx replied. "Gram and I were the first to arrive at the scene; we discovered Missy together."

"That room is tiny," Helen said. "How come you didn't see her snap some photos of the dead movie star?"

Slowly, three heads turned to stare at Alberta. It would've been four, but Lola had sensed the conversation had the potential to become belligerent, so she leaped from Joyce's arms for the safety of the living room.

"Remember, lovey, when I entered the room on my own to check that Missy was really dead?" Alberta asked.

"Of course; you took off your shoes first so you wouldn't contaminate the room," Jinx said.

"After I couldn't find a pulse and declared Missy was dead, I saw that you turned away to pray, so I took some photos of Missy with my phone," Alberta confessed.

"You took advantage of my moment in prayer to snap some photos of a dead woman?!" Jinx shrieked.

"That is one way to describe my actions," Alberta said.

"Gram, I have never been so proud of you!" Jinx exclaimed.

"*Subdolo!*" Helen proclaimed, raising her hand overhead and pointing her index finger to the heavens.

"Yes, it was sneaky," Alberta admitted. "And I don't know what possessed me to do it, but I did. All I could think of was that phrase everybody used to say when we were kids."

"Which one?" Helen asked. "'You're all gonna burn in hell'?"

"*Scatta una foto, dura più a lungo*," Alberta replied.

Joyce laughed involuntarily. "Take a picture, it lasts longer."

"So does this suspense," Jinx said. "I can't take it anymore, Gram, show us the results of your borderline spiritual transgression."

Reluctantly, Alberta stood up and grabbed her pocketbook from the kitchen counter. She sat back down and placed it on the kitchen table, and as if she were performing a pious ceremony, she unzipped the pocketbook, stuck her hand inside its confines, and slowly retrieved her phone. By the time she held the prize in her hand, the three other women had gotten up and stood behind her. Turned out she did have a flock. Alberta was the cleric and Jinx, Joyce, and Helen were her impatient congregation. It was revelation time.

When Alberta brought up the photo of Missy sprawled out on the settee, the three women crowded behind Alberta gasped. This was the first time Helen and Joyce had seen Missy in her role as a corpse, so they were shocked by the visual. Although Jinx had been one of the first to witness Missy's death, seeing it captured on camera gave it a grotesque appearance. Even Alberta grimaced when she looked at her screen. She closed one eye and turned her head away as she did when she watched one of those old horror movies Sloan loved.

There might not be any blood in the photo, nor was Missy's body disturbed in any way, it was still a gruesome portrait of the last moments of someone's life. Just knowing that the woman they were looking at was dead gave Missy's peaceful stare and supine position an aura of the macabre. Suddenly, Jinx expressed an unabashed enthusiasm for her grandmother's slightly unethical achievement that surprised the women more than the morbid screenshot.

"Oh my God, Gram, this is so gross, but at the same time so fascinating!" Jinx roared. "You have got to send that photo to me!"

"Ah *Madon*, why would you want such a thing?" Alberta asked.

"Do you know how much of a raise Wyck will give me for a photo like this?" Jinx asked rhetorically.

"Jinxie!" Helen cried. "You can't put Missy's dead face on the cover of *The Herald*."

"Why not?" Jinx asked.

"Because it's immoral," Helen replied.

"It's indecent," Alberta said.

"Also too, Vinny will blow a gasket," Joyce added.

"Joyce is right, lovey," Alberta said. "Vinny isn't your biggest fan and he'll be out for blood if you do that."

"I don't understand why the man doesn't like me," Jinx said. "I'm really very likable."

"*Voi due siete come l'olio e l'acqua*," Alberta explained.

"Which one's the oil and which one's the water?" Jinx asked.

"Let's not dwell on that right now," Alberta said. "Swear to me you won't publish that photo."

With her arms crossed, Jinx stomped her foot. "Fine!

But how does that photo prove Missy was wearing a lace curtain and not a lace shawl?"

The fact that the women had reacted so viscerally when they were shown the one photo Alberta had taken of the deceased woman, it was not surprising that they'd reacted in an even more heightened fashion when they discovered she had taken three.

Alberta swiped left to reveal a close-up photo of Missy's face and then swiped left again to reveal a close-up of the lace. For some reason, the group shrieked louder when they saw the photo of the material than when they saw the photo of a dead Missy's face with her eyes opened, but it was more of a reaction to the unexpected image than to what they were actually seeing. At every swipe, Alberta was surprising them, so they naturally expected the next image to be worse than the first.

"What in the world were you doing, Berta?" Helen asked. "Building a portfolio?"

"I was trying to capture a clue," Alberta replied. "Look closely at this photo and tell me what you see."

Helen, Jinx, and Joyce peered closer to the close-up. The women searched the photo for a suggestion that would indicate what they were looking at was a piece of a curtain and not a shawl, but all they saw was a piece of lace. They weren't able to see what Alberta had seen until she told them what was hiding in plain sight.

"Look closely," Alberta said. "You can see an opening for the curtain rod at the bottom of the hem."

Another gasp arose from the group.

"Wow, Gram, you're right," Jinx said.

"Look at that," Helen said, "it isn't a shawl after all, it's a curtain."

"Which means that it wasn't Missy's," Alberta declared.

"How can you be certain, Gram?" Jinx asked. "The photo confirms that it's a curtain, but Missy could've easily used that instead of a shawl."

"Think about it," Alberta started. "If Missy was going to go to the trouble of staging a symbolic suicide, don't you think she would put some effort into it and get a real lace shawl? Such a thing isn't hard to find, and being an actress, she would be aware of how important details are when creating a scene."

"That's really smart, Gram," Jinx said.

"Thank you, lovey, but I wish I was wrong about all this," Alberta replied.

"Why would you say that, Berta?" Joyce asked. "This is a very important clue."

"I know," Alberta said. "But it means that someone brought the lace curtain with them with the specific intention of staging Missy's murder in her dressing room so it looked like a suicide."

"That's a sobering thought that, unfortunately, makes sense," Joyce said. "If Missy were going to commit suicide, she would've waited until after the show opened for maximum publicity."

"Or at least she would've done it on the stage during rehearsal to make sure she was found by as many people as possible," Jinx hypothesized. "Not hidden away in her dressing room where no one knew where she was."

Helen shook her head. Not because she disagreed with what she was hearing; she just didn't like the implication. "Missy wanted to be back in the public eye, that's why she was reigniting her career. If she wanted to kill herself in darkness, without an audience, she could've done it at home."

No one had to say the words out loud because they all knew the truth. And it was a painful truth to admit. Their beloved star hadn't taken her own life. Someone had murdered Missy Michaels and they'd done it right under their noses.

CHAPTER 11

Meglio amico che nemico.

No matter how many times Alberta and Jinx walked through the front doors of St. Clare's Hospital, it never got easier. It didn't matter if they were entering the facility as visitors or investigators, death was always lurking nearby. As amateur detectives working on a case, they had no choice but to get used to the feeling of rubbing shoulders with the grim reaper. As women, however, they found these visits emotionally daunting.

"I'm really starting to hate this place," Jinx announced as she held open the door for Alberta to enter.

"I wish I could say it gets easier, lovey, but it doesn't," Alberta said. "My nerves always get rattled when I come to a hospital."

"Really?" Jinx replied. "I thought it was just me."

"It's most people," Alberta said. "You come to the hos-

pital because you're sick, you think you're sick, or someone you know is sick."

"That is so depressing, Gram," Jinx said.

"Hospitals are depressing," Alberta declared.

"Wait a second," Jinx said. "Women go to hospitals to
have babies. That's not a scary, nerve-racking experience."

Alberta laughed out loud and threw an arm around her
granddaughter. "That's because you haven't given birth
yet. Let me know how you feel after you've been in labor
for fifteen hours."

Folding into her grandmother's embrace, Jinx replied,
"As long as you're by my side, I'm sure I won't feel any
pain."

Alberta kissed Jinx's cheek and said, "*Possa Dio pro-
teggere.*"

"You want me to be God's protégé?" Jinx asked.

"I said 'May God protect,'" Alberta explained. "But if
we all acted like God's protégé, maybe we wouldn't have
to come to the morgue to visit another murder victim."

As optimistic and upbeat as Alberta had become ever
since moving to Tranquility, she could easily tap into her
more pessimistic roots.

"You really know how to be a killjoy, Gram," Jinx
joked.

When Alberta replied, her tone was devoid of any
humor. "Well, remember, we're here to start our investigation to find out who killed Missy."

The morgue looked exactly the same as it did the last
time they had visited. Gray walls lined with gray, metal
drawers that housed the gray-pallored bodies of the re-

cently deceased. It was a dreary room befitting a house of death, but it was also calming thanks to the soothing music that filled up the space.

"I see you still have your transistor radio dialed into the easy listening station," Alberta said.

Luke looked up from his computer and smiled his trademark toothy grin. He was a big guy, foreboding and goofy at the same time, a bit like Cerberus guarding the gates of Hell if the creature had undergone basic training to thwart its more ferocious tendencies. When he wasn't dabbling in community theatre, Luke's professional role was gatekeeper not only to the morgue, but to the medical examiner's office, which was at the end of the room behind him.

"Hi, Mrs. Scaglione, hey, Jinx," Luke said. "I'm riding a late '60s retro vibe lately."

Alberta listened closely and realized the instrumental music was Burt Bacharach's "I Say A Little Prayer."

"How appropriate," Alberta said.

The music might have been, but Luke's presence was not.

"What are you doing here?" Jinx asked. "You have rehearsal today."

"I had the early shift. I'm leaving in a few minutes," Luke explained. "But it isn't like we're going to be doing any rehearsing today without our leading lady."

"Nola's heartsick over it. She's going to break the news to the cast," Jinx said. "Most of them don't even know what's happened."

"I guess this is the tragedy part of theatre," Luke said. "I was really looking forward to the comedy side, though, given my usual surroundings."

"There'll be other shows," Alberta said. "And maybe

it's time for you to look for a position upstairs. The basement is no place for a young man like yourself."

"Thanks, Mrs. Scaglione," Luke said. "I've been exploring other opportunities."

"Good for you, and if you need a recommendation, I'd be happy to supply you with one," Alberta replied. "Is Vinny here?"

"He's in Pedro's office," Luke replied.

"Who's Pedro?" Jinx asked.

"The new medical examiner," Luke explained. "Started a few weeks ago."

"And already he's got his first mur—"

She couldn't think of a better way to stop Jinx from finishing her sentence, so Alberta hit Jinx in the chest with her pocketbook. It wasn't an artful maneuver, and while it achieved its goal, which was to stop Jinx from talking, it didn't silence her.

"Ow!" Jinx howled. "That hurt, Gram."

"Sorry, lovey," Alberta replied. "There was a fly on your jacket and I was trying to shoo it away."

"With deadly force?" Jinx asked.

"When in Rome," Luke offered. "You can go right in, they're expecting you."

"Thanks, Luke," Alberta said.

On the short walk to the medical examiner's office, Jinx wanted to know why Alberta had used her pocketbook as a lethal weapon.

"Why'd you haul off and whack me back there?" Jinx whispered.

"Because I don't want it to get back to Vinny that we're spreading rumors that Missy was murdered before the official announcement," Alberta said.

"Got it," Jinx said. "Leave the man his pride so he leaves us alone to investigate."

"Exactly," Alberta said. "A little pain in the boob is a small price to pay."

"I think it's the first time I'm glad I have little boobs," Jinx mused.

"Ah, *Madon.*" Alberta sighed. "Don't blame me for that. My boobs may sag, but they've never been little."

Alberta knocked on the door and entered, but Jinx lagged behind until she was certain she wasn't going to start laughing in response to her grandmother's slightly ribald comment. Vinny wasn't Jinx's biggest fan; no need to give him more of a reason to dislike her.

"Hi, Vin," Alberta said. "Don't yell at us for barging in, Luke gave us the go-ahead to enter."

"When does the chief ever yell?"

Even if Luke hadn't given them a heads-up, it would've been easy for Alberta and Jinx to figure out that the man who spoke was Pedro Suarez, the new medical examiner. Not only did the middle-aged man have the thick, black hair, olive complexion, and high cheekbones that were quintessential Latin features, he was standing behind the desk in the ME's office and wearing a spotless white lab coat with his first name sewn onto the breast pocket.

"How long have you known Vin?" Alberta asked.

"Since my interview last month," Pedro replied.

"Give it a few more days," Alberta said. "You'll hear the real Vinny D'Angelo loud and clear yelling from his office. His voice has a tendency to carry."

Vinny tried to maintain a jovial expression, but he clenched his jaw and his smirk looked like the start of a menacing growl. When he spoke, his voice sounded more exasperated than inviting.

"These are the ladies I was telling you about," Vinny said. "Alberta Scaglione and her granddaughter, Jinx Maldonado."

Pedro extended his hand to Alberta, who grasped it firmly. "Hello, Alberta, a pleasure to meet a woman with such a strong handshake."

"My father would always say, *Le strette di mano deboli sono per i pesci bagnati,*" Alberta said.

Before she could translate, Pedro replied, "He would be proud that his daughter didn't grow up to be a wet fish."

"You speak Italian?" Alberta asked.

"Italian, German, English, Portuguese, a little Mandarin, and, of course, my native Spanish," Pedro replied.

"*Dio mio!*" Alberta exclaimed. "You're like the United Nations."

"Pleased to meet you, Mister . . ." Jinx said, extending her hand to Pedro.

"Suarez," Pedro replied, shaking Jinx's hand. "I see the apple doesn't fall far from the tree. You have a firm grip like your *abuela.*"

"Thank you," Jinx replied.

Jinx turned to Vinny and adopted a different tactic from her usual blunt approach. She thought it might score her some brownie points if she were polite. "Excuse me, Vinny, is this a good time to fill us in on the autopsy report?"

It worked. Vinny stared at Jinx, surprised and momentarily silenced by her professional tone, before he replied, "It's, um, perfect timing, actually. Pedro was just about to fill me in on his findings."

"When the chief called me late last night, I knew it

must be important, so I worked through the night to have the report ready for this morning," Pedro replied.

"I can't believe you got a toxicology report so quickly," Vinny said. "I thought those things took at least a few days even if they were rushed."

"I didn't do a toxicology report," Pedro replied.

"What?!" Vinny cried. "I specifically told you that I wanted a toxicology report."

"Yes, that's exactly what you said," Pedro confirmed.

"Then why didn't you order one?!" Vinny shrieked. "If you want to keep this job, Pedro, you're going to have to do what you're told!"

Smiling, Pedro turned to face Alberta. "This must be the yelling you were talking about."

"Yes," she replied. "It's reared its pretty little head quicker than I thought."

"This isn't a joke!" Vinny shouted.

"I assure you, Chief, I never joke when it comes to my work," Pedro responded in a voice that was notably calm despite the tense conversation he was engaged in. "But in this instance, a toxicology report is unnecessary. Ms. Michaels didn't die from arsenic poisoning or anything else she might have ingested."

"She was strangled, wasn't she?" Alberta asked.

Pedro's thick, black eyebrows shot up like two startled caterpillars. "She most certainly was. Her hyoid bone was broken."

"Which bone is that?" Vinny asked.

"The soft bone between the chin and the Adam's apple."

Vinny would've accepted that answer unequivocally if Pedro had spoken, but it was Alberta who'd supplied the information.

"How do you know that?" he asked.

"I couldn't sleep last night, so I Googled physical signs of strangulation," Alberta explained.

"Were you out of warm milk?" Vinny asked.

"Getting answers always helps me sleep better," Alberta replied. "You should try it sometime, Vin, you wouldn't yell so much."

Once again, Jinx had to work hard to control herself from laughing out loud. She didn't only find Alberta's comment funny; the sight of Vinny contorting his face and clenching his fists so he wouldn't prove Alberta right and fill the room with his shouting was hilarious. Luckily, Pedro was focused on the actual matter at hand.

"You have very good instincts, Mrs. Scaglione," Pedro said.

"Thank you," Alberta replied. "Missy's eyes were another clear-cut sign that she died of strangulation."

"Her eyes were bloodshot, that's not so uncommon," Vinny said in a tone of voice that was dangerously close to a shout.

"You could've been a doctor, Alberta, or at least played one on TV," Pedro declared. "Missy had petechiae eye."

"Why don't you explain to the class what that means too, Alfie?" Vinny suggested.

Aware that the sarcasm that enveloped every word Vinny spoke was the result of his own inability to identify the physical clues that were right there on Missy's body, Alberta ignored him and continued to address Pedro when she spoke.

"Her eyes were more than bloodshot," she explained. "They were slightly distorted as well, both results of strangulation."

"You get an A-plus, Mrs. Scaglione," Pedro declared.

"I am one hundred percent certain that Missy Michaels died of strangulation."

He elaborated to advise that in his professional opinion someone strangled Missy with the lace shawl and put the arsenic bottle in her hand to make it appear that she had committed suicide. He confirmed that there were no other bruises, contusions, or traumas on Missy's body, so it appeared that she was killed in the dressing room and not brought there postmortem. Proving that he had thought about the scenario in detail, Pedro added that it meant she died rather quickly and didn't put up a fight, possibly because she knew her killer.

"How could she know her killer?" Jinx asked. "She didn't know anyone in town."

Vinny let out a deep sigh before he responded, "She knew Nola."

"Only on the phone and through e-mail," Jinx stated. "They never met in person."

"*Meglio amico che nemico*," Alberta muttered.

"I don't think it matters who kills you, friend or foe," Vinny said. "The result is the same."

"True, but if it was a friend, maybe Missy wasn't frightened in her last moments," Alberta proposed.

"That's an interesting way of looking at death," Pedro said. "I'll have to remember that."

"You also need to remember that she wasn't strangled by a lace shawl," Alberta said.

"Mi amiga, you're wrong about that," Pedro said. "The lace material left imprints on the poor woman's neck and throat."

"I'm sure it did," Alberta agreed. "But it was a lace curtain and not a lace shawl."

"How do you know that, Alfie?" Vinny asked.

"Simple, there's a hole running along the hem for the curtain rod," Alberta explained.

Pedro walked from behind his desk to a small box that was sitting on one of the chairs on the opposite side. He opened the box and pulled out the lace, which was still in the plastic evidence bag. He turned it upside down, sideways, and flipped it around until he was finally convinced that Alberta was right.

"*Caballa Santa,*" Pedro said.

"Holy mackerel is right," Vinny added.

"You're even smarter than Vinny said you were," Pedro gushed.

"You said I'm smart, Vin?" Alberta asked.

"No! I did not say you are smart!" Vinny yelled. "I said you're nosy."

"How dare you!" Alberta shouted.

"Come on, Gram, you really can't argue with that," Jinx said. "You are kind of nosy."

"And what about you?" Alberta asked.

"I'm an investigative reporter," Jinx replied. "I'm on a quest for the truth."

Unlike Jinx, Pedro had no problem filling the room with his laughter. "I am going to love working in this town."

As they walked to their cars in the parking lot, Vinny, Alberta, and Jinx felt that their work was just getting started.

"Do you think Pedro made the wrong decision not to run a toxicology report?" Alberta asked.

"No, I think it was the right call," Vinny said. "But I still may have him do one just to cover all our bases."

Jinx noticed a strange quality to Vinny's voice. She had never heard him sound contrite before, at least not in her presence. She was almost afraid to confront him on it, but then shifted her mindset. He might not be fond of Jinx, the person, but Vinny might find it easier to respond to Jinx, the reporter.

"Is something wrong, Vinny?" Jinx asked. "You sound as if you have more to say."

Vinny let out another sigh and replied, "I may have overreacted back there when I yelled at Pedro about the toxicology report."

"What do you mean?" Jinx asked. "You were totally within your rights."

"On the one hand, yes, because this is a high-profile case," Vinny said, "but on the other hand, no, because we know the arsenic bottle isn't real. Nola confirmed that it was a prop for the show."

They all stopped in front of Jinx's red Chevy Cruze, stunned by this announcement. Adding this clue to the fact that the lace shawl was actually a curtain and not part of Missy's own wardrobe meant that Missy's murder was definitely premeditated and not the result of a spur-of-the-moment act of violence. Whoever killed Missy brought both the lace curtain and the arsenic bottle prop to the dressing room. It also meant that the killer had something to do with the play or at least knew that Missy was going to star in *Arsenic and Old Lace*. Unfortunately, thanks to Sloan and Joyce's publicity efforts, everyone in town knew Missy had a role in the play.

"These clues do tell us one thing for certain," Alberta announced.

"What's that?" Vinny asked.

"That whoever killed Missy knew their way around the theatre," she replied.

"You're right, Gram," Jinx added. "It was pitch-dark backstage and there were no other props lying around the dressing room, so the killer must've known the landscape of the entire theatre."

Shaking her head, Alberta replied, "Something's not right."

"What're you thinking, Alfie?" Vinny asked.

"The killer didn't have a lot of time," Alberta started. "Why go to the trouble of including a prop bottle if they weren't going to poison Missy?"

Once again, Jinx noticed something different about Vinny. He opened his mouth to talk, then closed it. He tried again but was clearly struggling to find the right word.

"Vin," Alberta said. "Spit it out."

"Let's go back to my office," Vinny said. "I have something to show you."

CHAPTER 12

Quello che vedi non è sempre quello che ottieni.

The Tranquility Police Station wasn't as comforting as the rural playground found in Mayberry, but it definitely wasn't as disheartening as the decaying urban kingdom ruled by Barney Miller. The local law enforcement facility fell somewhere in between, and for Alberta and Jinx, who were spending more and more time there, it was beginning to feel like a home away from home.

The one-story building was clean, quiet, and well-organized, which meant it was nothing like any of the Italian homes either of the ladies had ever lived in, but it did mean that when they entered the facility, they weren't bombarded with a burst of frenzied activity. There was enough chaos out in the world, it was nice to know that in a place where that chaos was supposed to be controlled, they were confronted with calm. And a friendly face.

"Tambra!" Alberta exclaimed, disturbing the aforementioned peace. "Is everybody going to be late for re-hearsal today?"

"You'd better hurry," Jinx said. "Nola is on the verge of having an emotional breakdown, and tardiness will put her over the edge. It's a PTSD trigger for a schoolteacher."

"I'm leaving right now," Tambra said. "Who else is running late?"

"Luke," Alberta replied. "We just saw him at the morgue. And we met the new medical examiner, Pedro, who seems very competent. I like him very much."

"You only like him, Alfie, because he corroborated all your theories about Missy's death," Vinny said, entering the station behind the women.

Alberta stood in the doorway to Vinny's office and turned to address her old friend. "Like I said, he's a very competent man."

A smile started to form on Vinny's lips, but when he heard Tambra and the other officers begin to chuckle, his almost-grin turned into a definite glare. It put an end to any mirth. This was a place where serious business was to be conducted after all.

"Chief, okay if I still go to my nonrehearsal rehearsal now?" Tambra asked.

"Of course," Vinny replied. "Get a good look at the cast members who allegedly don't know about Missy's death when Nola breaks the news to them."

"You think they're suspects?" Alberta asked.

"As far as we're concerned, they're all suspects," Tambra replied. "I'll keep a sharp eye on them, Chief, in case one of them gives themselves away."

"Thanks," Vinny said. "Our murderer could be a cast member."

"Not Freddy," Jinx said. "He wouldn't hurt a fly."

"Or Helen or Father Sal," Alberta added. "They might actually hurt a fly, but definitely not a person."

"Benny's harmless too," Jinx said. "You can cross him off the suspect list."

Tambra and Vinny exchanged amused glances. Maybe the business conducted at the station wasn't always so serious. "Thanks, ladies," Tambra replied. "You've whittled down the suspect list so it's a bit more manageable."

"You're welcome, Tambra," Alberta said. "We're here to help."

"It's what we do," Jinx added.

Smiling broadly, Tambra grabbed her purse, the bright yellow leather surprisingly working nicely with her navy-blue uniform, and started to leave. "They're all yours, Chief."

"So, Chief," Alberta said. "What do you have to show us?"

Once the door to Vinny's office closed behind them, the ladies' attitudes changed. Alberta grew more relaxed because she was literally in the office of a dear old friend, a man she used to babysit. She threw her pocketbook on one of the sandy-brown faux leather chairs and stood with her hands on her hips, waiting for Vinny to start the show-and-tell. Alternatively, Jinx stood with her arms crossed in front of her chest, her purse still hanging on her shoulder, her overall stance giving the impression of someone who was not at all relaxed. Her appearance wasn't unfitting in the slightest because everyone in the room knew Vinny didn't like Jinx nearly as much as he liked her grandmother. But everyone in the room also knew it was time for Tranquility to have its own détente.

"Jinx, are you all right?" Vinny asked. "You look like you had too many helpings of Alberta's manicotti."

"You can eat a whole tray of my manicotti and not have a *mal di stomaco*," Alberta declared.

"I'm fine," Jinx lied.

"No, you're not," Vinny corrected. "I'm a cop, I know tense, and you, my friend, are tense."

"I didn't know we were friends," Jinx replied.

"We're not . . . not precisely anyway," Vinny admitted. "But the one thing I hate more than disloyalty from my team is unnecessary tenseness." Vinny took a deep breath and continued. "What do you say we start over?"

Startled by the unexpected proposition, Jinx instinctively glanced at Alberta, who understood her granddaughter was seeking direction as to how to receive Vinny's offer, and opened her mouth to speak. No words immediately rushed out of her mouth and no advice poured from Alberta, not because she didn't have anything to say, but because this was a moment between her friend and her granddaughter. Alberta was wise enough to know she shouldn't interfere, no matter how much Jinx wanted her to.

"Are you game?" Vinny asked. "Or would you rather we continue to butt heads?"

Jinx stopped looking at her grandmother and decided it was time to look within. She was ambitious and obstinate and, at times, full of herself and conceited. But she was also kind and hardworking and empathetic. She had long considered Vinny to be a roadblock to her success, an obstacle, when he really was an ally, and as the chief of police, his friendship would be an advantage to her that most other investigative reporters didn't have. He was right, there was no need for them to work at loggerheads; they were members of the same club, personally and professionally.

"I'd like that very much, Chief," Jinx replied.

She extended her hand to Vinny, who took it. Alberta had to turn away so neither of them would see the tears start to form in her eyes. She wasn't the stereotypical Italian woman prone to emotional outbursts, but seeing two people she loved pledge to move forward in peace was enough to make her cry.

"Now that that's settled, let's get down to business," Vinny announced.

As he walked around his desk like a lecturer preparing to address an audience, the women responded by each taking a seat in one of the chairs. They waited patiently as Vinny pulled open a drawer and placed the arsenic bottle, still safely contained in a plastic bag, on the desk. He could tell by their expressions that they were not impressed because they had seen this piece of evidence before. It was the response he expected, and it played perfectly into his setup.

He held up a finger and smiled, resembling a magician masterfully controlling a group of mesmerized spectators and reached into his drawer once again. What he produced this time roused an enthusiastic response, which was his goal. It was true that a picture was worth a thousand words.

"*Dio mio!*" Alberta exclaimed. "Did you find that inside the arsenic bottle?"

"We most certainly did," Vinny confirmed.

"Are those people who I think they are?" Jinx asked.

"They most certainly are," Vinny confirmed again. "This is a photo of Daisy and Teddy from the early days of their partnership."

Alberta and Jinx got up and leaned over the desk to get a better look at the photo in the plastic bag Vinny was holding.

"This was definitely a premeditated murder," Alberta said. "The shawl and the prop bottle possibly could have been last-minute additions to make Missy's death look more dramatic, but that photo wasn't lying around the theatre."

"Correct," Vinny said. "The killer either had possession of the photo or somehow took it from Missy."

"That latter scenario doesn't sound very likely," Jinx said. "If Missy's killer is this mysterious escort who walked with her from the Tranquility Arms to St. Winifred's, I can't imagine there was enough time to rifle through her pocketbook in search of a photo."

"Unless he got into Missy's room at the Arms beforehand," Alberta suggested.

"That's a possibility we're looking in to," Vinny said. "Of course, there are no helpful fingerprints on the photo."

"Are there ever?" Alberta said, sounding like a weary, hard-boiled cop.

"Rarely," Vinny replied. "But at least we have this photo as a clue."

"But what does it represent?" Jinx asked. "It isn't like Daisy and Teddy's relationship was a secret. Could the photo possibly implicate the actress who played Teddy as the killer?"

"I highly doubt that," Vinny said. "Inga Schumacher is in her late nineties now, if she's even still alive."

"You don't know if the woman is alive or dead?" Alberta asked.

"We're doing a search for her, but so far, we've come up empty," Vinny said. "We can't find any notice of her online other than some fansites that don't have information about the woman after the series ended. Plus, we're not even sure if her name is real."

"You think Inga Schumacher is a stage name?" Jinx asked.

"It could be," Vinny replied.

"Don't you think she would've gone for something less ethnic?" Jinx suggested. "Especially at that time period."

"I always liked Inga's name, it stood out," Alberta said. "But I know what you mean, lovey, movie studios liked actors to sound all-American. Like Rock Hudson and Doris Day. Though Rock and Inga has a nice ring to it."

"They would've made a great onscreen pair, Alfie," Vinny agreed. "They could've brought Rock on as Teddy's love interest and he could've adopted Daisy."

"They would've made a happy little family," Alberta gushed.

"At the risk of ruining our recent truce," Jinx interrupted, "could we stop the casting session and cast our attention back to the photo?"

"Sorry, I can get a little carried away when we start talking about the movies," Vinny said. "Where were we?"

"Trying to locate Inga," Jinx said.

"Right," Vinny replied. "The other glitch in the search could be that Inga may have changed the spelling of her last name."

"You think it could've been more ethnic than Inga Schumacher?" Alberta asked.

"Think about some of the relatives in our family trees, Alfie," Vinny said. "My cousin Patsy's full name doesn't exactly roll off the tongue."

"What's her full name?" Jinx asked.

"Pasqualina Benedetta Mastrangelico," Alberta replied.

"That flew right out of Gram's mouth with no problem," Jinx said.

"Your gram is an Italian woman in her sixties, not the head of a movie studio in the fifties," Vinny replied. "All of that's speculation for the moment anyway, right now we have to decipher the significance of this particular photo. It must have meant something to the killer, but what?"

All three of them took a closer look at the photo, but all three came to the same conclusion: The photo was insignificant. They weren't sure if the picture captured Daisy and Teddy on a photo shoot or Missy and Inga on a day off. All they knew for certain was that because of Missy's apparent age, it looked as if it was taken somewhere around the time the first film was released and they were standing in front of a house. Not exactly an abundance of clues. To find out more, they would definitely need to subject the photo to further examination.

Jinx took her phone from her bag and was about to take a photo of the photo when Vinny put up his hand to prevent Jinx from seeing anything except the crosscutting lines on his palm.

"Vinny, get out of the way, I'm trying to take a picture," Jinx said.

"You can't photograph this photograph," Vinny said. "It's evidence."

"Which is why I need to photograph it," Jinx explained. "To further examine the evidence."

"Sorry, but I can't risk this photo winding up on the front page of *The Herald*," Vinny said.

Jinx was about to protest, but she knew Vinny had a point. For the moment, she had no intention of using this piece of evidence as part of her article, but at some point during the investigation it might become important, and she could see that Vinny's worst nightmare could come true. Like any good reporter always trying to hustle for a lead and to manipulate a situation in her favor, Jinx knew it was time to negotiate.

"If you let me take a photo of this piece of photographic evidence so I can do some research," Jinx started, "Gram will delete the photo she took of Missy's corpse."

The second the words were spoken Jinx knew how damaging they sounded. Up until this point, Vinny was unaware that Alberta had surreptitiously taken photos of Missy's dead body at the crime scene, and that those photos were still on Alberta's phone, mixed in with the images of Lola playing with her new toy goldfish and Helen experimenting with a shade of lipstick even more garish than the bubblegum pink she had grown so fond of. Vinny's explosive reaction, therefore, was not unexpected.

"You took a photo of Missy's dead body?!"

Shrugging her shoulders, Alberta knew there was no sense in feigning innocence—Jinx had just outed her as a criminal. Or at least someone with a questionable fetish.

"I only wanted to take a photo of the lace around Missy's neck to prove it was a curtain and not a shawl," Alberta explained. "And Missy's body got in the way."

"Missy's . . . *body* . . . got in the way?" Vinny repeated in disbelief.

"Yes," Alberta replied. "If you remember, Missy was sprawled out on the chaise lounge. She took up a lot of space."

Vinny buried his face in his hands and ran his fingers through his hair. *What big hands Vinny has*, Alberta thought, *I never noticed that before.* She wondered if he was going to use those big hands to pull clumps of his own hair from his scalp, clench them into fists, and pound his desk, or reach forward and use them to strangle both ladies like someone had strangled Missy. When Vinny extended his hand toward Alberta, she thought, *Well, at least, if he just strangles me, Jinx will be able to escape.*

"Give me your phone, Alfie, so I can personally delete those photos," Vinny demanded.

Once she was certain that Vinny, in his angry, frustrated state, wasn't going to physically assault her—which really was never a possibility, was it?—she regained her composure and was able to respond without fear.

"Not until you let Jinx take a photo of this clue," Alberta said in an equally demanding tone.

Alberta watched Vinny stare at her and then at Jinx. Instinctively, she knew exactly what her old friend was thinking. She knew he understood that they were all working toward the same goal, but she also knew he was aware that she and Jinx had their own agenda. Would he play by the rules? Or play smart? Alberta held her breath and waited to see how Vinny was going to roll the dice.

"Jinx, we reached an agreement today to work as partners and I expect you to keep up your end of that bargain," Vinny said.

"I have every intention of doing that," Jinx declared.

"If this photo winds up in *The Herald*, I will personally arrest you for stealing evidence," Vinny said. "Is that understood?"

"I want to achieve a lot of things in my life, Vinny,"

Jinx said. "A prison record is not one of them. I hear you loud and clear."

"Good," Vinny replied. "Now take your photo and get out of here."

A few hours later, at Alberta's house, printed copies of the photo were sprawled out on the kitchen table. Jinx had stopped off at *The Herald* on their way back from the police station and printed out several copies, even enlarging the image so they would have blown-up versions to examine as well. The larger copies did distort the visual quality of the photo slightly, but it magnified the details of the picture, giving the viewer a different perspective. They were hoping it would also give them a clue as to the photo's significance.

It was a little early in the day to be sipping Red Herrings, so there was a pitcher of iced tea in the center of the table that was surrounded by a dish of cold cuts, cheeses, sliced tomatoes, lettuce, Italian bread, and a jar of mayonnaise and mustard, everything needed to make a sandwich for lunch. Not that the Ferraras and their friends ever needed an excuse to eat, but sleuthing did make them hungry.

Helen and Father Sal were at the theatre along with the other cast members and Freddy was working, so only Joyce and Sloan joined Alberta and Jinx around the table to examine the photo. They each had their own copy to examine, and after a few moments of silent perusal, Joyce pulled a magnifying glass from her pocketbook to enlarge her enlarged copy even further.

"Ah, *Madon,* Joyce!" Alberta cried. "Are you planning to go on *Let's Make a Deal*?"

"I've had this thing for decades," Joyce said. "Anthony picked it up for me at some junk store."

"That's not a very romantic gift, Aunt Joyce," Jinx said.

"It's better than romantic, honey, it's useful," Joyce replied.

"How so, Joyce?" Alberta asked. "You never even wore glasses."

"It's thanks to Arnold Brandenburg," Joyce replied.

"Who's that?" Alberta asked.

"Some guy I used to work with whose nickname all throughout Wall Street was The Jerk," Joyce said.

"Sounds like a charmer," Sloan said after taking a huge bite of a roast beef and provolone sandwich.

"Anything but," Joyce replied. "He would deliberately scribble his orders on tiny slips of paper, so it was incredibly difficult for anyone to read. I would always complain about it, so one day Anthony brought mc this magnifying glass and Arnold's chicken scratch finally became legible."

"I take it back," Jinx said. "That's actually very romantic."

"My husband had his moments," Joyce offered. "I wish this thing would work its magic on this photo, though. I don't know about you, but it doesn't look real to me."

"I'm having the same thought," Sloan said, still chewing on the same bite of his sandwich. "Maybe it's because the photo is so old."

"It could be a publicity still," Alberta suggested. "Like the ones the movie studios used to put out."

"That gives me an idea, Gram."

Without any further clarification, Jinx got up from the table and ran into the living room. Intrigued but not concerned, the rest of the group continued to eat their lunch and scour the photo for a clue that had not yet popped out at them. When Jinx returned, she brought with her Father Sal's DVD collection of all of Daisy's movies followed by Lola, who slithered into the kitchen behind Jinx. The cat, of course, was not delighted that Daisy received more attention than she did upon entering.

"Jinx, what a brilliant idea!" Joyce exclaimed. "Maybe we'll find the photo on one of the DVD covers."

"That's what I'm hoping," Jinx confirmed.

Fifteen minutes later, hope had crashed, burned, and disintegrated into a puff of smoke that was invisible but left the distinctive whiff of disappointment lingering in the air. The DVD inserts and cover jackets were strewn about the table, mixed in with the food, the photocopies, and a very bored Lola, and not one of the numerous images matched the photo that had been stuffed inside the arsenic bottle. All the visual footage used on the DVDs portrayed Daisy as a wealthy girl who lived in a swanky New York apartment. Even when she was photographed outside her home, the locations were sophisticated and urbane, nothing like the rural setting of the photo they'd found.

"There's something not right about this picture," Alberta said.

"It's the background," Sloan said. "Daisy and Teddy are all dressed up, but if you look closely, the house behind them looks dilapidated."

"And the street sign is about to fall over," Alberta said. "Joyce, can you make out the names on the sign with your magnifying glass?"

Joyce picked up Lola, whose bottom half was covering one of the blown-up photos, and put her in her lap, where she curled up into a ball. Then, looking through the glass, Joyce peered closer to the photo and replied, "It looks like the house is on the corner of Smith Street and Seventh Avenue."

"I don't think Daisy and Teddy would've been caught dead on Seventh Avenue," Sloan said.

"I agree with you on that," Jinx said. "But this photo definitely wasn't taken in New York."

"No, it looks like it's somewhere in the country," Joyce added. "I don't remember Daisy ever going to the country in one of her movies. Do you?"

"There was the time she dressed up like a boy and posed as a golf caddy at that country club," Sloan remembered.

"To get closer to Stone Jackson, a visiting matinee idol," Alberta finished. "Who, of course, turns out to be a *donnaiolo*."

"I assume that's a bad thing," Jinx said.

"Have you heard the stories of our cousin Ruggiero?" Alberta asked.

"The sleazy playboy?" Jinx replied.

"Bingo!" Alberta cried. "Stone Jackson was the same type of fella, a real *strisciamento*. But in the end, Daisy exposed him for the *due facce* he was."

"The what?" Jinx asked.

"Two-faced," Alberta translated. "It was like he was two men in one body. A womanizer and an all-American boy all rolled up into one."

"That's it!" Jinx cried. "That's what's wrong with the photo!"

Confused, Alberta, Joyce, and Sloan looked at one another.

"The photo was taken by a no-good, sleazy creep?" Joyce questioned.

"No! The photo's two-faced!" Jinx cried. "It's two photos in one. That's why it doesn't look right."

Once again, Joyce gazed into the magnifying glass and noticed a detail about the photo no one had spotted before. "Look at Teddy's hand."

Obediently, the rest of them picked up the photo in front of them and zeroed in on Teddy's left hand, the only one visible in the shot.

"It's tucked into her mink coat," Jinx stated.

"No, it only looks that way," Joyce corrected. "Look closer, you can only see her thumb, the rest of her hand is cut off."

"You're right!" Sloan cried. "This photo's been altered like Jinx said."

"*Quello che vedi non è sempre quello che ottieni,*" Alberta said, then quickly translated for the others, "What you see isn't always what you get."

"You're right about that, Gram. It looks like the people and the background are from two different pictures that were merged together to look like one," Jinx explained. "But why?"

"None of this makes any sense," Alberta said. "Why manipulate the photos to make a new picture and then stuff that into the arsenic bottle? And why make it look like they're on a country road? Like you said, Daisy wouldn't have been caught dead on Seventh Avenue."

"But she was caught dead in St. Winifred's Academy," Sloan said.

"If only Missy would've let Nola pick her up at the Tranquility Arms, nothing bad would've happened," Jinx remarked. "Instead, she was escorted right to her own death."

But who was Missy's executioner? Who was this mysterious person who intervened at the last moment and lured Missy away from the spotlight that awaited her and toward the darkness that was her demise?

Alberta ripped off a chunk of mozzarella cheese and plopped it into her mouth. "I think it's time we find out who Missy's escort was."

CHAPTER 13

Doni di nemici non sono doni.

The Tranquility Arms Hotel had been a mainstay in town for close to a century. And its history was almost as colorful—and tragic—as the goldenrod, emerald-green, and periwinkle-blue color scheme that adorned the structure itself.

The old, Victorian-style home was built in 1934 by its first owner, George Randolph, as a gift for his pregnant wife, Clara. An only child, George inherited his parents' entire fortune, which was vast even by today's standards, and included a steel mill, several industrial patents, and a robust stock portfolio. George was well-educated, well-liked, and, well, filthy rich, but unfortunately, after Clara died in childbirth, he was also a widower left as the sole caretaker of twin girls. He had been able to oversee the construction of the sprawling home, ensuring that it was built and fully furnished within six months, but he was unable to find the emotional strength to raise two daughters on his own. Bitter and distraught, George retreated to his family's estate in Brussels and left his daughters in the care of the good sisters of St. Winifred's of the Holy Well.

The church had been built two years before construction on Randolph House began, and the sisters lived in the convent on the same property that eventually became St. Winifred's Academy. The nuns were sturdy, pious, God-serving women who opened their hearts and their home to the two girls who were brought to them by Clara's midwife on a blustery February morning. The girls—still unnamed by their devastated father—were christened Beatrice and Bridget and grew up happy, content, and surprisingly unspoiled considering they were doted on by the entire convent.

As a result of the economic fallout from World War II, George found his finances suffering. In need of quick cash, he sold his home to an entrepreneur who was quietly buying up properties and turning them into hotels. Two weeks after George received his bill of sale, his Victorian home that had been built on the promise of a bright future, was turned into the Tranquility Arms. Luckily, the hotel's fate was much rosier than either George's or the house he abandoned.

As one of the first bed-and-breakfast hotels in the area, the Tranquility Arms drew guests from all over the Northeast. In the early 1950s it became the most fashionable venue for having a wedding thanks to the much-publicized double marriage of the twins. Being raised by a suite of Catholic sisters, the girls were an empathetic duo, and even though they had only seen their father in photographs and read about him in newspaper articles, they invited him to their wedding. Tragically, the ship George traveled on encountered rough seas resulting from an especially vicious storm and capsized, drowning all on board.

Beatrice and Bridget and their new husbands eventually left Tranquility to begin their married lives in New England, but their memory lingered on. The tangible result of the impact they made on the town could be viewed when you entered St. Winifred's Church. To the left near the entrance to the nursing room were two small, white marble statues of their saintly namesakes. The dedication underneath read, "For the children—who are gifts from God."

After the girls left, their birthplace prospered. The Tranquility Arms switched ownership many times over the years, but never lost its appeal as a premiere travel destination. It may have begun its life in the shadow of misfortune, but it had risen to stand triumphant. Standing in front of the bed-and-breakfast, Alberta hoped a similar happy ending would be born out of the most recent tragedy to devastate their town.

"What's the assistant manager's name again?" Alberta asked.

"Brandon Woolverton," Vinny replied.

"Damn, I was hoping he was Italian," Alberta said.

"Not everyone can be Italian, Alfie," Vinny remarked.

"I know," Alberta replied. "Isn't it a shame?"

More disappointment awaited Alberta when she entered the Arms. The person standing behind the front desk wasn't Brandon or Sanjay, the manager, but Helen.

"*Per l'amor del cielo,*" Alberta cried. "What are you doing here?"

"Waiting for you," Helen said, putting some papers in order.

"You said you were going to mass," Alberta said.

"Father Sal's sermon was a repeat," Helen remarked. "I know everything I need to know about Lot's wife. Curiosity kills."

"And you got curious and decided to join the investigation?" Vinny asked.

"*Join* the investigation?" Helen asked. "I had to start it because you two were late."

"Ah, *Madon*!" Alberta cried. "You weren't even invited, Helen. And what are you doing behind the front desk? Is this your new job?"

"I know my personality would help me find success in the hospitality sector, but no," Helen replied. "I'm holding down the fort while Sanjay puts out a fire in room twenty-seven. Apparently, someone is allergic to lavender. He had to bring emergency Benadryl and plain old Ivory soap."

"Where's the rest of the staff?" Vinny asked.

"The only other employee scheduled to work this shift was the assistant manager," Helen explained. "And he's out of town."

"Brandon?" Vinny asked.

"The Jamaican kid?" Helen asked.

"Yes," Vinny confirmed.

"That's the one," Helen confirmed. "He told Sanjay at the last minute that he needed to go back home to his family in Rochester for a few days."

"Wait a second," Alberta interrupted. "Brandon Woolverton is Jamaican? And from Rochester?"

"His family emigrated from Jamaica years ago and Brandon told me his name is thanks to his German ancestry on his father's side," Vinny conveyed. "He loved how his name always threw people a curve when they saw what he looked like. He said it made people realize there's a lot more to a person than the color of their skin."

"Lesson learned," Alberta said. "I can't wait to meet this young man."

"You'll have to wait until next week. He flew the coop and left me here to clean up the mess!" Sanjay cried. "And answer me this, who doesn't love lavender?"

Sanjay Achinapura was a small man with a big mouth. Standing at five-foot-six in his loafers with the specially made lifts that added an inch to his height and weighing in at 140 pounds when fully clothed in his manager's out-fit, Sanjay made up for his slight frame by talking in a consistent bellow. Whether he was barking orders or wel-coming guests, his tone was the same: loud.

Ignoring Sanjay's floral-scented query, Vinny asked, "When did Brandon leave?"

"Yesterday," he replied. "He texted me last night and said his family needed him, so he was taking a few days off. I texted him back and told him your family right here needs you, and he said thanks for thinking of me as fam-ily, there's nothing more important in the world."

"This Brandon sounds very wise," Alberta commented.

"What else could I do?" Sanjay asked, in a voice that was loud enough to elicit a response from the parish-ioners down the road. "I told him to take care of his fam-ily and get back ASAP. He replied TTUL." Sanjay paused to take a breath, but he wasn't finished talking. "In the name of Brahman and all that is holy, what is TTUL?!"

"It means 'Talk to you later,'" Vinny responded. "It's a shorthand lots of kids use."

"Wouldn't that be TTYL?" Alberta asked.

"The 'you' is silent," Helen replied. "Sanjay, I put these invoices in chronological order and you're low on staples."

"Do you want a job, Helen?" Sanjay asked. "It's hard to find good help these days."

"Thank you, but I must decline," Helen replied. "I'm a very busy woman."

"If you change your mind, let me know," Sanjay said. "I owe you."

"As Helen's sister, may I have her proxy?" Alberta asked. "Would you mind if I saw Missy's room?"

"The police have already gone through her room," Vinny said. "It's packed up and her belongings are being sent to her lawyer."

"I'd still like to see it for myself if you don't mind," Alberta said.

"Fine with me," Vinny said.

"On one condition," Sanjay stated.

"What's that?" Alberta asked.

"Get me a date with your sexy sister-in-law," Sanjay demanded.

"We don't have a sexy sister-in-law," Helen said.

"He's talking about Joyce," Alberta informed.

Helen's brow furrowed like the guest in room 27's must have when they started to wash. "Like I said, we don't have a sexy sister-in-law."

"Joyce is sexy and you know it!" Sanjay barked. "I am a patient man, I am a yogi, but I am out of shrimp curry recipes and I want a date with sexy Joyce!"

"Sanjay, you know that Joyce is technically still a married woman, don't you?" Alberta asked.

"So's my wife!" Sanjay bellowed.

"You have a wife?" Helen shouted.

"She's back in Mumbai with his three kids," Alberta replied.

"You see, I'm married, but I'm single!" Sanjay cried. "Joyce and I are a match made in Svarga."

"What in the world is Svarga?" Vinny asked.

"That I know," Helen said. "It has nothing to do with this world, it means heaven in Hinduism. Sanjay, let us up to Missy's room and I'll put a good word in for you when I get to Svarga, and with Joyce too. She and I are very close, you know."

"Thank you, Helen," Sanjay said, giving her the key to Missy's room. "You, unlike your sister, are a godsend."

"My father used to say the same exact thing," Helen replied.

Missy's room was on the porch side of the Tranquility Arms. The front porch wrapped around the right side of the bed-and-breakfast, and there was a separate entrance to the hotel at the very end of the corridor. Missy was in room 8, which was the last room on that side. Helen put the key in the door, and although they knew the room was empty and their sudden appearance wouldn't disturb anyone, they still entered slowly and quietly.

The bed was perfectly made, the drapes were drawn, and the only contents in the open closet were hangars, an iron, and a pillow. In the center of the room was a large, black suitcase on wheels and a black, leather duffel bag, Missy's belongings, which the police had already searched and packed up. The room looked as if someone had either just arrived or was about to leave.

"We've gone over the room and couldn't find any fingerprints other than those belonging to Missy and the staff,"

Vinny said. "If anyone else was in this room, they didn't leave a trace."

"If the police have already inspected the room, what are we looking for, Berta?" Helen asked.

"Some kind of clue that would explain why she really came here," Alberta explained.

"You think she came to Tranquility for some other reason than to star in the show?" Vinny asked.

"Costar," Helen corrected.

"I do," Alberta said. "She wasn't here twelve hours before she was killed. Someone was waiting for her to arrive."

"And you think Missy knew who that person was and arranged to meet them?" Vinny queried.

"It's a possible scenario," Alberta said. "And it makes more sense than her meeting a random stranger at a hotel she'd never been to before to act as her escort."

"Unless that person told Missy that he was sent by Nola to pick her up," Vinny said.

A look of shock appeared on Alberta's face. "I hadn't thought of that. You really think Nola is connected to Missy's murder?"

"She's definitely connected," Vinny replied. "I just don't know if the connection is innocent or a bit more nefarious."

"When's Brandon supposed to come back?" Helen asked. "I have a feeling he'll be able to fill in the blanks."

"Sanjay wasn't specific about his return date, but I have my team working on tracking him down," Vinny replied just as his phone beeped to indicate the receipt of a text. "Looks like my team needs to track me down."

"An emergency?" Alberta asked.

"There's been a break-in at the lumber yard," Vinny

announced. "I have to go, but feel free to keep looking around. Just don't take anything!"

Helen waited thirty seconds after Vinny left to speak. "You have no intention of following Vinny's orders, do you?"

Alberta didn't answer the question, but barked an order of her own, "Lock the door."

Dutifully, Helen complied and when Alberta heard the click, she picked up the black suitcase and hoisted it onto the bed. "I'll look through this and you rifle through the duffel bag. Let me know if you find anything out of the ordinary."

"Nothing out of the ordinary here," Helen remarked. "Just two crazy women searching through a dead woman's luggage."

As gingerly as possible, the women looked through Missy's personal items in search of a possible clue that would expose her link to this town, if such a link even existed. They sorted through all the usual items—toiletries, underwear, clothes, accessories—when Alberta suddenly stopped. Nowhere in the suitcase could she find anything personal. Missy was planning on being in Tranquility for almost two months—three weeks of rehearsal and then four weeks for the production—but nowhere could Alberta find photos, trinkets, or any other item that could be used to decorate her hotel room to make it appear homier.

How sad, Alberta thought, *to be away for so long and not want to be reminded of home.*

But maybe Missy didn't want to be reminded of home? Maybe she was longing for an adventure after so many years of residing in the outskirts of the public's imagination that she didn't want to bring anything familiar with her? Maybe she was simply a minimalist? Alberta zipped up the suitcase and realized that she and Missy might look a lot alike, but when it came to what was important and valued, she suspected they were very different.

The contents of the duffel bag didn't contradict Alberta's feeling. Helen had found pajamas, slippers, a plastic bag filled with crackers and raisins, and some celebrity magazines she most likely picked up at the airport. Was she searching to see if she could find her picture in any of the pages? Perhaps in a "Whatever happened to . . ." segment? Helen started to shove her findings back into the bag when she suddenly yelped in pain.

"What's wrong?" Alberta asked.

"Paper cut," Helen replied.

"From the magazines?"

"No," Helen replied. "This."

She pulled out a copy of the *Arsenic and Old Lace* script. She thumbed through it and saw that all of Abby's lines were highlighted in yellow, and there were notes scribbled in the margins.

"Dio mio!" Alberta exclaimed. "It's Missy's script."

"Filled with her notes," Helen said. "There could be a clue buried in here."

Helen didn't have to speak for Alberta to know what she was thinking because she was thinking it too. She was also thinking of Vinny's last words before he left.

"We can't take it," Alberta said.

"Why not?" Helen asked. "It could be riddled with clues."

"Because Vinny said not to take anything," Alberta said.

"It's not like we're stealing it," Helen replied. "We

have every intention of giving it back, we just want to borrow it for a while."

"For the sake of the investigation," Alberta said, trying to convince herself stealing the script wouldn't be viewed as breaking the law. "To solve this murder."

Without saying another word, Helen put the script in her pocketbook and snapped her purse shut. "What script? I have no idea what you're talking about."

They walked toward the front lobby instead of exiting out of the side door so they could return the key to Sanjay and thank him for letting them enter Missy's room. In exchange for the key, Sanjay had something for them.

He put the key back on its holder on the wall and bent down to pick up a small cardboard box. "This is for you," Sanjay said.

"Me?" Alberta asked.

"It's really for Missy," Sanjay explained. "But she's dead, so you should have it."

"Why me?" Alberta asked.

"Because you're the police and you're going to want to examine whatever's inside this box," Sanjay said.

"You've got it wrong, Sanjay, I'm not the police," Alberta said.

"Stop joking, Mrs. Scaglione!" Sanjay cried. "Everyone in town knows you're the real police . . . so take it! But remember, *Dushmanon ke upahaar koee upahaar nahin hain.*"

"You're not talking to your wife back home, Sanjay," Helen said. "Repeat that in English."

"Gifts from enemies are no gifts," he said.

"We have the same saying in Italian," Alberta said. "*Doni di nemici non sono doni.*"

"You think this is from Missy's enemy?" Helen asked.

"The woman was murdered!" Sanjay cried. "Of course I think it's from her enemy."

Alberta hesitated only slightly to once again rationalize her actions. Vinny had said not to take anything, and technically she wasn't breaking the promise she'd made to him. She was absolutely not taking this box that was meant for the recently deceased movie star, Alberta was being given the box. It was like a gift from Sanjay, which meant she was receiving the item, not taking it. Regardless of the semantic difference, the fact remained that Sanjay wanted a gift in return for his good deed.

"Get me a date with Joyce!"

Crossing her fingers behind her back like an untrustworthy teenager, Alberta swore, "I will do my absolute best."

In Helen's Buick, Alberta sat in the passenger seat with the package in her lap and waited for Helen to start the engine. The second she did, Alberta took her house keys from her pocketbook and used the serrated edge of one key to slice open the top of the box.

"You can't wait until we get home?" Helen asked.

"Sorry, I'm too impatient," Alberta said. "I'm dying to see what's inside."

"Let's hope Sanjay's saying doesn't hold any weight," Helen advised. "Because if there's a bomb in that box, you'll be dead before you find out who the enemy is."

"I don't think this will kill us," Alberta said. "Unless being cute is fatal."

She pulled a stuffed teddy bear out of the box and placed it on the dashboard.

"This is the clue I was hoping for," Alberta declared.

"You were hoping to find a stuffed animal?" Helen asked.

"I don't know what it means," Alberta replied, "but obviously this bear was sent to Missy because her grand-mother's name in the movies was Teddy."

"Is there anything else in there?" Helen asked.

Alberta reached into the box and pulled out a piece of paper. She unfolded it and stared at it for a few seconds before repeating it to her sister. "'Welcome home, Missy. Hopefully, by the time I arrive, you'll be dead.'"

CHAPTER 14

Avvocato, bugiardo, soldato, spia.

The first time Jinx met Nola Kirkpatrick she knew she had found a friend for life. Later, she understood Nola would also be her partner in crime.

Before she moved to Tranquility and while still living with her parents in Florida, Jinx answered an online ad at RoommatesNJ.com. She and Nola set up a FaceTime meeting, and the fifteen-minute interview to see if the schoolteacher and the budding reporter had enough in common to live together turned into a two-hour chat fest with both women leaving the conversation thinking they had found their new best friend. Two weeks later, Jinx had moved into the apartment and their lives had been entangled ever since.

In many ways they had become the sisters neither one ever had. They sat up late talking about guys, swapped clothes, and every once in a while, Jinx had to bail Nola out of jail. Jinx knew Nola had a good heart and wasn't one of the bad people she and her grandmother brought to justice; Nola just had a knack for being in the wrong place at the right time. During those periods it was a bit exhausting to be her friend, but it was a small price to pay to split living expenses and not have to go home to an empty apartment every night. Jinx, like her grandmother, was a practical girl.

She was also an impatient one.

Jinx looked around the crowded restaurant and sighed loudly. Nola was nowhere in sight. She tapped her red-manicured fingernails on the table so quickly, it sounded like she was galloping down a country lane. All she wanted to do was order the China Chef special with an extra spring roll and catch up with her friend, but in order to do that, her friend would have to arrive.

Just as Jinx pulled out her phone from her bag to send a text, the wording of which would not have been considered hashtag friendly, Nola plopped down in the chair across from Jinx and dropped her bag on the floor. She looked like she had just run a marathon.

"I'm so sorry," Nola panted. "I had to break up a fight at school."

"My aunt Helen always said that Catholic girls are tough broads," Jinx said. "Who threw the first punch? Was it that kid who played Belle a few years ago? She looked like she could arm wrestle the Beast and win."

"It wasn't a physical altercation," Nola said. "J. J. Yuskaukas claimed that Andrew Lloyd Webber's *Aspects of Love* is a better musical than Stephen Sondheim's *A Little Night Music* and, well, as you can imagine, the class went wild. It was complete pandemonium."

Jinx didn't know which musical was truly better because she had never heard of either of them before. One of the few things they didn't have in common was a love for the theatre. Nola lived for it, while Jinx only cared about it when Hugh Jackman decided to step away from Hollywood and strut his stuff on a Broadway stage.

"One can only imagine the chaos," Jinx deadpanned.

"It was bedlam, Jinx! Worse than that. It was hormones-out-of-control, teenaged bedlam!" Nola cried. "I tried to explain that everyone is entitled to their opinion, but my students weren't buying it, and I don't blame them. Don't get me wrong, J. J. Yuskaukas is a good kid, a baby-faced baritone, but just between you and me, he needs his head examined because *A Little Night Music* is a masterpiece. My kids know that. They are a savvy bunch of theatre devotees."

"That is one way to describe your students," Jinx said. "How did you calm them down?"

"Same way I always do when things get out of hand or if someone is triggered by a comment," Nola said, "I played 'No One Is Alone' from Sondheim's *Into the Woods*. It always works."

"I'll have to remember that the next time I find myself in the middle of a breakdown," Jinx said.

"Ever since what happened at the theatre, I've been listening to it nonstop," Nola said, her voice a hushed whisper. "I still cannot believe that Missy Michaels was murdered in one of my dressing rooms. I asked Father Sal to bless the room. The whole backstage reeks of sage and incense, but at least it's been spiritually cleansed."

"That's a relief," Jinx said.

A bigger relief should've been when the waitress asked them for their order, but it became another source of frustration.

"We'll have three China Chef specials," Nola said.

"I'm not that hungry, Nola, two will be enough," Jinx replied. "With a side of spring rolls, please."

"There will be three of us," Nola said. "I invited Kip to join us, but he's running late."

It was a good thing the waitress refilled their water glasses, it gave Jinx a few moments to decompress from hearing the news. She wasn't anti-Kip, but she wasn't pro-Kip either and didn't want to have lunch with him. However, she also knew her friend was going through a difficult time and didn't want to make matters worse by shouting her disapproval over the revised guest list. She hoped the way she posed her question would come off as curiosity and not inquisition.

"Oh, you didn't mention that Kip would be joining us," Jinx said. "Any particular reason you invited him?"

"I need to be surrounded by people who love the theatre as much as I do," Nola replied. "I know you're as devastated as I am over Missy's death, but I think we can both agree that you're not a supporter of the arts."

"I have a subscription to *Entertainment Weekly*."

"It's not the same thing."

"If you need emotional support, where's your boyfriend?" Jinx asked.

"Johnny went to New York to see some shows to re-fuel his creative juices."

"He went alone? He couldn't wait until you were free?"

Nola glared at her friend and then shook her head. "You don't understand artists, Jinx. Sometimes they need to process things by themselves."

"You don't understand how the boyfriend-girlfriend

thing works, Nola. You're supposed to rely on each other during the hard times."

"Don't get all superior with me," Nola said. "You have your relationship with Freddy and I have mine with Johnny. Don't compare them."

"Fine! If you're happy, I'm happy." Jinx took a sip of water and then looked her friend in the eyes. "Are you happy?"

Nola hesitated, and when she spoke, it wasn't about her boyfriend, but another important man in her life.

"Bruno!" Nola cried. "Come join us."

Her onetime defense attorney turned in their direction when he heard his name, and the moment he saw Nola his eyes lit up. It was obvious to everyone, except Nola and maybe even Bruno himself, that he had a crush on his former client. And it was obvious to Jinx that this was not going to be the quiet, girl talk infused lunch she'd hoped it would be.

"I was just picking up my takeout," Bruno said, holding up a bag adorned with the China Chef logo.

"Don't eat alone in that depressing office of yours," Nola said. "Join us."

"I don't want to intrude," Bruno replied.

"Too late," Jinx said. "Kip's already done that. He's allegedly on his way, but I'm sure he made a wrong turn and is cruising down to the Jersey Shore."

"He's right here, smart aleck," Nola said.

"Sorry I'm late," Kip said. "I seriously have no sense of direction. I graduated law school at the top of my class and I have trouble following the instructions on my GPS."

"Where'd you go to law school?" Jinx asked. "Guam?"

"Relax," Nola said. "You're here now and that's all that matters."

"I didn't know you were joining us, Bruno," Kip said.

"Neither did I," Bruno replied.

"Boys!" Nola cried. "I'm still your producer and I order you to sit down so we can have a proper lunch."

Dutifully, both men sat down, and the awkward pause that followed made Jinx feel like she was one of Nola's students and she had been summoned after class for detention. It also reminded Jinx that she was behaving like a brat. She couldn't really blame Nola for wanting to be surrounded by as many friends as possible; her entire world had been upturned a few days ago. She should be entering an exciting and creative phase of her life and instead she was sitting in a Chinese restaurant making small talk, trying to forget that a celebrity was murdered on her watch. It was time for Jinx to help her friend and stop adding to her stress.

"So, Kip, did I hear right? You're a real estate attorney?" Jinx asked.

"Yes, at Cohen, Cohen, Cohen, and Germinario," Kip replied.

"Sounds like one of those things doesn't belong with the others," Jinx said.

"It's three brothers and their cousin," Kip explained.

"The brothers are the Cohens, in case anyone's confused," Bruno joked.

"They're a great group of people and have really made me feel at home there," Kip said.

"I hope we've done the same," Nola said.

"You've all been wonderful," Kip replied. "I just wish the experience hadn't ended so quickly."

"I know," Bruno said. "I finally muster up the courage to be in a play and . . . well, I'm sure there will be another opportunity."

"Absolutely," Nola said. "Like I told everyone on Saturday at the nonrehearsal rehearsal, Johnny and I are in the process of exploring our creative options."

Before Nola could elaborate, the waitress reappeared with their lunch. Three plates overflowing with dim sum, pork fried rice, tofu with mixed vegetables, lo mein, and shrimp with lobster sauce. Coincidentally, Bruno had ordered the same meal, so it was China Chef specials all around. And, of course, a side of spring rolls for Jinx.

"You were right, Nola," Bruno said, scooping up a mixture of rice, lo mein, and shrimp. "This is much better than eating in my office."

"Speaking of my office," Kip said in response to his phone ringing. "I am so sorry, but I have to take this. It's one of the Cohcns."

"Which one?" Jinx asked.

"I can never tell," Kip replied. "They're triplets."

Excusing himself, Kip got up from the table and walked to a quiet corner of the restaurant. As he traveled, Jinx followed him with her eyes and glared daggers into his back.

"Hey, Jinx," Nola said. "You might want to dial down the death stare."

"I don't trust him," Jinx said unapologetically. "I think he's a liar."

"Avvocato, bugiardo, soldato, spia," Bruno replied.

"Do I need to warn Sloan that you've been hanging out with my grandmother in your spare time?" Jinx asked.

"My old law school professor, Mr. DiBenedetto, would always say that," Bruno said.

"What does it mean?" Nola asked.

"Lawyer, liar, soldier, spy," Bruno explained. "Silly little ditty, as he would call it, but it sums up what a lawyer does. We fight, we conceal secrets, and we lie. Doesn't make us sound like ours is the noblest of professions, but, alas, it is the truth."

"It really is a lot like acting," Nola said. "We lie all the time."

"Maybe that's why Kip aced his audition and got the lead in your play," Jinx mused. "He's a consummate professional when it comes to the craft of lying."

"Will you stop being so suspicious?" Nola said. "Kip got the lead because he's a terrific actor. He's also new in town, so we don't know him very well. That doesn't mean he's a liar."

"Five minutes after he arrives there's a murder," Jinx said. "To me, that's all the suspicion I need to question every lying word that comes out of his mouth."

"I know your grandmother is gaining this reputation as a superstar sleuth," Nola said. "But stop trying to emulate her. Not everyone is a murderer."

"Someone is," Jinx declared.

Knowing that she was only going to get an emotional response from Nola, she redirected her questioning to Bruno, hoping to engage in a more logical discussion. Of course, to do that, she would need to ask a logical, and not an emotional, question.

"Doesn't Kip have *liar face*?" Jinx asked. "I mean, can't you tell just by looking at him that he's hiding something? Like the fact that the only reason he moved here and auditioned for the play was to kill Missy."

"How reassuring to know that unbiased, balanced journalism is thriving in our fair city," Nola said, scooping up a forkful of lobster sauce.

"Jinx, I may have to side with Nola on this one," Bruno stated. "I don't know Kip extremely well, but I think he's a good guy. We met at a continuing education class and because he just moved here, I've been showing him around a bit. He even joined the ski group with me that Freddy runs."

"My Freddy?" Jinx asked.

"How many Freddys who own a ski and snorkel shop are there?" Bruno asked in return.

"Now who's Miss Illogical?" Nola proposed.

"Freddy never mentioned anything to me," Jinx pouted.

"Shocker!" Nola shouted. "Your boyfriend hasn't shared every minute detail of his life with you? That is completely unacceptable boyfriend behavior and you should break up with him pronto."

"Shut it, Nola," Jinx said. "Tell me more about this ski group."

"What's there to tell?" Bruno asked. "It's a bunch of guys who go skiing."

"I should ask Johnny if he wants to join," Nola said.

At the mention of Johnny's name, Bruno's body language changed. His mouth clenched, his hand, which was lying on the table, formed a fist, and his shoulders hunched up slightly. Jinx knew it was because the evil green monster called Jealousy had taken hold of Bruno's body, but she wasn't sure if Bruno was even aware of the transformation. When he spoke, his tone hadn't changed as much as his physical demeanor, but Jinx thought she detected an edge to his voice that wasn't previously there. "I didn't take Johnny for the outdoorsy type."

"You might be right about that, Bruno," Nola agreed. "Johnny is most comfortable in a dark theatre."

"Which is where I wish I was going to be."

Kip made the declaration as he slumped into his seat.

"Sorry about that call, I'm the new guy at the firm so I'm always expected to pick up when I'm summoned," Kip explained. "I only got out for lunch today because I have to go to a client's office right after this in some place called Newton."

"I could draw you a map," Jinx offered.

"You can follow me, Kip," Nola said. "I have a free period after this, so I don't have to rush right back to school. As long as I'm back for my sixth period English class, Donna won't harass me."

"The new principal's cracking the whip?" Bruno asked.

"Let's just say she's making her presence known," Nola said.

"When we met her at the party . . ." Jinx started.

"You mean the night Missy was murdered," Kip interjected.

"That's another way to describe the evening," Jinx said. "When we met Donna, she seemed nice—funny, actually—not like some parochial school dominatrix."

"I'm not sure if she literally has a whip that she uses on her staff, or a leather and lace outfit hidden in her office closet," Nola said, "but she is a no-nonsense administrator."

"Sounds like she's staking out her turf to let everyone know who's in charge," Bruno said. "She is the new girl in town, so to speak."

"Speaking as the new guy in town," Kip said, "I want to thank you all for making me feel so welcome. I'm super-bummed that we won't be having rehearsals because it's such a great way to get to know people and make long-lasting friendships."

Nola started to clamor on about all the different physical exercises Johnny was planning to do with the cast during the rehearsal period, as well as her ideas for the set and costume designs for the show. Kip, who could accurately be described as a theatre nerd, eagerly participated in the conversation, and even Bruno had surprisingly strong opinions about the dramatic journey his minor character would have taken over the course of the play. Jinx remained silent, eating her lunch, and observed them. Judgment quickly transformed into approval and then into opportunity.

Although she had nothing concrete on which to base her suspicions, Jinx didn't trust Kip. It was clear, however, that Nola and Bruno liked the guy and thought he was harmless and wouldn't even fall under the "suspect" column as a potential murderer. Because Kip didn't live or work in town, and now that *Arsenic and Old Lace* wasn't going to be produced, Jinx knew she would have a hard time keeping tabs on him. Unless she made it appear that she wanted to be part of the fun.

"Listen to you three," Jinx squealed. "You're making me want to jump on that stage and start memorizing dialogue."

"That'll be the day," Nola scoffed. "You hate the theatre."

Kip gasped and almost choked on his bok choy. "Please tell me she's wrong, Jinx. I was really hoping we could be friends. I'm already buddies with your boyfriend."

"Don't you worry, Kip," Jinx said. "You and I are gonna be besties."

"I would love that!" Kip gushed. "You were wrong, Bruno, Jinx is so not standoffish."

Jinx gave Bruno the stink eye and would have to remember to yell at him later, but for the moment, the fake smile she was wearing remained plastered on her face. She didn't want to give Kip any reason to think that she wasn't sincere about her proposition. It turned out that her happy expression was contagious. Across the table, Nola looked like Missy had just risen from the dead, the show had sold out its entire run, and there were talks of an extension.

"This is what I love about the theatre," Nola said. "The camaraderie, the togetherness, the creation of a whole new family." Nola looked at her mini-audience and tears came to her eyes. "I don't want it to end."

"Why does it have to end?" Jinx asked. "We could all remain friends, stay together, and be our own little theatrical family."

Nola and Kip cheered in agreement while it was Bruno's turn to give Jinx the stink eye. He knew how she felt about Kip, which meant that he didn't believe a word she'd just said. Nola, however, fell for it completely.

"I have just made a decision!" Nola squealed.

"What?" Kip asked.

"Nope, I can't say just yet, but you'll hear about it soon," Nola confirmed. "I need to tie up some loose ends, but I promise it is going to be life-changing. It'll make Missy Michaels the happiest dead child star who ever lived."

* * *

Later that night, Jinx was still contemplating what Nola had said and couldn't imagine what she was thinking. The good news was that she had made headway with her impromptu plan to get closer to Kip, who at the moment and without any substantiated evidence, was her prime suspect in Missy's murder. She knew that Bruno suspected she was manipulating the situation, but she also knew that as a public defender, he was on the side of Lady Justice and wouldn't tattle on her. If Jinx was wrong and Kip was nothing more than an innocent newcomer who was geographically challenged, there would be no harm. But if she was right and Kip was really a homicidal maniac, her investigation could help stop him before he caused anyone else any harm.

She started doodling in the notebook that she always carried with her. Taking notes on her phone or her laptop or any electronic device was a shortcut, but she did prefer the old-fashioned way, especially when she was working on a case. It created a stronger connection to her material.

She wrote down four names: Kip, Johnny, Donna, Missy. Her cutesy, bubble-shaped script was a visual contradiction to the very serious, underlying reason she was memorializing their names on paper. They'd all showed up in Tranquility around the same time, and Jinx wondered if they had anything in common or a connection that would lead to murder. She knew a little bit about each of them, but it was time she delved deeper. To do that, she needed some help.

"Gram, it's me," Jinx said into her phone.

"Hello, lovey," Alberta replied. "Is anything wrong?"

"I have to go to Philadelphia tomorrow to interview a former Tranquility resident who's turning one hundred," Jinx said.

"Ah, *Madon,*" Alberta replied. "God bless."

"And I was wondering if you could do some research for me."

"Of course, just tell me what the subject is," Alberta replied.

"Not what, who," Jinx clarified. "I think it's time we found out exactly who Missy Michaels was."

"We know a lot about her, lovey. There's tons of information about her online all about her movie career."

"I'm not talking about Missy the actress, I'm talking about Missy the person," Jinx said.

"You think there's a difference between the two?"

"Yes. I have a feeling there's a whole lot more about this woman that we never imagined," Jinx declared. "And it might just be the key to why she was murdered."

CHAPTER 15

Una stella senza luce.

Sometimes you can know someone and not know them at all.

That was how Alberta felt about Missy. When she saw her photo at St. Winifred's the night of her murder and was drawn in by the resemblance she had with the actress, Alberta thought she was getting closer to understanding the woman. But it had nothing to do with facts and everything to do with feeling. There was a visual connection because of their similar physicalities, but nothing more. The fact of the matter was the only thing Alberta or anyone knew about Missy was that once upon a time she starred in the movies. It was time they dug deeper to find out more. And the best digger Alberta knew was the man she dug.

Sloan was about to prove that he was not above a little skullduggery himself.

"Happy Anniversary!"

Standing in the middle of Sloan's office, Alberta was surprised by his singsong outburst. Was she already senile and not aware of it? What was so special about this Tuesday? And why was Sloan holding a bouquet of flowers?

"I'm so sorry, Sloan, I don't know what you're talking about," Alberta confessed. "What anniversary?"

"Our anniversary."

Alberta racked her brain and tried to remember what significant event occurred in their past that would warrant a celebration. The first day they met? The first time Alberta cooked for Sloan? Their first date? That had to be it. Their first date at the Tranquility Ball Waterfest, commemorating Tranquility's centennial. It had been a glorious night and the official start of their relationship, and Alberta had completely forgotten about it. She almost started to cry and then she saw Sloan's smile. *No tears*, she thought, *be grateful that you have someone to remind you of the special moments in your life.*

"I can't believe it's been two years," Alberta said. "And I can't believe I didn't remember."

There wasn't a trace of disappointment on Sloan's face. "Don't worry, I won't hold it against you, and I kind of like that I was able to surprise you."

"Never did I think that I'd have another anniversary with a man after Sammy," Alberta shared. "But I am so happy I'm sharing them with you."

"That, Alberta, is the best gift you could've given me," Sloan admitted.

Alberta felt her cheeks flare and she was filled with so much joy at that moment that she couldn't focus on words. Instead, she reached out to accept the flowers and kiss Sloan sweetly on the lips.

"*Il tempo vola quando ci si diverte*," Sloan said.

"Your lessons are working, you're starting to talk like a real native," Alberta replied. "And you're right, time has flown because we've been having so much fun."

"And it's my hope that we continue to have fun for a very long time," Sloan whispered, not taking his eyes off Alberta's.

She had no urge to break his gaze, she would be very happy to stare into his eyes for the rest of the day. Until she remembered she had come to his office with a purpose.

"That's my wish too, Sloan," Alberta said. "And I know the perfect way for us to have more fun."

"Let me guess," Sloan replied. "It has something to do with murder, mayhem, and a pint-size movie star from days gone by."

"Why, Mr. McLelland, it's as if you can read my mind," Alberta said.

She had tried to make up for her forgetfulness with a little flirtation and channeled Scarlett O'Hara as a young woman from the first part of *Gone With the Wind*. Not a born flirt, Alberta sounded more like a tipsy Carol Burnett from the famous spoof she did of the epic film.

"I'll do anything if you promise never to speak in that voice again." Sloan laughed. "That has got to be the worst Southern accent I have ever heard."

One major benefit of being in a relationship as an older woman was that Alberta could laugh at herself. If Sammy had said that to her during the early years of their marriage, she would've been hurt and taken it as yet another criticism and confirmation that everything she did was wrong. Now she took it the way it was meant, as a joke between two people who cared very much for each other.

Laughing, Alberta agreed to speak in a voice cultivated above the Mason–Dixon line. Sloan laughed even harder when Alberta told him the reason for her visit.

"I really am a mind reader," Sloan said. "I've been working on a surprise for you."

"You've already surprised me with these beautiful flowers and your sharp memory," Alberta said.

"Then let the surprises continue, madam," Sloan said. "I've uncovered the previously unknown history of Missy Michaels."

Sloan explained that he took a trip down the proverbial rabbit hole that is the Internet and did extensive online research using the library's resources to uncover the truth about the real Missy Michaels. He thought he was making progress when he found information on her fan club, but it was a dead end and the group must have disbanded years ago. Steadfast, Sloan soldiered on and did discover significant information in little-known websites that didn't seem to get much virtual traffic and additional details from a call he placed to a Hollywood memorabilia auction house that was selling a script of the first Daisy Greenfield movie signed by Missy. Luckily, Pierre, the chatty auctioneer who answered the phone, was delighted to show off his knowledge.

"Don't keep me in suspense, Sloan, tell me what you found out," Alberta said.

"Missy's story is really a Hollywood fairy tale," Sloan began. "She was discovered in 1956 when she was only six years old by a film producer who was on vacation in Deer Isle, Maine. He watched Missy playing with her family on the beach and saw more than a rambunctious little girl, he saw a cash cow."

"He could tell she would be a big box office star just from watching her play on the beach?" Alberta asked.

"It's their job," Sloan replied. "Producers and casting directors are trained to see not only talent, but someone's potential. He must've seen some inner spark in the girl because he whisked Missy away from her family, relocated her to Hollywood, and she became an instant star. She quickly eclipsed Shirley Temple's fame, but had even more heartache."

"I never read about any tragedies in her life," Alberta said.

"Because they were kept out of the papers at the time," Sloan explained. "Soon after arriving in Hollywood, the film studios pushed Missy's family to the side. Her mother, who had made the trip to the West Coast with her, was paid off to go back to Maine and essentially let the studios raise Missy."

"*Maria Santissima,*" Alberta gasped. "What kind of mother would abandon her own child?"

"The kind who was dirt poor and had three other children to feed," Sloan replied. "The kicker is that Missy's earnings were tied up with business managers for most of her career, so her family didn't get a penny other than the initial buyout her mother received to remove herself from Missy's life."

"How much did they pay her?" Alberta asked. "Not that any amount of money would be worth severing ties with your child, especially a baby so young."

"Pierre didn't say," Sloan said. "But when Missy was fourteen years old, she became emancipated and took control of her finances herself."

"Emancipated?" Alberta asked. "I don't think I know what that means."

"It's when a minor petitions to become an adult in the eyes of the court," Sloan explained. "Meaning a fourteen-year-old could make all her own decisions, financial and otherwise."

"Sounds to me like it means she disowned her family," Alberta commented.

"That's exactly what it means. She severed ties not only with her family, but her business managers as well," Sloan said. "It's a drastic measure, but there must have been a solid reason because the judge allowed it."

"What were the ramifications?" Alberta asked.

"By then Missy was already quite wealthy, but a little girl lost," Sloan said. "My guess is that she didn't understand that her mother was forced out of her life and assumed she just flew the coop. That's the only justification I can come up with to explain why Missy's family remained poor while Missy was one of the wealthiest girls in the world."

"I've heard about other child stars and how their business managers stole their money and misused their positions within their lives," Alberta admitted. "But to think that Missy turned her back on her own family. That's hard to accept."

"I'm sure there's a lot more to her story," Sloan said. "Consider these the bullet points."

"What happened after the final Daisy movie?" Alberta asked. "Did Missy reconcile with her parents?"

"According to Pierre, she did not, though all his information about her post-Daisy film career was strictly professional," Sloan said. "She made a few films and TV guest appearances as an adult, but the offers dried up and she officially retired from acting in 1979. If you remember, she did a few talk show appearances after that on Merv Griffin and Mike Douglas, and there was that big retrospective on Phil Donahue."

"I saw that!" Alberta exclaimed. "The entire hour was devoted to her. They had the whole cast on too. It was so wonderful to see them all together again."

"That was the last time that would happen," Sloan said. "The young man who played Daisy's boyfriend and then husband, Willie Mueller, died shortly after that reunion in a car accident. And the guy who played the grandmother's butler died the following year of a heart attack."

"What about Inga, the woman who played Teddy?" Alberta asked.

"There's nothing definitive on the Internet about her," Sloan confirmed. "If she's still alive, she's keeping a very low profile."

Unlike Inga, the actress who played Teddy, Alberta decided she didn't want to hide in the shadows and gave Sloan a big thank-you kiss.

"What was that for?" Sloan asked. "Not that I'm complaining."

"You have outdone yourself," she replied. "You've filled in so many blanks about Missy's life, you gave me flowers, and you remembered our anniversary."

"He's not the only one!"

Alberta turned around and for the second time that morning was flabbergasted. Helen and Joyce were standing in the doorway to Sloan's office. Alberta understood why Joyce was holding a tray of cupcakes, but she had no idea why Helen was holding a balloon in the shape of a goldfish.

"*Caro signore*," Alberta said. "What are you two doing here?"

"Wishing you and your fella a happy anniversary," Joyce declared.

"With a goldfish?" Alberta questioned.

"Your first date was at the Waterfest," Helen said. "I wanted to bring a water pistol with me to commemorate the occasion, but Joyce convinced me that you probably weren't wearing waterproof mascara."

"Thank you, Joyce, you always have my back," Alberta said. "And thank you, Helen, the thought and the goldfish are greatly appreciated."

"Ladies, this is incredibly thoughtful of you both," Sloan added. He grabbed a cupcake from Joyce's tray and took a bite. "Yum. Luckily, I'm a big proponent of a healthy breakfast."

"I see Sloan got you a lovely bouquet of flowers, Berta," Helen said. "What did you get him?"

Caught off guard, Alberta didn't have a chance to invent a gift, and Helen could tell by her agonized expression that she had completely forgotten there was a memory to memorialize.

"You forgot your own anniversary?" Helen barked.

"I've been so focused on solving this case, it slipped my mind," Alberta said.

"How hard could it be to remember?" Helen asked. "You've literally only had two men in your entire life."

"That's all right, Helen," Sloan said. "I'm not dating Alberta for her mind."

"Then this relationship might have some legs after all," Helen said.

"Basta!" Alberta cried. "How did you two know we were here anyway?"

Joyce laid the tray of cupcakes on Sloan's desk as Helen tied the balloon's string around the arm of one of the guest chairs in the office. They both sat down at the same time and acted as if they were going to give a presentation, which was exactly what they were going to do.

"Jinx called us last night and asked us to do some research into Missy's past," Joyce explained. "She thinks there's much more to her than just her childhood fame."

"She asked me to do the same thing," Alberta said. "That's why I'm here."

"We knew she asked you and we figured if you had some research to do, you would hightail it to Sloan's office first thing in the morning," Joyce said.

"Am I that predictable?" Alberta asked.

"When it comes to using Sloan, yes," Helen replied.

"Ah, *Madon!*" Alberta cried. "One of these days, Helen."

"What?" Helen replied. "Bang zoom, right to the moon?"

"Before the two of you start to brawl, I've already given Alberta permission to use me as she sees fit," Sloan announced. "Now why don't you and Joyce tell us what you've found out?"

Joyce explained that through one of her contacts she'd uncovered that although Missy married several times, she never had any children. Two of her husbands died, and while her third marriage ended in divorce, her ex was killed in a boating accident before he could change his will. Luck stuck as closely to Missy as death, because all three men chose Missy as their sole beneficiary and left her their entire estates.

She amassed about three million dollars in inheritance,

not a huge sum of money, but a much better amount than what most child actors were able to accumulate and an excellent amount for someone who hadn't worked in over four decades. She invested wisely in the stock market and made some smart real estate investments that all turned a hefty profit. Financially speaking, she'd had nothing to worry about.

She was also in good health. At least that's what Luke had told Helen. During a break in the meeting held on what was supposed to be the first day of rehearsal, Luke mentioned that according to the autopsy report, Missy hadn't been taking any medication and had no other physical ailments. Luke also mentioned that the autopsy report wasn't yet ready to be released to the public, so the information needed to be kept confidential and Helen couldn't tell anyone about it, including her sister or granddaughter. Helen swore she would never do that and immediately told the one person Luke hadn't forbidden her to tell: her sister-in-law, Joyce.

"You see, Helen," Joyce remarked. "I do come in handy."

"Sometimes," Helen added.

"That proves that Missy was healthy and wealthy, if not entirely wise," Alberta said.

"Why do you say that, Berta?" Sloan asked.

"She should never have come to Tranquility," Alberta said. "Had she stayed home and out of the public's eye, she might still be alive."

"She couldn't resist," Helen said. "We actresses understand the lure of the spotlight."

"Helen!" Alberta cried. "I'm sure you would've been *eccezionale* in the play, but you can't put yourself in the same category as Missy. She was a movie star."

"Actually, Helen and Missy had more in common than you might think," Sloan said. "You too, Alberta."

"I did notice that we bear a physical resemblance, and Missy used to wear her hair the same way I did," Alberta said. "But what could Helen and I have in common with that celebrity?"

"You're all Italian," Sloan announced.

"That's *pazzo*," Alberta said.

"It sure is. Daisy was a WASP," Helen added. "Her parents were originally from England."

"Daisy might have had British blood running through her veins," Sloan replied. "But Missy Michaels, or should I say Melissa Margherita Miccalizzo, was one hundred percent Sicilian."

"You can't get any more Italian than that," Joyce said.

"*Dio mio!*" Alberta exclaimed. "That's her real name?"

"It's so beautiful," Helen said. "Why in the world did they change it?"

"Back then they always changed actors' names to make them sound less ethnic and more majestic. The name needed to look good on a marquee," Sloan explained. "Rock Hudson was born Roy Harold Scherer and Lauren Bacall was originally Betty Joan Perske."

"Bogie and Betty has a nice ring to it," Alberta remarked.

"But Bogie and Perske sounds like an accounting firm," Helen added.

"Also too, despite her black hair, Missy doesn't look very Italian," Joyce added.

"The studio probably changed the little girl's appearance as well," Sloan said. "They were always transforming movie stars, like making Judy Garland lose weight, lifting Rita Hayworth's hairline, and revamping Marilyn Monroe's entire body."

"I wonder if Missy looks like the rest of her family," Alberta said.

"Hard to know," Sloan replied. "None of the photos I found online ever showed her back in Maine or with her relatives. They're exclusively photo shoots except for some rare candid shots, but in those Missy is only seen with Teddy or the other recurring characters from the films."

"Once Missy went to Hollywood, it's like her real family ceased to exist," Joyce said.

"What a sin," Alberta muttered. "To be torn from your family at such a young age."

"And then to have life torn from you at such an old age," Sloan said.

"Not for nothing, but this is the worst anniversary party I ever attended," Helen quipped.

"Sorry, Helen," Sloan said. "I'll make it up to you another time, but tonight I'm taking my girl out for dinner at that fancy new French restaurant in Lake Hopatcong."

"Ooh la la, that place is fancy," Joyce cooed. "Berta, you have to wear that new black dress you bought at The Clothes Horse, and I have a pink chiffon scarf and brooch to finish the outfit."

"That sounds perfect, Joyce, thank you," Alberta said. "I'll come over later and pick them up, but first I have an errand to run. And I need Helen's help."

St. Winifred's of the Holy Well didn't draw much of a crowd on a Tuesday afternoon, so when Alberta and Helen entered the church there were only two other people sitting in the pews. They dipped their fingertips into the holy water font, made the sign of the cross, and walked to the left, where the statue of the Blessed Mother was. They each lit a candle and silently said a prayer for Missy's soul. Their earlier conversation made Alberta realize that even if a family member knew that Missy died thanks to their long separation and fractured relationship, they might not care enough to offer up an invocation. It reminded Alberta of something her mother would often say, *una stella senza luce*—a star without light. And she imagined that without her family by her side, that's exactly what Missy was.

When they were finished, they gazed into the blue eyes of the statue and, as they always did, thanked the Blessed Mother for listening. It was a moment of grace and humility that the women felt was necessary. When they turned around, the last thing they expected to see were the glaring black eyes of Father Sal.

"Follow me, ladies."

Baffled but intrigued, Alberta and Helen followed Sal out of the church and down the walkway leading toward the rectory and the priests' offices. Unsure of why Sal wanted them to follow him, the ladies interlocked their arms to reassure themselves that he wasn't leading them down a path of some kind of spiritual destruction. With Sal, you just never knew.

Once they were in his office, they watched Sal climb on a small ladder to pull out a photo album from the top shelf of the floor-to-ceiling bookshelves that were chock-full of everything from first-edition hardcovers to pulp paperbacks to decades-old church newsletters. When he placed the item on his desk, they realized it was much more than a photo album: it was a Missy Michaels scrapbook.

"Sal, you weren't kidding," Helen said. "You really are a superfan."

"Thou shalt not lie, Helen," Sal replied. "I have similar handmade tomes on Doris Day and Lena Horne, as well as some others. Early in my career, when I was working far from home, these women became something of a substitute family to me."

Neither Helen nor Alberta commented on that revelation, but they were thankful that their friend felt comfortable enough to disclose a private truth to them. They also really wanted to dive into the scrapbook to see what private truths it would reveal about Missy.

The information Sloan had gathered came from reputable news sites. In contrast, the clippings Sal preserved in his book were culled from gossip rags and exposed a different side to Missy's life. Together, they began to create a more realistic picture of the former superstar.

Page after page was filled with articles and photos from supermarket newspapers and old movie star magazines, and few of them were flattering. They learned that Missy's stardom destroyed her family because they were never allowed to be with Missy while she was making movies in Hollywood. The pain and anxiety the separation caused took its toll on her parents, who divorced by the time Missy's second movie premiered. Her siblings— two sisters and a brother—were always jealous of her and never understood why she was the one the producer handpicked to be a star.

"Personally, I don't like to remember Missy this way, but life wouldn't be life if we only focused on the ripe fruit and ignored the rotting apples falling from certain family trees," Sal said. "I thought a tidbit or two in here could help with the investigation."

"You may be right, Sal," Alberta said. "Thank you for sharing these memories with us."

"I wonder if Missy even cared about seeing her family," Helen said. "She was probably surrounded by so many people in Hollywood and always working, she might not have had the time to miss them."

"It appears that they missed her money."

Alberta was pointing at an article that claimed Missy's family sued her for a portion of her salary. The claim was dismissed in court and corroborated the information Sloan discovered, that Missy was emancipated when she was only fourteen years old. She took control of her finances, and all the money she made from that point on was hers and hers alone. And from what the rest of the articles claimed, she never gave her family another penny.

"Do you notice that they refer to her family as the Michaels?" Alberta asked.

"That's their last name," Father Sal replied.

"Wrong," Helen said. "She's as Italian as the three of us."

"Holy Federico Fellini!" Sal shouted. "Are you serious?"

"Does Melissa Margherita Miccalizzo sound Irish?" Helen said.

Sal clutched his heart and closed his eyes, seemingly lost in a recurring daydream. "I always knew she and I could be related."

The last page of the scrapbook was a full-page article with the headline WHATEVER HAPPENED TO MISSY MICHAELS? It was mainly a recap of Missy's career and they gleaned nothing new from its content. But the accompanying photo was the clue they were looking for. Sal was right, his scrapbook might help them find out who'd killed Missy.

"*Santa Madre di Dio!*" Alberta exclaimed. "Look at this photo."

Immediately, Helen and Sal focused on the picture on the page. It showed Missy with her parents and three siblings on a country road in front of a dilapidated house. The street sign behind them showed they stood on the corner of Smith Street and 7th Avenue.

"That's the house in the photo!" Helen exclaimed. "The one that was stuffed inside the arsenic bottle."

"You're right!" Sal squealed. "The background is the same, except in this photo the people are different."

"This confirms it," Alberta said. "The murderer didn't kill Missy Michaels."

"Then who'd the killer kill?" Helen asked.

"Melissa Margherita Miccalizzo."

CHAPTER 16

Una voce dal passato.

Melissa Margherita Miccalizzo might be dead, but Missy Michaels was still alive and kicking.

Based on the bustling activity taking place on stage and in the theatre at St. Winifred's Academy, it was obvious that despite the rumors of her grisly demise, the old girl wasn't yet ready to make her final exit from this world. The entire cast was milling about, chattering, discussing characters they wouldn't get to play, and reciting lines they wouldn't get to say. The large, blown-up photo of Missy still stood on the tripod at the back of the theatre, and to the left of the entrance were stacks of programs with the same before-and-after photos of Missy plastered on the cover announcing her as the unequivocal star of *Arsenic and Old Lace*. But how could there be an *Arsenic and Old Lace* if the lead actress and box office draw was—what was the delicate way to put it?—otherwise engaged?

Ever since Nola bolted from her lunch with Jinx, Bruno, and Kip, she had been acting odder than usual. At home she was sequestered in her bedroom, so Jinx hadn't seen her, and when Jinx texted her at work during the day, she received an automated response stating that "The person you are trying to contact cannot be reached at this time." Nola was always busy, but she was always responsive. No one had heard from her until she e-mailed a missive to the cast and creative team of the show at 5:45 a.m., asking them all to meet her at the theatre later that night for an emergency meeting.

As they entered the lobby of the theatre, Jinx turned to Alberta and paused.

"What's wrong, lovey?" Alberta asked.

"Nola's making me nervous," Jinx admitted. "I haven't even been able to fill her in on Missy being Italian and being from Deer Isle, Maine, which, incidentally, does not sound like a town that would have any kind of Italian population."

"We're everywhere, lovey, don't ever forget that," Alberta replied. "But your not being able to share any of the information we found with Nola might be a good thing."

"You don't think Nola had anything to do with the murder, do you?" Jinx asked.

"Not Nola," Alberta said, "but possibly someone she knows. Better to keep what we found out private for the moment. These are clues that might help in the investigation."

"That makes sense, Gram. I got so caught up in the excitement of what you found out, I wanted to share it."

"It might not be the Italian way to do things," Alberta stated, "but sometimes it's best to keep quiet."

Tell that to Helen.

"Nola's lucky I took a sabbatical from volunteering at the animal shelter!" Helen said, joining Alberta and Jinx in the lobby. "I'm not always free on Thursday nights."

"Don't make it sound as if you had anything else to do," Alberta replied. "Now that the show's been canceled, you have all your nights free."

"Aunt Helen, do you have any idea why Nola called this meeting?" Jinx asked.

"I suspect it has to do with everyone returning their scripts," Helen said. "She mentioned that at the first rehearsal meeting. Do you think I should return the script we swiped from Missy's hotel room?"

"Let's keep it for a while longer," Alberta said. "No one's missed it and it still might hold a clue."

"Jinxie, has Nola said anything about Missy's script?" Helen asked.

"I haven't been able to get a hold of her since our lunch on Monday, but I know this has been so hard on her," Jinx said. "She's really been quite upset."

She still was.

"Don't yell at me!"

The women turned toward the box office, and although the blinds were down on the ticket window, they could see that a light was on inside the small room. From the sounds emerging within the space, they could also hear that a fight was brewing.

"Don't call me that!"

Despite the venom lacing each spoken word, it could

be nothing more than a lover's quarrel. The women looked at one another but remained silent so they could hear more of the argument between Nola and Johnny. Yes, it was eavesdropping, but yes, it was also entertaining.

"How many times do I have to ask you that?" Johnny yelled.

"I slipped, I'm sorry!" Nola yelled back. "What difference does it make anyway?"

"Just drop it!" Johnny barked.

"You can really drive a person crazy!"

"Like you're not deeply maladjusted!"

"And you're never to be trusted!"

"You're a crazy person yourself, Nola!"

Suddenly, the fighting stopped. Instead of bickering and shouting, the women heard the unmistakable gurgles and smacking sounds of a couple making out.

"Are they kissing?" Alberta asked.

"How could they be kissing after insulting each other like that and saying such hurtful things to each other?" Helen asked.

"They weren't fighting," Jinx said.

"Lovey, I know there's a generation gap and couples act differently nowadays, but didn't you hear them?" Alberta asked. "No matter what your age, you have to admit what we heard was fighting."

"They were reciting lyrics from a Stephen Sondheim musical!" Jinx shouted. "Nola plays that song constantly, I'd have recognized the words anywhere."

"That must be one angry musical," Helen said.

"Ah, *Madon!*" Alberta cried. "That doesn't sound like anything from *The King and I.*"

"It's from a musical called *Company,*" Jinx explained.

"Revolutionary for its time, according to Nola, otherwise known as the walking encyclopedia of American musical theatre. I just call it annoying. Nola! Get out here!"

Following Jinx's outburst, the kissing immediately stopped and was followed by the sounds of Nola and Johnny quickly making themselves presentable and emerging from the box office room into the lobby. When Nola spoke, it was made very clear why her role in the theatre community was not on the stage but behind it. She was a terrible actress.

"Oh, hi, everybody!" Nola said in a tone of fake surprise. "I had no idea anyone was out here."

"Obviously," Jinx replied. "Or else you wouldn't have been carrying on like you were on your own private soundstage."

"There are no soundstages in theatre," Johnny corrected. "Only in film and TV."

"Don't challenge my metaphor, Johnny!" Jinx yelled. "I've had enough of these private little performances you two put on. Fight like normal people from now on! And get this meeting started and tell us all what this emergency is!"

"Now that your grandmother is here, I can do just that," Nola declared.

"Me?" Alberta said. "I'm just here to lend moral support."

"That and so much more, Mrs. Scaglione," Nola said mysteriously. "Let's go into the theatre and I'll explain everything."

Unsure as to where Nola was leading the conversation, they followed her into the theatre. One person who didn't seem to be thrilled by the direction Nola was taking them was Johnny. Alberta couldn't tell if he was embarrassed to have been caught canoodling with his producer behind closed doors or if he was still angry about whatever they were fighting about before the canoodling began, but he didn't look as excited and energetic as he did when she first met him during the auditions. Maybe he was having another panic attack based on whatever big, secretive announcement Nola was about to make?

Inside the theatre, the entire cast had already taken their seats. Crew members sat as a group in the first row, Jinx had grabbed a seat next to Tambra, and sitting in front of them were Bruno, Luke, Kip, and Benny. Joyce, Sloan, and Father Sal came rushing over to Alberta, and Helen asked if they knew why Nola had gathered them all together, but they revealed they were in the dark just like the rest of the group.

When Nola stood in front of the microphone, center stage, she didn't have to say a word for her curious audience to stare at her in rapt attention. She had them in the palm of her hand. And like any good producer, she held the dramatic pause before speaking.

"Thank you all for coming here tonight, and forgive me for being cryptic," Nola started. "After the devastating turn of events last week, I've been doing a great deal of thinking, and I've come to the conclusion that Missy wouldn't want our show to end because she could no longer be a part of it. She was an actress and she understood the importance and the cathartic nature of theatre and I know in my heart that she'd want the show to go on. So that's exactly what we're going to do."

"How can we go on without our star?"

Even Helen was surprised by Father Sal's outburst, but he only said out loud what everyone else was thinking. After he spoke, the rest of the company, one by one, asked the same question. Nola didn't respond, but raised her hands, palms facing her audience, until they quieted down.

"We're going to go on because one superstar is going to take the place of another," Nola announced. "Tranquility's very own celebrity, Alberta Ferrara Scaglione, will take over Missy's role as Abby Brewster and share the stage alongside her very own sister, Helen."

A huge gasp was followed by enthusiastic applause. The only people in the theatre not joining in the ovation were Alberta and Johnny. Alberta because she was in shock and Johnny, based on his glowering stare and pursed lips, because he didn't support the idea. Alberta wasn't insulted because she understood what she believed Johnny was thinking: There was no way in the world she could take Missy's place.

"What do you say, Mrs. Scaglione?" Nola asked. "Will you join our merry band of players?"

Looking around the room, Alberta couldn't argue with Nola's comment. The faces staring at her in anticipation indeed looked merry, all except Johnny of course. There was something about his expression. Now that she looked at him closer, Alberta wasn't convinced he was upset because of Nola's odd casting choice. It wasn't just that he didn't want to be involved in the show now that Missy was no longer part of the production, there was another reason that he was hiding. When he flicked his nose with his forefinger, it dawned on her. Johnny was acting like Lola did when she got caught doing something wrong like stealing a biscotto from the kitchen counter. He looked guilty.

"Say something, Berta."

Helen's whisper and nudge in the ribs ripped Alberta

from her contemplation and back into the conversation Nola was trying to have with her.

"Please say yes, Alberta," Nola implored. "You're our only hope of fulfilling Missy's last wish to return to the stage."

Alberta forced herself not to roll her eyes at Nola's overly dramatic comment and remembered where she was. This was the theatre. This was where drama took center stage. But it wasn't a place Alberta was used to being, and although she enjoyed the time she spent sitting in a chair as an audience member, the thought of standing on stage and performing as part of a cast and working with a director frightened her. But wait . . . If she was with the director, that would mean she'd be working side by side with Johnny. And what better way to find out why he was acting so strangely and looking so guilty than to get close to him as an actress instead of an amateur detective? It was the perfect disguise.

It was also the perfect way for Alberta to make a complete fool of herself in front of the entire town. She wasn't an actress, she didn't know the first thing about being in a play, and the only time she performed in a show she'd wound up beheading Jesus. No, she couldn't do it. And if she hadn't turned to see Helen staring at her, she would have told everyone that she was very sorry, but she wouldn't be able to honor Nola's absurd request. However, when she saw Helen's lips moving, she knew she was saying a Hail Mary and literally praying that Alberta would accept Nola's offer. It wasn't something she wanted to do, but she would do it for her sister. Before she could change her mind, she gave everyone the only answer they wanted to hear.

"I'll do it."

Raucous applause erupted and Alberta sat in awe as she received her first standing ovation. Nola ran over and threw her arms around her, thanking her for saving their production. One by one, the rest of the company hugged her, kissed her on the cheek, and clutched her hand. Laughing and shaking her head, she couldn't believe how excited she had made everyone by simply agreeing to step into Missy's role. When Kip stood in front of her, tears welling in his eyes, she realized that their euphoria had nothing to do with her and everything to do with themselves.

"Thank you for giving us the chance to do what we love."

Kip embraced Alberta warmly and she could feel his heart beating. These people truly loved the theatre. It was a passion that Alberta didn't possess, but she felt humbled to be in their presence. She wasn't stepping into the footlights for the same reasons they were, but she felt a rush of adrenaline course through her body knowing she had made a choice that was going to make so many people happy. Especially her sister.

"This is going to be so much fun, Berta," Helen gushed uncharacteristically. "It'll be nothing like Headless Jesus."

"You'd better pray it isn't," Alberta said.

"We'll run lines, and I know that it'll be a stretch because you're going to be playing the older sister and I'm the younger one, but follow my lead and you'll be fine."

Now Alberta felt the tears well up in her eyes hearing her sister speak so fervently about their joint venture. She gave Helen a tight hug and said, "If you can be a chauffeur, I can be an actress."

"Are you sure about that, Alberta?"

Johnny's question did what he meant it to do. It created tension. It brought the effervescent scene to a screeching halt. It made everyone in attendance hold their breath. Except for Alberta. She had expected Johnny to challenge her seemingly impulsive response and it gave her the opportunity to do what smart actresses have done since the first time they were permitted to perform on the stage with their male counterparts. She fawned all over her director.

"Honestly, Johnny, I'm not," Alberta said. "But if you guide me with your expertise and your experience, I have no doubt I'll be in good hands and will be able to give you a performance you'll be proud of."

If Johnny saw through her sycophantic pledge, he didn't make his disbelief apparent. Instead, he responded like a typical director when confronted by an insecure performer. He vowed to lift her up to the rafters so her inner light could shine.

"Welcome aboard, Alberta," Johnny announced, his scowl turning into a smile. "And get ready to have the time of your life."

The following Saturday at the rehearsal reboot, Alberta sat in row J, her script with all her lines highlighted in bright orange clutched in her hand and a cluster of caffeine-saturated butterflies starting to flutter in her stomach. She wasn't prepared to perform; she also wasn't prepared to hear from the woman whose footsteps she had to follow.

A movie screen began to lower from the ceiling above the stage and everyone looked up at the technical intrusion. Alberta thought it was odd to see a film screen on a stage, but then realized that because the theatre was part of a high school, the space most likely doubled as an assembly room and the screen was used for instructional videos. She didn't know what its purpose was at the moment, but Sloan and Joyce, who stood in front of the fully revealed screen, looked like they were about to tell everyone.

"The reason we're all here is because of Missy Michaels," Joyce started. "And because she couldn't be here today in person, we thought the next best thing would be to let her appear in video."

"On loan from Father Sal's private collection, we'd like to show you Missy's last TV appearance," Sloan said. "This is from an interview with *Good Morning Michigan* that Missy did in 1982."

"We think you'll agree that it's important for us to see the woman that we, unfortunately, never got to see in life," Joyce said.

The lights dimmed and the familiar sound of a tape cassette being put into a VCR filled the room. Someone hit a button and the sound shifted to the whirl of tape rotating around the reels growing louder when static appeared on the screen. The grainy lines soon gave way to the image of two women sitting in club chairs made of olive-green leather. They were facing each other and between them was a small glass table on which there stood a vase filled with flowers the same color as the purple popcorn rug that covered the entire floor. Behind them was the logo for the show's segment, "Five Minutes With . . ." The woman on the left of the screen didn't look familiar and was obviously a local news reporter, but the woman on the right was unmistakable. It was Missy.

"Welcome back, everyone, I'm Jessica Westin and this is 'Five Minutes With' . . . Missy Michaels."

Jessica waited for the applause to die down to speak again. When she did, she turned to face Missy, and her tone, while professional, couldn't suppress the hint of a true fan.

"I know it's been quite a while since the last film," Jessica said. "But do you think there's a chance we might get to see Daisy Greenfield back on the big screen?"

The question gave Missy pause and she appeared to be deep in thought. It was almost as if the sound of her alter ego's name came as a surprise to her when she must have known that the two were forever conjoined; one could not exist without the other. Then again, Missy was probably fully aware of this fact, and it might simply be a truth she was comfortable with.

Smiling the same way she had done since she was a child, Missy replied, "I would love to bring Daisy back to life and share her story with the public." She paused briefly, and her eyes still shone, but her smile faded. "But I don't know if Daisy would agree."

Jessica laughed nervously, unsure what Missy's response meant. Did this woman think Daisy Greenfield was a real person? "Doesn't Daisy do whatever Missy tells her to do?"

"Not always," Missy said. "She's been having such a wonderful time with her husband since their marriage, I'm not sure the girl has the time to go back to New York and stay in one place for a few months. Even though her grandmother's penthouse is palatial."

This time Jessica, along with rest of the studio audience, laughed genuinely. "So in your mind, Daisy's had a good life?"

"Picture-perfect," Missy said. "She's had the life every little girl ever dreamed of."

"It is important to point out that Daisy's life didn't start off like a dream," Jessica said. "She was orphaned as a little girl."

All traces of smiles and laughter left Missy's face. "What really is family? What really is the bond between a child and their guardian? Daisy lost her parents, but she had unconditional love from her grandmother and the servants in their home treated her like she was their own."

"That's very true," Jessica said, surprised by the change in Missy's tone. She attempted to bring levity back to the conversation with her next question. "Plus, she was filthy rich."

The audience appreciated the comment, but Missy did not.

"Money never meant anything to Daisy," Missy said. "She would've given up every penny if she could have had her parents back, but even at a young age, Daisy was a realist, a survivor." Missy took another pause and bowed her head. No one dared to interrupt her because they weren't sure if they were listening to Missy or Daisy. When she continued to speak, they still weren't sure. "She knew her parents were gone forever and so she accepted her life and made the best of it."

When she spoke again, Missy turned from her interviewer to face the audience and, as a result, looked directly into the camera.

"That's why every single one of you loved Daisy Greenfield," Missy continued. "Because she was strong and wise beyond her years. She was tough and intelligent, but she was also a lost little girl. Every one of you felt like you had to protect her and wrap your arms around her to make sure she felt safe and loved. I'd like you to know that we felt every loving embrace, and because of that and on behalf of myself and Daisy Greenfield, we'd like to thank you."

The camera remained on Missy's face. Like every person sitting in the theatre at St. Winifred's and more than likely every studio audience member who saw the interview live, it couldn't look away. The qualities Missy exuded as a child actor were amplified as an adult and, ironically, she was even more vulnerable later in her life than she was at the beginning of her career.

The video cut off and a layer of silence filled the theatre, as if each person was paying their respects to the murdered star. They reflected on the last words they heard from Missy, *una voce dal passato,* a voice from the past. Not a sound was heard until the back door swung open and Kip shouted his arrival.

"I'm sorry I'm late! I swear, it won't happen again."

Now that the spell was broken it was the perfect time to get to work.

Johnny went into full-on director mode and called Alberta, Helen, Kip, and Bruno to the stage. Jinx saw Nola retreat back to the lobby and thought it would be the ideal time to get a few quotes from her so she could write an article about the new casting. Rushing as always, she didn't notice Kip racing down the aisle in her direction until the two collided with each other.

"I'm so sorry," Kip said, sprawled out on the floor.

"You keep saying that, don't you?" Jinx replied, lying in a similar position a few feet away.

Jinx stood up and saw that Kip was now on his knees,

unhurt and shoving papers back into his briefcase, which had opened when he fell. Feeling partially responsible for their fender bender, Jinx crawled on her knees to where Kip was to help gather the files and documents that were strewn all around them.

"I had to go into the office this morning and file some reports," Kip explained. "Which is why I was running late."

"I know the feeling," Jinx replied, remembering to keep her tone friendly and conversational. "I'm officially on duty myself and need to interview Nola."

"Our work is never done, is it?" Kip asked.

The question was rhetorical, but it was true. Jinx stared at the letter on the top of the pile of papers she was holding and it took all the self-restraint she had not to scream. Before Kip turned around to face her, she shuffled the pile, making sure that letter was now mixed in with all the others. Maintaining her composure, she gave them all to Kip, but she couldn't find the strength to speak.

"Thanks so much," Kip said. "I'd better get up on that stage before Johnny recasts my part."

When Kip turned to run toward the stage, Jinx felt all the energy leave her body. She slumped into an aisle seat until she caught her breath from the shock. The letter Kip had received was addressed to him at his former address in Deer Isle, Maine. He and Missy were from the same hometown.

CHAPTER 17

Non tutti i ragazzi crescono per essere uomini.

Being part of an amateur detective team meant always being able to rely on your partners. Except for those times when your partners were too busy to help.

Alberta and Helen were onstage working with Johnny to lock in the blocking for their opening scene and Joyce was huddled over a desk with Sloan working on the revised publicity campaign that had to highlight the new star of the show, while being sensitive to the reason the old star had been replaced. Jinx was on her own.

She slipped out of the theatre unnoticed without any thought of where to go, but by the time she was behind the steering wheel of her car she had a destination. It was Saturday, so there wouldn't be anyone at *The Herald* and she'd be able to do some research uninterrupted. And if a colleague also gave in to the urge to work over the weekend, she'd say she needed peace and quiet from her large, loud Italian family to put the finishing touches on an article she was working on. Which wasn't far from the truth.

As expected, the office was empty, which allowed Jinx free rein to work unencumbered without worrying if Calhoun, her main rival at the paper, or anyone else for that matter, would be lurking nearby, trying to snoop around and sneak a peek at what she was investigating. Or, more specifically, who.

Jinx couldn't believe Kip was from the same hometown as Missy. What were the odds? It had to be more than a coincidence, especially because Kip had kept the fact a secret. When he was asked where he came from, he had told her grandmother he was from the Boston area, which was a generalization at best, but very far from the truth.

In the short time Jinx had known Kip, she had not taken him for the quiet type. He was a lawyer and an actor, two professions that required bravado and noise and were not suited for those with shy or tiny egos. Kip wasn't obnoxious, but he was gregarious and talkative. He'd deliberately chosen to keep his origin confidential. But why?

Using the online search resources available to the newspaper, which were more extensive than those used by the general public, Jinx quickly connected Kip Flanigan to the address in Deer Isle, Maine, that she saw on the letter. It wasn't an error, it wasn't an optical illusion born out of wishful thinking on her part to connect Kip to the murder victim. At some point in his life before relocating to New Jersey, Kip had lived in the same town where Missy was born.

Energized, Jinx continued her search to delve deeper

into Kip's past and came up with innocuous bits of information. He graduated from Deer Isle-Stonington High School, went to Bowdoin College, and received his law degree from Boston University. According to the date on an old driver's license and an obituary on the Jordan-Fernald Funeral Home in Mt. Desert, Jinx was able to cobble together a portion of Kip's history.

Instead of moving out into the world as an adult, he returned to Deer Isle after the death of his father, who died suddenly of a heart attack while Kip was in law school. He stayed for almost two years and appeared to live an uneventful life; at least there were no events worthy of online testimony. Until Jinx stumbled into a chat room at JazzHands.com that listed all the community theatres in southeastern Maine.

In a thread for a production of *Joseph and the Amazing Technicolor Dreamcoat* at New Surry Theatre in Blue Hill, Maine, Kip was singled out, not for the kudos he received for his portrayal of the title character, but for the criminal charges filed against him that forced him to leave the show prematurely.

"Ah, *Madon,*" Jinx muttered, sounding more like her grandmother than she realized. "Kip is a criminal?"

Leaning in closer to her computer, Jinx read that most of the posts debated who was better, Kip or his replacement, Alan Doohey, with the consensus tipping slightly in Kip's favor, though, to be fair, a huge percentage of chatters agreed that Alan had a more defined six-pack.

The more interesting posts, however, referenced a mysterious arrest that resulted in Kip spending several nights in jail until the charges were dropped. It was his stint in the clink that forced him to miss the final week of performances and allowed Alan to take over the lead.

"What charges?" Jinx asked the screen. "What crime did Kip commit?"

She looked up quickly to make sure she was still alone and that no one had overheard her talking to herself. Once satisfied that she was still the only one in the office, she continued to scour the seemingly endless chat posts in search of specific details of Kip's crime. Fifteen minutes and an exhaustive online search later, all she'd uncovered were posts that argued his innocence or guilt, but none that detailed the crime itself. The only clue was the mention of someone named Wes. Was he the victim of whatever crime Kip was involved in? Was he a cohort, the whistleblower? Everyone in the chat room seemed to know the details of the crime so no one felt the need to mention it.

"Thanks a lot, JazzHands.com!" Jinx cried.

She was still no closer to finding out why Kip was arrested. What could he have done that would've kept him in jail for a few nights? Confident she wouldn't find what she was searching for on the Internet, she decided to go directly to the source. Not Kip, but the Deer Isle police force.

"Hello, my name is Jinx Maldonado and I'm a reporter at *The Upper Sussex Herald* in Tranquility, New Jersey."

Jinx hoped that her professional credentials, not to mention the speaking voice she adopted when trying to sound, well, professional, would convince the police officer on the other end of the line to cooperate and give her whatever information she requested. When she heard the officer's friendly response, she thought they were off to a promising start.

"Hello, Ms. Maldonado from New Jersey, this is Detective Perreti from Deer Isle. How can I help you?"

When she heard that she was speaking to an Italian, she knew the rest of the conversation would be smooth sailing.

"I'm doing research on cold cases throughout the country, kind of a state-by-state profile for a series of articles I'm writing for the paper," Jinx said, impressed with her on-the-spot lie. "And I'm looking to get more information on a case in Deer Isle involving Kip Flanigan."

"I can't help you with that," the detective replied.

So much for working with a fellow paisan.

"Is there someone who can help me?" Jinx asked.

"No."

This time the detective's voice sounded even less cooperative.

"Perhaps I could speak to your chief, perhaps he—or she—is aware of something called the Freedom of Information Act," Jinx stated.

"I'm fully aware of the FOI, but you're still not going to get what you want, no matter who you talk to," the detective replied.

Suddenly, all professionalism and decorum Jinx was trying to maintain disappeared in an angry poof and all that was left was her stubborn and very high-voltage Italian personality. "And why the hell not?!"

"Because those case files are sealed," the detective replied.

"Sealed?" Jinx said. "Why in the world would Kip's case files be sealed?"

The detective didn't answer Jinx's question because he had already hung up.

What kind of crime could Kip have committed? And why would the files on his case be sealed? If he had been arrested for a petty crime and no charges were pressed against him, there wouldn't be any reason to seal his file. He must have done something huge, then perhaps cut a deal with the DA's office, and in return his file was being kept secret from prying eyes like nosy reporters several states away.

Government red tape was no match for the Ferrara Family Detective Agency, and by the time Alberta, Helen, and Joyce returned from rehearsal they found Jinx waiting for them in Alberta's kitchen with a fully formulated plan.

"You want us to do what?" Alberta gasped.

"You and Aunt Helen need to invite yourselves over to Kip's apartment under the pretense that you want to rehearse lines in order to give me the opportunity to search his place for clues so we can find out why he lied to us about living in the same hometown as Missy and uncover what kind of crime he committed back in Maine."

When Jinx finally finished speaking so she could take a much-needed breath, the rest of the women took her pause as their chance to tell her how crazy they thought her idea was.

"You want us to invite ourselves over to a criminal's apartment?" Alberta asked.

"You want me to act as if I don't know my lines?" Helen asked.

"Also too, with your guts you should play the stock market," Joyce added.

"If I ever make enough money to gamble it away, Aunt Joyce, I'll remember that," Jinx said. "But for now, I'd rather stick with a sure bet. If you follow my plan, this will all work out. Do you trust me?"

Alberta and Joyce said "Absolutely" at the same time

Helen said "No," but luckily, they believed in majority rule, so the ayes won out.

"I still can't believe Kip could be a criminal," Alberta said. "He's such a nice boy."

"Nice boys can have shady pasts, Berta," Helen said. "Remember Louis Pantoliano?"

Alberta didn't respond verbally; she gasped and made the sign of the cross, kissed her fingers, and offered them up to the heavens.

"What was so shady about Louis Pantoliano?" Jinx asked.

"Never you mind, lovey," Alberta said. "Some pasts are better left alone."

Helen grabbed the pitcher of Red Herring on the table and started to pour everyone a glass. "Let's hope Kip's isn't one of those."

The next morning, Alberta called Kip to ask if he would be available to rehearse privately. She explained that because she was so new to the theatre and very nervous about working with such established actors, she needed the extra rehearsal time to be on par with the rest of the cast. Alberta was thrilled when Kip immediately agreed. She was less excited to hear that Kip agreed that Alberta needed additional rehearsal time because he said her thespian skill set was practically nonexistent. So much for instilling confidence in a fledgling actor.

They discussed a time to meet and Kip told her that he was available later in the day if she wanted to come over. Alberta said that she'd bring the food if he brought his theatrical know-how.

"I'm a bachelor, Mrs. Scaglione, I'll do anything for a free meal," Kip said. "I'll see you at around three."

The drive to Parsippany took about thirty minutes, but it gave the women time to fine-tune their plan. Jinx drove them in her car and would explain to Kip that Helen's Buick was in the shop and Alberta was almost as bad with directions as Kip, so Jinx had to be their chauffeur. It was a plausible reason for her to be tagging along. It would also allow Jinx the freedom to search his apartment while the three actors were rehearsing their scene.

"What if he catches you, lovey?" Alberta asked. "If he really is a criminal, he might not appreciate someone searching his place."

"Number one, he *is* a criminal, Gram."

"That's right, Berta, don't get soft on us now," Helen said.

"I'm not getting soft," Alberta said, not entirely believing herself. "I'm keeping an open mind."

"*Non tutti i ragazzi crescono per essere uomini,*" Helen said.

"Really?" Alberta asked. "Then what do boys grow up to be?"

"Murderers," Helen replied. "Odds are fifty-fifty that this sweet-faced boy has grown up to be a cold-blooded killer. Remember that and we all might drive back home in this Chevy instead of a stretcher with white sheets over our faces."

"Wowza, Aunt Helen," Jinx said. "You don't really think Kip would murder all three of us, do you?"

"Why are we forcing ourselves into his apartment to force out his secrets into the light of day if we don't think he's capable of murder?" Helen asked. "It's similar to the plot of *Arsenic and Old Lace*. My character, Martha Brewster, is a sweet-faced old lady who's killed over a dozen people with her equally homicidal sister. You never know what people are capable of."

"I should've known you'd become a method actress," Alberta said.

"I am committed to my craft, Berta," Helen replied.

"You know something, maybe this was all a mistake," Jinx announced, steering the car into the parking lot of Kip's condo complex. "Why don't you call Kip and tell him that you have to cancel."

"*Sciocchezza!* Let's not get ourselves worked up," Alberta said. "I have a feeling we're going to have a lovely afternoon."

"Mrs. Scaglione, how nice to see you," Kip said as he greeted Alberta at the door. "And you too, Helen." By the time he said hello to Jinx, his smile appeared strained. "Jinx, I didn't know you were coming too."

"It's my fault," Helen said. "We usually take my Buick, but the distributor is on the fritz."

"And I'm almost as bad with directions as you are," Alberta declared.

"Which left me to play the role of the chauffeur," Jinx lied.

"I didn't want to cancel, Kip," Alberta said. "I am in way over my head with this acting stuff and you're such a good actor, I really could use your help."

A genuine smile returned to Kip's face.

"Like Thespis and Suzanne Pleshette who came before me, it is my duty to guide those less fortunate," Kip declared.

Helen gasped. When she could speak, she asked, "You appreciate the acting prowess of Suzanne Pleshette too?"

"It all starts with the voice, Helen," Kip replied. "And no one had a better voice than Ms. Pleshette. In fact, when you say certain vowel sounds you remind me of her."

"You're right, Berta," Helen said. "We're going to have a lovely afternoon."

"If you don't mind, I always like to begin a rehearsal with some stretching and breathing exercises," Kip said.

"It would be blasphemy to begin any other way," Helen agreed.

Alberta and Jinx had no idea if Helen was being serious, but they wouldn't dare mock her for her newfound passion. It was wonderful to see her giving her all to this play. And if it helped with their investigation by making Kip feel in control, that was even better.

Kip took the tray of food Alberta had brought into his kitchen as they all agreed they would eat after they rehearsed. When he returned, Jinx sat in a chair off to the side and watched the three of them raise their arms, breathe in through their noses, exhale, make soft vowel sounds, and thank the theatre gods for allowing them the opportunity to perform and bring their characters to life. She sat in awe and fought the urge to laugh at the spectacle, but then she realized she was no better. When Joyce first opened the doors of the closet that housed a wardrobe that had been cultivated over four decades, Jinx practically got down on her knees and wept with joy. No one passion was better than another. She loved clothes, Kip loved acting.

She also loved being able to play the detective without Kip detecting she was playing such a role.

Sitting in a chair that had its back to the front door, Jinx was able to survey the area and deduced that Kip's condo provided the perfect floor plan for her to investigate without getting caught. The front room was L-shaped and comprised the living and dining rooms. To their immediate right were two doors; one was a closet, and based on the whirring sound emanating from the other, it housed the washer and dryer. The kitchen was off to the left of the dining room, but a wall separated it from the living room, blocking any line of vision. Behind the kitchen was the bathroom and to the right were two more doors that presumably led to the bedrooms. As long as Alberta and Helen kept their working space to the left side of the living room and made sure Kip's back was facing the bulk of the apartment, Jinx shouldn't have any problem looking into each room without being seen by Kip.

The one tip Jinx had picked up from this crash course in theatre was that one of the most difficult things to learn was timing. Just as Kip was setting up the blocking for the first scene all their characters had together, Jinx whispered that she had to use the bathroom. As expected, Kip was so engrossed in his work that he hardly acknowledged her comment and simply pointed toward the back of the condo without ever taking his eyes from Alberta.

It was Jinx's turn to perform.

She went into the bathroom and turned on the light and the overhead fan, but instead of staying in the room, she closed the door behind her and tiptoed across the hall to the door that she assumed led to Kip's bedroom. When she opened it, she saw that she was right.

Kip had only recently moved in, so the bedroom wasn't fully furnished and there were boxes stacked in a corner. She took a deep breath to calm her nerves and slow her racing heartbeat and began to move about the room. She opened the closet and found nothing but clothes and shoeboxes. The boxes could contain something other than shoes, but she didn't have the luxury to open each and every one. Her time was limited and she had to use it wisely.

She closed the closet and focused on the boxes in the room. She took the lid from the top box and, true to Kip's nature, it contained scripts and books about theatre. The second box was filled with law books and the bottom box was labeled office supplies. If there was a box that was labeled office supplies, presumably there had to be an office, which was a much more likely place for Kip to store incriminating evidence than in his bedroom. Who would want to sleep every night with a reminder of past evil deeds literally a few feet away? Buried secrets needed to be buried as far away as possible.

Jinx closed the bedroom door behind her and glanced to the left. She couldn't see anyone, so that meant they were still utilizing the far left side of the living room as their mock stage. Still, she had been gone for quite a while, and her absence might not ignite alarm, but it would definitely be noticed. Erring on the safe side, Jinx flushed the toilet, washed her hands, and turned off the bathroom lights, but deliberately kept the fan on to create additional noise.

"I don't mean to interrupt, but I'm starving," Jinx declared, peeking into the living room. "I'm going to cut a piece of Gram's lasagna."

"I set out plates and you can heat it up in the microwave," Kip said.

Again, Kip's instructions came as a tangential thought

as his focus remained on the scene they were rehearsing. Just as Jinx retreated into the back of the condo, Alberta caught her eye and Jinx shook her head back and forth, indicating that, so far, she hadn't found anything.

While the lasagna was spinning around in the microwave, Jinx went to open what she hoped was the door to Kip's office, but the doorknob wouldn't turn. Discovering that the door was locked made Jinx's heart start to race again. Kip lived alone; there was no reason for him to keep a door locked, so he must have locked it once he knew he was having company.

Ever since Jinx and her family embarked on careers as amateur detectives, she'd found herself carrying items that would be useful for investigations. She never went anywhere without latex gloves, plastic Ziploc bags, and, thankfully, safety pins. She took one out of the back pocket of her jeans, opened it up, and started to jimmy the lock. It took a few minutes, but just as the microwave oven beeped, the doorknob twisted, and Jinx gained entry into the room.

She knew that she was supposed to be quiet, she knew that she needed to prevent Kip from finding out what she was doing, which was immoral if not borderline illegal, but she couldn't help herself. The scream fled from her mouth and echoed down the hall before she even realized she had made a sound. And no one would blame her for screaming after what she saw.

Standing in the middle of the room was like being in a Missy Michaels museum. Kip had created a shrine to the star, and everywhere she looked there was memorabilia of the former child actress. A bookshelf filled with videos, DVDs, a Daisy Greenfield lunch box, two hanging shelves filled with Missy Michaels dolls in various shapes and sizes, and, most disturbing, a whole wall covered in her eight-by-ten glossies and newspaper clippings.

On the small table underneath the one window in the room, there was a framed article from *The Ellsworth American*. Jinx didn't recognize the name of the newspaper or the little boy in the photo, but the headline was undeniable: IS KIP FLANIGAN THE NEXT MISSY MICHAELS?

Jinx was so mesmerized by what she saw that she only heard Kip the third time he yelled her name.

"Jinx! What the hell are you doing in here?"

She stared into Kip's eyes and was terrified because all she saw was rage. The only thought racing in her mind was that this must have been the last image Missy saw right before Kip killed her. And Jinx had no doubt that he was ready, willing, and able to kill again.

CHAPTER 18

Amor di madre, amore senza limiti.

"I said, what are you doing in this room?"

Jinx didn't hear Kip's words, she only saw his fury, which frightened her into silence. She looked at her grandmother and aunt, standing in the doorway behind Kip, and all she could think was that she'd single-handedly lured them all into a death trap.

"I asked you a question and I don't want to repeat myself again," Kip said. "What are you doing in this room?"

Swallowing hard, Jinx inhaled deeply and then let the breath flow out of her. Somehow words followed. "The door was open, and I was curious what the rest of the condo looked like because I'm thinking of buying a place of my own."

"That door was locked," Kip stated. "I made sure of it before you three came over."

"Why?"

Kip turned around to face Alberta, and although Jinx knew that he was staring at her and Helen with the same frightening expression, she was thankful she was given a reprieve and didn't have to look into his eyes any longer. She then realized his movement was an opportunity for her to change her position.

With his back to her, Jinx walked clockwise until she was once again facing Kip, but at least this time she had Alberta and Helen behind her. There was strength in numbers and if Kip lunged forward, he would attack her first, giving them a chance to run out of the condo.

"Why did I lock the door?" Kip asked. "Because it's my door and I have every right to lock it if I want. On the other hand, you don't have the right to break into a room because you feel like it."

"You're right, Kip, we don't," Alberta said, her voice, if not, her heart rate, calm. "But we're here now, so why don't you explain why this room is a shrine to Missy?"

"Because she's the greatest star who ever lived, that's why," he replied.

"That's true, she was the greatest," Alberta said. "But you told us you didn't even know about her before you started rehearsal. Why did you lie to us?"

The rage that had gripped Kip's body seemed to seep out of his body and was replaced with sadness. A few seconds ago he looked like he could rip the women limb from limb and now he looked like he needed their limbs wrapped around him in comfort.

"I knew what people would think, it's what they always think," Kip said. "That I'm this obsessed fan, some kind of fool."

"We don't think you're a fool, Kip," Helen said.

The kindness in her voice, whether real or manufactured, convinced Kip that she was telling the truth. It gave him the strength to explain why he had turned this room into a sanctuary where one could bathe in the glory and the spirit of the former child star. It was because he couldn't let go of the child within him. A child with a lot of wounds.

"Then you're a better person than the rest of my family," Kip said.

He looked at the swarm of photos decorating the room and was lost in memory. The women weren't sure if that memory starred him or Missy, but for a few moments he was far away from them. They sensed the crisis was over and Kip no longer posed a physical threat, so they waited quietly for him to return to them.

Kip walked toward the window and picked up the framed article and asked the question out loud. "'Is Kip Flanigan the next Missy Michaels?' That was the question on everyone's lips when I was seven years old." He stared at the photo and looked confused, and the women weren't sure if he recognized the little boy or if he was trying to remember who he was. He placed the photo back on the table, and when he turned around, they saw pain in his eyes, they understood he not only remembered exactly who that little boy was, but he was feeling the same emotions from all those years ago.

"I got the lead role in our community theatre's production of *Oliver!* and for the first time in my life I felt like I belonged somewhere," Kip explained. "My older brothers and even my younger sister were all athletes; I didn't know the difference between a hockey puck and a football, so I wasn't exactly the apple of my father's eye. But when I stepped on that stage for the first time, I felt like I found my home."

Alberta was fascinated. Just as Nola had done previously, Kip was comparing the theatre to home. It never occurred to her that the stage could give its inhabitants such comfort.

"I was very young, but for the first time I understood what peace felt like," Kip admitted. "I was surrounded by people who shared my interests and didn't make fun of me. Do you have any idea what kind of a revelation that is for a seven-year-old?"

Alberta thought back to when she first moved to Tranquility and looked out her window to the sprawling Memory Lake in her backyard. It was the first time in her life that she was an independent woman. The feeling Kip had described came to her much later in life, but still, she knew the power of change.

"I have an inkling," Alberta said.

"Some talent agent from New York saw our show and told my parents that with the right management, I could be a star," he recalled. "I had no idea what he was talking about, but if it meant that I could stay on that stage and feel as good as it felt to be up there with all those people, I was all for it."

"The agent wanted to do to you what that producer did to Missy all those years ago," Jinx said.

"Exactly," Kip confirmed. "But my parents weren't as accommodating as Missy's."

"They wouldn't let some strange man take their son away from them," Alberta said.

"Like they would have even missed me!" Kip cried. "All they did was point out how different I was from every other boy in town. My mother would say that the nurses must have switched babies at birth because she didn't know where I came from."

Kip turned away from them so he could cry without an audience, and the women bowed their heads in both pity and shame. They ached for Kip because no child should be made to feel that he doesn't belong in his own family and prayed that his mother asked for forgiveness for making such a hateful comment.

Alberta remembered a phrase she heard the older women in her family repeat frequently, *Amor di madre, amore senza limiti.* A mother's love knows no limits. It was always a comforting thought until now. A mother's love, like all other emotions, could get twisted, and the things she said out of love for her child could tear at their heart instead of heal it. Alberta shuddered because she had done the same thing to her own daughter.

When Kip was finally in control and had shed enough tears for the boy he used to be, he wiped his eyes and turned back to face the women. It was like they were looking at a different person. He was smiling and his eyes were welcoming instead of threatening. He looked like the Kip they all thought they knew.

"Ultimately, my parents relented and let me go on a few auditions in New York," Kip said. "My mother came with me and we spent the best two weeks of our lives." He paused and then corrected his comment. "Well, it was the best two weeks of my life, my mother never stopped complaining about how much she hated the city and wanted to return to Maine."

"I take it your mother didn't travel much," Helen said.

"That was the one and only time she ever stepped across the Maine state line," Kip declared. "For me, it was the first time I realized there was a life for me outside Deer Isle. None of the auditions panned out and the agent's interest in me fizzled, but I will always consider that trip to be a turning point in my life." Kip once again stared at the photos on the wall. "And it's how I was introduced to Missy Michaels."

"You met the woman?" Alberta asked.

"No, I was never that lucky, but before I left for New York, our local paper ran that article on me," Kip replied, pointing at the framed photo on the table. "I didn't know who Missy was, of course, but once they made the comparison and set the stage, so to speak, that I could be as famous as Missy, I was hooked. I guess you could say I became obsessed."

"I think you could safely say that," Helen said, looking around the room.

Unexpectedly, Kip laughed. It wasn't just a nervous chuckle, it was a full-on release of all the energy that had been stored up inside him. The feelings Jinx sensed might be exhibited with a burst of violence were transformed into an outpouring of laughter.

"Thank you, Helen," Kip said, still laughing. "Everything they say about you is true."

"And what exactly do they say about me?" Helen asked.

"That you tell it like it is and have no filter," Kip replied.

Helen shrugged. "I can't really argue with that."

"I keep this room locked because I'm embarrassed by what I've created. Not because I don't truly admire and love everything Missy Michaels did with her life and her legacy, but because I know people aren't going to understand that in some really weird, tangential way, it's my legacy too."

"How so?" Jinx asked.

"Missy and I are connected," Kip explained. "I almost

had the same life she did. Who knows? Maybe in some parallel universe I'm a bigger star than she is. The truth is that this room reminds me of what my life could've been like."

"I know how you feel, but trust me, Kip, it isn't always smart to hold so tightly to the past," Alberta said.

"Many a therapist has told me that before, Mrs. Scaglione," Kip said. "I'm just not ready to let go. Especially now."

"Because of the murder, you mean?" Jinx asked.

"Yes," Kip replied. "Which is why I made sure the room was locked before you came over here. I know what this looks like and I know that you're all thinking that I killed Missy, but I swear to you, I wanted to work with Missy, I wanted to celebrate our time together, I would never have killed her."

"Even though she had the life you always wanted?" Alberta asked.

"That wasn't her fault," Kip said. "If I was going to kill anyone, it would've been my parents. After we got back from New York, they refused to entertain any more thoughts of my being an actor, they wouldn't even let me try out for any more shows in town. It wasn't until I went to college that I got to perform again. I was hoping this play would finally bring Missy and me together, not sever our relationship before it even started."

All three women stared at Kip, pondering whether he was telling them the truth or thinking quickly on his feet to get out of the jam he had been caught in. They were all wearing their best poker faces, even Jinx, who had a tendency to allow her emotions to creep to the surface, so Kip had no idea what they were thinking. Naturally, he thought the worst.

"You still think I killed Missy, don't you?" Kip asked.

Alberta spoke for the trio. "No, but you're going to help us find out who did."

Thirty minutes later after they had devoured Alberta's lasagna, Kip poured coffee into an assortment of cups and placed them in front of the women sitting around the kitchen table. When he placed a box of Entenmann's Chocolate Chip Cookies—original recipe—next to the coffee pot, the woman knew Kip was friend and not foe. Once again, food proved to be the common denominator that brought people together.

"I don't know how I can help you find out who murdered Missy," Kip said.

"You're arguably her biggest fan," Alberta said.

"Even bigger than Father Sal," Helen said.

"Which means you may know more about her than anyone else," Jinx added.

"That's true," Kip said. "I have been compiling data on her since I was a kid. I have journals, newspaper clippings, a whole video library of her talk show appearances. I even created a family tree."

"About the real Missy or Daisy?" Alberta asked.

"Missy, of course," Kip replied. "Would you like to see it?"

"Does the pope enter the world in a puff of smoke?" Helen asked rhetorically.

Kip retreated to the now-unlocked room and returned with a rolled-up poster. Familiar with how to turn a kitchen table into an evidence desk, Jinx took away the box of cookies and Alberta and Helen each grabbed two coffee cups so Kip could unfurl the poster and spread it out on the surface. After he did, they placed a coffee cup on each corner of the poster so it would remain flat and they could examine Kip's artwork. Even though they were only interested in the information contained in the poster, they couldn't help but be impressed by the artistic talent that was also on display. Kip clearly was a renaissance man: actor, lawyer, and now artist.

The family tree was impressive. It was an illustration in black ink that was then filled in with watercolor paint. But the intricate and well-executed details were what transformed it from a simple drawing created to preserve history into a piece of art that would transcend time.

The trunk of the huge oak was thick, its bark creviced and rough. It stood on a patch of uneven ground that was also a home to wildflowers, rocks, and twigs. To the right of the tree, a cardinal had successfully plucked a worm from the ground, and to the left, a fox with a long, fluffy, white-tipped tail was scurrying off the page. Kip had even drawn the roots of the tree underneath the ground that burrowed into the earth. Some of the roots twisted around one another for strength and company, while others ventured off alone into their own private space, just like a real family.

The tree itself was lush and several shades of green. Its branches varied in size and length: some were empty, some held squirrels, one was home to a bird's nest, but all held the names of Missy's family members written in black ink and beautiful calligraphy. Although the women were primarily interested in the information the tree contained, it took them a moment to zero in on the words because they looked like decorations.

"Kip, this is a work of art," Alberta said.

"Thank you. I took a few art classes in college, but ultimately took a more practical route," Kip replied.

"You're like my sister-in-law, Joyce," Helen said. "You do a little bit of this and a little bit of that."

"Helen, if I didn't know better, I'd say you just gave Joyce a compliment," Alberta said.

"And if you repeat what I said, I will not be responsible for my actions," Helen warned.

"What's most fascinating and pertinent are all the names of Missy's relatives," Jinx reminded everyone. "Could you talk us through how they're all related?"

Kip's eyes lit up. "It would be my pleasure."

Missy, of course, was in the center of the tree because she was the epicenter of her family as far as Kip was concerned. Above her were the names of her parents, Alfredo and Carlotta Miccalizzo, with dates underneath indicating their births and deaths. They died within two weeks of each other, and Alberta thought that must have been comforting for the two of them but devastating to the rest of their family. There was another row of names above them for their parents, and then the names of their siblings were written on the branches on their same level.

On either side of Missy were the names of her siblings: Alfredo, Jr., or "Fredo," Benno, and Angela. According to the tree, Fredo and Benno died without getting married or having any children. Angela married Enrico Petrocelli and had twin boys, Tony and Santino. Tony died a bachelor, but Santino married Elsa Horvalt, and together they had one child, Adrienne. The date under Angela's name showed that she outlived most of her immediate family and died less than ten years ago. Almost every name on the tree had two sets of dates underneath their names, all except one.

"Is Angela's granddaughter the only living member of the Miccalizzo family?" Alberta asked.

"As far as I can tell, yes," Kip replied. "Adrienne Petrocelli is the last Miccalizzo standing."

"That's weird," Jinx said. "I can't believe there aren't cousins or some distant aunt still alive."

"Unlike the traditional Italian family of that time, no one had a lot of kids," Kip explained, pointing at various sections of the tree. "Missy's brothers were both childless, so several branches of their tree died off early."

"*Che peccato*," Alberta said. "What a sin to have no more family around."

"Speaking of having family around," Helen said. "Where is Adrienne?"

"I don't know," Kip answered. "She lived most of her life in Michigan, which is where Angela died, by the way, in a nursing home, but at some point since then, Adrienne moved."

"How do you know?" Alberta asked.

"Right before the auditions when I knew that Missy was going to star in the play, I tried to reach out to Adrienne," Kip said. "I thought it would be nice to stage a family reunion and bring Missy and Adrienne together."

"It's true, then, that Missy hadn't met any members of her family?" Jinx asked.

"Yes, Missy was estranged from her entire family," Kip replied. "I don't think she saw them again once she went to Hollywood."

"We know all about that and Missy's emancipation," Alberta said.

"And the fact that while Missy got richer, her family got poorer," Helen added.

"I'm sure a lot of family secrets died with Missy and they'll be sealed up along with her when she's laid to rest," Kip remarked.

Alberta and Helen were a bit surprised by Kip's graphic description, but Jinx was alarmed by the use of one specific word: sealed. It reminded her that Kip was not only the holder of Missy's heritage, but the holder of his own secrets, which were sealed up in a police station in Deer Isle, Maine.

"Do you have any other sealed-up secrets you'd like to share, Kip?" Jinx asked.

Alberta understood why Jinx would ask such a question. Although she believed Kip was harmless, the fact remained that he had been mixed up in some kind of criminal affair, so his innocence could not be proven until he was exonerated of his guilt. However, Kip had given them quite a bit of information with little coercion and they would most likely need his help if they wanted to connect with Missy's only living relative; challenging him was not the way to ensure his continued cooperation. Alberta did the only thing she could think of to end Jinx's line of questioning: She kicked her in the shins.

"Owww," Jinx cried.

"Are you all right?" Kip asked.

"I'm fine," Jinx replied, rubbing her shin. "Just a charley horse."

Once again, Alberta's quick thinking had kept Jinx quiet, but she had another relative at the table who was harder to control.

"You didn't answer Jinx's question, Kip," Helen said. "Do you have any more secrets to reveal?"

Helen was fixed on Kip's expression, so she didn't see Alberta and Jinx staring at her. If Kip noticed their surprised expressions just inches from him, he gave no indication. He simply leaned back in his chair and smiled.

"None at all," Kip said. "Now that my Missy memorabilia has been uncovered, I have no more secrets to hide. I feel like a free man and I owe it all to you three. Thank you."

The women didn't think Kip would thank them if he knew that they knew he was lying. They would keep quiet and let him continue to think that he was as good an actor as he believed himself to be.

"Then it's case closed," Jinx said.

For now.

CHAPTER 19

Bella donna o belladonna.

Behind every strong woman is a wise man. Or, in Jinx's case, a wise dude.

"You want me to team up with Vinny?" Jinx asked.

Jinx and Freddy were snuggling on her couch, a TV mystery movie about a psycho Pilates instructor playing in the background, as they shared a plate of Alberta's left-over lasagna. Nola was staying over at Johnny's apartment, so Jinx had been able to fill Freddy in on the whole Kip-is-an-obsessed-Missy-fan portion of her day without fear of being overheard. When Freddy suggested that she team up with Vinny to unlock the secrets of Kip's past, she thought she heard him wrong.

"You want me to be Vinny's partner?" Jinx repeated.

"Is my girlfriend going deaf?" Freddy asked. "That's what I said."

"Why would you suggest something like that? You know I'm not Vinny's favorite Tranquilitarian."

"For that reason exactly," Freddy said. "And watch your vocabulary please, you know how big words turn me on."

Ignoring her flirting boyfriend, Jinx continued her line of interrogation. "Vinny and I have finally gotten to a place where we don't scream and yell at each other, why would I risk ruining that by working alongside him?"

"Because the two of you will get to know each other better and you'll each find out what I already know," Freddy said.

"What's that?"

"That you're both great guys."

Jinx playfully stabbed Freddy with her fork. "Is that what I am to you? One of the guys?"

Smiling devilishly, Freddy replied, "You're one of the sexiest guys I know, Jinxie boo."

Groaning, Jinx rested her head on Freddy's shoulder. "I think I prefer when you call me 'dude.'"

"You don't like 'Jinxie boo?'" Freddy asked.

"It makes me sound like a cat."

"Well, you are purr-fect."

Jinx had officially had her fill of flirting. She abruptly sat up and faced Freddy, almost upturning the plate of lasagna in the process. "Promise me two things."

"I'll promise you two-thousand-million-thousand things, Jinxie . . ."

"First, do not ever call me 'Jinxie boo' again," Jinx interrupted.

"That's gonna be a tough one, Jinxie boo, but for you, I promise," Freddy said.

"Thank you."

"What's the number two promise?" Freddy asked.

"If I agree to work alongside Vinny and our partner-ship doesn't become all hunky-dory, as Gram would say, I get to say I told you so for like . . . I don't know . . . all eternity."

Freddy took the plate of lasagna from Jinx and placed it on the coffee table. He then held Jinx's face with his hands, and Jinx could feel that they were warm, but slightly trembling. His brown eyes with their flecks of gold dancing in the light stared at her. He was silent, but Jinx was so connected to Freddy at that moment that she heard every word he didn't speak. He loved her. She re-turned his feelings, so no words needed to be spoken. But when Freddy did finally speak, she melted in his arms.

"As long as I get to spend all eternity with you," Freddy whispered, "I grant you that promise."

It was a good thing Freddy kissed her because Jinx felt all the words she wanted to share with her boyfriend catch in her throat. It was also a good thing Nola didn't come back to the apartment the next morning and went straight to work from Johnny's place because she would've found Freddy and Jinx wrapped in each other's arms sleeping on the couch.

After they each showered, dressed, and had a quick breakfast of some anisette cookies and coffee, Jinx still wasn't convinced working side by side with Vinny was the smartest idea Freddy ever had. But watching him bent over his chair at the kitchen table lacing up his sneakers, his hair falling into his eyes, his big ears looking bigger than ever, she realized that had he suggested she try to swim across Memory Lake underwater, she would've made a valiant attempt. Love really made you do crazy things sometimes.

Other times it made you realize how crazy you'd been acting.

Vinny was standing underneath the ornate, wrought-iron archway that was the entrance to Tranquility Park when Jinx arrived. She smiled, not because she was determined to put forth an optimistic attitude, but because Vinny reminded her of her father, Tommy. If her father ever wore a tweed jacket with an orange V-neck sweater and jeans. The only piece of Vinny's clothing she had ever seen her father wear were beat-up hiking boots, but the resemblance between Vinny and her father wasn't physical. Tommy Maldonado wasn't as tall, as wide, or as Hollywood handsome as the chief of police, but when she looked at Vinny she saw the same compassion and fatherly affection she saw when she caught her own dad looking at her. She had never noticed this side of Vinny before. Maybe she did need her boyfriend to open her eyes to the world around her.

"Good morning, partner," Vinny said, "or is it too early to award Freddy a victory?"

Despite the commitment she made to herself to appear aloof and professional, Jinx felt her mouth form into a broad smile before she could stop the transformation. She decided to adopt her boyfriend's outlook on life: relax and see where the ride takes you.

"If that extra coffee you're holding is Joey Vitalano's special dark roast blend with no sugar and extra soy milk, I'll deliver Freddy's prize myself," Jinx declared.

"Then the fifteen minutes I spent waiting on line at Vitalano's Bakery this morning was worth it," Vinny said, handing the coffee container to Jinx. "And might I add that Freddy is one lucky guy."

Jinx couldn't disagree, but she also didn't want to get off track as to the reason why she and Vinny were joining forces. There was another guy who had gotten lucky and she wanted to know why.

"You could say the same thing about Kip Flanigan," Jinx said. "How do you go about getting your court documents sealed so no one finds out that you committed a crime?"

Instead of imparting some fatherly and/or chief-of-police wisdom, Vinny howled.

"Did I say something funny?" Jinx asked.

"No, you just reminded me of your mother," Vinny explained, still laughing.

Suddenly, thoughts of Kip flew away on the cool breeze gliding through the park and Jinx was left with a yearning to hear more of Vinny's memories of her mother. She had never connected the two of them before, but it made sense that Vinny would remember Lisa Marie because he had grown up with Alberta. It wasn't just the mention of her mother, it was how casually Vinny did it. Most people actively avoided talking about her mother because of her fractured relationship with Alberta, but Vinny shared his thought without a hint of hesitation or regret afterward. Maybe it was because it was just the two of them on a Monday morning talking a stroll through the park. Their defenses were down and they could speak honestly.

"My mother was funny?" Jinx asked.

"No, the complete opposite," Vinny recollected. "She was very serious. Even when she was little, four, five years old, she didn't have time to fool around, she was always direct and to the point. Like you were just now."

Jinx looked off to the left and saw the tree house that had been in the park since before it had officially been a park and remembered a past case she had worked on. She shook the memory from her mind because she didn't want to be distracted from the conversation. If she had learned one thing from her grandmother, it was that cases weren't nearly as important as family.

"What else was she like as a little girl?" Jinx asked.

Vinny hesitated, and Jinx wasn't sure if it was because he had no further information to share or if he felt as if he would be betraying his friend if he spoke openly about his friend's estranged daughter.

"I only ask because, well, you know that my grandmother doesn't really talk about my mother, and because she doesn't say anything, no one else in the family does," Jinx said. "Plus, my mother never liked to talk about her life in New Jersey, which means I don't really know much about my mother when she was growing up in Hoboken. If you could maybe fill in some of the blanks, that would be cool."

Jinx took a deep breath and Vinny smiled. "As Freddy likes to tell people, I really am a cool dude," he said. "Guess I should prove it."

As they walked through the park, Jinx sipped her coffee and listened to Vinny share stories of Lisa Marie. He started with the one when she insisted Alberta return the black patent leather Mary Janes she bought for Lisa Marie's first day of kindergarten because they would get scuffed too easily while playing in the schoolyard. Alberta was furious that she had to send her daughter off to St. Ann's in a pair of navy-blue boat shoes.

Then there was the time during her seventh or eighth birthday party, Vinny couldn't remember precisely, when Lisa Marie told the clown to stop making balloon animals and blow up something more practical, like a spatula or an oven mitt. Alberta was actually quite proud of her that day.

Just as they were exiting the park, Vinny told Jinx one final story of how Lisa Marie demanded Alberta teach her how to sew so she could raise the hemline of her skirt. Alberta refused, on the grounds that Immaculate Conception High School was no place for *cattive reggaze* and that she could transfer to Hoboken High if she wanted to be a bad girl. The only reason Alberta relented and started giving Lisa Marie sewing lessons was because the kid actually registered at Hoboken High, saying she recently moved to town from Sicily and was living with relatives.

"My mother went that far to hike up her skirt?" Jinx asked.

"She would've gotten away with it too, if it wasn't for Raffaella DeFilippo," Vinny said.

"I'm almost afraid to ask, but who's Raffaella DeFilippo?"

"She was the principal's secretary and also your grandmother's cousin's brother-in-law's wife."

"My family's tree grows bigger every day," Jinx said. "Ah, *Madon*! I almost forgot about what we found thanks to Missy's family tree that Kip put together. We have to find out where Adrienne lives."

"You're talking about Adrienne Petrocelli?" Vinny asked.

"Yes, you know about her too?"

"I am the chief of police, it's kind of my job to know who the next of kin is."

They stopped walking when they reached the front steps of the police station. Jinx looked up at Vinny and smiled, partially because she was happy to have spent the morning with him and partially because she was embarrassed that it took a forced morning rendezvous for her to realize she and Vinny had always been on the same side. It was time to get things back on track.

"Do you have any leads on her?" Jinx asked. "Kip said she used to live in Michigan, where most of Missy's family moved to, but he lost track of her after she moved."

"We're working on a lead as to her whereabouts and should have confirmation shortly." Before Jinx could ask, Vinny answered, "I'll let you know where she lives the moment we find her."

"Thank you." But Jinx wasn't done. "Now back to Kip and whatever crime he committed in Maine. You never answered me; how does somebody get their court documents sealed and what do we have to do to get them unsealed so we can find out what kind of criminal Kip really is?"

"First of all, Kip's an alleged criminal," Vinny said. "When someone's court case is sealed, it often means their record has been expunged, and in the eyes of the court they have not been convicted of any crime."

"Semantic distinction duly noted," Jinx said. "But why does the court allow that? The public has a right to know if they're living next to a guy who, let's just say, got away with murder."

"The judge must have felt that the need for secrecy to perhaps ensure Kip's safety was more important than the public's need to access information," Vinny explained. "And to answer your next question."

"How do you know what my next question is going to be?" Jinx asked.

"You're going to ask me how we can get sealed documents unsealed, aren't you?" Vinny replied.

"You're like an old Italian lady, you can read my mind," Jinx teased.

"You hang around enough old Italian ladies, they start to rub off on you," Vinny joked. "To unseal a document, you have to bring a motion to the judge stating you have a serious privacy or public safety concern."

"We totally have that!" Jinx exclaimed. "There's been a murder, Kip might be a murderer, what more evidence do we need?"

"None," Vinny agreed. "Which is why I've asked Tambra to prepare a motion to submit to the Deer Isle courthouse to have Kip's documents unsealed so we can know what kind of person we're dealing with."

Jinx stepped back and leaned into the railing at the front steps and nodded her head. "This working together thing really is a lot better than being at odds all the time."

"I'm glad you agree," Vinny said. "There is one glitch, though."

"That sounds a bit ominous," Jinx replied.

"Sometimes when documents are sealed, the judge orders them to be destroyed," Vinny explained.

"Like shredded into little bits or thrown into a fire?" Jinx asked.

"Both of those methods would work," Vinny replied. "But let's see what happens when we file our motion."

"Agreed," Jinx said. "And I also agree that from here on in we share information and don't keep secrets from each other."

When Jinx saw Donna Russo strut on up to Vinny, her curly hair bouncing with each step, she wondered if Vinny was distinguishing professional information from personal. She wondered about some other things too.

Shouldn't Donna be at St. Winifred's on a Monday morning? Were false eyelashes appropriate to be worn by high school principals? And why was she shoving the manila envelope she was carrying back into her purse? *Bella donna o belladonna*, Jinx thought. Was Donna a pretty woman or a deadly poison? She wanted to remain in Vinny's presence for a while longer to look for clues that might help her answer that question, but both Vinny and Donna had other ideas.

"I hope I'm not too early for our meeting, Vin?" Donna asked.

"Nope, you're right on time," he replied. "Jinx and I were just finishing up."

"We were?" Jinx asked.

"Yes," Vinny confirmed. "I'll let you know when we find the address and what response we get on that other matter."

"Talking in code," Donna gushed. "Looks like I stumbled into the middle of some hush-hush tête-à-tête." Vinny opened his mouth to protest, but Donna interrupted. "Don't try to deny it. I know when a person looks suspicious."

Jinx thought to herself that she could say the same thing about Donna.

Later that night, Jinx was in Donna's lair, so to speak, but she wasn't at St. Winifred's Academy to investigate its principal; she was there to figure out the best way to publicize what was becoming known as the show that would not die. Even if its star had.

She sat at a table in the back of the theatre along with Nola, Sloan, and Joyce as they brainstormed on how to let the public know the Tranquility Players were back in business. Father Sal, Benny, and Bruno were rehearsing on stage with Johnny while Helen and Alberta were going over their lines in one of the last rows. Jinx could see that Helen never opened her script and had already memorized her part. Alberta, on the other hand, kept looking down at her script to help her get through the scene. Helen had had a head start because Alberta had just joined the cast, but it was clear that Helen was taking her foray into acting very seriously. Jinx wasn't worried that Alberta wouldn't learn her lines in time because she had the best scene partner possible, her own sister. They were a terrific team on- and offstage. That was it! They had been searching for a publicity angle and it was staring them all in the face the whole time.

"Put Gram and Aunt Helen on the cover of the new poster and you'll sell out every night," Jinx announced.

"That's a brilliant idea, Jinx," Sloan agreed. "Capitalize on the fact that real-life sisters are playing sisters in the show."

"I love it," Nola said. "But do you think they'll go for it? They aren't what I affectionately refer to as publicity whores."

"Alberta might need some convincing," Joyce said. "But Helen will be all for it."

Turning around in her seat, Helen addressed the group, "Helen will be all for what?"

"Appearing on the new poster for the show alongside Alberta," Joyce explained. "The Ferrara sisters as you've never seen them before."

"I don't know about that," Alberta said. "People might think we're doing this for our egos."

"Why else are we doing it?" Helen asked. "We'll do it!"

Helen's enthusiastic cry was heard throughout the theatre, including the stage, where Johnny was trying to direct a scene.

"Do you mind keeping it down?!" Johnny bellowed. "I'm trying to direct a show, if you haven't noticed!"

"Sorry," Helen said. "Carry on Macduff."

Unperturbed by Johnny's outburst, Helen and Alberta resumed running lines. Jinx, however, could still hear the rough tone of Johnny's voice.

"Does he always yell like that?" Jinx asked.

"You don't understand theatre people, Jinx," Nola replied, dismissing the comment with a shrug.

"Theatre people have no right to yell at one another like that and you know it," Jinx said. "He'd better not yell at you like that."

"Jinx, I love you, but I'm warning you to back off where Johnny's concerned," Nola said.

"She's only concerned about you, honey," Joyce intervened. "Also too, we all are."

Nola sighed, and it looked as if she was going to scream louder than Johnny, but instead when she spoke, her voice was hardly above a whisper. "Thank you."

She didn't need to say anything more for them to understand how grateful she was that she had people looking out for her. It was the same comforting feeling that raced through Jinx's body when she saw Vinny walk through the door.

"Excuse me," Jinx said. "Joyce, could you come with me for a sec?"

Jinx, with Joyce right behind her, greeted Vinny and led him to where Alberta and Helen were sitting. Whatever he had to share, he'd need to share with the four of them. No more secrets.

"We found out where Adrienne lives," Vinny said. "And she's right here in New Jersey."

"Missy Michaels's only living relative is living here in Jersey?" Alberta asked, stunned by the revelation.

"That's correct, Alfie," Vinny replied. "And not too far away, in Parsippany."

"Parsippany?" the ladies hissed.

"Granted, it's no Tranquility, but you're making it sound like a dirty word," Vinny said.

"Because it is, Vin," Alberta said. "It's where Kip lives."

Vinny let some air escape his lips and whistle into the air. "That does put a little blemish on the facts, doesn't it?"

"Do you think Adrienne and Kip know each other?" Helen asked.

"Not according to Adrienne," Vinny replied. "She didn't mention his name when we spoke with her earlier."

"You spoke with Adrienne already?" Jinx asked.

"Of course, we did," Vinny said. "And I'm sharing that fact with you now like I promised."

Softening, Jinx backpedaled. "You're absolutely right and we thank you."

"Do you think Adrienne has anything to do with Missy's murder?" Alberta asked.

"I don't know, Alf," Vinny replied. "She doesn't have a record, and other than being Missy's only living blood relative, she doesn't seem to have any ties to her. We're looking into her alibi, so we'll know more in a bit, but from my first meeting with her, she seems like a good kid. Maybe a little shy and nerdy, but I didn't come away thinking she has what it takes to commit murder."

Alberta crossed her arms and looked at Jinx, Joyce, and Helen, then returned her gaze to face Vinny. "We'll be the judge of that."

CHAPTER 20

Molto lontano da casa.

For the second time in almost as many days, Jinx and Alberta drove to Parsippany to investigate another unsuspecting person of interest. Instead of Jinx driving, however, Alberta was behind the wheel of her BMW. They would tell Adrienne that Jinx's Chevy was in the shop so her grandmother, who just happened to be a life-long Missy Michaels fan, was more than willing to play chauffeur so Jinx could keep her appointment to interview Adrienne for *The Herald*. They just had to remember never to tell Helen, who might not appreciate someone taking over her designated role in the family business.

Although Alberta and Jinx had both lived in the area for several years, there were still many parts of New Jersey and even nearby towns that they knew by name only. Parsippany was one of them. Whereas Tranquility was a small lakeside community where everyone knew almost everyone else and it took effort to remain anonymous, Parsippany was a sprawling city. Which meant that even though Kip and Adrienne shared the same zip code, it was very possible they would never bump into each other.

Officially, Parsippany was a municipality. Which meant it was large enough to be called a city but had a geographical makeup more appropriate of a town. It wasn't urban, like Hoboken, where Alberta grew up, but filled with parks, lakes, even a golf course. Visually, it was like Tranquility, only supersized.

When Jinx pulled into the parking lot of the Troy Hills Village apartment complex, where Adrienne lived, they realized they hadn't even entered this part of town when they visited Kip. He lived several miles away on the other side of Lake Parsippany. Still, it was quite a big coincidence that Missy's only living relative and her number one fan just happened to live in the same New Jersey town. Hopefully, once they started chatting with Adrienne, they'd find out which type of murder her presence in the area was like: accidental or premeditated.

The complex itself was the typical garden apartment setup: a collection of two-story, L-shaped brick buildings, well-manicured lawns, a few trees on the edges of the property, with swimming pool behind the buildings. It all looked nicely maintained, but not a suite of luxury units. Which made sense because they were meeting with a twenty-five-year-old woman who was living alone.

As they walked up to the front steps, Alberta marveled at how the world had changed. "I didn't live alone until I was sixty-four."

"I guess that's why you're always up for an adventure," Jinx said. "You're making up for lost time."

"As if I could back out of participating in any of our

little adventures," Alberta remarked. "You would never let me live it down."

"Don't put it on me, Gram, you love the thrill of it," Jinx said. "Like ringing the doorbell of a woman who, for all we know, could've killed her great-aunt."

"I'll just act like I do whenever I have to visit my cousin Diana," Alberta replied. "My mother never trusted that one."

"The more I hear about our family, Gram, the less surprised I am by our hobby."

The bell hardly rang before the door opened and they were greeted by a young woman who, even if they hadn't known was Missy's niece, they'd certainly know was Italian. Adrienne had thick, black hair the same length as Jinx, but without any of her waves. Her eyes were the same color as her hair, and she had dark circles under her eyes that appeared to be the result of her olive complexion rather than poor health. She stood a few inches taller than them both, even though she was wearing flats while Alberta and Jinx were both wearing heels. If the woman had introduced herself as Alberta and Jinx's long-lost relative, they would've welcomed her into the family with open arms.

"Hi, I'm Adrienne and you must be Jinx."

"I am, and this is my grandmother, Alberta, who drove me because my car battery decided to lapse into a coma this morning," Jinx fibbed. "I hope you don't mind the extra company."

"Not at all," Adrienne said. "Please come on in."

The women entered the apartment, and as Alberta walked by Adrienne, she smelled a powerful floral scent. She recognized the perfume but couldn't remember its name.

The apartment was larger than Kip's, but not as nicely decorated. For every piece of furniture there were at least two unopened boxes stacked next to the wall. The space was actually a duplex, with the first-floor layout almost identical to Kip's, with a laundry room where his bedroom would be located and a staircase instead of the Missy Michaels museum. Alberta couldn't tell if Adrienne had just moved in or if she was planning a quick getaway.

"I'm sorry for the way things look," Adrienne said, perhaps reading the expressions on their faces. "I've been living here for almost a month, but I've been so busy with work and acclimating myself to the area that I haven't gotten around to unpacking, let alone decorating."

"No apology necessary," Jinx said. "It took me a good six months to stop living out of boxes when I moved."

"What makes it worse is that I'm not one of those girly-girls, if you know what I mean?" Adrienne said. "I don't have the home decorator gene in my blood, so I have a feeling it's going to take me a while to get this place to look like someone lives here."

"As long as you're comfortable, Adrienne, that's all that matters," Alberta said. "A person's home should be just that, their home, and it shouldn't have to impress anyone other than the people who live there."

"I like your attitude," Adrienne said. "It reminds me of my grandmother."

"Angela?" Jinx asked.

"Yes," Adrienne replied. "She was more like my mother actually, she raised me after my parents were killed."

"I'm so sorry to hear that," Alberta said.

"Thank you, but it was such a long time ago and I was so young, I almost don't remember them," Adrienne said.

"Listen to me, already babbling before you even get your tape recorder out."

"That's all right," Jinx said. "And I can't thank you enough for agreeing to do this interview."

"The chief of police gave you a glowing recommendation," Adrienne said.

"He did?" Alberta and Jinx replied at the same time.

"Yes, he said I absolutely didn't have to grant any interviews, but he guaranteed me that you would treat me fairly in the press," Adrienne said. "I figured I might as well get it over with because the reporters will be banging on my door soon enough. This way I can tell them that I already gave at the office."

"I'm honored that both you and Vinny trust me to tell your story," Jinx said. "Should we set things up in the kitchen?"

"We have to, it's the only horizontal surface in my apartment," Adrienne said. "Let me clear off the table first."

Adrienne grabbed the stack of papers and what looked like a tablecloth with a paisley motif that was rolled up in a ball and placed them underneath the stairs. The only thing left on the table was one of those inexpensive decorative boxes sold at craft stores. This one was covered in daisies.

Maybe it was Adrienne's favorite flower, or maybe she chose that box because it reminded her of the character Missy played in the movies. Regardless of the reason, Alberta and Jinx had to find out what was inside it. Noticing their curious expressions, Adrienne decided to make it easier for them.

"The cops had the same expression on their faces that you two have," Adrienne said. "The box was my grandma's and I assume she got it because my aunt played a character named Daisy in some old movies, but I can't be sure because we rarely talked about her."

"It is a common design after all," Alberta said.

"But you have to admit that it would lead people to think there was a connection between your aunt and whatever's in that box," Jinx said.

"Decide for yourself," Adrienne said. "Take a look, I have nothing to hide."

The same thought went through Jinx and Alberta's mind at the same time. Was Adrienne calling their bluff? Was she testing them to see if they'd give in to their curiosity? Could she really be hiding a major clue that could crack this case right on her kitchen table? There was only one way to find out: accept Adrienne's challenge and do as she suggested.

"Well, if you insist," Alberta said.

With Jinx at her side, Alberta lifted the lid of the box, and they both tried to act as if they weren't thoroughly interested in finding out what was inside. If they told the truth, they would have to admit they were disappointed to see that it housed Post-its, pens, and some old CDs.

"It's just an old junk box," Adrienne admitted. "One of many, I'm sorry to say."

"We're the ones who are sorry," Alberta confessed. "We shouldn't have assumed there was anything worth seeing."

"Trust me, I know what you and the cops are thinking," Adrienne said. "I come to this state at the same time my famous aunt is killed. Even I understand it's a weird coincidence."

"That's still no reason for us not to be hospitable," Alberta said.

"Don't think twice about it," Adrienne replied. "It

really is nice to have company. Which reminds me, I'll make us some coffee or tea and we can start."

"I can do that if you don't mind," Alberta said, "That way you two can get right to the interview."

"That would be great," Adrienne said. "I'm sure you know your way around a kitchen much better than I do."

"That, Ms. Petrocelli," Jinx said, "would be the understatement of the year."

Jinx and Adrienne sat across from each other at the table and Jinx pulled out her microcassette recorder. She advised Adrienne that she would be recording their entire conversation and would only press the Stop button if Adrienne gave instructions that she wanted to speak off the record. Adrienne commented that she had watched enough crime procedurals on TV that she was well-versed in the rules of how reporters and cops conducted business.

Jinx began her interview by asking factual questions to collect as much information about Adrienne's background as possible. Adrienne revealed that she was born in Camden, Maine, but her family moved to nearby Bath following her birth. After she graduated high school, she attended the University of Michigan and decided to stay in the area after college because the job market back home wasn't nearly as diverse as it was in the Midwest.

When the teakettle whistled, Alberta plopped the tea bags into the cups she found in the top cupboard and poured the boiling water over them. She knew that Jinx liked honey in her tea and was surprised to find a squeezable jar next to the cups. She squirted some honey into one cup and poured some milk into another for herself, but she wasn't sure how Adrienne took hers.

"Sorry to interrupt," Alberta said, "but how do you take your tea, Adrienne?"

"A spoonful of sugar," she replied.

Jinx took back control of the conversation and asked Adrienne what her major was in college, and Alberta set about searching for sugar while the song from *Mary Poppins* was playing in her head on an endless loop. It made it even worse because like most of the world, she only knew two lines of the lyrics, so the same words kept repeating themselves over and over again. By the fourth time she silently heard a voice sing about medicine, she found the sugar in one of the cabinets, and then realized she needed a spoon. She pulled open one of the drawers and found what she needed, and a few more things as well.

The inside of the drawer resembled the contents of the box with the daisy motif. It contained a collection of mismatched silverware, matchbooks, a bottle of spirit glue, a rubber band ball, candlesticks, and a bunch of business cards. Alberta noticed that one of the cards had Adrienne's name printed on it, identifying her as a customer sales representative for BioMedique. Alberta had never heard of the company but assumed it must have something to do with the medical industry. When she took out a spoon from the drawer, she made sure to take the card as well. It would come in handy later, when she would be able to investigate the company further.

Alberta found a plastic tray hiding behind some paper towels underneath the sink and put the cups on it so she would only have to make one trip from the kitchen to the table. It was hardly far, but Alberta was hoping to be a more active participant in the interview, not just a de facto waitress.

"Tea with honey for you," Alberta said, placing a cup in front of Jinx. "Tea with a spoonful of sugar for you," she said, placing the other cup in front of Adrienne. "And tea with milk for me."

Alberta pulled out a chair at the table and sat down. "I hope you don't mind if I sit here," Alberta said. "There really isn't anywhere else for me to go."

Alberta hoped Adrienne wouldn't point out that she could sit on the couch in the living room, but the young woman proved to be a cooperative hostess.

"Not at all," Adrienne said. "And feel free to ask me any questions you want as well. Like I said, I have nothing to hide."

"I wouldn't want to interfere while Jinx is working," Alberta said, "but I wonder what you think about Missy's movies. Which one is your favorite?"

"I don't have one," Adrienne replied.

"How can you not have one?" Alberta asked. "You must have a favorite."

"I've never seen them," Adrienne declared.

It was Jinx's turn to kick her grandmother under the table to make her shut up and not go off on some tirade about how it was inconceivable that Missy's only living relative had never seen one of her films. Adrienne was a few years younger than Jinx, and the Daisy Greenfield movies were long gone from the silver screen before they were born. Just because Missy and Adrienne were related didn't mean there was any emotional connection between the two women. From what Jinx had gleaned thus far, they were more like strangers than relatives.

"Look, family is the most important thing in the world, but Missy Michaels is nothing more than a name from my childhood," Adrienne explained. "My family rarely talked about her and when they did, it was almost always about her as an actress."

"Did you know she was coming out of retirement to act once again?" Jinx asked.

"How could I know?" Adrienne replied. "Nothing was in the papers and Missy hadn't had any contact with my family in years, not since the lawsuit."

"What lawsuit?" Alberta asked.

Adrienne took a long sip of tea. "I don't have all the details and from what my grandmother told me the lawyers handled everything." Adrienne took another sip of tea, then asked, "What else can I tell you?"

They weren't sure if she was trying to be helpful or avoid talking about her famous dead relative. But neither Alberta nor Jinx wanted to give Adrienne any reason to stop talking or ask them to leave, so Alberta glared intently at Jinx, willing her granddaughter to take a different approach to the interview to ensure it continued. Jinx understood what she had to do.

"Why did you move here?" Jinx asked.

"I had to get away from the Michigan cold," Adrienne explained. "This past winter was the worst in years, and I couldn't deal with another one. I thought about moving to Florida, but I know how hot it can get down there, and I felt like I would be going from one extreme to the other."

"You made the right decision," Jinx said. "I grew up in Florida and I never want to experience another hot, humid Florida summer for as long as I live."

"But why New Jersey?" Alberta asked.

"Work," Adrienne replied. "I decided I wanted to move back to the East Coast, so I applied to a bunch of places and the place in Jersey made the best offer. I do customer service for a company right here in Parsippany. I start next week."

"Do you know Kip Flanigan?" Alberta asked.

At the mention of Kip's name, Adrienne's cup slipped through her fingers, and if she hadn't caught it at the last second, it would've crashed onto the table. "I'm such a klutz," she said. "I haven't eaten much today."

Alberta fought her maternal instinct to feed Adrienne and instead fed her the same question in hopes of getting an answer this time. "I said, do you know Kip Flanigan?"

"No, should I?" Adrienne asked.

"He's a very nice young man who's going to be in the show that Missy was supposed to star in," Alberta explained. "He lives here in Parsippany too and I thought you might know him."

"Parsippany is a big town, Gram, if you haven't noticed," Jinx said.

Adrienne glanced up at the clock on the wall. "Oh, wow! I didn't notice the time. I'm sorry, but I have to get ready for an appointment. We can schedule a time for you to come back if you'd like."

"I'll let you know if that's necessary," Jinx said. "But I think I've gotten everything I need."

"I don't think I got anything useful out of Adrienne!" Jinx cried.

Joyce refilled her glass with Red Herring and Helen cut her another slice of Entenmann's cherry pie. Alberta was the only one who didn't move at the table. She was also the only one who knew Jinx was wrong.

"You got everything you needed out of her, lovey," Alberta said.

"How can you say that?" Jinx asked.

"Because we know she was lying," Alberta declared. "I don't know what she was lying about, but she was definitely lying."

"How can you be so sure, Gram?"

"Because I don't care what Adrienne says about not ever talking about Missy," Alberta said. "No one turns their back on their family like that and never sees them again."

"That's exactly what my mother did."

Jinx's words landed like a thud on the kitchen table. It was as if the big, old Italian elephant in the room was lifted up and thrown on the table for dinner. Helen and Joyce eyed each other, not sure what to say or do. They knew Lisa Marie was the literal link that connected Alberta and Jinx, but they also knew that link had been severed over a decade ago. Alberta, however, wasn't upset, she wasn't angry, she was relieved. She was thrilled Jinx had brought up her mother and hadn't minced words about how she left New Jersey to start a new life far away from her family.

"You're right, lovey," Alberta said. "But I need you to understand that I have not turned my back on your mother. If she ever reached out to me or needed me, I would go to her in a heartbeat, no questions asked."

"Despite my mother's silence, I know that she'd do the same thing for you," Jinx said.

"That's because we're family," Alberta said, the tears falling easily from her eyes. "She's my daughter and I'm her mother. We have this . . . *thing* between us, but nothing can change who and what we are to each other."

"Gram, I'm sorry, I didn't mean to make you cry," Jinx said, her own tears racing down her face.

"Crying is just a way to wash your heart, lovey," Alberta said. "Sometimes it needs a good scrubbing."

"Sanjay told me the same exact thing," Joyce said. "I think it's a Buddhist saying."

The mention of Sanjay's name abruptly ended the sentimental spell cast around the room.

"You talk to Sanjay now?" Helen asked.

"As part of the investigation," Joyce said. "I was going to fill you all in after you told us what you learned from Adrienne."

"We're finished with Adrienne," Jinx said. "Tell us about Sanjay."

"I asked him about the security footage the night of the murder and whether it showed Missy leaving with her escort," Joyce explained.

"Did it?" Helen asked.

"He doesn't know," Joyce replied. "Sanjay said the video is missing."

"Missing?" Alberta cried. "How could a videotape just disappear?"

"And why are they still using videotape?" Jinx asked. "Hasn't Sanjay upgraded?"

"Sanjay's cheap, Jinxie," Helen said. "An upgrade costs money."

"He thinks the tape was stolen and he's hoping Brandon will be able to tell us more now that he's back from helping his family," Joyce said. "He was working the night of the murder and saw Missy leave with her escort."

"Brandon works all through the night, doesn't he?" Alberta asked.

"Yes, someone's at the front desk twenty-four-seven," Joyce confirmed.

"Then I think it's time we paid Brandon a visit," Alberta said. "Let's go."

"I'd love to, Gram," Jinx said, "but if I don't post five hundred words online before midnight about the new bill on the docket overhauling how Jersey recycles plastic, Wyck will have my head."

"And I need to work on my blocking or else Johnny's going to have my head for lunch," Helen said. "If I sit still, I know all my lines, but once I move, I'm like a silent film star."

"Then it's just me and you, Joyce," Alberta declared. "Let's see if Brandon can shed some light on this mystery."

When they arrived at the Tranquility Arms, the only mystery was why Sanjay was standing behind the front desk and not Brandon.

"He's still not back yet!" Sanjay cried. "He texted me to say he'd be back today, but today is now tonight and still no Brandon! I bet that lazy bum is taking a nap at his apartment!"

As Joyce began to placate Sanjay and tell him that maybe Brandon's family still needed him, Alberta hit Joyce's pocketbook so it fell to the ground. Alberta bent down to pick it up at the same time Joyce did and whispered in her ear, "Find out Brandon's home address."

"Like I was saying, Sanjay, maybe Brandon is taking a nap," Joyce said, contradicting herself.

"That's what I said!"

"I have an idea," Joyce said. "Do you have Brandon's address? I could go over there and see if he's home."

"It's 492 Maple Lane Road!" Sanjay cried. "And take these, you might need them."

Sanjay slammed down a set of keys onto the counter.

"What are these?" Joyce asked.

"The spare keys to Brandon's apartment!" Sanjay shouted. "He kept a pair here because he was always locking himself out!"

"If you had his keys, Sanjay, why didn't you go over to his place yourself?" Alberta asked.

"Because if I found him there taking a nap, I would kill him in his sleep!" Sanjay exclaimed. "And then who would send money to my sixty-seven relatives back in Mumbai?"

Standing in the middle of Brandon's ransacked living room, Alberta and Joyce held on to each other tightly because someone had beaten Sanjay to it. The young man was lying on his couch, his bloodshot eyes open and still looking fearful, a green scarf wrapped and knotted around his neck. From the odor emanating from his body, it was apparent that he had been in that position for several days.

Brandon never left town to take care of a family emergency, he had been strangled to death.

CHAPTER 21

Due omicidi meritano due sospetti.

Joyce let out a cry and turned her back on the corpse. Alberta stared at the young man a moment longer and then did the same. Sometimes the truth was just too hard to face.

"The poor boy, he was so young," Joyce said.

"I know, he was younger than Jinx," Alberta added. "It isn't fair."

Holding on to Alberta's hands and shaking her head, Joyce asked, "How could these things happen? Here of all places?"

Alberta squeezed Joyce's hands tighter. "I ask myself that all the time."

"I want to do something, but I feel so helpless," Joyce admitted.

"We can pray."

Together, hands still entwined, Alberta and Joyce prayed

for Brandon. They asked God to have mercy on his soul and to receive him in heaven with a full heart and a loving embrace. They also prayed for Brandon's family, that they would be able to endure this shock and recover from the pain they undoubtedly would feel to lose such a young member of their family. They still had enough faith to believe God had heard every word. If not, it would have been difficult to remain in the room.

Joyce took a handkerchief from her pocketbook and handed it to Alberta, who instinctively placed it over her mouth and nose as a way to block out the smell that was starting to become overwhelming. Joyce then removed the brooch that was keeping the thick, cotton scarf pinned to her jacket, so she could give the accessory a similar use. She dropped the brooch into her pocketbook and looked around the room.

"Should we open a window, Berta?"

"I'd like to, but we shouldn't touch anything. For all we know, whoever killed Brandon came in through the window; he does live on the first floor."

"Honestly, Berta, I don't know how you keep your wits about you in times like these," Joyce remarked. "You've got the strength of Moses."

"I also know when to call in reinforcements," Alberta said.

As they waited for the police and ambulance to arrive, Alberta and Joyce stood in place to prevent any accidental disturbance to the crime scene but look around the room for clues. They felt as if they were playing one of those optical illusion games, straining their eyes in search of things that didn't belong, not knowing what they were looking for but sure they would know when they found it.

"Berta, over there," Joyce said. "That's a VHS case."

"You're right, but where's the video?"

"It might be around here, but I don't see it."

"Ah, *Madon*!" Alberta cried. "That has to be the case for the security footage."

"You think that's why Brandon was killed? Because of whatever's on that footage?"

"That has to be the reason," Alberta said. "The footage shows Missy being led out of the Tranquility Arms by her escort. But why would Brandon bring the video here? He should've given it directly to the police."

"I hate to speak ill of the dead, Berta, but maybe he was blackmailing Missy's escort."

"Now who's keeping their wits about them?" Alberta asked. "You're starting to think like a real detective, Joyce."

"Just trying to keep up with my fearless leader."

"Whoever escorted Missy to the theatre must have killed her," Alberta said, "and that same person must have killed Brandon because he was the only person to see the video."

"If we only knew who this escort was."

"Maybe we do."

"What do you mean?" Joyce asked. "You figured out who killed Missy already?"

"No, but look over there, at the base of the floor lamp beside the window."

It took a few seconds for Joyce to see what Alberta was pointing at. "That's a rubber band," Joyce said. "How's such a common item a clue?"

"Because it's what Johnny uses to tie back his hair into a ponytail," Alberta replied.

Even with her scarf covering her mouth, her gasp could be heard in the hallway.

"Everything all right in here?" Vinny asked as he entered the apartment.

"Just a little post-traumatic shock," Alberta said.

"Tambra, help Joyce outside," Vinny ordered. "And Alfie, explain to me how you two happened to be in the presence of yet another dead body."

Alberta explained that they had gone to the Tranquility Arms to ask Brandon about Missy's escort the night of her murder, but Brandon was nowhere to be found. She filled Vinny in on what Sanjay had told them about Brandon never showing up for his shift, and that he gave them the keys to Brandon's apartment so they were able to let themselves in when Brandon didn't answer the doorbell.

In anticipation of what she knew was going to be Vinny's next question, Alberta said, "No, we haven't moved from these spots."

"I guess I should thank you for doing our work for us," Vinny said. "I was planning on questioning Brandon tomorrow. We tried to reach him in Rochester, but his family said they hadn't heard from him in months."

"He wasn't the devoted son we thought he was?" Alberta asked.

"That wasn't the impression I got from speaking to his parents," Vinny said. "From what I know of Brandon, he was more devoted to himself, a bit of an opportunist, kind of like the hustlers we grew up with. Not bad necessarily, but they would turn a blind eye to their morals if it meant they could make a buck."

"Sounds like Brandon had what it takes to be a blackmailer," Alberta said.

"What are you talking about, Alfie?" Vinny asked.

Alberta pointed toward the VHS tape box Vinny hadn't

yet seen and explained their theory to him. She then alerted him to the rubber band and its potential connection to Johnny. She wasn't being egotistical, but she knew her old friend would be impressed with her deductions. And she was right.

"It's time we called Johnny Fenn in for questioning," Vinny said.

"You should make it a two-for-one sale," Alberta said.

Vinny had known Alberta for a long time and had become fluent in Alberta speak. "There's another suspect?"

"*Due omicidi meritano due sospetti*," Alberta said. "Two murders deserve two suspects."

"Don't keep me in suspense," Vinny said. "Who's suspect number two?"

"Kip," Alberta replied. "He doesn't have an airtight alibi for the night Missy was murdered, and there is his obsession."

"Full sentences, Alfie," Vinny said. "Speak in full sentences."

"Kip has a whole room covered in Missy memorabilia," Alberta said. "Jinx found it when we were over at his apartment rehearsing. Honestly, after talking with him I thought it was harmless; creepy and *strano* but nothing to worry about."

"You realize Kip has some kind of criminal past, right?" Vinny asked rhetorically.

"Yes, but who among us should cast the first stone?" Alberta mused.

Vinny's silence led Alberta to believe he was stymied by her biblical reference. She was wrong.

"Me! That's who, 'cause I'm the chief of police!" Vinny declared. "And I'm telling you what I told Jinx: from here on in, we share whatever information we learn. The next time you stumble upon a room filled with a dead woman's tchotchkes, tell me about it! No more secrets."

"You should practice what you preach, Mr. Chief of Police," Alberta said.

"What's that supposed to mean?" Vinny asked.

"Excuse me, Chief," Tambra said. "The team needs to start collecting evidence."

Reluctantly, Vinny turned his attention away from Alberta's veiled accusation and toward the dead body in the room. "Of course I want a report on their findings in the morning, and we need to bring Johnny Fenn and Kip Flanigan in for questioning."

By the time he turned back around, Alberta had slipped out of the apartment to join Joyce, who was waiting for her in the hallway. Vinny would have to interrogate his old friend later, he had two new suspects to grill first.

"You let them both go?!"

Alberta's voice blared through the phone and exited from the receiver on the other end so clearly that Vinny was glad he'd closed his office door before dialing. He explained the details of the investigation, knowing full well that Alberta wouldn't want to hear the facts, but the truth was both Kip and Johnny had alibis that didn't seem fabricated, although they were being checked out. The police had searched both apartments for the security footage videotape but came up empty, and only Brandon's fingerprints were found on the tape cover with the results from the rubber band coming back inconclusive. It wasn't what Alberta wanted to hear, but with no legal reason to hold either suspect, Vinny's only recourse was to let them both go.

"Did you at least tell them not to leave the state?" Alberta asked.

"Yes, Alfie, I know how to do my job."

"*Mi dispiace,* I'm frustrated," Alberta said apologetically. "As much as I didn't want to believe it, I thought for sure it was one of them, Vinny."

"Me too, especially when I saw Kip's cinematic sanctuary, *mucca sacra*! He literally worships that woman. Creepy isn't the word for it, it's downright macabre."

"What do we do now?" Alberta asked.

"We don't take our eyes off either of those boys," Vinny said. "Just because we couldn't hold them doesn't mean they're innocent. If one of them is the murderer, trust me, they're going to crack."

Later that night as Jinx, Freddy, Nola, and Johnny were having dinner at the girls' apartment, it seemed as if Vinny's prediction was starting to come true.

"This whole town thinks I'm a murderer!"

No one could disagree with Johnny, but Nola, being the devoted girlfriend she was, tried to mollify his fears. She only made the situation worse. "Not just you, Johnny, the police also suspect Kip."

"That doesn't make me feel any better, Nola!" Johnny cried. "Kip is the one who killed Missy. Why can't anyone see that?"

"Why would you say that, Johnny?" Jinx asked.

"He comes from the same small town in Maine that Missy does," he stated.

Jinx hid her surprise at this comment and asked, "How do you know that?"

"Everybody knows he's been lying because he's guilty!" Johnny cried, slamming his fist on the table.

"Dude! Knock it off!" Freddy yelled. "We're trying to have a nice dinner and all you're doing is yelling."

"I'm sorry, but I didn't sign up for this," Johnny said. "All I wanted to do was direct a play and get noticed."

"Well, you kind of got your wish," Freddy said.

Just as Johnny was about to unleash yet another verbal tirade, Jinx's cell phone rang, filling the air with the theme song from *Murder, She Wrote*. She told everyone that she was only binging on the show because she was doing professional research, but if she was being honest, she had developed a serious girl crush on Angela Lansbury.

"It's my boss, I have to take this," Jinx said, getting up and walking into the galley kitchen. "Hi, Wyck, what's up?"

"I need an article tying Brandon's murder to Missy's," Wyck demanded.

Jinx of course couldn't see Wyck, but she knew exactly what he was doing. He was leaning forward, his forearms on his desk, as he spoke into his speakerphone. His ears were beet red and he was bouncing in his chair like a toddler on a sugar high. It was how he got whenever he was excited about a new angle to an article.

"I'm already on it," Jinx replied.

"I want you to talk to everybody—the only Miccalizzo left standing, the obsessed fan, and that director guy," Wyck ordered.

Jinx glanced at Johnny stealthily and replied, "I've got them all covered."

"And don't forget Inga," Wyck said.

"Who's Inga?" Jinx asked.

"The woman who played Teddy in the movies with Missy."

"Right, the grandmother. She's still alive?"

"Alive and well and living in that actor's retirement home in Englewood," Wyck explained.

"What?" Jinx cried. "I can't believe she's still alive, she's ancient."

"She's old, but we still send Christmas cards to each other every year."

"Wyck, why haven't you called her already to interview her?"

"Because that's your job! I'm the editor and you're the reporter."

"Do you really think an old lady in a nursing home is going to be able to shed any light on Missy's murder?"

"Probably not, but her story will make for a great human-interest piece," Wyck said.

"I still can't believe you've never gone to see her. You're such a fan."

"I didn't want to destroy the illusion of only knowing her from the movies," Wyck said. "You know these actor types are mesmerizing on the big screen, but up close and personal, they can be the most annoying creatures on God's green earth."

"I'll visit her tomorrow," Jinx said. "Thanks for the tip."

When Jinx turned around, she saw Freddy, Johnny, and Nola staring at her from the dining room table. Freddy and Nola looked curious, but Johnny looked like he was about to explode.

He didn't disappoint. "I have had it! My career is imploding, we're trying to have a relaxing dinner, and all you can do is talk about murder."

"She's trying to find out who really killed that old lady and clear your name, ya *stunod*!" Freddy bellowed.

"*Vai all'inferno!*" Johnny shouted. He stormed off into Nola's bedroom and slammed the door behind him.

"You know something, Nola?" Freddy started. "You're boyfriend's a jerk."

Shaking her head placatingly, she replied, "He's just an artist."

"Stop making excuses for him," Freddy said. "You deserve better than him and you know it."

He wasn't done giving orders. He turned to Jinx and started to put on his jacket. "Get your things, you're staying over at my place tonight. If she wants to stay in this apartment with that loose cannon that's her choice, but I am not leaving you to spend the night in this apartment with him one door down."

A throng of emotions flooded Jinx's body and she had to hold on to the back of the chair to steady herself. She was disturbed by Johnny's aggressive outburst, she was saddened that her best friend had such little self-respect, but most of all she was proud of her boyfriend's passion. She knew she should probably be scared, but she was exhilarated.

The next morning, Jinx was still overflowing with joy. Part of it had to do with the romantic evening she had spent with her very protective boyfriend, but part of it also had to do with that day's scheduled road trip.

The Actors Fund Home was located on six acres in Englewood, New Jersey, about an hour from Tranquility.

The home was first established in Staten Island at the turn of the twentieth century but was relocated to its current location a few decades later. As its name implied, the first-rate facility catered to retired actors and, as a result, focused as much on the personal touch as providing the most up-to-date medical care. The residents were former actors, they had earned their livings communicating with others, expressing emotions, and sharing their souls with countless audiences. It was only fair that they received the same attention in their golden years.

Inga Schumacher had no idea that she was about to receive more attention in one afternoon than she had in the past decade. But when she saw the four Ferrara ladies flanking Father Sal in the doorway of her private room, the ninety-eight-year-old suddenly turned into the great film star Greta Garbo and wanted to be left alone.

"Get out!" Inga shouted. "I'm not ready for my last rites!"

She might look old and frail, but the former movie actress was just as feisty as she was when she portrayed Teddy Greenfield decades ago. She was also as compassionate. Once Alberta explained who they were and that they wanted to speak to Inga about her former costar, Inga instructed the young nurse who ushered them into the room to find two more chairs so her guests could be comfortable while they talked. Despite the dreadful reasons that prompted the visit, Inga was grateful for the company.

When everyone was seated around Inga's bed, the woman was ready to hold court. She sat up, folded her hands in her lap, and said, "What do you want to know?"

On the drive over, the group had decided to let Jinx lead the conversation and speak for the group. If they all bombarded her with questions at once, Inga would probably call for the hook and have them thrown out of her room.

"When was the last time you spoke with Missy?" Jinx asked.

"Just a few weeks ago," Inga replied. "She told me all about how she was going to star in *Arsenic and Old Lace.*"

"Was she excited about the opportunity?"

"She was thrilled," Inga replied. "She couldn't wait to work with Johnny the director. She said that over and over again, Johnny the director, never just Johnny, always Johnny the director."

"It sounds like she trusted Johnny with making her look good for her comeback," Jinx said.

"She most certainly did. You know she had never performed onstage before. I gave her a few tips from when I was on the boards, but that was a long time ago. She said she wasn't worried about making her debut and her comeback at the same time, she felt like she was in good hands with Johnny the director. She thought it might open some new doors and lead to other jobs," Inga explained. "She even got her own website, it got her so excited, like she was little Missy again."

"She has her own website?" Jinx asked.

"Missy said every serious actress these days has one," Inga replied. "I'm sure she got ripped off, though, I mean, I don't know anything about websites, but one hundred thousand dollars seems like a lot of money."

"To create a website?" Joyce interjected.

"That's what she told me she paid for it," Inga replied. "I didn't say anything. Lord knows she has almost every dime she ever made. It's not like she ever helped out her family."

"Could they have used her help?" Alberta asked.

"What family can't use a little financial help now and again?" Inga replied.

She leaned back against her pillows and everyone remained silent. Whatever Inga was thinking about was making her sad; she shook her head a few times in response to whatever memory was playing out in her mind and waved a wrinkled hand in the air.

"I tried to get Missy to reunite with her family, but she had been on her own since she was practically a baby and she had become tough and isolated by the time she was thirty. She wouldn't listen to me." Inga sighed deeply and continued, "I could've tried harder, I'm sure, but I had my own family problems. I never had children of my own, mind you, but I took care of my parents and sister before they all passed," Inga explained. "And now Missy's gone. But her death was inevitable, one way or the other. At least Johnny the director made her happy in her final days."

Her emotional words moved everyone in the room. Especially Father Sal, who sat on Inga's bed and took her hands in his. "If Johnny made Missy as happy as you, Inga Schumacher, made all of us by watching you cavort up there on that big silver screen, she passed over into eternal life with a huge smile on her face."

A similar smile grew on Inga's face, and then the rest of the ladies in the room.

"Thank you, Father," Inga said. "Thanks to all of you for making me feel like I had an audience again." She then said what everyone else was thinking. "What a splendid way to spend an afternoon."

* * *

The feeling stayed with them when they returned to Alberta's house. Jinx, for one, couldn't believe that even while investigating two murders that were almost assuredly linked and committed by the same diabolical person, she felt joyful. It looked as if Lola felt the same way.

When Alberta placed a plate of cut-up meatballs on the floor and called for Lola, the cat uncharacteristically didn't respond. Usually, she bounded into the kitchen, and although she might play the role of Miss Finicky from time to time, she could never resist the aroma of Alberta's meatballs for very long.

"Lola! Come and eat!" Alberta cried, but still there was no response.

"Gram, come look!" Jinx yelled from the living room. "Lola's playing with the teddy bear you found in Missy's room at the Tranquility Arms."

"It's a sign," Father Sal said. "We just met the real Teddy and now Lola's playing with her namesake."

"That isn't playing," Helen said. "That's a catfight."

They all examined Lola more closely and realized Helen was right. What might have started as a playful encounter with the stuffed animal was turning into an all-out brawl. Alberta intervened before the teddy bear suffered a fatal injury.

"Lola, give me that," Alberta said, trying to pry the bear from Lola's claws and teeth.

"I've never seen Lola so aggressive," Joyce said. "Is there a meatball tucked away in the belly of the bear?"

No, but there was a message.

Alberta grabbed the bear and pulled in one direction while Lola bit down on the head and yanked in the opposite direction, resulting in the cute little teddy bear being torn in two.

"Oh, my eyes!" Father Sal cried. "I feel like I've been transported back to the Inquisition!"

There was no bloodshed, but the aftermath was just as frightening.

There was a piece of paper sticking out from the torso of the now-headless bear. Jinx instructed everyone not to touch the note and ran out to the kitchen to find the latex gloves she kept in her bag. Her hands covered appropriately, she pulled out the note, noticed a faint smell of catnip or perfume, which was what probably had aroused Lola, and smoothed out the note so it could be read.

"What does it say?" Alberta asked.

"It's addressed to you, Gram," Jinx replied.

"Me? Sanjay said the package had been delivered to Missy," she explained. "Why would the note be addressed to me?"

"Whoever wrote it knew you ultimately would find it," Jinx said. "It's a warning."

Jinx held up the note so the others could read it. There was no other way to interpret its message, the note was a direct threat. **"Alberta, stop snooping or you'll wind up as dead as Missy."**

And just like that, the joy everyone had felt all day long vanished from the room.

CHAPTER 22

Non si può aver il miele senza la pecchie.

Never fear, this wasn't the first death threat Alberta had ever received. One had even come in the sixth grade, decades before she became an amateur sleuth, and was written in green magic marker by Joanne Rutigliano, who was angry at Alberta for beating her in the school spelling bee. As was the case back in grammar school, Alberta refused to allow a cowardly missive to prevent her from living her life.

Alberta had the same message for whoever was threatening her now that she had for Joanne: *Se hai qualcosa da dire, dillo alla mia facia.* She knew her anonymous admirer had something to say, Alberta just wished they would say it to her face. The irony didn't escape her when she was face to face with Sloan and knew she should say something to him about the note, but decided to keep her mouth shut instead. Somewhere Joanne Rutigliano was saying, *You can give it, but you can't take it.*

Ignoring the voice in her head, Alberta was determined to have a leisurely lunch with Sloan at Mama Bella's Café without once uttering the words Missy Michaels, murder, Brandon, strangulation, or anything related to theatre. They were halfway through their meal and it looked as if Alberta was going to see her goal fulfilled. It was Friday, so they had decided to go old-school Italian and order fish. Shrimp cocktail for an appetizer, followed by a warm octopus salad and, for their entrée, bay scallops over squid pasta. As the waiter swapped out empty salad plates for pasta bowls, Alberta saw Bruno picking up a takeout order from the front and all her hopes for a private lunch were killed.

"Bruno, so nice to see you," Alberta said as Bruno approached their table.

"This is like déjà vu," Bruno said.

"Why, have we met here before?" Sloan asked.

"No, I was at China Chef last week picking up my takeout and I bumped into Jinx and Nola having lunch, so they invited me to join them," Bruno explained.

As much as Alberta truly liked Bruno, she knew she was going to hate herself for her next statement. "I can't allow my granddaughter to have better manners than me, come join us."

"Are you sure?" Bruno asked. "I don't want to intrude."

Sloan was already pulling out a chair for Bruno. "Don't be silly, you and Berta are going to share the stage with each other shortly, why not share a table for lunch?"

Bruno sat down and pulled a large container out of his

bag. He took off the lid and the aroma of lemons and herbs filled the air. Alberta didn't even need to look at Bruno's meal to know he'd ordered the salmon as it was one of her favorite dishes at the restaurant. Bruno, unfortunately, wanted to talk about one of her least favorite topics.

"How do you think rehearsals are going, Alberta?" Bruno asked.

"I finally learned my lines for the opening scene, which was a huge hurdle to get over, so for me they're getting better," Alberta said. "Though I do wish Johnny would stop his yelling. *Dio mio*! He likes to hear himself shout."

"He's a blithering idiot if you ask me," Bruno said.

No one had asked Bruno how he felt about Johnny. However, now that he offered his unadulterated opinion, Alberta forgot all about her desire not to engage in any theatre talk and wanted to know more about why Bruno had critiqued their director so harshly. Knowing that Bruno had a soft spot where Nola was concerned, she made the assumption that his comment about Johnny was less about his being a loudmouthed director and more about his being a bad boyfriend.

"Are your feelings about Johnny somehow connected to your feelings about Nola?" Alberta asked.

Sloan seemed much more surprised by Alberta's comment than Bruno, who silently mulled over her question before responding. "As her former lawyer, I still feel protective of Nola," Bruno said. "She always finds herself unwittingly in a bad situation through absolutely no fault of her own."

"Nola's the one who brought Missy to Tranquility in the first place," Alberta said. "Not for nothing, but she kind of created a bad situation for herself by setting things into motion."

"No, she didn't," Bruno corrected. "It was Johnny's idea to do *Arsenic and Old Lace* and to cast Missy in the lead."

Sloan and Alberta looked at each other, matching confused expressions on their faces. Sloan turned to Bruno and asked, "Are you sure? Because that's not what we heard."

"Nola wanted to do a Neil Simon comedy, like *The Odd Couple*, because everybody loves Neil Simon, well, everybody except Johnny," Bruno explained. "And God forbid Nola contradict Johnny. I don't know what it is, but he sure does have a hold over her."

Sensing that Bruno wasn't yet ready to admit the hold that Nola had over him, Alberta decided they had talked enough about facts and thought it safer to discuss fiction.

They continued to dissect the rehearsal process and how everyone was starting to flesh out their characters. Bruno said he knew Father Sal was a born comedian but was surprised how well he handled his character's more sinister traits. Sloan agreed and surmised that it might be the result of delivering so many fire-and-brimstone sermons.

They all had nothing but praise for Helen. She had learned all her lines so quickly and now that she had mastered her blocking, she was finding the funny bits and nuances of Martha Brewster. Alberta beamed like only a proud sister could when Bruno admitted that no one could deny that Helen was doing a great job portraying a crotchety old lady with homicidal tendencies.

When he finished his meal, Bruno threw the container back into the bag and apologized for rushing off but confessed that he had to meet with a new client in fifteen minutes, so he had to run back to his office. After he left, Sloan grabbed Alberta's arm, and his words delighted her.

"Are you thinking what I'm thinking?" he asked.

"If you're thinking that Nola's a liar, then we're thinking the same thought," Alberta replied.

"Why do you think Nola would tell us that casting Missy was all her idea?"

"Maybe she was hoping to take all the credit?" Alberta suggested.

Sloan shook his head. "That really isn't like her, and considering how she feels about Johnny, why would she deny him a bigger spotlight?"

"Johnny could've told her to lie, or it could've been an innocent slip of the tongue on Nola's part," Alberta said.

Sloan's face scrunched up as if he didn't want to say what he was about to say. "I don't think Nola is all that innocent. But we're overlooking the most important piece of this new puzzle."

Alberta raised her eyebrows. "What's that?"

"Why would Johnny even think of Missy?" Sloan asked. "He's too young to know who she was. I mean, it's possible that he saw one of her movies on the late show."

"There's only one way to find out why Johnny is the real mastermind behind Missy coming to Tranquility," Alberta said.

Sloan took a deep breath before he spoke. "I'm afraid to ask this, but how?"

"It's time Jinx and I found out the real story about Johnny Fenn."

* * *

There was no rehearsal on Friday night, so they knew the theatre would be empty. They also knew that for a young woman, Nola had an old-fashioned work ethic and didn't readily embrace technology. Everything she did in connection with the theatre was done with pens and paper, not keyboards and computers, and Alberta knew that every person associated with the play had to fill out an application form. If they could see Johnny's application, maybe they could find a clue that would reveal the real man behind the director.

To avoid being noticed in case anyone was working late at the school, Alberta and Jinx parked a block away and entered the theatre from the back entrance. Jinx had swiped Nola's key and would put it back on her key ring in the morning while she was in the shower getting ready for rehearsal. It would mean Jinx would have to get up early on a Saturday, but she was hoping whatever facts they uncovered about Johnny would be worth not being able to sleep in.

Now that a show was being rehearsed, a ghost lamp was kept lit on the stage at all times. It was a bit of superstition acknowledging that theatres were often haunted by the ghosts of actors past, but it had a practical side effect: It prevented Alberta and Jinx from bumping into things backstage.

They were about to open the doors leading to the lobby when they heard someone talking. At first, they thought it was Nola doing work in her office, but realized that it couldn't be her because Jinx had her key. The voice got louder, and they immediately recognized a Jersey accent trying very hard not to sound like a Jersey accent.

"I left some papers at the theatre and I needed to pick them up, but I'm leaving now," the voice said.

There was silence for a few moments as the woman who was speaking listened to whoever was on the receiving end of the call. But Alberta and Jinx had heard enough to know the woman doing the listening was Donna Russo.

"I understand this has to be kept secret, and believe you me, nobody wants this Missy Michaels nonsense to be behind us more than I do," Donna barked.

There was another pause and Donna said, "I'm on my way."

A door slammed shut and Alberta and Jinx were quite certain they were alone, but to be on the safe side, they didn't move for a full minute. Once they creeped over to open one of the doors and look around the lobby, they were confident Donna had left the premises and they were the only two people inside the building.

"Should we follow Donna?" Jinx asked.

"No," Alberta replied. "I know enough about Donna Russo to know that she's harmless."

"Really? What do you know about her, Gram?"

"Nothing important, lovey, at least not anything to do with this case."

"What we just overheard kind of implicates her in this case," Jinx said.

"Let's focus on one suspect at a time," Alberta said. "And right now that suspect is Johnny Fenn."

Inside Nola's office, there was only one filing cabinet, so it didn't take them very long to find the paperwork they were looking for. When they found Johnny's application, with copies of his Social Security card and passport attached, they realized they were focusing on the wrong suspect. Johnny Fenn technically didn't exist, but Gianni Fennacacculi did.

"Ah, *Madon*!" Alberta cried. "That's almost as Italian as Melissa Margherita Miccalizzo!"

Now that they had concrete evidence that Johnny had lied to them about his real name and Nola, for some reason, had covered up the fact that it was Johnny's idea to stage Missy's comeback, they were ready to confront Johnny with the truth and expose him for the fraud they knew he was. They weren't sure if it would lead to him confessing to Missy's murder, but it was a possibility. Alberta and Jinx formulated a simple but surefire plan to get Johnny to reveal his true identity, but for it to work, they needed Helen to participate.

The next morning at rehearsal, the eldest Ferrara proved she was a trouper. "This is what they call meta theatre, Berta," Helen stated, standing center stage and opening her arms wide, as if presenting to an audience.

"All of a sudden you're Melina Mercouri?" Alberta said. "What's this *meta* theatre?"

"It's a play within a play," Helen explained, crossing to stage right. "You, me, and Johnny will be rehearsing *Arsenic and Old Lace*, but really, you and me will be acting out *Will the Real Gianni Fennacaculi Please Stand Up?*"

"I never heard of this meta theatre before, but yes, that's what it'll be like," Alberta said. "We need Johnny to admit he's been lying to us about his real name and who knows what else."

"I've got it covered, I've been acting far longer than you have, Berta," Helen said. "I understand how to use a scene to my advantage."

"As long as you get Johnny to admit he's really Gianni, I don't care what you do in the scene," Alberta replied.

"It makes no sense to me, though," Helen said. "Why would he change his name? Just listen to it . . . *Fennacacculi* . . . it sounds like the song of Sicily."

"Maybe all the yelling he does has made Johnny tone-deaf," Alberta said.

The lobby doors slammed shut, announcing their director's arrival.

"Places!" Helen cried. She then continued in a hushed whisper, "Let our scene begin."

The door to the theatre was flung open and Johnny entered. He was wearing the same outfit he'd been wearing since the beginning of rehearsal: jeans, a white T-shirt, and his navy-blue baseball cap with the gold M embroidered on the front. Alberta assumed he had several T-shirts in the same style because despite his downtown look, he always smelled fresh and clean. But perhaps he went home every night and washed his clothes. Or maybe he just yelled at his shirts until any odors disappeared in fright.

"What a nice change of pace, ladies!" Johnny bellowed. "You're on time."

Helen remembered an old Italian phrase, *Non si può aver il miele senza la pecchie*, which roughly translated to honey is sweet, but the bee stings. Yelling was part of Johnny's charm, but his words still had some bite. Although she had quietly taken his verbal abuse as an actress in his play, she was looking forward to seeing how the bee would react when it got stung.

"Rehearsal started five minutes ago, Johnny," Helen remarked. "You're the one who's late."

"Already in character, I see," Johnny replied. He placed his left palm onto the stage, flung his body to the right, and didn't stop moving until his two feet landed on the stage. "Let's take this scene from the top."

They ran through the scene once as directed, but when Johnny told them to do it again, this time with more feeling, Helen changed the stage direction. Instead of crossing stage left to where the couch would be, she crossed stage right to the front door.

"Stop!" Johnny shrieked. "You're supposed to cross stage left!"

Suddenly, Helen's face transformed into an innocent gaze and Alberta thought she was auditioning to play the lead in a stage version of *Rebecca of Sunnybrook Farm*. When she spoke, however, Alberta detected the venomous tone of the housekeeper in *Rebecca*. "Are you sure about that?" Helen asked. She then placed one hand on her hip and gave what could only be described as a come-hither look as she said, "Mr. Fennacacculi?"

The blood drained from Johnny's face and he looked as if he was playing out the last scene of *Witness for the Prosecution*. He opened his mouth to speak, but he had clearly forgotten his lines. Helen needed to prompt him.

"Should I check my script notes to see what the stage direction is?" Helen asked. "Mr. Fennacacculi?"

"How . . . how do you know my name?" Johnny stuttered.

"That's beside the point, Gianni," Alberta stated. "What matters is why you've been masquerading as Johnny Fenn when that's not who you are."

Johnny was still in such shock he could hardly speak. "I . . . I . . ."

"Spit it out, Johnny!" Helen cried. "How do you expect them to hear you in the balcony?"

"This theatre doesn't have a balcony, Helen," Alberta whispered.

"It's a theatrical reference, Berta!" Helen yelled. "Come on, Gianni, it's your line."

"I never meant to lie, I swear," Johnny said, finally in command of his voice. "But I learned a long time ago that I could get more work if my name sounded less ethnic and not so, you know, not so . . . Italian."

"Holy Bobby DeNiro!" Alberta cried.

"Haven't you ever heard of Martin Scorsese?" Helen asked. "He's Italian and his career hasn't suffered."

"I know, but Fennacacculi is hard to spell, and if you can't spell a name, you can't Google it," Johnny said. "I was thinking about changing it for a long time and one day my ex created a website for me, JohnnyFenn.com, and it was a done deal. Gianni Fennacacculi died that day and Johnny Fenn was born."

"That was a smart business decision," Alberta said. "That website is easier to type out than GianniFennacacculi.com. But that isn't everything you're hiding, is it?"

"What else is there?" Johnny said. "I anglicized my name to push my career forward. I'm not proud of turning my back on my heritage, but there's nothing more behind the change."

"I'm not talking about your name, I'm talking about the real reason behind why you're directing this show," Alberta said. "It was your idea—not Nola's—to bring Missy Michaels here, wasn't it?"

Once again, Johnny started stuttering. "Nuh-nuh-nuh . . . no!" For a director who was constantly telling his actors to articulate, he clearly wasn't taking his own advice.

"Stop lying!" Helen barked. "We know it was your idea,

we want to know why Nola told everyone it was her brainchild."

"Because I told Nola to say that!" Johnny confessed. "I wanted Nola to take the credit, it's her theatre after all."

"You expect us to believe you were just being . . . *nice*?" Alberta asked, her question filled with sarcasm.

"Yes!" Johnny shouted. "I know I'm a loudmouth, I know I can sometimes come off like a jerk, but I love Nola."

Alberta and Helen looked at each other, surprised by Johnny's confession about the severity of his feelings for Nola. He could easily be lying, but because they wholeheartedly agreed with the first two thirds of his statement, they figured they might as well believe the final third as well. That part of Johnny's deception, at least, was motivated by emotion.

"I found an old DVD of one of Missy's movies in my ex-girlfriend's collection and one thing led to another and I came up with the idea to do this play and have Missy star in it," Johnny explained. "But I knew how important it was for Nola to create something special for the Tranquility Players, so I told her to tell everyone that it was her idea."

"Was it also your idea to swindle Missy out of one hundred thousand dollars?" Joyce asked.

Alberta didn't know the terminology for a play-within-a-play-within-a-play, but when she saw Joyce at the back of the theatre with Vinny and Tambra standing behind her, she knew that their scene had taken a new twist. Joyce had not played a role in their original plan, but Alberta was curious to see where her sister-in-law would lead them.

"What are you talking about?" Johnny asked.

"I asked an investment banker friend of mine to do a little digging," Joyce said.

"That one really does have more friends than Carter has liver pills," Helen replied.

"He confirmed that Missy sent a check for one hundred thousand dollars for the creation of her website to Dirigo, Inc.," Joyce said.

"I have no idea what Dirigo, Inc., is," Johnny claimed.

"Then allow me to explain," Joyce said. "It's a newly formed company that was originally named Spider Web's Design, Inc., but changed its name about a month ago. The only transactional activity has been the receipt of one hundred thousand dollars from Missy Michaels's savings account and a subsequent transfer into another account. Do you want to guess where that money was transferred to?"

"No," Johnny replied. "But I have a feeling you're going to tell me."

"It was deposited into the account of Gianni Fennacacculi aka Johnny Fenn," Vinny announced.

"What?!" Johnny shouted. "That isn't true! I never got any money from Missy. I never even met the woman!"

"You didn't need to meet her to rob her of her money," Joyce declared. "According to the security footage at the Tranquility Trust, you're seen depositing the money into your account the night Missy Michaels was killed."

"That's impossible!" Johnny cried.

"You are a director, aren't you?" Joyce asked. "Isn't it your job to make the impossible look possible? According to the video, you succeeded."

"I don't know what this is about, but I didn't take any money from Missy and I didn't deposit it into my own bank account!" Johnny cried. "You gotta believe me!"

They didn't.

"Gianni Fennacacculi," Vinny said, "you're under arrest for the murder of Missy Michaels."

CHAPTER 23

Se non è unmessaggio di posta elettronica, è l'altra.

Courts, like turtles, move at their own slow pace. Which is why despite Johnny's screaming and bellyaching, he spent the weekend in jail.

At Alberta's request, Bruno agreed to represent Johnny. She wasn't convinced of the director's innocence, but she knew that Bruno would be a fierce advocate. The lawyer hedged at first, his unspoken reluctance being his strong feelings for his potential client's girlfriend, but in the end his oath to uphold the law was stronger than his desire to hold Nola in a tight embrace. Unfortunately, Alberta turned out to be more persuasive than Bruno because the judge didn't agree with Bruno's request to fast-track the bail hearing and kept it on the docket for Monday morning. Sometimes you could finagle the system and sometimes you couldn't.

"Fifty thousand dollars!" Nola cried.

"This is a murder case, Nola, the judge didn't even have to offer bail as an option," Bruno explained.

Looking around the courtroom, a shiver gripped Nola's spine. She had been in this location before, and she had been in the situation Johnny was in now, and the terrible memories of that ordeal were rising up from the tucked-away place in her mind where she had stored them. She didn't like the feelings that were resurfacing and this time it was worse because she wasn't the only victim. Johnny was sitting in a jail cell, desperate to get out but knowing he didn't have the financial means to post bail. Nola didn't have the money either, but she knew how to get it.

"Mrs. Scaglione," Nola said, her voice already starting to shake. "You were once very kind to me, and I hope you can find it in your heart to be kind again. Johnny isn't perfect and I know that, but I also know that he's innocent. I'm the only one here who knows what it feels like to be in that position and you're the only one I can ask who can help him like you once helped me." Nola took a pause to control her breathing, which had begun to accelerate. She then took a deep breath and asked the question she never thought she'd have to ask. "Could you please pay Johnny's bail?"

Alberta could hear Sloan, who was standing behind her, inhale deeply. He was surprised by Nola's request, but she wasn't. She also wasn't surprised by her quick reply.

"Yes, I will."

Tears sprang from Nola's eyes and she began to sob. She clasped her hands and held them to her chest; she didn't try to hide her face because she had nothing to hide. When Alberta sensed that Nola's crying was ending, she wrapped her arms around her. They stood there for a few seconds until Nola whispered in Alberta's ear, "You are my very own guardian angel."

The time for emotional outbursts was over and practical matters took over. Bruno advised Alberta to get a cashier's check ready, and he and Nola set off to advise the court and Johnny that bail would be paid. When they were alone, Sloan grabbed Alberta's hand and stopped her from dashing out of the courthouse and heading over to the bank.

"Sloan, what's wrong?"

"Are you sure you want to do this?" he asked.

"Yes, I am," Alberta said.

"And you aren't doing this out of any sense of guilt?" Sloan asked.

"I'm doing this because I'm not entirely convinced of Johnny's guilt," Alberta replied. "But even if I'm wrong, he isn't a flight risk; he isn't going to skip town."

"How can you be so sure?" Sloan asked.

"*L'innocenza di un bambino.*"

"Did you call me a baby?" Sloan asked.

"Sometimes you're as innocent as a baby," Alberta replied. "Which is something I love about you."

"I sense that there's something you don't love," Sloan said.

"You can be a little *stunod* sometimes," Alberta said as sweetly as possible. "Now that Johnny's going to be directing the show while out on bail with a murder charge looming over his head, Nola's little play is going to get more publicity than it ever would if Missy were starring in it. There's no way Johnny's going to miss out on being the center of all that attention."

"*La saggezza di una dea.*"

Sloan's accent was improving and so was his word choice.

"Did you call me a goddess?"

"You are a wise one," Sloan said. "And to be clear, I was not trying to tell you how to spend your money, I just wanted to make sure you weren't suckered in by Nola's performance. As honest and heartfelt as it might have been."

Once again, Alberta was reminded how different Sloan was compared to all the other men in her life. And, once again, she was reminded how happy she was that he had come into hers.

"I did know that," Alberta said. "But thank you for saying it out loud."

As they passed Vinny's office on their way out of the police station, they heard someone else who had no problem sharing her thoughts out loud.

"I'm not sure if you can hear it by the tone of my voice, Vinny, but I'm not thrilled to have a murder suspect in my school!"

The door to Vinny's office was ajar, so they could see that he was sitting in his chair listening to Donna scream at him. His face wasn't contorted in anger or flushed from trying to contain his rage, as it was when he fought with Alberta or Jinx; he looked almost amused by Donna's harangue. Which only made Donna's tone grow shriller and more strident.

"How am I going to convince the church and the parents of the students at St. Winifred's that allowing Johnny Fenn, or whatever his name is, to continue working on this play is a responsible thing for me to do?" Donna asked. "Tell me, Vin, how am I supposed to do that?!"

Vinny leaned forward, clasped his hands on his desk, and smiled. "You tell them that in this country a man is innocent until proven guilty. It's the ultimate lesson in civics playing out in real time for all to see. If you word it properly, you might even be able to increase tuition for the unprecedented experience."

"That is a novel way of looking at things," Donna replied. The volume of her voice had softened noticeably, and its tone was almost submissive.

"Plus, you can tell them that I'll have two cops seated in the back row of the theatre at all times whenever Johnny's on the premises," Vinny added.

Her response practically dripped with honey-scented oil. "I told you we'd make a good team, Vin, didn't I?"

Vinny didn't answer, but his impish grin told Alberta her suspicions about the couple had been right and they were, in fact, a couple. Before they could be seen, Alberta grabbed Sloan's hand and pulled him away from Vinny's open door and toward the exit.

"What in the world was that all about?" Sloan asked. "Have Vinny and Donna, you know . . ."

"Shacked up?" Alberta said, finishing Sloan's thought.

"I wasn't going to put it that vividly," he replied. "But now that you mentioned it, have they?"

"I don't know where they are in their relationship," Alberta admitted. "But I do know my old friend's bachelor days are finally over."

A few hours later, Alberta and Sloan found themselves right back at the police station, this time inside Vinny's office, not standing outside eavesdropping. His tone of voice was much less conciliatory than it was when he was speaking to Donna, even though the subject matter of both conversations was the same. Perhaps it was because the person yelling at him this time was twice Donna's size and a different gender.

"I can't drop the charges!" Vinny yelled.

"Why not?!" Bruno yelled back.

"Because I said so, that's why!" Vinny yelled even louder.

It was hardly a defense and only served to render Bruno speechless for five seconds, after which he railed against Vinny even louder.

Before Alberta could interrupt, Bruno said everything that was on her mind. He reminded Vinny that Johnny had no past criminal record, he had absolutely no motive, an alibi that admittedly couldn't be corroborated, but also couldn't be invalidated, and even if Johnny did deposit the $100,000 into his own bank account, there was no crime in accepting money.

Instead of responding to Bruno, which was the logical response, Vinny directed his reply to Sloan. "I guess you haven't told your girlfriend and her posse about the e-mails."

"What e-mails?" Alberta asked.

"Why don't we go to your place, make a pitcher of Red Herrings and I'll explain everything," Sloan suggested.

Back at Alberta's, the pitcher was full, the *antipasti* was on the table, Helen and Joyce rushed over to join them in response to emergency text messages Alberta sent them, yet Sloan still hadn't told them anything about the e-mails.

"Bruno and I have been more than patient, Sloan," Alberta said. "It's time you explained why you and Vinny are in cahoots."

"Vinny and I aren't in cahoots per se," Sloan hedged. "But he did discover what I've been up to . . . with someone else."

"Someone else?" Helen said. "Are you two-timing my sister?"

"Of course Sloan isn't two-timing Berta," Joyce said. "Sloan, please tell me you're not two-timing Berta."

"Heavens no!" Sloan cried. "If you'll all just wait a little bit longer, I'll explain everything."

"I really don't have time for this, Sloan," Bruno said. "I have a client facing a murder charge."

"We just have to wait for one more person," Sloan replied.

"I told you, Jinx is down the shore on an assignment," Alberta said. "She won't be back until tonight."

"We're not waiting on her," Sloan said. "It's someone else."

"Who?" they all asked in unison.

With perfect timing, the kitchen door flung open to reveal Father Sal. "None other than me! Your friendly neighborhood ecclesiastic."

"Have a seat, Padre, so we can get this show on the road," Helen commanded. "And no, don't get any ideas about taking our play on tour."

"We would be a hit upstate," Father Sal said, sitting at the table. "They do love when their elders take charge."

"*Basta!*" Alberta cried. "I don't want to hear you two bicker like Ma and Pa Kettle, I want to hear what Sloan has to say."

"So do I," Bruno said. "I'm the lawyer here, I'm the

only who can keep Johnny out of jail, and you've been keeping information from me. That isn't how this works!"

"I'm sorry, I needed to wait because Father Sal plays a large part in what I have to say," Sloan admitted.

"You're like the Gladys Kravitz of the Catholic Church, Sal," Joyce stated. "You've got your eyes and ears everywhere."

Sal rolled his hand in front of him as he bowed his head at the compliment, "It is a gift."

"You owe us the gift of an explanation!" Alberta yelled. "Now talk!"

"Father Sal and I hacked into Johnny's e-mail account with the help of an ex-con Sal has been working with who's serving time on parole," Sloan explained.

Except for Bruno, all those gathered were accustomed to engaging in slightly unorthodox methods of operations in their search for clues while investigating a case, and everyone, including Bruno, knew that Father Sal was not averse to following a morally ambiguous path if it led to some kind of gilded prize. However, no one ever thought they'd see the day when Sloan stepped over the line and joined them in participating in an illegal activity.

"Let me get this straight, Sloan," Bruno started. "You and a priest used an ex-con trying to go straight to commit a crime and jeopardize his parole?"

"We asked him nicely," Sloan said.

"And we bought him dinner," Sal added.

"*Santa Madre di Dio.*" Alberta sighed and made the sign of the cross. "We finally did it. We corrupted the innocent."

"Your boyfriend isn't a saint, Berta," Helen said. "What did you find out?"

"We could only see his e-mails for the past six months,

but there were no exchanges between him and Missy," Sloan said.

"That's more like noninformation," Joyce said.

"Correct, but we didn't stop our hacking there," Sloan replied, "thanks to Father Sal."

"You know how to hack into e-mails?" Alberta asked.

"No, but I listen when people talk, and I remembered that Inga said Missy always referred to Johnny as Johnny the director, so I had Bartholomew—he's the ex-con—hack into the account for Johnnythedirector@gmail.com," Sal explained.

"Se non è unmessaggio di posta elettronica, è l'altra," Alberta said and then translated for Sloan. "If it's not one e-mail, it's the other."

"And as Father Finley would say," Sal added, "we hit the trifecta."

"He was the gambling addict, right?" Helen asked.

"Yes, my oh my, how he loved his horses," Sal confirmed. "But he was a good priest. In fact, he won first prize for Best Homily three times in a row at the Cathys."

"What's the Cathys?" Alberta asked.

"The New Jersey Diocese Catholic Church Awards," Sal explained. "He won in the Non-Holiday Category."

"I didn't even know there was such a thing," Joyce said.

"Like many things that come out of the Vatican," Sal confided, "it's very hush-hush."

"Will you hush up about the gambling priest?" Bruno ordered. "Tell us what you found out when you read the e-mails between Missy and Johnny the director."

"Johnny e-mailed Missy saying that he was her number one fan," Sloan said.

"I think Kip would disagree with that claim," Joyce interrupted.

"He might not have the proof to back it up, but it is how Johnny presented himself," Sloan replied. "He then told Missy that he wanted to build a website for her to remind the world of what a great star she was."

"That doesn't make sense," Alberta said.

"I agree," Father Sal said. "The world already knows Missy Michaels is a great star."

"No, Johnny told us his ex-girlfriend created a website for him," Alberta corrected. "If he couldn't create his own, why would he suggest he would create one for Missy?"

"For the money," Sloan explained. "He charged her one hundred thousand dollars, which is an exorbitant price, but Missy paid it without any hesitation, which is an indication that she either didn't know any better or she was so desperate to get back on the public's radar that she didn't care that she was getting ripped off."

"Maybe Johnny implied that he wasn't tech savvy to throw us off the track," Alberta suggested.

"Or he paid someone five thousand dollars to make the website and pocketed the rest," Helen proposed.

"Also too, maybe he was framed," Joyce added.

"All very real possibilities," Sloan hedged.

"How terrible to be duped right before you die," Alberta commented.

Sloan and Father Sal exchanged very serious glances, which was a signal that their tale had yet to completely unfold.

"Are you seriously going to tell us that there's more to the story?" Bruno asked.

"Yes," Sloan confirmed.

"And it gets worse?" Bruno asked.

"Much," Sal replied.

"Then give me your glasses, everybody," Bruno said. "It's time for refills."

No amount of alcohol could prepare them for what Sal and Sloan were about to share with them, but it was good that they were slightly anesthetized by the Red Herrings, as it helped lessen the shock. They had uncovered some nefarious plots before, but what they were about to hear topped the list.

"About a week before she arrived in Tranquility, Missy sent Johnny an e-mail telling him that she had been diagnosed with Alzheimer's," Sloan conveyed. He paused as Alberta, Helen, and Joyce each made the sign of the cross, kissed their fingers, and offered their acknowledgment to God. "In that same e-mail, she expressed her desire not to live out her life like a victim, but to take control of her circumstances."

"I can't blame her," Helen said. "Alzheimer's is a horrible disease. It robs you of every human right."

"You might want to hold your approval until you hear what Missy proposed," Father Sal said. "She told Johnny that she wanted him to kill her after the play was over."

They were all so shocked by this revelation, they couldn't find any words and instead let out one communal gasp.

"She told him that she'd pay him one hundred thousand dollars now and would have another hundred thousand dollars released to him after her death," Sloan explained.

"So Missy agreed to pay such an exorbitant amount to Johnny for him to build her website, but it was, well, a red herring of sorts. The money was really a down payment to murder her," Bruno surmised.

"It seems that way," Father Sal said.

"These are extreme measures," Bruno said.

"The way Missy rationalized it," Sloan said, "she'd get to die on her own terms, and Johnny would garner huge attention as Missy Michaels's final director and be catapulted to stardom."

"She instructed Johnny not to respond to the e-mail and that she would wire the money into his Dirigo, Inc., account," Father Sal said, continuing the explanation. "If he deposited the money into his own account, she would know that he agreed."

"*Diabolica!*" Helen cried.

"I agree, Helen," Alberta said. "But forgive me, it makes sense."

"Berta, how in the world could that vile proposal make sense?" Joyce asked.

"Don't you remember, Inga told us Missy would die one way or the other," Alberta reminded them. "If she hadn't been murdered, it would only be inevitable that the Alzheimer's would have killed her."

"But having an untreatable illness and orchestrating your own death are two entirely different things," Joyce said.

"Plus, Johnny would have to go along with it, and that's the ultimate long shot," Helen said.

"It seems he did agree," Bruno said.

"But hold on, according to the e-mails, Missy told Johnny to kill her when the show was over, not before it started rehearsals," Alberta said.

"True," Sloan said, "but Vinny thinks they have enough info to make the charges stick."

"He also demands that this information remain silent," Sal added. "Which means we cannot tell Jinx."

"Why not?!" Alberta cried. "She's as much a part of this as we all are."

"She's also a reporter, Berta," Sloan said. "And Vinny will throw us all in jail if this information leaks out. I know it'll be hard for you, but please keep this a secret for a little while longer."

Sighing, Alberta threw up her hands and agreed. "There's so much I don't get about this whole thing anyway, it'll be easy to keep my mouth shut. Like what in the world is a dirigo?"

"You don't know?" Sloan asked.

"Of course not," Alberta said. "Does anyone know what a dirigo is?"

Everyone remained silent until Sloan filled them in. "It's the state bird of Maine."

"Maine?!" Alberta cried.

"Yes," Sloan replied. "Which makes perfect sense because that's where Missy was born. Johnny probably thought it would be a clever tribute."

"I don't think Johnny set up that account at all," Alberta said.

"Who else could have done it?" Sloan asked.

"Kip is from Maine. He's obsessed with Missy," Alberta said. "Don't you think it's possible that Kip set up all this and he's framing Johnny for a murder that he actually committed?"

"In the immortal words of Alberta Ferrara Scaglione," Sloan said, "ah, *Madon*!"

CHAPTER 24

Tondo e tondo e tondo lei va, dove si ferma, nessuno la sa.

The next two days made the Ferraras and their friends feel like they were on a merry-go-round. One minute they were convinced Johnny was the murderer and then someone offered an opinion that made them question his guilt and the pendulum would swing in Kip's direction. A little while later, another comment was made and they were right back where they started, pointing the finger of blame at Johnny. After all the clues they unearthed, after all the information they discovered, they still didn't feel any closer to solving the case.

They knew all about Missy's childhood in Maine, how she became a movie star, and how she turned her back on her family and didn't offer them any financial support. They knew that Kip was from the same small town as Missy and nurtured an unhealthy preoccupation with the former star. They also knew he had some kind of criminal past, but its severity was still a secret.

They also knew Missy's family moved from Maine to Michigan and that Missy's only living relative, Adrienne, recently made a move from Michigan to Parsippany, which happened to be the same town Kip was currently living in. They knew that Brandon was probably the only person who could have identified Missy's killer because the killer more than likely escorted Missy from the Tranquility Arms to St. Winifred's Academy, but Brandon would never be able to identify the escort because the escort, who also had to be the killer, strangled Brandon the same way the escort/killer murdered Missy.

And finally, they knew that whoever the murderer was knew about Missy's childhood in Maine because of the doctored photo that was found in the fake arsenic bottle Missy was clutching when her body was found. They knew a lot and yet they still knew very little.

Besides the investigation into the two murders, there was the whole theatrical side of things that for most of the Ferraras was like stepping into an entirely new world. Memorizing lines, remembering stage blocking, late-night rehearsals, working on publicity, building the set, searching for costumes and props, rigging the lights—it was all exhausting. They'd never realized that theatre people took the phrase "the show must go on" literally. It was a religious vow, a medical oath, a sworn testament that they would uphold and never, ever break. No. Matter. What.

The leading actress was killed before rehearsals even began. Replace her with a woman who has never acted on stage before. The director was charged with murder. Have him continue to direct the show as if he didn't have a cloud of doom hanging over his head. And then when things couldn't possibly get any worse, a flat from one of the sets fell onto the actress playing the ingenue, causing her to tumble off the stage and break her ankle. Which was precisely what happened to Tambra in the last few minutes of Tuesday night's rehearsal.

Fortunately, Luke was at the theatre and was able to manually reset the break while they waited for the paramedics to arrive. His quick and efficient action meant that Tambra would heal quicker and only be in a cast for four weeks instead of a few months. She'd be able to shift over to desk duty instead of having to take a short-term disability leave from work, but it also meant she would be the second cast member to have to withdraw from the production. Tambra was an optimist, however, and while she was devastated that she wouldn't be able to share in the opening night glory with the rest of the cast, she was grateful that, unlike the first actress who had to be replaced, she was still alive and could cheer them on from the audience.

But who was going to take Tambra's place in the role of Elaine, the young woman engaged to Mortimer, the nephew of the two elderly homicidal sisters, who was played by Kip? Nola initially asked Jinx to step in, but Father Sal quickly turned down the role on Jinx's behalf. He said he had seen her go undercover during one of her first forays into being an amateur sleuth, portraying a young novice named Sister Maria, and claimed Jinx didn't know the first thing about committing to a character. Jinx couldn't disagree.

While everyone else was panicking and frantically trying to find someone, anyone, to take over the role, Nola remained calm. Alberta, in particular, was impressed with her cool demeanor given the high-level of anxiety everyone else was experiencing. She had always thought of the young woman as emotional and capricious, but seeing the way she responded to this latest obstacle, Alberta pivoted in her perception of her. Nola was actually a competent, levelheaded leader. Alberta had no idea how she was going to solve the current problem she was faced with, but she was confident she would find a solution. And she did. In only two days.

Before the Thursday night rehearsal, which was mandatory for the entire company, Nola gathered everyone into the theatre, walked up to the microphone stand in the center of the stage, and addressed her cast.

"Don't worry, I'm not going to make another long speech," Nola said. "I'll make this short and sweet. As you know, Tambra had an unfortunate accident a few nights ago and has had to withdraw from the production."

The inevitable groans rose up from the crowd.

"I know, it's a total bummer," Nola said. "But in theatre when you have a flop, you flip it. As your producer, that's what I did. Please welcome the newest addition to the *Arsenic and Old Lace* family, Missy Michaels's only living relative, Adrienne Petrocelli."

A huge gasp erupted from the group and then shouts and applause. In contrast, Alberta, Helen, Jinx, and Joyce stared at the young woman on the stage with dropped jaws. Alberta let out a slow whistle and muttered, "*Tondo e tondo e tondo lei va, dove si ferma, nessuno la sa.*"

"You can say that again, Berta," Helen said.

"I didn't catch that, Gram," Jinx whispered in Alberta's ear. "I'm still trying to recover from the shock."

"Round and round and round she goes, where she stops, nobody knows," Joyce translated.

"That sums up Nola all right," Jinx said.

"She's got *faccia tosta*, that one, I'll give her that," Alberta said.

"Are you giving Nola a compliment or taking a swipe at her?" Jinx asked.

"Both," Alberta replied. "She's got real chutzpah to traipse out Missy's niece like a sideshow exhibit."

"That's a little harsh, Berta, don't you think?" Helen asked. "The kid's got a show to put on, and desperate times call for desperate measures."

"Now you're Nola's biggest fan?" Alberta asked. "You used to make fun of her."

"When she was a director, because she was terrible," Helen said. "As a producer, she's top-notch."

"As much as it pains me, I have to agree," Joyce said. "Getting Adrienne to fill in for Tambra is a brilliant marketing ploy."

"Why does it pain you to have to say that, Aunt Joyce?" Jinx asked.

"Because now Sloan and I are going to have to create a whole new marketing campaign to highlight the newest star of the show," Joyce explained.

"That's showbiz, kids," Helen said.

"Isn't it the most exciting business in the world?" Nola asked, joining the group. "One minute you feel like closing out of town and the next a star is born. It's so thrilling, and the fact that you're all involved just makes the journey so much more exciting."

"Congratulations, Nola," Alberta said. "You really pulled the rabbit out of the hat on this one. But I didn't know Adrienne was an actress."

"She isn't professional by any stretch of the imagination," Nola said. "She did perform in college, but mainly because her ex was a theatre major, and she said she knew the play, so when I asked her if she would join us, she said she'd be honored to appear in the show her aunt was supposed to headline."

"She said that?" Alberta asked.

"I think it's going to help her gain closure," Nola said.

"I'm not one to put a damper on things," Helen said.

"You're not?" Alberta asked.

Ignoring her sister and costar, Helen continued, "But is Adrienne going to be able to get up to speed with the rest of us? We open in less than a week."

"That is a concern, and we talked about it and decided it would be best if Adrienne stayed in Tranquility for the next week so she could rehearse during the day with me and Johnny and any other available cast members," Nola explained. "Sanjay even agreed to let Adrienne take over Missy's room at the Arms and stay there for free."

"How much is that gonna cost me?" Joyce asked.

"Just a dinner with him," Nola said. "I hope you don't mind."

"Nah," Joyce replied. "It could be worse. He could want to whisk me off to India for a long weekend."

"That was his first suggestion," Nola confessed. "But I got him to compromise."

"Looks like I owe you," Joyce replied.

"You're doing so much for me and the show already— all of you are—that I'm the one who owes you," Nola said.

"Honey, we're having the time of our lives," Alberta said, fibbing a bit. "You just put all your energy on making this show the best it can possibly be."

"With all of you helping out and Johnny steering the

ship," Nola said, "this show is destined to be a critical and commercial smash."

Unfortunately, from the sound of Johnny's bellowing, it sounded like the show was headed for disaster.

Standing on the stage, he yanked the microphone out of the stand and shouted into it. His voice boomed throughout the theatre. "If party time is over, we still have a show to rehearse! We open in less than a week, people, and we are far from ready. I want my actors on stage now!"

As the night wore on, Johnny's demeanor only got worse once it was evident that Adrienne was not sliding into the role as easily as Nola had implied she could. When Alberta and Jinx met with Adrienne, they'd found her to be straightforward and talkative. The Adrienne who showed up onstage was the opposite; she was shy, quiet, and unsure of herself. She also knew nothing about proper theatre etiquette.

During the blocking of a scene between Adrienne and Kip's characters, Elaine and Mortimer, her cell phone rang and the old song by The Flamingos, "I Only Have Eyes for You," played at full volume.

"You have got to be kidding me!" Johnny shouted. "Do you mind turning off your phone?"

"I'm so sorry," Adrienne said, fumbling with the phone in an attempt to silence it. "It's a marketing call from my alma mater. Like I have money to give to the University of Michigan."

She finally hit the right button and turned her phone off, but not before Johnny started yelling again. "This isn't going to be easy, Adrienne, so I need you to concentrate."

"I will, I promise," she said. "It's just a bit more emotional being here than I thought it would be."

"Whatever you need from me, Adrienne, just let me know," Kip offered.

"What I need is for the two of you to start the scene over from the top," Johnny barked. "Do you think we could make that happen?"

They did make it happen, but they only made it through half of the scene because Adrienne, affected by the tender way Kip was delivering his lines, started to cry. At first, Johnny and Kip thought she was crying in character, but when her crying intensified and it was evident that she wasn't even making an attempt to continue the scene, they realized this was a real-life crying jag. One that quickly looked like it could transform into a real-life breakdown.

Alberta contemplated going up onstage and trying to console Adrienne, who was obviously distraught, when Johnny did what a good director is supposed to do: he consoled his actress. To Alberta's surprise, Johnny embraced Adrienne, who wrapped her arms around him, clearly desperate for physical contact, and whispered something in her ear. Alberta couldn't hear what he was saying, but it seemed to be working because Adrienne's body was no longer shaking and her crying came to an end. But if Johnny had saved the day, why did he look so miserable? And why was he looking over at Nola as if she were his mortal enemy instead of his girlfriend?

"Why don't we take a five-minute break?" Johnny said. He then added through clenched teeth, "Nola! Could I speak with you?"

"Excuse me," Nola said to Jinx. "Johnny needs me."

Jinx watched Nola speedwalk over to the far left of the

theatre where Johnny was waiting for her. As she got closer, Johnny walked behind a large dining room hutch that was going to be used as one of the set pieces in the show and Nola followed him. They were now both out of Jinx's line of vision, but when she raced over to stand on the other side of the hutch, they were still within earshot and she was able to overhear their conversation.

"Do you think you could've warned me about Adrienne?" Johnny hissed.

"I wanted to surprise you," Nola replied.

Jinx was disgusted by the placating tone of Nola's voice. If Freddy ever spoke to her the way Johnny spoke to Nola, she would channel her inner Cher and slap him so hard across the face, his neck would snap. She wished she could slap Johnny and knock some sense into him. He was lucky to have Nola as a girlfriend and should treat her like a princess instead of the scullery maid.

"All you did was make me look like a fool," Johnny seethed.

"How did I do that?"

"By blindsiding me!"

"What was I supposed to do? Just let the show close?" Nola asked. "I couldn't do that after everything we've gone through to get to this point. I thought I was doing you a favor by recruiting Adrienne."

"All *you* had to do was convince her to be in the show," Johnny said. "I have to take this woman, who couldn't shine Missy's shoes, and turn her into a real actress in under a week."

"Johnny, Adrienne's character doesn't have a lot of scenes, and they're mainly with Kip, who can help Adrienne if she goes up on her lines or forgets her blocking," Nola said. "Kip's a pro."

"He's also Missy's killer," Johnny hissed.

"You don't know that."

"So, you think I did it!"

"I didn't say that, stop putting words in my mouth," Nola said. "I think you're both innocent."

"You're half right, I'm innocent and Kip's guilty," Johnny replied. "But I'm the one with a murder charge on his head."

"Because the evidence points to you."

"Nola! You're not making me feel any better."

"The evidence they have at the moment, which is all circumstantial, by the way," Nola added.

"If the cops would do their job, maybe they'd find evidence that would prove Kip murdered Missy and I could get on with my life. Until then, do me a favor, Nola?"

"What?"

"Stop doing me favors!" Johnny yelled.

Johnny was so infuriated that he didn't notice Jinx crouching in front of the hutch when he stormed past her and hoisted himself back up on the stage. He told the cast that their break time was over and he wanted to take it from the top of Act Two. When Nola emerged from behind the hutch, she looked as if she wanted to restart the whole day. She looked weary and upset and frustrated. Mainly, she looked like she could use a friend.

"Don't be mad at me, but I overheard every word Johnny said and innocent or guilty, he shouldn't take out his frustrations on you," Jinx said.

"You have no idea what he's going through, Jinx," Nola replied.

"It doesn't matter," Jinx said. "He's acting like a total jerk and someone has got to tell him to stop."

"And you've appointed yourself the person to do

that?" Nola asked. "Stay out of my relationship, Jinx, I'm warning you."

"Nola, how can you defend him when he could have committed murder?" Jinx asked.

"Because I know that he's innocent."

"How can you be so sure?"

"Because I know how frightening it is to be accused of a crime you didn't commit," Nola replied. "He's acting the same way I did."

"No, he isn't, Nola. I was there, remember? You weren't lashing out at people who were trying to help you," Jinx said. "This is all a game to him, an act, and he's lying too."

"He is not a liar!"

"I know that his real name is Gianni Fennacacculi?" Jinx confessed.

"What are you talking about?"

"Johnny Fenn is a made-up name, he changed it," Jinx explained. "I can tell from your expression that this isn't news to you. You already know Johnny's lying."

"You're lying."

"Grow up, Nola! Maybe Johnny isn't a murderer, but he's definitely not good enough for you."

Nola turned to get as far from Jinx as she could and ran right into Bruno's arms. Bruno grabbed Nola's shoulders to steady her and held on a few seconds longer than necessary. He looked down into her eyes, and Jinx could see that he was searching for the right thing to say, but before he could speak, she broke free and ran out of the theatre.

"What did you say to her?" Bruno asked.

"I told her that her boyfriend is a liar, and she knows it's true, but for some reason she won't break up with him," Jinx replied.

"Nola's not going to leave him now that he's facing a

murder charge," Bruno said. "She's too decent a person to do that."

"You mean she's too dumb a person," Jinx said. "She needs someone who's going to treat her with respect and protect her, instead of accusing her of making his life more miserable than it already is."

She looked up and saw that Bruno wasn't even listening to her, he was staring at the doors leading to the lobby, where Nola might be at this very second if she hadn't left the building.

"Someone like you," Jinx said.

"What do you mean, someone like me?" Bruno asked.

"You have to stop lying too, Bruno," Jinx said.

"Lying about what?" he asked.

"Your feelings for Nola," Jinx replied.

"I'm not in love with Nola," Bruno protested.

Jinx didn't respond, she just smiled at him and waited for him to realize what she already knew.

"I shouldn't. I mean, she's given me more legal headaches than any woman ever should," Bruno said. "But . . . there is just something about her that despite all my misgivings and my better judgment makes me want to protect her and hold her and, well, there you have it, I'm in love with her. Are you happy now that I said it and proved you right? I hope you're happy, because I'm not happy because it doesn't matter what I think or feel, Nola's only got eyes for the loudmouthed director."

Jinx smiled. Hearing Bruno's nervous confession was heartwarming, but she also figured out how he could tug at Nola's heartstrings. "I know the perfect way to make Nola forget about Johnny and fall in love with you."

"This is not the time to toy with me, Jinx," Bruno

warned. "Swedes don't condone violence, but Sicilians have a history of aggressive behavior."

"I'm not toying with you," Jinx said. "All you have to do is make her jealous."

"And how am I going to accomplish that?" Bruno asked.

"By going out with another woman," Jinx said, smiling a very pleased-with-herself smile as she put her hands on her hips.

"Nola isn't going to get jealous if she sees me going out on a date with you," Bruno said. "Freddy might punch me, but Nola wouldn't raise an eyebrow."

"You're not going to go on a date with me," Jinx replied.

"Then who am I going on a date with?" Bruno asked.

"Adrienne."

CHAPTER 25

I bravi ragazzi non finiscono sempre per ultimi.

"You're playing matchmaker between Bruno and Adrienne?" Alberta asked. "Lovey, that's playing a dangerous game."

"Gram, we're investigating two violent murders," Jinx replied. "How can playing Cupid be dangerous?"

"Because once you're dead the pain is gone," Alberta said. "If Bruno gets his heart broken, he's going to carry that ache around with him for the rest of his life."

Jinx held Lola closer to her face and rubbed her cheek on her fur. She wasn't receiving any comforting words from her grandmother, maybe she'd get some solace from her favorite cat. Lola, however, proved she was her mother's cat daughter and let out a noise that was part meow and part purr and jumped from Jinx's arms to the kitchen floor. She stretched her lean limbs, did a quick, full-body shake, and sauntered off into the living room. There would be no more Lola love this morning.

"You think I made a big mistake butting my nose in where it doesn't belong?" Jinx asked.

"I think your intentions came from a good place, lovey," Alberta said as she placed the plate of scrambled eggs and tofu bacon in front of Jinx. "I'm just worried that this isn't going to end well."

"Because you don't trust Adrienne?" Jinx asked.

"I don't trust the heart," Alberta replied.

"Sorry, Gram, I don't understand."

Alberta turned to the stove and transferred the rest of the eggs onto her plate, but added real bacon instead of the imitation meat Jinx preferred. The bacon was crisp on the edges, with a healthy proportion of fat, just the way Alberta liked it. It was good to be fortified with a hearty meal when you had to tell your twenty-seven-year-old granddaughter about the birds and the bees. Not the physical elements of the story, but the emotional ramifications.

Once again, Alberta was fascinated that Jinx could be so self-assured and mature in certain aspects of her life and yet be so ignorant in others. She didn't know if it was a quality Jinx shared with other young women her age—Nola certainly was more street-smart—or if it was unique to her granddaughter.

"Even in the best matchmaking scenarios, there's always a chance the relationship between the two people you're setting up will go *fuori dai binari*, off the rails." Alberta paused and took a bite of bacon, savoring its smoky flavor before she continued. "But here you have four people involved."

"But only Bruno and Adrienne are going to go out on a date," Jinx said.

"And they're going to bring Johnny and Nola along for the ride as emotional baggage," Alberta explained.

"I never thought of it like that, but it makes sense," Jinx said. "I mean, the whole reason behind Bruno hooking up with Adrienne is to make Nola jealous."

"Exactly!" Alberta cried. "But it isn't just Nola's emotions you're playing with, it's Johnny and Adrienne's too."

"And if three's a crowd, what does four make?" Jinx asked. "A hostile gang?"

"Nothing may come of it, lovey, but we know Nola's emotional and impetuous. She has a long, complicated history with Bruno, and I suspect she has feelings for the boy she's never truly explored," Alberta said. "We also know Johnny has a temper, so who knows how he'll react if he catches his girlfriend getting upset that Bruno's out with somebody other than her."

"And then there's Adrienne," Jinx said.

"She's the wildest wild card of them all," Alberta said. "I mean, what do we really know about her?"

"On the surface she appears to be pretty cool, but she's kind of a contradiction, Gram," Jinx said. "When we interviewed her, she was blasé about Missy, she didn't get emotional, and, in fact, told us she didn't even consider the woman to be part of her family."

"Then, when she was onstage, she suddenly burst into tears," Alberta said.

"And why was she onstage in the first place?"

"What do you mean, lovey?"

Jinx gobbled up her breakfast and, in between bites, described her concerns. "She isn't an actress, she has no sentimental connection to her dead aunt, and yet when Nola suggested she take over Tambra's part in the play, she immediately said yes and even agreed to move to Tranquility for a few weeks when she works a half hour away in Parsippany," Jinx said. "When you break it down, it doesn't make sense."

Alberta scooped up a healthy forkful of eggs and chewed it slowly, ruminating on the details Jinx laid out. Once she had a chance to digest the information as well as the thick and fluffy eggs, she reversed her original position. Jinx hadn't made a mistake grabbing hold of Cupid's arrow, she'd made an insightful maneuver that might actually help them solve this case.

"It makes all the sense in the world, lovey," Alberta declared.

"What?" Jinx asked. "You were just telling me I was playing with fire trying to shove Bruno into Adrienne's arms."

"I was wrong. We need to learn more about Adrienne, and what better way to do that than when her defenses are down while she's on a date? Especially if Bruno keeps refilling her glass with wine," Alberta said. "And do you know what will make the date even better?"

"If we strap a wiretap on Bruno and listen in on their conversation?" Jinx asked.

"Why use a wiretap when you can be there yourself?" Alberta asked. "You and Freddy are going to join them and make it a double date."

"Gram, for an old lady of a certain generation you are totally with it!" Jinx exclaimed.

"That's exactly what Sloan said to me last night," Alberta said.

Jinx's howls of shocked laughter roared throughout

the house and sparked Lola's interest. The cat returned to the kitchen and placed her front paws on Jinx's knee. Unable to resist Lola's public display of affection, Jinx grabbed her around the belly and lifted her high up in the air. Unafraid, Lola closed her eyes and purred, and Jinx lowered her arms and cradled the cat like a baby.

"I'd love to play with you all day, Miss Gina Lollabrigida, but I have to get ready for a hot date," Jinx said.

"Do you think Freddy will go along with the plan?" Alberta asked.

"Freddy'll do whatever I tell him to do," Jinx said. "But I am worried Bruno is going to chicken out."

Alberta got up and walked around the table to take Lola from Jinx's arms. The cat did not appreciate Alberta's interference and voiced her displeasure loudly.

"*Zitto!*" Alberta cried. "Shoosh, Lola, we have to let Jinx alone so she can go play *paraninfa.*"

"What's that?"

"Matchmaker," Alberta said.

She kissed Jinx on the cheek and said, "Now go on and get out of here, and make us all proud and prove once and for all that *I bravi ragazzi non finiscono sempre per ultimi.*"

"Whatever that means," Jinx said, "I'll try to prove it."

Jinx returned a kiss to Alberta's cheek, planted one on the top of Lola's head, and dashed out of the kitchen. Alberta swayed Lola from side to side and sighed. "I have a feeling Jinx isn't going to make good on her promise, Lola. Because no matter how hard they try, nice guys always wind up finishing last."

* * *

When Freddy's electric-blue Ford Ranger pulled up in front of Bruno's condo complex, Jinx was afraid her plan had gone awry before it was even set into motion. The most important part of the equation was Bruno, and he was nowhere to be found. Without him there could be no double date. And if there wasn't a double date, she wouldn't be able to find out what Adrienne was hiding.

"Did you tell him to be outside at 7:30?" Freddy asked.

"Yes, and I texted him when we left," Jinx replied.

"Dude's got cold feet," Freddy said.

"Dude cut himself shaving and had to wait for his chin to stop bleeding."

Freddy turned to look out the driver's side window and saw Bruno glaring at him.

"Bruno, what're you doing over there?" Freddy asked.

"I live in this complex," Bruno said, pointing behind him. "Not the one over there."

"Sorry, Bruno, my fault," Jinx said. "Kip's poor direction must be rubbing off. Hop in so we can pick up Adrienne."

Since the Ranger was a two-door, Bruno ran around to the passenger side and struggled to get into the back seat while Jinx leaned forward and pulled the back of her seat up so Bruno could squeeze in.

"Tell me again why I'm playing along with this charade?" Bruno asked when he finally got into the car and Freddy started to drive off.

"Freddy, speed it up if you could," Jinx said. "I made reservations at the Black Forest Inn for eight o'clock."

"I made reservations there too, for the same time," Bruno said. "Klaus, the maître d', is going to kill me."

"Klaus is cool," Freddy said. "I saved his life on a diving trip once, so he owes me."

"You see Bruno, there's absolutely nothing to worry about," Jinx said.

"Then why do I feel sick to my stomach?" Bruno commented.

"Has it been that long since you've been on a date?" Freddy asked.

"This isn't a date," Bruno declared.

"You're right about that, Bruno," Jinx said. "This is a top-secret mission and it's time to get serious."

Clearly Adrienne didn't get Jinx's memo about the serious nature of the evening's festivities because when she saw Bruno struggle to get out of the back seat of the truck, she threw back her head and let out a raucous laugh.

"Madame," Bruno said, trying to make the best of an awkward situation. "Your, um, chariot awaits."

As Adrienne climbed into the back seat, she turned to Bruno and smiled, "I feel like I'm back in the boondocks."

"I can promise you one thing," Bruno said.

"What's that?" Adrienne asked.

"The restaurant has indoor plumbing."

Once again Adrienne's laughter filled the air. Maybe the evening wouldn't be so bad after all.

True to his word, Freddy was able to smooth things over with Klaus and the maître d' didn't even mention the reservation snafu. They followed Klaus to a spacious booth that was much more comfortable than the bucket seats in Freddy's truck and overlooked a lush expanse of trees that looked like an enchanted forest when the moon-glow shined down on them.

Jinx was relieved to see that Bruno started to lighten up after drinking his first glass of merlot and even began asking Adrienne questions about her life back in Michigan and how she was enjoying living in New Jersey. Their conversation was flowing nicely, Adrienne seemed forthcoming in her responses and, surprisingly, a tad flirtatious given that Jinx and Freddy were inches away. The double date was off to a successful start and Jinx almost felt guilty about what she was going to do next. But if she wanted to find out the dirt on Adrienne, she was going to have to manipulate the conversation.

"Did you grow up in Deer Isle, Adrienne?" Jinx asked.

"No, I grew up in Rockport, which is close by," she explained. "When my grandmother, Angela, married Enrico Petrocelli, they moved there and opened up a small lobster fishing business on the Penobscot Bay."

"Whenever I think of Maine, I never think of it having any kind of Italian population," Freddy said.

"The Miccalizzos were fishermen from Sicily," Adrienne said. "When they came to the States, they felt right at home in Maine."

"Then how did everyone get to Michigan?" Jinx asked, refilling Adrienne's glass with more wine. "That's in the middle of the country, there can't be that many fishing opportunities there."

Bruno opened his mouth to respond to Jinx's comment, but Adrienne proved to be a much faster talker.

"Michigan is part of the Great Lakes region," Adrienne said. "My grandparents moved there to open up their own fishery operation, and for a while business was booming, but after a few years the whole area was over-populated with fishermen all trying to make an honest living and they went bankrupt."

"I'm so sorry to hear that," Jinx said. "What did they do after that?"

"Moved around the area, taking odd jobs, finally set-tling down in the little town of Harrietta, on the western side of the state," Adrienne said, draining her second glass of wine.

After a while, the boys stopped trying to participate in the conversation and just listened to Jinx and Adrienne talk. It also gave them more time to devote to their meal, which was authentically German and authentically deli-cious.

"It's such a sin that your grandmother and her sister never reconciled," Jinx said. "It's like my mother and my grandmother."

"They don't talk to each other?" Adrienne asked.

"Nope, they had some silly fight years ago and now it's been over a decade," Jinx shared. "I know they both still love and miss each other, but I guess they're too stubborn to admit they were wrong and reach out."

"From what I know, Missy let her business managers handle all her money and alienate her from her family so they could control her and make her a big star," Adrienne said. "By the time Missy was an adult, there was too much water under the bridge for her to reconcile with anyone. I don't even know if she knew where my grand-mother lived."

"Family dynamics can be a minefield," Jinx said. "I've only started to feel comfortable enough to talk about my mother in any detail in front of my grandmother."

Adrienne took another gulp of wine and agreed. "I remember my grandmother getting drunk and saying the worst things about her sister, and then the next day she'd profess her love for her and say that Missy Michaels was the most wonderful woman who ever lived." Adrienne poured herself some more wine from the second carafe the waiter had placed on their table only moments earlier. "My grandmother was a very complicated woman."

"I suspect Missy was too," Jinx said.

"She was a bitch."

The only one who didn't react to Adrienne's catty comment was Adrienne. But that was because Adrienne was rip-roaring drunk. The wine was finished before dessert was served, but Adrienne jumped on the waiter's suggestion that German coffee spiked with Kirschwasser brandy would be the ideal liquid companion to their peach kuchen, a standard German dessert.

By the time they left the restaurant, Bruno needed to hold Adrienne up at the waist to make sure she remained vertical until they got to the truck. It took Freddy's assistance to get Adrienne safely in the back seat, but once Adrienne was seated, she started to nod off. In the front seat, Jinx felt bad for her role in getting Adrienne blitzed, especially because she didn't think any of the gossip she'd shared about her family would prove useful to their investigation.

When they pulled up to the Tranquility Arms, Bruno had to nudge Adrienne several times until she woke up from her nap on the drive there.

"Let me help you up to your room," Bruno offered.

"No!" Adrienne yelled. "I want Jinx to take me."

"It's no problem at all," Bruno said, not fully understanding the reason for Adrienne's protest.

"I'm drunk and you want to take advantage of me," Adrienne slurred.

Now that he understood why Adrienne wanted Jinx instead of him as her chaperone, he was shocked. "I would never do that, I swear."

"They all swear, all you men lie," Adrienne said, grabbing onto the headrest in front of her in an attempt to sit up. "Just ask my ex."

"I can assure you, Adrienne, I'm nothing like your ex," Bruno affirmed.

"You know who my ex is?" Adrienne asked.

For a split second, Adrienne was lucid; all the alcohol had seeped out of her body as she stared at Bruno with fear in her eyes. Bruno didn't see Adrienne's fright; he was still more concerned with trying to convince her that all he wanted to do was get her safely to her room. Jinx, however, could tell by looking at Adrienne that she would never let that happen.

"It's all right, Bruno, I'll take her," Jinx said.

The two women slowly walked around the front porch to room 8, where Adrienne was staying. When they got to the door, Adrienne twisted the doorknob and walked right in. Before Jinx could make a comment about her entering the room without putting her key in the lock, Adrienne turned around and said good-bye.

"Maybe I should come in," Jinx said. "To make sure you get to bed safely. You really did have a lot to drink."

"I'm fine," Adrienne replied, suddenly more sober than she'd been for most of the night. "The nap I took on the ride home cleared my head."

Jinx tried to peer into the room, but Adrienne stood tall and blocked her view. "If you're sure."

"I am," Adrienne said. "Thanks for a fun night, and please thank Bruno for me too. I didn't mean to come off as rude."

Before Jinx could reply, Adrienne shut the door. Jinx stood on the other side for a moment, not sure why but suspecting that Adrienne was hiding something. After half a minute of silence, Jinx retreated back to Freddy's Ford.

It wasn't until they started to drive away that Jinx realized her suspicions had been right. Some*one*—not some-*thing*—had been hiding nearby. Across the street from the Tranquility Arms was parked a yellow Jeep. It was the same kind of car Kip drove.

CHAPTER 26

Alcuni bambini non crescono mai.

One of the best and worst things about putting on a show was technical rehearsal. Or simply *tech*, as theatre savvy folks referred to it. Some people relished the experience, others would rather deliberately cut themselves and then swim with sharks.

Tech is when the actors are forced to play second fiddle to the behind-the-scenes technical designers and stage crew. Finishing touches were made to the set, lighting cues were implemented, quick costume changes were refined, and the sound system was fine-tuned. And the days were long. They were known in the industry as *10 out of 12s*, referring to the ten hours Actors' Equity, the union for stage actors, will allow its members to work in a twelve-hour period. On a Broadway show, tech rehearsals could last over a week; at St. Winifred's Academy, everything had to be completed in one day.

With opening night looming on the very near horizon and only twenty-four hours to make sure all the technical details of the show were locked-in, safe, and artistically acceptable, it was no surprise to even a stage novice like Alberta to find the air fraught with tension. Anxiety levels were high, stress was palpable, and patience was an extinct commodity. Luckily, Alberta had grown up in a loud, crowded Italian family, so she felt right at home.

"This is so much fun!"

By the look on Nola's face, Alberta could tell the woman disagreed with her exclamation.

"You don't have any antacid in your pocketbook, do you?" Nola asked.

"I'm sorry, honey, I don't," Alberta replied. She then pulled out something from her purse wrapped in tinfoil. "I do have part of a prosciutto and capicola sandwich—oh, and fresh mozzarella, the tiny balls like in my *antipasti*; that might settle your stomach."

"Mrs. Scaglione, you know I love you and your food, but if I took a bit of any of that, I'd hurl," Nola said.

"Don't be so nervous," Alberta said. "This is the exciting part. Your dream is about to come true."

Nola smiled a queasy smile. "It's thrilling, it really is, and I love tech rehearsal, but there's so much that can go wrong from here on in."

Alberta was going to tell Nola that she was imagining things but stopped herself because the woman was right. A two-time murderer was still at large and was quite possibly in the theatre with them at that moment, two actors in the cast—Alberta included—had barely memorized their lines and still forgot some of their blocking, and they had yet to run through the entire show from start to finish. When Alberta thought about it, the potential for disaster was high. For some reason, however, she wasn't concerned. It probably had to do with the fact that she was a novice and didn't really understand the pressure of performing in front of an audience, but mainly it was because she was going to be onstage in every scene with her sister. She trusted Helen with her life; why shouldn't she trust her with her performance?

"You're much more experienced than I am," Alberta said. "But from where I'm standing, it looks like everything is under control."

Someone shouted from backstage and the lights shut off just as a loud crash was heard from somewhere in the wings.

"You call that under control?" Nola asked.

"Honey, this is calm and orderly in comparison to what happened at my cousin Matty's second wedding," Alberta said. "Let's just say it involved several doves, a flame thrower, and a belly dancer. I don't see any birds, nothing's on fire, and as long as you don't expect Helen or me to dress like harem girls, we're ahead of the game."

Nola burst into ripples of laughter and threw her arms around Alberta.

"Thank you for that, Mrs. Scaglione," Nola said. "I know you made up that story to make me feel better, but it worked."

"Nola!"

This time it was Johnny's voice that reverberated through the theatre.

"Sounds like somebody needs me," Nola said. "Excuse me."

Nola nearly collided into Helen and Jinx as she ran down the aisle, she was so focused on getting to Johnny she didn't even notice them.

"That girl is going to collapse from exhaustion if she doesn't slow down," Alberta said.

"She's in charge of a million little details that need to be taken care of before we open," Helen said. "She'll relax once the rave reviews come out."

"I told her that we got through Cousin Matty's wedding and she thought I was making it up," Alberta said.

"The first or the second wedding?" Helen asked.

"The second of course," Alberta replied.

"What's the difference between the two of them?" Jinx asked.

"After his first wedding he had to spend his honeymoon in jail," Alberta explained. "But at the second wedding, the police weren't even called."

"Sounds like the night I had last night," Jinx said. "I got in too late to call you, and then you've been tied up with tech all morning."

"That's all right, lovey, tell us now," Alberta said.

"I got Adrienne drunk like you suggested, Gram, and she confirmed a lot of what we already knew about Missy," Jinx said. "But after we dropped her off, guess whose car we spotted across that street from the Tranquility Arms?"

"Johnny's?" Alberta guessed.

"Nope, the other suspect," Jinx replied.

"What was Kip's car doing parked across the street from where Adrienne is staying?" Alberta asked.

"He was either stalking Adrienne and broke into her room," Jinx surmised, "or he had rehearsal last night and parked there; it's only a block away."

"He's a stalker," Helen said.

"How do you know?" Alberta asked.

"I was here last night with Joyce, Father Sal, and some of Nola's students painting the set," Helen explained.

"*Dio mio!*" Alberta exclaimed. "Every time I cut that boy some slack, he does something to make me think I've been duped. I want to trust him, but I just don't think I can."

"Kip!"

And now it was Helen's voice that echoed throughout the theatre.

"Helen, what are you doing?" Alberta asked.

"I've had it with him and his lying," she replied. "Every time I'm onstage with him, I'm thinking the only one in the cast *not* playing a murderer could really *be* a murderer. He's pulling me out of character and I won't stand for it anymore."

"Helen, is something wrong?" Kip said, running up to them.

Helen pointed her finger at Kip's face and shook it wildly, "Why are you stalking Adrienne?"

"I'm not stalking Adrienne," Kip stated.

"Thank God," Alberta said. "At least we settled that."

"I'm stalking Johnny," Kip said.

"Why are you stalking Johnny?" Alberta asked.

"Because I know he's the one who killed Missy and I want to prove it," Kip said.

"We all want to find out who killed Missy," Jinx said, "but that doesn't explain why your Jeep was parked across the street from the Tranquility Arms last night. We saw you when we brought Adrienne home."

"I saw you too," Kip said. "I was crouched down in the front seat of the car."

"But that still doesn't explain why you were there in the first place!" Helen cried.

"Because last night I was following him! And I followed him right to the Tranquility Arms!"

Every head in the theatre snapped in the direction of where Kip was pointing, which meant that every head in the theatre was now looking at Johnny. The noise of tech died away and in its place was a hushed silence as everyone waited for the scene to play out. The next line didn't come from either Johnny or Kip, but from Nola.

"Why were you at the Tranquility Arms last night?" Nola asked.

As the director, Johnny was the one who told everyone else what to do; he was not used to having to perform in front of an audience. He was also not used to being confronted by an angry girlfriend in public.

"I can explain everything, Nola," he said, trying to keep his voice calm. "Let's go into your office so we can talk privately."

"I'm not going anywhere with you until you tell me the truth!" Nola cried. "I covered up your lie about your real name and now you lie to me about where you were last night. You said you needed to rest, that's why you couldn't help us paint the set."

"I wasn't lying," Johnny said.

"You were just cheating on Nola with Adrienne!" Kip shouted.

"Shut up, Kip!" Adrienne screamed. "Johnny isn't cheating on Nola with me."

"I'm not cheating on Nola with anyone," Johnny cried. "*Especially* Adrienne."

Alberta turned to Helen and whispered, "What does he mean, 'especially Adrienne?'"

"I have no idea, Berta, but if our scenes are this good

on opening night," Helen replied, "*The Herald* is going to give us five stars."

"If you're not sleeping with Adrienne, what are you doing with her, Johnny?" Nola asked.

"Come on, Johnny, tell her!" Kip yelled. "Then tell everyone how you killed Missy!"

"I didn't kill Missy!" Johnny shouted. "You killed Missy!"

"*Oh caro Dio in cielo*," Alberta said, throwing a fist into the air. "If either one of you killed Missy, you know we're going to be able to prove it, don't you forget that. But first, Johnny, you need to tell Nola what you were doing at Adrienne's last night."

"And if you don't tell me right here and now, I swear to God I will cancel this show before we even open!" Nola shouted.

The entire cast started screaming at Johnny to start talking and explain what he was doing with Adrienne when he was supposed to be with Nola. Alberta thought she was suddenly cast in the stage version of *Frankenstein* and they were rehearsing the scene where the villagers storm the castle with pitchforks and torches.

"I was with Adrienne because of you!" Johnny shouted. "I was giving her private acting lessons so she would shine in the part like everyone else is. I got to her room early and the door was open, so I waited for her until she got back. I know I can be a jerk, Nola, but I've been trying to make this the best damn play you ever produced because I love you!"

The entire group sighed with delight as the horror show suddenly turned into a romantic comedy.

"You love me?" Nola asked.

"Yes, you idiot!" Johnny cried. "I would never look at another woman when I can look at you."

Nola was on the verge of tears, but perhaps remembering what Alberta had told her earlier, she shook her head to prevent them from flowing and embraced her boyfriend. They kissed passionately and almost all the onlookers swooned.

Out of the corner of her eye, Alberta saw Adrienne walk up the aisle from the lip of the stage and thought she was going to leave the theatre; instead she marched right up to Bruno, who was standing nearby. "Tell me the truth, Bruno, was our date last night a setup so Jinx could get into my room?"

Alberta knew before Bruno spoke that he was going to tell the truth. He was, after all, one of the good guys. "It was a setup, but I swear to you it was never our intention to search your room."

"Like hell it wasn't," Adrienne barked. "You stay out of my things, Bruno, do you understand me?"

"Loud and clear," Bruno replied.

Adrienne stood stock-still for a few moments, staring at the floor, her fists clenched. Alberta thought she looked like one of her children when they would have a temper tantrum. She thought of something her grandmother Marie would say when she saw an adult acting like a baby, *Alcuni bambini non crescono mai*. Some children never grow up. She wondered what her grandmother would say about Adrienne. It was understandable that the woman would be upset that her date had been fake, but why did she assume Jinx wanted to search her room? What did she have to hide?

"I need the following people onstage right now," Johnny shouted. "Bruno, Father Sal, Luke, Benny, Kip, and Adrienne. The rest of you have a twenty-minute break, but don't go far, we're in a time crunch, people. We open tomorrow night!"

Those four words made everyone forget about Johnny the loudmouth and Johnny the cheater; from this critical moment on, he was only Johnny the director, just as Missy had dubbed him. As much as Alberta wanted to see if any more fireworks would start while he was directing the explosive trio of Kip, Bruno, and Adrienne in a scene, she wanted to use her time wisely.

Alberta turned to her sister, but before she said a word, Helen spoke for her. "We're going to break into Adrienne's room at the Arms, aren't we?"

"I love that you can read my mind," Alberta gushed.

"It'll come in handy when we're in side-by-side cells," Helen replied.

"If we're going to sneak in without Sanjay calling the police, we're going to need Joyce's help," Alberta said.

"I already texted her," Helen replied. "She's waiting outside for us with Sloan."

"Helen, you've thought of everything," Alberta said.

"What are big sisters for?" Helen asked.

Alberta was grateful that her sister-in-law was a fashionista. Regardless of where she was going, Joyce was always dressed to the nines. So even though she thought she'd be spending the entire night at St. Winifred's in tech, she was perfectly outfitted to play the femme fatale. And judging from the way Sanjay was ogling her, Alberta could tell that he couldn't think of anything else except how beautiful Joyce looked standing in the middle of the lobby of the Tranquility Arms.

Her black crepe pants tapered at the ankle and were topped with a gold, cashmere V-neck sweater. Instead of a belt, she wore a black-and-gold-striped silk scarf tied in a knot at her waist that fell to her knee. In place of her trademark gold hoops, her earrings were three black pearls stacked on top of one another that matched perfectly with her chunky, black pearl necklace. Black, backless pumps completed the outfit that Joyce described as "1940s glam meets 1980s disco." Joyce loved the look and, better yet, so did Sanjay.

Peeking out from around the corner of the hallway, making sure she couldn't be seen, Alberta watched Sanjay. Her plan was working, he couldn't keep his eyes off of Joyce.

"Joyce Perkins Ferrara!" Sanjay screamed when he saw her. "Have you finally come to your senses and decided to run away with me?"

"I can't run anywhere," she cried. "I was walking to my car from St. Winifred's and twisted my ankle."

Falling right into her trap, Sanjay ran out from behind the front desk as Joyce plopped into one of the chairs in the lobby. Sanjay dropped to his knees and grabbed Joyce's ankle to examine it.

"It's the other ankle," Joyce said.

Dutifully, Sanjay dropped one ankle and picked up the other. Joyce moaned at his touch, and when she saw Sloan enter the lobby, she let out a cry to camouflage the sound of the door opening. Sanjay let out an even louder cry when he thought he hurt Joyce, which hid any sound Sloan might have made as he grabbed the key to Adrienne's room from the hook behind the front desk.

Joyce maneuvered herself in the chair, causing Sanjay to have to turn slightly right as Sloan ran from behind the front desk to the hallway where he met Alberta. Joyce let out a sigh of relief now that her part of the plan was completed. Alberta gave her a quick nod before disappearing with Sloan down the hallway. Her part was just beginning.

Sloan ran down the hallway, followed by Alberta, and met Helen in front of room 8, waving the key triumphantly in his hand. They silently cheered Sloan on as he opened the door. Alberta only had time to give him a quick celebratory kiss on the cheek before following Helen into the room; the clock was ticking and they only had a few minutes to scour Adrienne's room for clues.

They found what they were looking for in literally less than one.

Sitting right on the bench at the end of the bed was the cardboard box decorated in daisies that Alberta had seen in Adrienne's apartment. What was it doing here? Surely Adrienne didn't need to bring Post-its, paper clips, and old CDs with her to prepare for her stage debut. Alberta didn't have time to wonder what was in the box, she just opened it. She did not find what she hoped she would. The box didn't contain anything about Missy, but what it did contain would tell them everything they needed to know about Kip.

CHAPTER 27

*Onorevoli colleghi, vi prego di dare il benvenuto alla
signora dell'ora.*

Since Alberta started her foray into the investigative
arts, she'd prided herself in trusting her instincts. For
decades, she'd ignored the ping in the pit of her stomach
that tried to alert her to a dangerous situation or a person
who was better avoided than accepted. She assumed the
men around her knew better than she did, and if they
weren't voicing concerns or noticing red flags, why should
she? Everything changed, however, when she moved to
Tranquility and started working with her female relatives.
For the past few years, instead of refusing to listen to her
intuition, she turned up the volume, so not only could she
benefit from her sixth sense, but those around her could
as well. She had finally found her girl power.

But as she held the box that she found in Adrienne's
hotel room, a very large part of her wished she hadn't lis-

tened to her inner voice. If only she had turned a blind eye to its nagging, as Sammy had often turned away from her. Had she done that, she could have kept thinking Kip was a good guy: quirky, possessing a very active imagination, but ultimately harmless. The contents of the box proved otherwise.

Jinx, Joyce, Helen, and Sloan sat around Alberta's kitchen table, glasses filled with Red Herrings in front of them, a half-eaten Entenmann's blueberry crumb cake awaiting further destruction, and although they had all sat around this table many times before, they knew this time was different. Alberta wasn't eager to share the information she'd uncovered and they, sensing her apprehension, were not eager to hear it. But when they formed the unofficial Ferrara Family Detective Agency, they promised that once they took on a case, they would see it through to the end. They would do whatever they could to expose criminals even if one of those criminals had quickly become a friend.

Alberta made the sign of the cross and kissed the gold crucifix she never removed from her neck. The others knew it was an indication that Alberta was asking for guidance, and possibly forgiveness, for what she was about to do next. Which was to reveal Kip's hidden past.

"What's in this box fills in the blanks about Kip's criminal record," Alberta announced. "And it is worse than we could ever have thought."

"But Gram," Jinx said. "That's the same box we found at Adrienne's and it contained nothing but junk."

"It's either a different box with the same design," Alberta said. "Or she replaced her old junk with old evidence."

"What kind of evidence, Berta?" Sloan asked.

"The kind that tells me I misjudged the boy all along," Alberta replied. "And proves that Johnny may be right: Kip could be our murderer."

"Whatever's in that box is obviously disturbing," Helen said. "But it's late, we're tired, and we need to know what we're dealing with, so tell us."

"Whatever it is, Berta, we'll all handle it together," Joyce added.

Alberta lifted the top from the box and took another look at the papers inside. She pulled them out and placed them on the table. "These are Kip's unsealed court documents."

"Oh my God!" Jinx exclaimed. "How did Adrienne get her hands on those?"

"Vinny told me they're impossible to get without a court order," Jinx said. "He's still waiting on a response to the motion he filed to get them unsealed."

"She must have stolen them from the court or bribed someone on the inside to make copies for her," Sloan said.

"I don't know how she got them, but they're here," Alberta said. "Read them yourselves."

Alberta passed around the papers, and one by one, they gasped when they read the indictment and the charges that were brought against Kip. They were devastated, and the findings made them rethink their entire investigation.

"Two years ago, Kip's boyfriend, Wesley Henderson, vanished and Kip was arrested for his murder," Alberta exclaimed. "Eyewitnesses testified that in the weeks leading up to Wesley's disappearance, the couple had been fighting, there was at least one physical altercation, and they found traces of Wesley's blood in the driveway of the house they shared in Deer Isle."

"Wes!" Jinx cried. "That's the name that was mentioned in that theatre chat room I found. No one said who he was, but they must all have known."

"According to the documents, the weekend Wesley disappeared, Kip was attending a legal conference in Bangor," Alberta continued. "But the hotel security camera captured him leaving the hotel at one a.m. and not returning until four. He was never able to adequately account for what happened during those three hours, but a round-trip car ride from Bangor to Deer Isle and back takes a little over three hours."

"His absence is suspect, but three hours wouldn't be long enough for Kip to drive home, kill his boyfriend, dispose of the body, and return to his hotel," Joyce said.

"That's exactly what his lawyers argued," Alberta replied. "His absence during that time was questionable but hardly airtight evidence to prove he killed Wesley."

"But was Wesley really killed?" Jinx asked. "His body was never found."

"There needs to be significant circumstantial and forensic evidence to support corpus delicti," Sloan said. "Or a charge of murder without the presence of a dead body."

"The court believed Wesley was murdered and that Kip did the deed," Alberta said, "but the jury believed otherwise, and Kip was acquitted."

"But why were his documents sealed?" Helen asked.

"From what Vinny told me, the safety of the person being charged, in this case Kip, has to be seen as more important than the public's right to know the details of the case," Jinx explained.

"Maybe with the body never being found and the fact that the real murderer could still be at large, they worried about Kip's safety," Sloan suggested.

"Anything is possible," Alberta said. "All we know is that Kip has now been involved in two murders, possibly three if you count Brandon, and I know that it all may be a coincidence or really bad luck, but it makes me question everything I've thought about that young man."

"I can't believe all of this is unfolding on the night before we open," Helen said. "I was really starting to find my groove as Martha Brewster, I hope this doesn't derail me."

"Helen, you're going to steal the show tomorrow night and you know it," Alberta said. "But the rest of us should get a good night's rest. We have a big day tomorrow."

"I hate to be accused of mansplaining," Sloan said, "but don't you think this information you found about Kip should be turned over to the police?"

"You know, Sloan," Alberta said, "for a man, you can sometimes be right."

Despite the late hour, Alberta knew that Vinny would want to be briefed on Kip's backstory. When she called him, however, he didn't want to listen to her, he wanted her to open her back door.

"Vinny!" Alberta exclaimed, opening up her kitchen door. "What the hell are you doing here at this hour?"

"You're the only one I know in this town who still has a VCR, Alfie," Vinny replied. "Where else would I go to watch a videotape?"

They all sat on Alberta's couch as Vinny put the video into the VCR; even Lola woke up to join the impromptu screening. He faced everyone and said, "*Onorevoli colleghi, vi prego di dare il benvenuto alla signora dell'ora.*"

"I caught the ladies-and-gentlemen part," Jinx said, "but lost everything else."

"Please welcome the lady of the hour," Alberta said.

"What lady?" Joyce asked.

Vinny pressed Play and they were shocked to see Missy's face once again on a TV screen. She was the lady of the hour, but this time it wasn't vintage Missy Michaels, it was what she looked like during the days leading up to when she was killed.

She wasn't in a fancy New York penthouse like her alter ego, she wasn't even in a television studio as a guest on a talk show as she was the last time they watched her, she was sitting in a high-backed chair, an ivory wall behind her that was bare except for half of a painting that was cut off by the camera. They saw enough of the painting to know that it featured a gray vase filled with white daisies against a lush, black backdrop.

At the start of the tape there was silence. Missy stared into the camera—collecting her thoughts, creating ambience, searching for her lines—who could tell, but the result was magnetic, no one could take their eyes away from the screen and everyone held their breath until Missy spoke. It was worth the wait. Her voice was clear and strong, her eyes glistened, her smile proudly showed off her wrinkles; it wasn't clear if she was talking or performing, but it didn't matter, the result was mesmerizing.

"Hello, my name is Missy Michaels and if you don't know who I am, don't be upset, it's been quite a while since I've been relevant, as they say these days. But all that is about to change." Missy paused and leaned closer to the camera. "I'm going to the sweetest little town, maybe you've heard of it—Tranquility, New Jersey—and I'm going to star in a new production of *Arsenic and Old Lace* with the Tranquility Players. We're putting on this show at the beautiful theatre at St. Winifred's Academy and I couldn't be happier. I'll be playing Abby Brewster, one of the spinster aunts who, along with her sister, does some naughty things, but it's all in the name of fun. So come see me in the show, I would love to see you."

Missy stopped, and for a moment, it looked as if she had lost her train of thought, but then they realized she was trying to compose herself. What had started as a piece of promotional fluff, a video she'd put together to announce to the world that Missy Michaels was making a comeback, suddenly became something more important. Missy was using the video to share her thoughts with the world. But what was she thinking?

"It would be nice to have a place in your hearts one final time."

She paused again, and it looked as if she would continue speaking, and they hoped she would, they wanted to hear more from her, they wanted to spend hours listening to her, but that was it. The screen faded to black and Missy's face was gone. The impact of her words remained.

"She wasn't talking about having one last moment in the spotlight," Alberta said. "She was talking about acting in public once more before she died."

"There was most assuredly a finality to what she said," Joyce agreed.

"Like she somehow knew she was going to die," Helen added.

"Do you think she had some kind of premonition that she'd be murdered?" Jinx asked.

"I hope not, lovey," Alberta said. "But she knew something, it was right there in her eyes."

"How'd you get this tape, Vin?" Sloan asked.

"It came in the mail addressed to me, personal and confidential," Vinny explained. "We haven't been able to trace it, but Forensics is checking for fingerprints and DNA, though I doubt we'll find anything."

"It might not hold any clues," Alberta said, "but it is a lovely gift."

"Thanks for letting me use your machine, Alfie," Vinny said, "and I'm sorry I kept you all up. Tomorrow's the big night."

Vinny walked over to the TV and was about to eject the tape from the VCR when Alberta stopped him.

"May I keep the video until tomorrow?" Alberta asked. "I'd like to watch it again for inspiration."

"In return Gram can give you this," Jinx said.

Vinny took the daisy-covered box. "What's this?"

"Kip's unsealed court documents we gound in Adrienne's room," Alberta said.

Kip smiled. "Now this is teamwork. Thank you."

"I'll drop it off at the station on my way to the theatre," Alberta said.

"Speaking of being dropped off," Helen started, "Joyce, can you drive me home?"

"Of course," Joyce replied. "Sloan, I can take you too."

"Thanks," Sloan said. He turned to Alberta. "Are you nervous?"

"About the show?" Alberta said. "A little, but if I get

scared, I'll look at you in the audience, and if that doesn't work, I'll just let Helen say all my lines. She knows the entire show by heart."

Alberta noticed that Jinx was playing with Lola instead of putting on her coat and following everyone out the door. She wondered if her granddaughter had come to the same conclusion she had.

When they were alone, Jinx revealed that she had. "I think I know who the killer is, Gram."

"Me too, lovey."

"The only problem is, how do we prove it?"

"I have an idea," Alberta said. "Nola may hate me for it, but if all goes like I hope it will, we'll expose the killer when we take our final bows and there's nowhere to hide."

"What do we have to do?" Jinx asked.

Just as Alberta was about to explain her plan, they heard another voice in the house. They looked around but didn't see anyone.

"Who's there?" Alberta called out.

"Gram, it's coming from the TV," Jinx said. "It's Missy."

They walked into the living room and saw Missy's face on the screen.

"Vinny didn't stop it before he left, the videotape must have been running this entire time," Alberta said.

"But it's a different scene," Jinx said. "At least her outfit's different, and so is the location."

They stood and listened to what Missy had to say, and it was as if she really was speaking to them from beyond the grave. She was giving them exactly what they needed so they could put her killer behind bars.

* * *

Alberta's plan was simple, but it had two crucial parts that she and Jinx needed to execute immediately. The next morning, Jinx went to see Pedro Suarez, the medical examiner, at St. Clare's, and asked him to run a test on Missy's blood.

"For arsenic?" Pedro asked.

"No."

"Some other kind of poison?" Pedro asked.

"No."

Jinx handed Pedro a piece of paper and saw his eyes widen. "I can do this right now."

On the other side of town, Alberta met with Donna at her office. The principal wasn't thrilled to be summoned to her own office on a Saturday morning, but Alberta had said it was an emergency. She also warned her not to tell Vinny about their meeting. When Alberta arrived at St. Winifred's, Donna was already sitting behind her desk, wearing a tracksuit instead of a power suit, but still the epitome of authority.

"What's this all about, Alberta?" she demanded. "And why do you want to keep it a secret from Vinny?"

"Don't worry, I'm not going to tell anyone about you and Vinny," Alberta said.

"You know about us?" Donna asked.

"I've known Vinny since we were kids," Alberta said. "I know when he's in love."

Donna snickered. "You think we're in love?"

"Don't try to deny it," Alberta replied. "I know you want to keep it under wraps until Missy's murder is solved, and that's what I've come to talk to you about. I need your help."

"In solving a murder?" Donna asked. "I'm a principal, not a detective."

"Neither am I . . . officially . . . but I've got a pretty good record," Alberta replied.

Donna gave Alberta a long, hard look. Whatever she saw, she liked. "How can I help you?"

"Nola told me that the Academy has their own little film studio here, where kids can learn how to make movies," Alberta said. "Is that true?"

"Yes, we're very proud of it," Donna replied. "We received a grant from the state's film department and got the whole thing set up last year; it's been an instant hit with the students, as you can imagine. But I don't see how I can help you."

"Can you recommend a student who has film editing skills, who you can trust to keep his mouth shut?" Alberta asked.

"No, I can't," Donna said. "But I can recommend a student with excellent editing skills who I trust implicitly to keep *her* mouth shut."

"A girl can do that kind of stuff?"

"Alberta, I'm disappointed in you, a girl can do any kind of stuff."

"*Errore mio*," Alberta said. "Do you think you can call her and ask her to come here now? I can pay her for her work."

Donna was already dialing the phone, and when her student answered, she put it on speaker. "Farrah, this is Principal Russo."

"Am I in trouble?" Farrah asked.

"No, you're not in trouble," Donna replied. She shrugged her shoulders and looked at Alberta. "Why does every student think they're in trouble when the principal calls?"

"Why else would the principal call?" Farrah asked.

"Because I have a woman here who has an offer that I don't think you're going to be able to refuse," Donna replied.

"I'm listening," Farrah said.

"Farrah, this is Alberta Scaglione, how'd you like to make a hundred dollars and help solve a murder?"

CHAPTER 28

La commedia è difficile, è un omicidio che è facile.

Alberta and Helen were running around Alberta's house like teenagers getting ready for a first date. They were excited, they were scared, and they knew that when the night was over, they would never be the same. For different reasons, of course. Helen was going to make her stage debut and Alberta was going to reveal to the entire audience who killed Missy Michaels.

Helen decided she would get ready for the show at Alberta's so they could do one final read through of all their lines as Abby and Martha Brewster. No one was more surprised than Alberta that she had actually memorized all her lines; she assumed it was in large part because she was playing a sister to her own sister onstage, so there was a built-in comfort level. Plus, even though it was a starring role, it wasn't a huge part and there were lots of other people in the cast, which meant the spotlight wasn't on her the entire time.

Alberta gathered her costume, character shoes, and makeup bag, took one last look around her living room to make sure she hadn't forgotten anything, kissed Lola on the top of her head, and headed into her kitchen to leave. Helen was sitting at the table already dressed in character, but not making any attempt to move.

"Helen, c'mon, we're going to be late," Alberta said.

"I want to give you something first," Helen said as she pulled a small, black velvet box from her pocketbook.

"*Cosa del mondo*," Alberta muttered. "Helen, it's not my birthday."

"Today is even more special," Helen said. "I know you don't want to be in this play and you're only doing it for me."

Alberta started to contradict Helen, but she knew that was useless, they'd both know she was lying. "You know I'd do anything for you."

"I do know that," Helen said. "And that's why I want you to have these."

Alberta opened the box to reveal a delicate strand of rosary beads made out of balsa wood. "Helen, these are beautiful, but they're yours."

"The church sent a group of us to the Amazon rain-forest to work with the missionaries," Helen said.

"I remember," Alberta interjected. "That was back in the eighties."

"It was 1987, to be exact," Helen said. "The indige-nous people weren't very welcoming—not that I blame them, we were intruding on their land—but there was this one boy, Baku, no more than eight years old, who was fascinated by us. He followed us everywhere, me in particular. He never said much, but each day he'd watch while he was whittling away at some balsa wood. The day we left, he gave me that rosary, and he said something to me that I've never forgotten."

"What did he say?" Alberta said.

"I had to have it translated of course, but he said, 'Keep these until you find someone who shares your soul,'" Helen replied.

"*Dio mio!*" Alberta cried. "Eight years old and so wise."

"We've always been close, Berta, but these past few years have shown me that I could not live without you," Helen said. "Which must mean we share a soul."

"I know you want everyone to think that you're grumpy and cantankerous, which you are, *mia sorella*," Alberta said. "But I've always known you are the heart of this family."

The sisters hugged each other tightly, and it was lucky that they hadn't yet put on their makeup because the tears fell freely. They pulled back and looked at each other for a few more seconds and then Alberta grabbed Helen's hands and stood up. "Let's show everybody that the Ferrara girls have still got it."

When they arrived at the theatre, it was a bustle of activity. All the actors were nervously walking around wearing half their costumes and reciting their lines to themselves, which made them look like they had recently escaped a psychiatrist's care, the stage crew were making last-minute adjustments based on last night's tech rehearsal, putting little pieces of black tape all over the stage, shouting orders to one another and speaking in a theatre shorthand that Alberta didn't understand. Despite never wanting to perform onstage before, the energy was infectious, and for a while she almost forgot there was still a murderer loose.

Jinx and Joyce ran up to Alberta and Helen just as they were about to go backstage to their dressing rooms. No one spoke, they just screamed in delight, hugged one another, and jumped up and down with sheer happiness. The gift-giving continued as Joyce presented them both with opening-night gifts, small portraits that she'd painted of them in their costumes. As a sentimental touch, she included a small bouquet of daisies in memory of Missy.

"Joyce, these are beautiful," Alberta said.

"After all this time, you're finally starting to improve," Helen said.

"Also too, notice how I smoothed out your wrinkles to make you look younger," Joyce added.

Helen laughed the loudest among the ladies. "Just this once I'll forgive you for trying to play God."

Jinx was the next one to dole out the gifts. She presented her grandmother and aunt with two hardcover copies of the play signed by the playwright, Joseph Kesselring, and the two original stars, Jean Adair and Josephine Hull, who played Martha and Abby.

"This is starting to feel like Christmas," Alberta said. "Lovey, these are lovely! So is your scarf by the way."

Jinx ruffled the bright red, orange, and yellow scarf she was wearing and dramatically threw it over her shoulder. "Another fine piece of vintage fashion from Aunt Joyce's never-ending closet."

"I really did buy a lot of Pucci back in the day," Joyce said. "I'm glad someone can put it to good use."

"Thank you, Jinxie," Helen said, kissing Jinx's cheek. "This is a very thoughtful gift, especially for Berta."

"Why's it so special for me?" Alberta asked.

"You could use it as a prop during the play and if you go up on your line, you can just make like you're reading a book," Helen replied.

"Ah, *Madon*!" Alberta cried. "I knew Sweet Helen had a short shelf life."

Nola's voice boomed from some unknown place, but her announcement set them all into action.

"We're going to open up the house, people," Nola said. "All actors and crew, please go to your dressing rooms."

No one wanted to use the star dressing room where Missy had been found dead, so the women were all sharing one room and the guys were in another. When Alberta and Helen arrived, they were greeted by two finely dressed gentlemen, who were waiting inside. Sloan looked resplendent in a navy-blue suit, white shirt, and a baby-blue tie that matched the bright shine of his eyes. Father Sal looked considerably less dreamy, but that was because he was dressed in his drab black suit and was wearing considerably more stage makeup than even the ladies because his character was described in the script as looking like Boris Karloff.

Alberta involuntarily let out a little gasp when she saw Sloan, she was that taken with his appearance. Helen, on the other hand, let out a loud laugh when she saw Sal.

"You're going to frighten all the little children, Sal," Helen said. "Which will be no different than at nine o'clock mass."

"And you, my friend," Sal started, but then paused. He smiled at Helen, and at first it looked as if he was searching for the right barb, for the cleverest bon mot, to toss back at her. But then his expression changed and his smile faded, although his eyes still shone bright. This was no time for jokes; the one-liners would come later when the lights dimmed and the play started. Now was the time for honesty.

"You, my friend, are gonna knock the socks off everyone in the audience," Sal said. "Because do you know what you are?"

"I'm almost afraid to ask," Helen replied.

"You're an actress, and a fine one at that," Sal said. He took something from his jacket pocket and showed it to the others. "This is a medal of St. Genesius, patron saint of actors, and that is what you are, Helen." He pinned the medal to the lapel of Helen's dress. "No matter what happens tonight, you will be guided by your patron saint."

Helen traced the medal with her finger and shook her head. "You're a constant surprise, Sal DeSoto."

"Likewise," he replied.

"I guess it's my turn," Sloan said. "This is for you."

"All these gifts!" Alberta cried. "No wonder theatre people are always broke, all they do is buy people things."

"This actually didn't cost me anything," Sloan said.

"I'm not sure that's how a fella worms his way into a woman's heart," Helen remarked.

"Shoosh you," Alberta said. "Gifts that don't cost anything are even more thoughtful."

Alberta opened the beautifully wrapped gift, and the sight of the photo of her and Sloan on their very first date in a delicate antique lace frame brought tears to her eyes. She almost laughed out loud as well, because she realized she was becoming a sentimental old lady and wasn't sure if it was because she was surrounded by so many emotional theatre people or because she was simply an old lady. Not that it mattered; it was nice to have something to cry happy tears over. And someone.

"Sloan, this is so thoughtful and I know exactly where I'm going to put it," Alberta said. "Right on my nightstand, so it'll be the last thing I see at night and the first thing I see in the morning."

"I have a copy of the same photo and that's exactly where I put mine," Sloan replied.

"I'm sorry to douse this moment with the unromantic seeds of reality," Sal said. "But didn't you say the gift didn't cost you anything? You certainly didn't get that frame at the discount store."

"It was a gift from my daughter Shannon," Sloan said. "She picked it up when she and her family were on that African safari."

"In other words, you regifted," Helen said.

"One more word out of you, Helen, and Martha Brewster's going to be an only child," Alberta scolded.

Nola's voice once again boomed from the unknown, announcing that the time for gifts was over as they had a show to do. "Five minutes, people, the curtain goes up in five minutes."

"Get out of here, fellas," Helen said. "We have to finish our makeup and I have to screw on this wig so it doesn't fall off."

"Have a wonderful show, everyone!" Sloan cried.

He left the dressing room, allowing the actors to ready themselves for their adoring public, who they could already hear chattering and laughing as they patiently waited for the curtain to rise. Alberta took a deep breath and wondered how they were going to react when the curtain finally descended and she took center stage to introduce them to a murderer. At least they wouldn't be able to say they didn't get their money's worth.

At exactly eight o'clock, Nola assembled the entire

cast on the stage and the closed house curtain was the only barrier between them and the enthusiastic audience. She told everyone to gather in a circle, clasp hands, and close their eyes, which they did. Johnny, Father Sal, Bruno, Alberta, Helen, Kip, Adrienne, Benny, Luke, and the others all became one unending circle, and a new family was born.

"This hasn't been an easy ride, folks," Nola started. "We have had our share of obstacles literally from before day one, but we pushed forward, we persevered, and here we are on opening night. Let's remember why we're on this stage, to share our energy, to entertain, to make our audience forget about their troubles for a few hours. Life doesn't always make us smile, so it's vital that we, as actors, remind the world that it's okay to laugh.

"Thank you for sticking with this show and never giving up," Nola continued. "I am so proud of what we've been able to accomplish, and I know that Missy Michaels is looking down on us, and she's already giving us a standing ovation."

At the mention of Missy's name, Alberta was jolted back to reality and she opened her eyes. She received another jolt when she found herself staring right into the eyes of the killer. Alberta felt a tingle in her gut; she knew the show must go on, but she knew it was going to be a very different show than the one anyone had expected.

Based upon the audience's reaction twenty minutes into the show, *Arsenic and Old Lace* was a hit. There were howls of laughter, brief snippets of spontaneous applause, and one very loud "Bravo" was heard when Alberta made her entrance, but she suspected that was Sloan and didn't feel she had earned such praise. However, during a scene with her, Helen, Father Sal, and Benny, who was playing Dr. Einstein, a more interesting scene was developing backstage.

During their dialogue, they could hear loud voices coming from behind them. Although the four actors were novices, they knew the protocol was for anyone who wasn't on stage to be quiet and if they had to have a con-ve̶̶̶̶̶̶̶̶̶̶̶̶uld whisper, not shout, as Kip and

line that Father Sal expertly ̶̶̶̶̶̶̶̶̶̶ the silence that came in between, y could be heard telling Kip to "just admit you did it." The audience also heard it and a murmur of giggles and hushed chitchat immediately erupted, causing the next few lines of the scene to barely be heard and definitely ignored.

Alberta was the only one of the actors standing, so she moved closer to peer out the stage window to see if she could catch someone's eye and use hand signals to get them to stop yelling. What she saw made her want to start yelling. Lying on the ground was Jinx's scarf, which meant she must be nearby, and Alberta knew that there was no reason for her to be backstage; she should be in the audience with Freddy. Jinx was in trouble, she felt it, and there was no way she was going to ignore her instinct if there was a chance her granddaughter was in danger.

"I do wish Freddy would stop lounging in his chair and go help his girlfriend," Alberta ad-libbed. "I think she's somewhere in the back and she's in trouble."

Helen, Father Sal, and Benny had no idea what Alberta was talking about, but luckily, the person she was trying to reach understood completely. In the darkness of the theatre, they heard a commotion, and Alberta knew that Freddy was stepping over people making his way to the aisle so he could run backstage to Jinx's aid. Freddy might not have any acting chops, but he was born to play the hero.

Unfortunately, there was no way for Freddy to get backstage without running onstage and onto the set where the actors were performing.

"Where is she?" Freddy asked Albe_____ he was in her house on Memory L_____ in front of an audience.

"Follow me," Alberta said. She then tu_____ confused Helen and said, "We'll be right back."

Freddy followed Alberta out the front door of the set and Helen, in her trademark deadpan expression, turned to Father Sal and said, "Looks like my sister's got herself another hobby."

The ad-lib worked, and the audience howled, immediately forgetting about the unorthodox entrance and once again paying attention to the scene. While the rest of the scene was being reconstructed without one of its principal players, another scene was playing out hidden from the audience. Behind the set, Alberta picked up the scarf from the stage, pulled back a curtain, and practically had to shove the scarf in her mouth to prevent her scream from further disrupting the play. Freddy immediately dropped to his knees and pulled out the gag that had been shoved into Jinx's mouth and started to untie the ropes that were knotted around her wrists and ankles.

"Who did this to you?" Freddy asked.

"I don't know," Jinx replied. "Someone hit me from behind."

She witnessed history repeat itself, because Johnny

came running up behind Freddy and whacked him in the head with a gun.

"Why did you do that?" Jinx screamed.

When Freddy rolled over and Johnny saw who he had struck, he was stunned. "Oh my God! I thought it was Kip."

"Why would you want to knock out Kip?"

They all turned around to see Nola standing right off stage left. She was wearing a headset and carrying a clipboard because she was doubling as the stage manager. She played a third role as she stared at Johnny, that of the confused girlfriend.

"I'm putting an end to all of this right now," Johnny said. "I'm going to make Kip pay for killing Missy, framing me, and, most of all, ruining our play."

"I'm not the one who's ruined this lousy play, you are."

They all turned in the other direction to see Kip standing stage right, pointing a gun directly at them.

"Excuse me," Nola said. "This play is *not* lousy."

"The direction stinks and you know it," Kip hissed. "I'm going to make you pay for that, Johnny, and prove to everyone that you're the one who killed Missy."

Standing in between the two men wielding guns, Alberta stretched out her arms to both of them and put up her palms to stop them from talking any further. "I know exactly who killed Missy, and when this show is over, I'm going to tell everyone."

Untied, Jinx was kneeling next to Freddy, cradling his head in her lap. "Gram, we have to be careful, the killer is on this stage and they're desperate."

Jinx looked from Johnny to Kip, and both men responded in unison, "I didn't do it."

"Shut up, both of you!" Alberta yelled. "From here on in, Jinx and I are running this show."

"Sorry, Gram, I think you have to fly solo on this flight," Jinx said. "I need to stay with Freddy until he wakes up."

"Of course, lovey," Alberta said. "I know what I have to do."

"What you have to do is get back onstage and finish out the scene," Nola ferociously whispered.

"First, you need to tell me how many prop guns are used in this show," Alberta asked.

"You know there's only one," Nola replied. "I went over all this during my gun safety lesson. Were you not paying attention?"

"I was hoping I was wrong," Alberta said. "Because if there's only one fake gun, that means one of these two is holding a real gun."

Terror gripped Nola's face as she looked at Johnny. Could this man she loved be a murderer? Would he use the gun in his hand to murder again? "Johnny, please tell me you didn't kill Missy. Please tell me you have nothing to do with all this."

"I'm sorry, Nola, but he can't tell you that," Alberta said.

"I knew he was the murderer," Kip cried.

"No one said you were innocent, Kip," Alberta stated.

Helen's booming voice interrupted their confrontation. Alberta recognized it as her cue and she knew the time had come. She had wanted to wait until the end of the show to expose the killer, but there had been a rewrite and the play would have to change. In spite of the grave circumstances, she chuckled to herself. *La commedia è difficile, è un omicidio che è facile.* Comedy was hard, but murder, for some, came easy.

Alberta walked through the front door of the set and rejoined her castmates. Their dialogue bore no resemblance to the script, but you could hear a pin drop in the audience as they sat enraptured by what they were watching.

"Sorry, that took longer than I expected," Alberta said.

"Is everything all right outside?" Helen asked. "It sounded like the boys were causing some ruckus out there."

"They were arguing, but it's all resolved now," Alberta said.

"What on earth were they arguing about?" Father Sal asked.

"They're under the impression that my sister and I are the only killers in town," Alberta said. "But they're wrong."

"They are?" Helen asked.

"We might have killed all those men with arsenic, but we didn't kill Missy Michaels and Brandon," Alberta announced.

Alberta couldn't see the faces of the people in the audience, but she was certain they looked as shocked as Helen and Father Sal did.

"If we didn't kill those two," Helen said, "who did?"

"The new girl in town," Alberta replied. "We know her as Elaine Harper, but everyone else calls her Adrienne Petrocelli."

CHAPTER 29

Non è finita fino a quando la signora morta parla.

"I wasn't due back until Act Two, but it seems like one of the old ladies is going rogue."

Adrienne didn't even bother entering the living room through the front door. Instead, she emerged from the stage left wing and spoke her line as she crossed in front of the set, then stepped onto the deck of the playing space. She continued walking until she took her position at the far right wall. She possessed far more stage presence than she let on during her brief rehearsal period; either she'd lied about her experience or Johnny really was a terrific director.

"You sound as if you think you've solved this whole mystery, Alberta," Adrienne said.

"Her name is Abby," Helen whispered loudly. She shook her head and directed her next line to Father Sal. "Why is everyone breaking the fourth wall?"

Nervous laughter rose up from the audience. They didn't know if they were watching the play or a real confrontation; they also didn't know if whatever they were watching was being played for laughs or if they should take everything they were seeing seriously. They may have been confused, but they were completely invested.

"Please allow me to introduce not only Missy Michaels's only living relative," Alberta said, "but Johnny Fenn's ex-girlfriend."

"What?" Adrienne cried.

"I apologize," Alberta said. "Johnny Fenn's *jealous* ex-girlfriend."

A slow, sinister smile spread across Adrienne's face as she bent over and leaned on the back of Helen's chair. "Tell me more."

Alberta hesitated, because she knew the young woman had killed twice, and she didn't like the fact that she was now hovering so close to her sister. When she started to talk, Alberta walked toward Helen and extended her hand, and Helen, understanding her sister's motivation, took it, got up from her chair, and crossed to the other side of the stage. Once she was standing in between the two-time murderess and her sister, Alberta spoke much more freely.

"As I was saying, the two of you went to the University of Michigan," Alberta said. "You told us you went there and the M on Johnny's baseball cap that I thought was in honor of our fallen star was really in honor of his alma mater. You're both the same age, so I'm guessing that's where you met."

"I'm impressed Alberta," Adrienne said. "The rumors I heard about you were true. But the fact that we went to the same school hardly means we dated."

"Of course not," Alberta said. "Two things told me that. First, Johnny said he would never cheat on Nola *especially* with Adrienne, and you were pea green with envy when Johnny professed his love to Nola in front of everyone at tech rehearsal. If looks could kill, Nola would've been your third victim."

Adrienne stood, literally, with her back against the wall and her face contorted into a mask of hatred. The audience shuddered, but Adrienne didn't hear them; she was in her own private world.

"Johnny doesn't love Nola," Adrienne spat. "They have this idiotic bond for their love of the theatre, and he loves the opportunities he thinks she can give him."

"Is that why you wanted to get back at Johnny?" Alberta asked.

"I warned him not to dump me!" Adrienne howled. "I told him I would find a way to make him pay."

"When you found out he was going to direct your aunt, the only other person you hated more than him, it was like the forces of destiny presented you with your revenge on a cold, silver platter," Alberta said.

"You're piling it on a little thick, don't you think, Berta?" Helen whispered.

"We do have a paying audience," Alberta replied. "I want to make sure they get their money's worth."

"That's all Johnny ever wanted too," Adrienne said. "His piece of the pie."

"At some point, I assume you told Johnny that you were Missy Michaels's niece maybe when you showed him your DVD collection of her movies," Alberta said.

"How did you know that?" Adrienne asked.

"Johnny said he discovered Missy because his ex-girlfriend had her DVDs," Alberta replied. "But then

Johnny met Nola, they started dating, he broke up with you, and when he found out she was a producer, he came up with the brilliant idea to lure his ex-girlfriend's aunt to star in his current girlfriend's play."

"You all think Missy Michaels was some kind of saint! Let me tell you something, she was evil!" Adrienne screamed. "Why do you think I put that doctored photo in the fake arsenic bottle? To show the world that she literally turned her back on her family and let them suffer and struggle while she went on and made millions."

"Is that why you killed her and framed Johnny for the crime?" Alberta asked.

The audience screamed, and it was only when Alberta saw Johnny standing stage left, a gun dangling from his hand, that she realized they were responding to his entrance and not her line delivery.

"That's ridiculous!" Johnny shouted. "Adrienne wouldn't do that to me."

"Why not?" Adrienne shouted. "You treated me like dirt! You tossed me aside the same way my aunt disowned her own family!"

"Adrienne, when we broke up you said you understood that it was for the best!" Johnny cried.

"The best way for Adrienne to put her plan for revenge into motion," Alberta said.

"I don't care what it looks like, I don't care what you might think she's done," Johnny said. "Adrienne isn't the murderer, Kip is."

The audience erupted in another series of screams, this time in response to Kip's entrance on the other side of the stage. The gun he was holding wasn't hanging at his side, it was pointed directly at Johnny.

"You shut your mouth, Johnny!" Kip yelled. "I loved

Missy, I would never have killed her. You're the one who saw it as an opportunity for publicity because the only thing you care about besides yourself is your lame career!"

"Speaking of careers, Adrienne," Alberta said. "How's the customer service business?"

"What are you talking about?" she replied.

"I didn't expect you to remember," Alberta said. "You told us that was your job, but I found your business card in your kitchen drawer and called your office. You don't work in customer service at BioMedique, you're one of their top IT people."

The first crack in Adrienne's tough armor started to show. "Big deal, so I work in IT."

"It's a very big deal, because it means that you're an expert when it comes to technology," Alberta started. "It also means that you're the ex-girlfriend Johnny was talking about who built his website. The same one who was going to build Missy's website."

"You're insane!" Adrienne cried. "I wouldn't lift a finger to help that woman."

"And you didn't," Alberta confirmed. "But you did swindle her out of one hundred thousand dollars and hacked into her e-mails, created a new account for Johnny theDirector@gmail.com, and made it look like Missy and Johnny were communicating, all in your attempt to frame Johnny for the murder that you committed."

"Adrienne . . . please . . . tell them this is all a lie," Johnny begged.

"You should know all about lies, Johnny," Nola said. "Why didn't you tell me that she was your ex-girlfriend?"

Johnny turned around and saw Nola staring at him with a look of utter despair on her face. She didn't have to say a word for him to know what she felt, he could tell just by looking at her; in fact, the entire audience could tell that she was deeply hurt because the man she was in love with had lied to her about something so incredibly important. Most of the people in the audience knew Nola's less-than-ideal personal history, so they were devastated by this betrayal. Especially Bruno, who came running onstage behind Nola and started to lunge toward Johnny. Instinctively, Johnny raised his gun and pointed it at Bruno, who immediately put up his hands and started to back away.

"Don't do anything stupid, Johnny," Bruno pleaded. "there's a full house watching your every move."

Johnny turned and had to squint to see Vinny standing in the audience, Tambra leaning on a crutch next to him, with Donna on his other side. The combined sight of the police and the very stern-looking principal made Johnny's hands shake, which wouldn't have mattered if one of his hands wasn't holding a gun.

"I haven't done anything!" Johnny cried. "And neither has Adrienne. Kip's the killer."

"I told you to stop blaming me for something you did!" Kip cried.

"*Basta*! Both of you!" Alberta shouted. "I'm sorry, Johnny, you may not want to believe it, but Adrienne framed you, and did a good job at it too. She even impersonated you when she deposited the hundred thousand dollars into your checking account at Tranquility Trust's ATM machine."

"I may be a lot of things, Alberta," Adrienne said. "But I look nothing like Johnny."

"You're the same height and build as he is," Helen said.

"Put on the same clothes he always wears, pull back your hair into a ponytail, don a University of Michigan baseball cap, slap on a fake beard and voilà, instant Johnny," Alberta said.

"A fake beard?" Adrienne howled. "Now you're grasping at straws."

"You should really keep your facial glue hidden better," Alberta said. "It was in your drawer next to your business card. I couldn't imagine what you needed it for until I found the rubber band in Brandon's apartment."

"That we can prove matches the ones in the rubber band ball Gram found in your kitchen drawer," Jinx said.

Adrienne turned around to see Jinx and a still-not-completely-steady Freddy at her side standing behind Kip. "I should've killed you when I had the chance!"

"You're not impulsive, Adrienne, you don't strike back quickly, you play the long game," Alberta said. "But had you only waited a few months, you would have seen your aunt die and, thanks to her, you'd have become a very rich young woman."

"You don't know what you're talking about," Adrienne said. "No matter when she died, that woman wasn't going to leave me a dime. She ignored me her entire life, you think she was going to remember me when she died?"

"She did remember you and I can prove it," Alberta said. "That's your cue, Farrah honey."

Suddenly, a projection screen slowly descended from the ceiling, causing everyone to move downstage.

"Farrah Fogarty, are you responsible for that?" Nola asked.

"Yes, Ms. Kirkpatrick," Farrah said from the control booth at the back of the theatre. "I did some video editing for Mrs. Scaglione. The principal said I could use it for my final project."

"Vinny," Alberta said, "I'm sorry I didn't tell you about this part, but remember the video you let us watch?"

"What about it?" Vinny shouted from the audience.

"There was more on it. We never stopped the tape, and after you left Missy came back on screen," Alberta explained. "I had Farrah splice it together with the other videos Father Sal had and, well . . . Missy has a lot more to say."

"Well, don't keep us in suspense, Alfie!" Vinny shouted. "Roll the tape!"

"I guess it's true what they say, *Non è finita fino a quando la signora morta parla,*" Alberta said.

"I hate to interrupt," Father Sal said, "but I don't believe anyone in the history of the theatrical arts has ever said 'It isn't over until the dead lady speaks.'"

"It's called artistic license, Sal," Helen scolded. "Keep going, Berta, you're doing just fine."

"Play the tape, Farrah," Alberta instructed.

"What the hell are you doing?" Adrienne cried.

"Letting your aunt speak for herself," Alberta said. "Listen up, Adrienne, you'll be shocked to hear what she has to say."

When Missy's face appeared on the huge screen, Adrienne fell back onto the flat and gasped. She was literally looking into the face of death.

A louder gasp rose up from the audience. Even though they'd been robbed of seeing the opening-night performance of a time-honored classic comedy, they were seeing a one-of-a-kind production that could never be duplicated. Had Nola known the evening would turn out this way, she could've charged triple the ticket price.

After a montage of clips of Missy as a child, a young woman, and in her final days, words slowly appeared on the screen, The Final Confession of Melissa Margherita Miccalizzo, more famously known as Missy Michaels. The words faded and the woman herself appeared.

"If you're watching this tape, it means that I'm dead," Missy announced. "Don't waste a second feeling bad for me, I've had a wonderful life filled with the same ups and downs everyone faces. I've had successes and failures, triumphs and regrets. Lots of regrets actually, the biggest one that I let my family down."

Missy looked away from the camera until she regained the strength to look into the eyes of whoever would one day watch the tape and resume her final thoughts. Adrienne was stunned by what she heard.

"This wasn't on the tape!" Adrienne cried.

"Had you watched the entire thing before sending it anonymously to the police, you would've seen it," Alberta said. "And you would've finally heard your aunt apologize for how she treated you."

"I'm not going to bore you with excuses, but the facts are that when I was young, I had greedy managers," Missy began. "It's a cliché, I know, but it's true. Ironically, when I got older, I became the greedy one. I knew I was going to be typecast as a child actress and my career was probably over, so I guarded my money with my life. I married well, my husbands didn't seem to last very long, but their money did. I invested, I bought real estate, and I kept it all for myself. I didn't even think about giving it to my family because I hadn't heard from them in years. No one ever reached out to me until a few years ago, when I received a lovely card from my niece."

All heads turned to Adrienne, but she didn't even notice she was being stared at. She was entranced by the vision of her aunt.

"I'm so sorry I never wrote back to you, Adrienne," Missy continued. "I'm not asking for your forgiveness, only a little understanding. I've been on my own since I was six years old; that's a long time, and it's a little too late to teach this old broad a new trick, but it's my problem to deal with wherever I am when you hear this video."

Missy took a deep breath and angrily wiped away some unexpected tears.

"I hate women who cry," she said. "Tears don't solve problems, actions do. To make up for my very rude behavior and for a lifetime of turning my back on my family, I'm leaving you everything I own. My house, my stocks, all my money, every last cent, and it's not a bad sum, if I say so myself, for an actress who hasn't worked in decades. Use it well, Adrienne, to have a wonderful life with as few regrets as possible."

An image of Missy from her first movie as Daisy appeared on the screen, but Alberta could see that Adrienne was getting restless, and she had to get on with her presentation. She felt bad not allowing Farrah to show off her editing skills, but it was more important to make sure Adrienne was captured.

"Farrah, honey, you can pause it right there," Alberta said.

Missy's smiling six-year-old face froze on the screen.

"It's eerie that you almost predicted this Adrienne," Alberta said.

"I don't know what you're talking about," Adrienne replied, without taking her eyes off of Missy's image.

"As part of your plan to blackmail Johnny, you fabricated a story that Missy was dying of Alzheimer's," Alberta explained. "You were half right. Your aunt was dying, but not from Alzheimer's. She had stage four pancreatic cancer and only had months to live."

"No!" Adrienne's scream rocked the entire theatre. "That can't be true!"

"It's all in the medical examiner's report," Jinx said. "We asked him to check for any cancer drugs in Missy's body and he found traces of Xeloda and Abraxane, two drugs used to combat pancreatic cancer. They weren't caught before because a toxicology report wasn't done."

"There was no need for you to kill her," Alberta said. "Her body was already doing that for you."

"If you'd only refused to give in to your quest for revenge a little while longer," Jinx said. "You would be able to live out the rest of your life in the lap of luxury instead of living it out in prison."

Adrienne looked around the stage wildly, she looked into the audience, but saw nothing but darkness. Alberta imagined it was what she'd see if she looked into her soul.

"You can't prove I did any of this!" Adrienne screamed.

"We'll be able to trace the fake e-mail account you created to frame Johnny back to you," Vinny shouted from the audience. "We can also link the rubber band found in Brandon's room back to you and I'm sure the Tranquility Arms security tape footage showing you were Missy's escort will be found."

"And if they don't find that, they'll discover you're the one who hacked into Kip's sealed court documents," Alberta said.

"You did what?!" Kip screamed.

"What the hell did you do that you have sealed court documents?" Johnny asked, raising his gun at Kip.

"I didn't do anything!" Kip protested, raising his gun at Johnny.

"I knew you couldn't be trusted!" Johnny shouted.

"Both of you shut up!" Adrienne screamed. "Once I found out Kip was in the show, I researched him online and found out his nasty little secret. I knew I could use his past against the two of you."

"I can't believe you would do this to me, Adrienne!" Johnny cried.

"That's because you're weak! The two of you are!" Adrienne screamed. "Just like Brandon!"

Sanjay stood up from his seat in the audience and yelled, "Is that why you killed my Brandon?!"

"He blackmailed me and wanted me to pay for the security footage," Adrienne said. "Like I would *ever* pay him! I killed that sniveling idiot like I killed my no-good aunt. Like I should've killed you, Johnny, for dumping me!"

Lightning fast, Adrienne reached out and grabbed the gun from Kip's hand and shot Johnny in the leg. Stunned, it took him a moment to grasp what had just happened, but when Johnny felt the searing pain ignite like a torch in his leg and race up his entire body, he screamed and fell to the ground. He aimed his gun at Adrienne, but when blood poured out of his flesh, it was apparent that the gun he was holding was a useless prop.

"Dammit!" Johnny shouted, tossing the gun onto the floor.

Vinny raced down the aisle and jumped onto the stage. He stood next to Johnny and told him that an ambulance was on its way.

"An ambulance isn't going to help a dead man," Adrienne said. "If you hadn't left me, Johnny, none of this would've happened."

She raised her arm to shoot again, but Helen swung her pocketbook wildly and let it soar through the air. It hit Adrienne in the face, causing her to stumble into the wall just as Jinx sprang forward and grabbed her arm. They struggled for a few seconds until the gun fell out of Adrienne's hands, crashing right into the prop gun that was lying on the floor.

Vinny scrambled forward at the same time Adrienne did, they struggled to get the real gun, and, as a result, the two guns spun around in a circle. Adrienne got hold of one gun, while Vinny hit the other with his shoulder, making it slide right next to Alberta's feet. Instinctively, Alberta bent down to pick up the gun, but when she stood and pointed it at Adrienne, she froze, because she had never held a gun before. Unfortunately, Adrienne felt very comfortable aiming her gun at Alberta.

"Don't do this, Adrienne," Vinny said. "You'll only make things worse for yourself."

"That's impossible and you know it," Adrienne said. "Are you a gambling woman, Alberta?"

"No, I'm not," she replied.

"Too bad, because what are the odds that I have the prop gun and you have the real one?" Adrienne asked. "One way to find out is for you to pull your trigger, but I don't think you have the guts to do it."

Alberta felt everyone's eyes on her. Helen, Jinx, Vinny, the cast spread out onstage, the entire audience. They were all watching her, waiting to see what she would do. She was waiting to find out as well.

Alberta was not a violent person, but she was fiercely

protective of her family and friends. She felt heat, adrenaline, and anger rise up her body and she realized she was fiercely protective of something else: her own life. She had spent the past few years creating a new life for herself, experiencing the world as she had never done before, trusting her own instincts, gaining self-respect and independence and now this young, disturbed woman threatened to take it away from her with one small gesture. All Adrienne had to do was pull her finger back on the trigger and release a bullet that may or may not be real, a bullet that could end Alberta's life. Alberta couldn't deny what she was feeling, she was frightened. But she was also infuriated.

"I was right," Adrienne said. "You're just like the rest of them, you're a coward. You don't have the guts to fight back."

Alberta stared directly into Adrienne's black, hateful eyes and replied, "Watch me."

Alberta pulled the trigger, but instead of the bullet racing toward Adrienne, she shot at the metal contraption that held the sandbag directly over the girl's head. The heavy bag fell onto Adrienne's shoulder and knocked her to the floor. As she lay there, unconscious and unmoving, Vinny scrambled to her and kicked the gun off the stage to where Tambra was standing. The cast, tight-knit as ever, let out a sigh of relief and some of them collapsed to their knees. The audience, who had been watching in rapt attention for the past ten minutes, was finally able to release its contained energy and rose to give them a standing ovation.

Helen grabbed Alberta's hand and squeezed it tightly before dragging her to the lip of the stage. At the last second, Helen stepped back leaving Alberta alone in the spotlight so she could take the bow she had so rightfully earned. The audience went wild. Unaccustomed to being in front of such a large crowd, Alberta felt a little foolish, but the rush, she had to admit, was undeniable. It was nothing, however, like the feeling she got when she looked all around her and saw Jinx, Helen, and Freddy clapping for her on the stage, and Joyce and Sloan running up to the stage with tears in their eyes.

She felt her own tears welling up behind her eyes. If Alberta never stepped on another stage for the rest of her life, she knew the people who loved her would still consider her a star.

And when you had your family's love, who needed applause?

EPILOGUE

Un uccello non lascia mai veramente il nido.

The rest of the show's run went off without a hitch. No performance ever matched the intensity and surrealism of opening night, but the cast banded together like soldiers in a foxhole and for the next three weekends, they played to sold-out audiences who showered them with flowers, praise, and more bravos than Patti LuPone and Nathan Lane had ever received.

Tambra stepped back into her role after Adrienne was carted off to jail to await her trial. and although she had to hobble around the stage using a crutch and wore an ankle cast that clashed with her 1940s dress, with its cap sleeves and flouncy skirt, the slightly disabled detective was an upgrade from the two-time murderer who previously played the role.

Nola hosted a closing night party at the theatre that turned out to be a bittersweet affair. She officially ended her relationship with Johnny. He had told her too many lies, and she could no longer trust him. Bruno was there to pick up the pieces, but it was too soon to tell if Nola would finally notice the good guy standing in front of her.

Instead of running away in shame, Kip was relieved that his past had been exposed. He explained that his relationship with his boyfriend had hit a rough patch, but he swore he had nothing to do with Wesley's disappearance or his murder. He confessed that the hours he was gone from the hotel in Bangor were because he had a rendezvous with a guy he met online. He wasn't proud of his actions, but he knew if he didn't explain himself, a cloud of doubt would follow him around for the rest of his life. He didn't want his newfound friends to always look at him suspiciously.

A week after the show closed, Joyce and Sloan showed up at Alberta's with Helen and Jinx in tow and threw a huge bag on Alberta's kitchen table.

"*Dio mio*, Joyce!" Alberta cried. "What's all this?"

"This, my celebrity sisters-in-law, is your fan mail," Joyce said.

"Are you kidding me?" Alberta asked.

"Why are you surprised Berta? We were a smash hit," Helen said. "I'm already talking to Nola about our next production. I'm thinking of the female version of Neil Simon's *The Sunshine Boys.*"

"Not on your life, Helen," Alberta said. "That one show almost killed me, literally; if you want to risk fate and do another one, you're on your own."

"Fine," Helen said. "There are a few one-woman shows I've been eyeing as my next vehicle."

When they were halfway through the pile of mail, there was a knock on the door. When Alberta saw that it was Vinny and Donna she said, "Can I finally tell everyone your secret?"

"You know?" Vinny asked.

"That you and Donna are a couple?" Alberta asked. "Of course I know."

"You don't know anything, Alfie," Vinny said.

"That's what I tried to tell her," Donna said. "But she's a little stubborn, that one, if you haven't noticed."

"You two have been scurrying around town having a clandestine affair for months," Alberta said.

"We're not a couple," Vinny insisted. "Donna's been helping me with this."

Vinny tossed an envelope onto the table. It wasn't as big as the bag of fan mail, but it caused the same amount of commotion.

"What's that?" Sloan asked.

"My novel," Vinny said proudly.

"You wrote a novel?" Joyce asked.

"Yup," Vinny said. "And Donna helped edit it."

"Vinny's a wonderful writer," Donna said. "He just needed some nips and tucks here and there."

"*Stupefacente!*" Alberta cried. "I can't believe you wrote a book. What's it about?"

"You," Vinny said.

"Me?" Alberta replied.

"It's a murder mystery about an old lady who turns out to be one helluva detective," Vinny said. "It's called *What's Murder All About, Alfie?*"

The group roared with laughter and loved the title, but the celebration was short-lived. One of the cards in the bag had a very distinctive handwriting that Alberta recognized immediately. And she should because the writing was her daughter's.

"Gram, what's wrong?" Jinx asked.

"This card is from your mother," Alberta said, her face suddenly pale.

"Lisa Marie sent you a card?" Joyce asked.

Her hands shaking, Alberta ripped open the envelope and took out the card as everyone around her grew silent. She stared at the picture of the blue hydrangeas on the cover, the same flowers that grew in her backyard. She was filled with so many emotions; she was thrilled to hear from Lisa Marie after all these years, but she was also ashamed that she hadn't been the one to reach out first. When she opened the card, however, she gasped, and was frightened by the few words her daughter had written.

"Gram, what is it?" Jinx asked. "What does my mother say?"

"Just one sentence," Alberta replied. "'I need your help.'"

Recipes from the
Ferrara Family Kitchen

Joyce's Low Carb Eggplant Bruschetta

1 large eggplant
6 fresh basil leaves, chopped
4 tomatoes, diced
½ cup artichoke hearts, quartered
¼ cup kalamata olives, halved
¼ cup capers
3 tablespoons balsamic vinegar
¾ teaspoon onion powder
¾ teaspoon salt
½ teaspoon pepper

1. Combine basil, tomatoes, artichoke hearts, olives, capers, vinegar, garlic, onion powder, salt, and pepper in a bowl. Cover and refrigerate for 2 hours.
2. Preheat oven to 400 degrees.
3. Slice eggplant in ½ inch slices. Drizzle with balsamic and sprinkle with salt and pepper.
4. Bake for 10 minutes. Flip 'em and bake for another 10 minutes.
5. Top each eggplant slice with the bruschetta mixture.

Bruno & Alberta's Swedish Sicilian Meatballs

1 pound ground beef
1 egg
½ cup Italian flavored breadcrumbs
1 onion, minced
½ teaspoon salt
¼ teaspoon nutmeg
2 tablespoons vegetable oil
2 cups milk
⅓ cup water
1 package McCormick Swedish Meatball mix
4 cups of cooked spaghetti

1. Mix ground beef, egg, breadcrumbs, onion, salt, and nutmeg in a large bowl. Shape the beef into about 20 meatballs. The nutmeg and the Italian breadcrumbs make for an interesting taste combination!
2. Heat a skillet over medium-high heat and add the oil.
3. Add the meatballs and cook until brown.
4. Drain meatballs and set aside on a paper towel.
5. In another skillet stir in milk, McCormick mix, and simmer on medium until it boils. Reduce heat and simmer for about another minute to thicken.
6. Add in meatballs and cook for another few minutes.
7. Serve the meatballs and sauce over the spaghetti.

Alberta's Favorite Bacon-Wrapped Mushroom

2 pints mushrooms
1 pound bacon
1 quart white vinegar
2 teaspoons salt
2 teaspoons pepper
1 tablespoon oregano
1 cup extra virgin olive oil
2 lemons

1. Cut the bacon slices in half.
2. Wrap each mushroom with half a piece of bacon and secure them with a toothpick.
3. Mix the vinegar, olive oil, salt, pepper, oregano in a bowl.
4. Squeeze in the lemons.
5. Add the mushrooms and refrigerate for at least two hours.
6. Preheat oven to 375 degrees and bake for 30 minutes or so until the bacon is done.
7. Place on paper towels to absorb the grease.

Jinx's Gluten Free, Non-Dairy Baked Ziti with Fauxsage

1 16-ounce package of gluten-free ziti
2 packages of Tofurky Italian sausage
1 15-ounce container of non-dairy ricotta cheese—
   Kite Hill is my fave
1 egg
1 onion, minced
2 teaspoons of minced garlic
1 teaspoon dried oregano
½ teaspoon salt
½ teaspoon black pepper
1 26-ounce jar of pasta sauce
1 8-ounce package of non-dairy shredded Italian cheese—
   Daiya brand is fab
1 teaspoon basil

1. Preheat the oven to 350 degrees and grease a 9x13 inch baking dish.
2. Stir the gluten-free ziti into boiling water and cook uncovered for about 8 minutes.
3. While the ziti is cooking, heat a large skillet over medium heat. Add the fauxsage and cook for about 10 minutes. Drain those babies and set them aside.
4. Stir the non-dairy ricotta, egg, onion, garlic, and oregano in a large bowl and then stir in the ziti, fauxsage, salt, pepper, and ½ jar of pasta sauce. (Do not let my Gram or any Italian woman over the age of 50 know that you're using sauce from a jar. Trust me!)
5. Cover the bottom of the baking dish with sauce, then layer in the ziti/fauxsage mix, and add ½ of the

shredded cheese. Repeat this step and sprinkle with basil or whatever spice you like. Cover tightly with aluminum foil.

6. Bake in the oven for about 20 minutes. Take off the foil and bake for another 5-10 minutes or until the cheese is melted.

Connect with

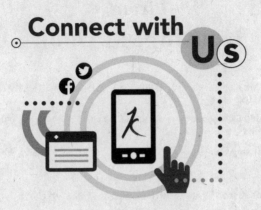

Us

Visit us online at
KensingtonBooks.com
to read more from your favorite authors, see books
by series, view reading group guides, and more.

for sneak peeks, chances to win books and prize packs,
and to share your thoughts with other readers.

facebook.com/kensingtonpublishing
twitter.com/kensingtonbooks

Tell us what you think!

To share your thoughts, submit a review,
or sign up for our eNewsletters, please visit:
KensingtonBooks.com/TellUs.

Grab These Cozy Mysteries from
Kensington Books

Available Wherever Books Are Sold!

All available as e-books, too!

Visit our website at **www.kensingtonbooks.com**